DAMNUM FATALE

Book Two of the Resonance of Souls Trilogy

VICTOR BELLA AZENZIK

Published by: AR PRESS
Roger L. Brooks, Publisher
roger@americanrealpublishing.com
americanrealpublishing.com

TABLE OF CONTENTS

Chapter 1: Western Pennsylvania, 1987 ... 1

Chapter 2: Boston, 2025 ... 7

Chapter 3: The Massage ... 14

Chapter 4: Corrina ... 23

Chapter 5: Victoria's Kindness ... 34

Chapter 6: Uninvited Stranger ... 38

Chapter 7: The Father ... 50

Chapter 8: Nephilim ... 56

Chapter 9: Centralia ... 65

Chapter 10: Cassian Begins ... 71

Chapter 11: Lines in the Sand ... 79

Chapter 12: College ... 85

Chapter 13: The Son ... 93

Chapter 14: Unexpected Stranger ... 99

Chapter 15: The Pizza Chronicles ... 107

Chapter 16: Chelsea ... 117

Chapter 17: The Matriarchy ... 129

Chapter 18: Ariel ... 138

Chapter 19: Friz Knows ... 142

Chapter 20: Abbadon and Diobalst ... 149

Chapter 21: Bad Decisions ... 159

Chapter 22: Doti ... 166

Chapter 23: Loss of Control 175

Chapter 24: So That Happened 181

Chapter 25: Malcom in the Dark 190

Chapter 26: Vengeance 207

Chapter 27: End of the Tunnel 213

Chapter 28: The Breakup 222

Chapter 29: The Love of Jazign 229

Chapter 30: Consequences 247

Chapter 31: The Search 255

Chapter 32: The Dragon's Wisdom 270

Chapter 33: Katabasis 279

Chapter 34: Asmodeus 287

Chapter 35: The Justice of Emotion 295

Chapter 36: A Brother's Love 304

Chapter 37: Messages 313

Chapter 38: Descent 317

Chapter 39: Reunions 330

Chapter 40: Deeper into the Truth 338

Chapter 41: The Holy Ghost 348

Chapter 42: Plans 357

Chapter 43: Here Comes Trouble 368

Chapter 44: The Story of Lynn 376

Chapter 45: Nuclear Option 384

Chapter 46: The Builder's Mercy 394

Chapter 47: Devastation 403

Epilogue 410

About the Author 417

WHAT HAPPENED LAST TIME IN ENVIOUS, BOOK ONE OF THE RESONANCE OF SOULS TRILOGY?

ALL STORIES, EVEN THOSE WITH legendary or sacred status, risk embellishment and adulteration over time. Changes through translation or interpretation occur over generations. The metamorphosis appears circumstantial or accidental.

But what if they were not?

What if the curators of historical information skewed stories to suit the prevailing ideology of the time? Now imagine that those curators are not benevolent. In fact, they have a nefarious agenda to stop the progression of life by shaping dogma to end the creative process among humans.

The most published piece of literature in the current history of Earth, The Bible, has been translated into over seven hundred languages with over three thousand versions. Many stories in the Bible have been twisted by the hand of humans. Key stories, consistent with other biblical tales, have been altered. The truth has been bent to plant seeds of conflict. The prologue of *Envious* tells of one such story. The *intended* story of Cane and Abel. A story that divulges the origin of the Spurs.

You know nothing about Spurs because, as the curators of your history, they have hidden their own existence. They cleverly conceal their presence by obscuring their misdeeds with outlandish fictional tales.

Creatures such as vampires, ghosts, witches, and warlocks are historically dismissed as horror stories.

But these creatures are very real. Spurs are the most devasting force of evil on Earth.

The tale of *Envious* begins in a small town of Western Pennsylvania. A young man named Cassian broods over the forsaken love of his first girlfriend, Lynn. He learns of an incident of betrayal at a party held by the Bosco family—a small-time criminal organization with deep control of the town government and businesses. Over the phone, Cass laments the story with his best friend, Malcom, while sitting at home drinking cheap wine from his mother's liquor cabinet.

His next memories are a blur of unbelievable pain, strange experiences, and horrifying dreams. During this time, Cass has an extraordinary encounter with a beautiful woman who claims to have granted him a gift along with an ominous warning.

Cass begins to wake from his coma and realizes he is in a hospital following a severe car crash. He learns that he must accept the devastating loss of his right eye and left foot. During his long and transformative rehabilitation, he believes that, at times, he may have *jumped* into other people and seen from their perspective.

Cassian is a logical person and assumes that he must be imagining these events. He fears that brain damage from the head trauma is causing hallucinations or insanity.

Before leaving the hospital, he *jumps* into his hospital roommate. To Cassian's astonishment, his own body speaks to him. An entity calling himself Stu claims to be a celestial steward of universal knowledge.

Stu tells Cassian an unsettling truth regarding the universal increase in entropy. It is God and the angels that want chaos while Satan and the demons seek order. But their conversation is disrupted.

Once out of the hospital, Cass hijacks the body of his slightly inebriated older brother, Mike, to continue his conversation. Stu informs Cass that he has been shrouded by an angel. Shrouding is the term angels prefer over possession (they claim they do not control those they *possess*). But the angel grants Cassian the power to possess any person he wishes. However, there are things that Stu is not allowed to say. These are things that Cass must learn on his own. What Stu explains is that the gift is intended to eradicate Spurs.

A Spur, Stu continues, is a Hell-bound, human soul that is offered the opportunity to escape Hell and live on Earth. To do this, the Spur must convince desperate souls in the Dream World to allow them entrance to their body. Once a person *chooses* to acquiesce and allow the Spur entry, they are entrapped in their own mind until the body dies or the Spur leaves. The Spur, now in possession of that body, awakens the next morning to begin its reign of terror. But not in the ways you may imagine.

Stu warns Cass that Spurs are terrified of his power. Any who discover he is shrouded will send people to kill him. Stu emphatically warns Cass that *he* must destroy all who come to harm him.

Cass rejects suggestions that he may be in danger and discards any ideas of killing another person. The last thing that Stu explains before he leaves is that Cassian's nightmares are more than just nightmares. The Spurs want Cass among their ranks.

As Cass recuperates at home, he is fortunate that friends and teachers work with him to complete his coursework to graduate high school with his class. He is intending to go to the University of Pittsburgh in the fall.

Cassian's Anatomy and Physiology teacher is a young, beautiful woman who offers to help him with his studying. One evening, lust drives Cass to abuse his power. Through his actions, he learns an awful secret. Shamed by his betrayal of her trust, he quickly and carelessly tries to undo what he has done. The tragic consequences will haunt Cassian forever.

Cassian's grandmother, Betty, and step-grandfather, Bill, live nearby. Bill is wealthy and holds his money over the heads of everyone. He treats Cass and his immediate family like a pariah. After Cassian's car wreck, Bill chastises Cassian's mother, Pamela, at Easter dinner. Cass uses his power to make Bill take three (rather than one) pain pills prescribed to him. To the relief of everyone, Bill is soon rendered unconscious.

After this night, Bill begins the heavy consumption of alcohol, which he quit five years earlier. Cass hears about this during his grandmother's regular visits. She is disturbed by Bill's erratic behavior. Feelings of guilt cause Cass to see his power as a curse, only bringing about horrible events.

Against the wishes of his friend Malcom, Cass insists on going back to school to finish his senior year. Excited and terrified to see Lynn, Cass hears from Malcom just before his first class that Lynn is not at school. She is pregnant and living with her aunt in Virginia. Cass is furious with Malcom for not telling him sooner but eventually understands his friend's reasoning. He is now faced with the possibility that Lynn may be carrying his child.

While at school, Cass runs into Mary, Lynn's younger sister. This meeting brings back a flood of emotions. It seems Mary had always had a crush on Cassian. Cass is torn between his feelings of love and anger with Lynn and his rising interest in Mary. As the school year ends and summer begins, Cass begins to quietly date Mary.

When Lynn's older sister, Beth, who never liked Cass, learns that he is dating Mary, she furiously confronts Cassian. In his rage, he takes control of Beth and brings her to a party being held by the Bosco family. He hopes to learn the truth about what happened to Lynn on the night of her betrayal. What he does places him and his family on the radar of bad people. Cass jumps back to his own body, leaving Beth at the party, unconcerned about what horrors she would face.

Mary confronts Cassian about her sister's odd proclamation that Cass somehow drugged her. He can honestly respond that he did not but struggles to keep his deeper secret. Mary is much too sharp for Cass to deceive, but she seems to accept his story.

While on a date at a movie theater, Cass and Mary are confronted by a group of his former classmates. One of them, Williams, becomes belligerent with the couple. He says nasty things to both Cass and Mary. Cassian's sometime friend (and Williams's best friend), Jimmy, steps in with two other guys to pull Williams away before a fight occurs. Mary and Cass go to the other side of the theater to see a different movie.

Angry with what happened, but not strong enough to fight, Cass sneaks into the theater Williams is in and uses his power for revenge. This triggers a cascade of events that lead to catastrophic outcomes. Cass is forced into horrendous actions, just as Stu warned.

During these events, Cass is aided by the angel, Ex, that is shrouding him. Ex suggests immediate actions he must take to prevent similar situations from occurring in the future.

Following the advice of Ex, Cassian banishes his first Spur with the help of his two close friends, Tony and Malcom. Jimmy is freed from the Spur but is now mentally reduced to the ten-year-old boy he was when the Spur first took possession of him. Jimmy sees Cassian as a saint who released him from Hell. He becomes passionately loyal to Cassian.

Cass swears the three of them to secrecy after revealing his power to Tony and Malcom to assure that neither was possessed by a Spur. Now, three others know of Cassian's secret.

When Mary gets back from visiting Lynn, she informs Cass that Lynn had her child and named him Samuel. Cass tells Mary about what recently happened but still tap dances around being shrouded by an angel. Mary knows he is lying to her and gets angry. But Cassian assures her that he is not lying and that the Boscos have gotten Beth hooked on heroin. He warns Mary to stay far away from the Bosco family.

Bill gets arrested for killing two people while drinking and driving. Again, Cass feels responsible. Grandma Betty frets about losing Bill's wealth with no concern for the people he killed. Later that day, Cass learns the horrifying truth about the identity of the victims—Lynn and Samuel Richter. His guilt begins to turn into anger.

The next day, Bill and Betty humbly approach Cassian and Pamela offering to pay for Cassian's education. Bill attempts to negotiate a seedy deal where Cass must take full responsibility for fathering Samuel. It comes to light that Bill has business ties with the Bosco family. If Cass refuses the deal, Bill threatens that the Boscos will kill Cass and his family. Furious, Cassian makes the deal with Bill, but on *his* terms, not Bill's.

Cass tries to figure out why the Boscos would want to kill him. He considers that they may be Spurs and suspect he is shrouded. While continuing to keep his secret from Mary, Cass tells her about the Bosco threat. Her ability to break down the complexity of the situation helps Cass to see more clearly.

Cass finally and fearfully confronts the angel who has possessed him. The angel, Ex, explains to Cassian that they must prepare for his new purpose in life—the banishment of Spurs. Cass is terrified to learn that his life will henceforth be a roller-coaster ride of danger.

Ex considers the coming events to be an ideal training scenario for Cassian. The angel begins with lessons about the Dream World and the theories behind it. There are two aspects to dreams—Freewill dreams and Devotion dreams. Freewill dreams are normal dreams where you are free to make choices. This is where Spurs or demons attack to possess a body. Devotion dreams are spiritual dreams where astral projection allows one to travel to other places and other worlds to help fuel creation, thus the term *devotion*.

That night, Cassian's dream takes him to a room hidden deep within a cavern. The room contains eleven large books. In the middle of the room sits a stranger with a blurred face. Cass knows that this stranger is possessed by either a Spur, a demon, or another angel. The deep voice of the stranger makes Cass mentally label him with the nickname Vader. Vader will not speak about himself and advises Cassian not to let others know his identity in the Dream World.

In the conversation, Cass learns that not only are they not speaking the same language, but they are not even from the same world. Vader explains that the books are not for them and that the room housing the books is a sanctuary from the eyes of all others. If Cass can find the room again, he may be able to find some peace in the Dream World. Then the stranger leaves.

Cass attempts to touch one of the books set in the middle of the series. It causes him great pain. As he inspects the books, he moves down the line noticing more intricate work on the covers of the books as he moves from right to left. The last book is the smallest and has the most intricate cover. When he tries to touch that book, the pain is so intense that he awakes from the dream with his hand numb and sore.

The next day, Cass does not tell Ex about this room with the books. Ex continues his lessons by describing the origins and rules about Spurs. Ex tells him that while he is using his power, Spurs and demons can see the aura around the person he possesses as well as his own body. This is why he must be careful with the use of his gift.

While Mike is away at college, Cassian asks his mother to leave and take their dog, Sholette, to his aunt Susan's home. Pamela and Susan have not spoken in years, but Pamela will go if Cass agrees to go with her. Cass explains that he must confront this problem, and so Pamela refuses to leave. To help her understand, Cass reveals his secret to his mother. He tells her that they are in great danger. She eventually understands and agrees to help him, but she will not leave her son.

Tony's brother, Darren is one of the only uncorrupted cops in town. Tony informs Cass that his home was bugged because they suspected him of being involved in the heroin trade. It may only be the phones, but he can't be sure. Anyone listening could now know the secret he told his mother.

Cassian had been suspicious for a while that something was off about his grandmother. He visited her home and banished the Spur possessing her. Together, they question Bill and find out that he bugged Cassian's living room and Eric Bosco knows that Cass is shrouded. In the end, Grandma Betty shoots Bill in the chest.

Events begin to unfold quickly as the Boscos move to execute Cass. Ex teaches Cassian how to use his powers in this situation while they dispose of his would-be assassins. Oddly, though, they are armed with tranquilizer darts. Ex finds this to be strange. Historically, demons and Spurs have only ever tried to kill the angel's host.

After they are finished, Cass decides it's time to end the reign of the Bosco family. Afraid he may not survive, Cass gets his favorite food and goes to a peaceful place where he once spent a wonderful day with Mary. He awaits nightfall as he enjoys his (possibly) last meal.

Mary finds Cassian at this place and elaborately, yet violently, reveals her own secret to Cass. She has known that Cass was one of the shrouded since the night at the movie theater. She had been living in fear of him because she is possessed by an ancient Spur named Khalima.

Mary claims that Khalima is not evil, but very kind. Khalima helped Mary, and Mary loves her. She begs Cassian not to banish Khalima without at least hearing her story. Cass agrees for Mary's sake.

Khalima was once the wife of Cain. She was present when Abel was murdered by the hand of her husband. An angry God and bold Satan bargained over their dominion. The souls of Khalima, Cain, and eleven others were given to Satan that day. They became the original thirteen Spurs.

After centuries as a Spur or residing in Hell, Khalima changed her philosophy of life. She strongly warns Cass to be careful with his trust. She leaves Cassian to speak with his angel and advises that he learn the story of the origins of the serpent.

Cassian needs a host body to speak with Ex. He has Mary find Malcom and send him to a place they both know well. As he is parked in the location waiting for Malcom, he has an odd experience where he jumps from lifeform to lifeform. He can feel the energy of every living thing and the power is overwhelming.

Cass falls into a deep sleep that leads him to the worst nightmare of his life. He begs God for help. When he does this, the sky opens and a creature reminiscent of a large stingray floats above him. It is wearing what looks like a parachute pack on its chest. When over him, the pack opens and a white rain falls upon Cass and the horrors that are tormenting him.

The demons and Spurs are burned and driven away by the white rain. Cass then experiences the truth about his life. He is confronted by the good and the bad, both done to him and what he has done to others. Then he feels love and hate in the same way. Other emotions swing back and forth, weaving a pattern around the backbone of his lifeline. He sees other lifelines interacting with his own. He sees how he hurt other people. He learns a personal lesson on forgiveness and kindness.

When he emerges from this experience, he meets Ex face to face. Ex shows him the true image of the angelic form. Ex then guides Cass through his crisis of conscience over killing people. Cass is warned that he must get over it because he is going to have to kill again…soon. They are now able to communicate without a host conduit.

As they drive to the Bosco home, Ex then tells Cass the original, untainted story of the Garden of Eden. This leaves Cassian confused as the story reflects the actions of Khalima. Her good faith in not harming Cass may be a ploy to entrap a gullible teen that may be thinking with his hormones. He must decide if he can trust her.

When he gets to the Bosco estate, Ex and Cass learn that they have been lured there by two willing demons, Eric and Mitch Bosco. This is more than Ex can handle, and they are soon captured.

They want Cassian for his ability to resonate with other life forms, as he had done earlier that night. His power in their hands would allow the demons to find and destroy other angels in the world.

They torture him to accept a fellow demon into his body. As they force him to sleep, Cass goes into the Dream World to find help. Once there, his faithful dog, Sholette, appears to guide him.

With the help of his friends, Cassian escapes to bring a fiery wrath upon Eric Bosco. Meanwhile, Jimmy has led Mitch away from Eric into the woods using his knowledge of the Dream World. When Cass is free, he attempts to save Jimmy, but it's too late. Mitch killed him.

Cass confronts Mitch only to find that he is wearing a strange device that prevents Cass from accessing the power of Ex. The demon gets the better of Cass and tries to convince him to join forces with him.

Mary and Khalima disrupt the device, allowing Cassian to break free and kill the demon inside Mitch. As Mitch begins to beg for his life, Malcom and Tony shoot and kill him.

But there was a third demon. Barry Bosco was the worst of the three. He attacked Cassian with the same device that Mitch wore. As he was about to kill Cassian, Mary begs God for help as Cass had done earlier. The sky opens and angels begin to surge through the rift, pouring the white rain on everything. But they are too late to save Mary. Barry Bosco killed her as she sat unprotected with her hands to the sky.

Cassian kills both Barry and the demon possessing Barry.

Khalima then speaks to Cassian. She has been forgiven by God and allowed to become a steward. Though Mary and Jimmy are dead, their souls will live on, and Cassian must begin his new life as one of the shrouded.

CHAPTER 1

WESTERN PENNSYLVANIA, 1987

SATURDAY

CORRINA RAN FRANTICALLY INTO THE dark woods with only a trace of moonlight coming through the thick trees. She had no idea which direction to run, but she knew she was getting away from that terrible house. Her clothes were torn, and she could feel the cool night air passing over her chest and backside. She hurt in so many places.

Her shoulder slammed into a thin tree that spun her around as she fell to the ground. The soft forest floor with leaves and scrub brush eased the fall. Pushing herself up, she looked back in the direction she came. *Was that the direction she came from?* There were no lights and no other noise but the subtle background of crickets in the night. She listened carefully for sounds of pursuit. Nothing.

She turned back to the direction she thought she was running and began to walk. She felt around her body for injuries. Her thighs were sticky from blood and ached like someone punched her inner thigh muscles. Her right hip hurt so bad. Her mouth and throat were dry and it caused pain to swallow. Her head felt foggy with the creeping sensation of a headache starting. How did she get here?

Her friend, Carol, talked her into going to this house party in the woods. It was a long drive out of town along dark roads. There was a house with lights and music…and a swimming pool. Did someone give her a drink? Maybe. She didn't like the taste of alcohol and always turned it down. *Why can't I remember?* she thought.

She blinked her eyes and a burst of light and cloudy images filled her mind. Pain. Pain in her private parts. *No!* she screamed as the man pushed her down. *What happened?!* She tried to remember.

She was on a sofa…or was it a chair? The French doors were right in front of her. She tasted blood. She flew up in an instant and ran for the door, sprinting for the line of trees off to the right. It didn't seem like anyone was chasing her. But she kept running. Her feet were bare, but she paid no attention as fear pushed her onward. She had no idea where to go. That was as far back as she could recall. Everything else was completely gone. How was that possible?

Panic overcame her again, and she started to run in the faint moonlight. The pain soon kicked in so she slowed to a walk, feeling the weight of her situation. Lost in the dark. She must have been drugged or something. She reached up and felt around her head. There were some aches on her face, but no large, painful bumps like she was knocked unconscious. Most of the pains she was feeling were…inside.

She knew what happened. She fell to the ground and began to cry. Her mother and father warned her about this kind of thing. She never believed it could actually happen. Corrina curled up in a ball and wept tears of shame. Her mother was going to be so mad at her. She would be grounded for weeks…probably months. Her clothes were torn and bloody. She was going to be in so much trouble.

• • •

The sound of chirping birds filled her ears before she realized the cold on her side. Corrina opened her eyes and saw dried leaves and broken twigs in the forefront of trees with light shining through. Stiffly, she began to push herself upright. The pain in her right leg and hip screamed as she stood and looked around, listening for sounds of civilization.

Based on the amount of dew on the ground, it must still be early morning. The sun was off to her right. Corrina recalled that they were going north and west out of town the night before. She put the sun on her left and began to walk in a southern direction. Twenty minutes later, she heard the sound of a car on a road. She altered her direction slightly to the east, in the direction of the noise, and continued walking.

Corrina broke through the trees and found herself on an embankment overlooking an isolated road. She climbed down the steep slope and began to trudge toward the east. She covered herself the best she could with her torn clothing. When the trees opened, she stopped and stood in the warm sun, hoping to chase away the chill she felt in her whole body. Her throat hurt to swallow, and she could feel the glands in her neck were swollen. She was sure she must be getting sick.

The hopelessness of her situation crashed on her, and she began to weep as she continued walking along the road. The sound of a car approaching around the bend ahead frightened her. She considered running into the woods to hide. The embankment was nearly ten feet high, and it looked like there was poison ivy covering the hill. Before she could make a decision, a blue Ford Bronco rounded the bend.

The shocked look on the face of the man behind the wheel made her cry even harder. *What must she look like?* Beat up, bloody, limping, and crying. She heard the car stop behind her. She didn't turn but kept walking.

Someone was running up to her. She couldn't look.

SIX YEARS LATER...

"I know it is you who resonates with one of the shrouded, Tinilfasela," Unfamiqua said.

"It's no secret. To be forthcoming with you, I was not too happy that you started here as a Karma steward. It would have taken me many cycles to get to that level under normal circumstances. And yet you simply walk into it…without ever being shrouded," Tinilfasela said.

"When will you be speaking with him again?" Unfamiqua asked. "I need to get a message to him."

"You are amazingly unfazed by my confession. It was meant to be off-putting to you if not outright offensive."

"Yes. I did notice. When will you be speaking with him again?" Unfamiqua repeated.

Tinilfasela looked quizzically and said, "You are supposed to know *nothing* about this shrouded. What message could you possibly have for him? This is no business of yours. You were told to stay away from him or anyone related with the incidents that freed you. Can you not simply learn from the three major realms of existence and be happy?"

"No. I cannot. You may have been shrouded when you carried a mortal body, but have you ever experienced the qualia of pain of being held down by possession?"

"I have not," Tinilfasela said, "but I know of the pain it brings to a mind in our realm of consciousness."

"So, you have no experience with it in any way. You have never felt the endless remorse of time passing in Hell. You and your fellow stewards could learn much from me if you would open your minds and free yourselves from the Grad machinations," Unfamiqua said.

"You suffered in Hell from your own decisions. You were given a choice, and you chose to become a Spur. The Spurs and demons are enemies to our kind.

"As you seem to have information about the shrouded with whom I resonate, any hint of betrayal, and I will be looking at *you*," Tinilfasela said.

"You disappoint me, Tinilfasela. He needs and deserves better than that. You should know that calling the Spurs and demons *enemy* is foolish. They serve God as surely as any angel or steward. And do not act like there are not stewards serving their side as well. It is not me betraying him or you. Those stewards were in your ranks before I got here.

"What I need to tell him is important. Can you please listen to what I have to say? If you decide not to help me, then I will not ask you again. I will find another way to get my message to him," Unfamiqua said.

Tinilfasela paused for a moment thinking, then said, "Tell me what you want. I will listen and decide." Sighing, Tinilfasela added, "I pray this is not my greatest folly. You know the Grads are watching me closely and Illoc cannot stand my presence. If you stir the wrath of that buffoon against me, I will do what I can to make your studies difficult."

Unfamiqua said, "Your terms are acceptable. I have no intention of drawing their wrath or even their slightest attention. As you stated, I am not supposed to be interfering. The Grad stewards as well as the rest of you want a reason to rid yourselves of me. But none can do that without great cause.

"I vowed that I would *end* possession and shrouding if I could. And I will attempt to fulfill that vow. In return, I can tell you about Hell. I can tell you much about Limbo as well. I know things that the second tome of knowledge may not have recorded."

"I said I would listen to you. I do this more out of concern for my resonant than for you or what you claim to know. I would rather not be associated with you…especially while the Grads are monitoring my actions," Tinilfasela said.

"I have spent thousands of years being isolated and treated as an outcast. I expect no different treatment from beings claiming to be of a higher order or in some way intellectual. I turned my isolation around and learned to feel love and peace and compassion…more than I have been shown in my time *here*. I carry that love with me, Tinilfasela. Not you, the Grads, the angels, the demons—or even Azazel himself—could take that from me. I have no room in my heart for vengeance against these beings, but I will do what I can for those I love.

"The demons are planning something against your resonant. I know this, but I do not know what. I believe they are being helped by a high-level steward. I need to warn him. I would like you to send a Cysistal stone. If I cannot convince you to help me in my endeavor, I will find a way to do it myself, even if I must breach the forbidden knowledge in the thirteenth tome," Unfamiqua said.

"A Cysistal stone! Maybe one of my arms too. I would need approval for that."

"Yes. Will you help?"

"I said I would listen. Can you please get on with it. My next window to speak with him should occur in about seven to ten Earth years. I'm not sure you will have enough time to tell me what you want at the rate you are going!" Tinilfasela said sarcastically.

Unfamiqua smiled and said, "It is good you resonate with the boy. You remind me of him. I don't know what you have heard about me or about what you may have read. You Watchers have been privy to much knowledge unknown to me. For instance, I only recently learned in book one about the four thousand years of Matriarchy before the Flood. I spent most of that time in Hell and knew nothing of what transpired with the Nephilim, the Elioud, and the truth of what they call the Antediluvian era.

"You may not trust me, Tinilfasela, but I am your ally. I will not betray you and certainly not the identity of your resonant. I earned my redemption from God through his trust. I will nevertheless continue to do everything I can to right the wrongs of my past. I was one of the thirteen souls never given a choice. I was known by the name Khalima, wife of Cain, son of Eve."

CHAPTER 2

BOSTON, 2025

Franklin Germane awoke on a Thursday morning with a stiff neck. Unsurprising, after the stressful interaction from his previous day at work. Not the first time his neck hurt after a high-stress situation. It would be better in a few days.

Confrontations with his boss and line manager always had him treading dangerously close to the grounds for termination. His proclivity for sarcasm, abhorrence of coerced, meaningless servitude, and lack of sensible filtering never served him well in his professional life. But nothing ever made him fight more than the yoke of oppression being lowered onto his neck…which seemed to be aching worse by the minute.

He had been an employee at Abbadon Pharmaceuticals for nearly ten years. The company paid well, but vacation, or any kind of time off, was kind of a joke. Three weeks of vacation for the first ten years, then a fourth week. You also had unlimited days off for illness. Officially, all employees are encouraged to form a great work–life balance for their physical and mental well-being.

Of course, realistically, most employees were pressed so hard by timelines that they rarely took off more than two weeks in a year. Even when ill, many pushed to keep working. The pandemic made it much easier for people to work from home too. If you balanced that with an average ten-hour workday and weekend work, Abbadon got their employees for a bargain.

The argument with his boss started as a calm explanation about why there was no way he, or anyone else for that matter, could accept the new project timelines without major changes to the current software platform. It wasn't that he objected to working hard, but the massive amount of valueless work required with the existing software was not even close to possible in the projected timeframe. Months—not days—would be needed.

The software platform in question was conveniently brought to the company several years ago (when Franklin was laid off) by his sycophantic line manager, Azizullah, who went by Aziz in the office. Aziz promoted the product to the department vice president and other leaders as a "future-proof" tool designed specifically for flawless protein sequencing and structure determination.

In reality, the product was an antiquated sack of crap built with a clunky old language, layered with so much useless code that it could barely function. Modifications were made by writing scripts to fix problems. These always created more problems. Franklin thought, *Who even wrote scripts anymore?*

There were at least two competing platforms that were superior to this one in every way. That didn't matter to Aziz as he would never have to personally use the software. He merely directed others to use it.

For a man who prayed five times a day and proclaimed to detest lying, he certainly mastered the art of deceit. Aziz openly displayed a subservient and ingratiating façade to peers and superiors. But as soon as they were gone, he clamored relentlessly about how they were so "dumb and stupid" as he put it. Franklin found this amusing coming from someone as close-minded as this guy.

Probably the worst thing Franklin witnessed from Aziz was the deep respect he displayed for women in their presence…and the utter contempt he demonstrated toward them when they left the room. He was no different than the old, two-faced church biddies he recalled from his youth. Franklin occasionally told people, but nobody believed him since Aziz appeared to be so polite and respectful to everybody. *What a joke!* he thought. *Why are the uber-religious so often like this?*

After an hour-long battle that did not end nearly as calmly as it started, they eventually came to a compromise. This was not so much a compromise as an acceptance of a pathway destined to fail. But it did serve as lip-service to get him away from the pointless discourse. He agreed to upgrade his computer to one with more processing speed and RAM to fix the software issues. *Upgrading RAM is the first sign of a shitty software*, he thought.

He left work that evening reflecting on his great luck that he wasn't fired after insinuating Aziz was receiving kickbacks to push this garbage product. Of course, that was much better than some other comments he withheld; particularly the one reducing Aziz to a life-support system for the bacteria in his shit.

Just thinking about the argument sent a fresh surge of pain up his cervical region. He could feel tension from the top of his head down to the base of his neck. Looking in the mirror, he noticed he was hunched over like a question mark. He reached up and tried to massage the knotted muscles around his spine as he stretched his head around in circles. It hadn't been this bad since his grandmother died.

Maybe a few Ibuprofens and a hot shower would help. It was a small comfort that Friday was almost there and it was a three-day weekend for Memorial Day.

Once Franklin completed his morning routine, he went downstairs to the kitchen to drink the protein shake that his wife, Victoria, made for him. She was always up and out the door by 6 a.m. He wouldn't see her until he got home around 7 p.m. or so.

She was an emergency room doctor and never knew when she would be finished. They didn't get much time together during the weekdays but always did nice things like this for each other.

Victoria was fifteen years older than Franklin. They met online in 2015 when he was twenty-seven years old. They had been dating for several weeks before he found out that she was forty-two. She looked like she was in her twenties. It didn't bother him at all, but he did worry that she may feel less secure dating someone so much younger. He soon realized that the last thing Victoria Penner felt was insecurity.

They were married seven months after their first date. It was hard to believe that was ten years ago. She was now fifty-two but looked younger than him. Whatever she was doing to keep her youth was working marvelously.

As he drank his breakfast, his phone buzzed with a text. It was from Victoria. "Good morning! Did you sleep okay? Around 3 a.m. or so, I thought you were having a seizure."

He wrote back, "No, I didn't sleep well. Neck is stiff and sore."

"Not surprised. It was like your whole body spazzed! Hope you feel better. Take some Ibuprofen."

The drug had been coursing through him for the last half hour. He was losing hope that it was going to help. He texted back, "I'll be fine. Just the (poop emoji) I told you last night…about work."

"Fuck those people. Just do your job and get out of there. I'm going to see if Wendy can fit you in tonight for a massage," she wrote back.

That sounded like a great idea. He hadn't had a massage in months. Surprising how sedentary work produced more muscle knots than physical labor. He would know, after spending years in the lab and in the field for his job. Only in the past three years did he get promoted to a desk job directing the science.

Some promotion. He was making less money salaried than hourly, and he could feel himself getting fatter every year. At least until Victoria said something to him, and she started him on a fixed-calorie diet that seemed to be working.

Damn my neck hurts, he thought as he recalled this happening to him several times in his life, but this was so much worse. He continued trying to stretch it as he texted Victoria, "Yes, please. See if Wendy can fit me in. It doesn't even have to be Wendy."

"What if it was Scott?" she texted back.

"Fine with me. I don't care about getting a man-sage. LOL."

"Ok, but no complaints later (shrugging girl emoji). I'll text you later. Love you (heart emoji)," she responded.

"Thank you! (kissy face emoji) Love you too!" It was going to be a long day.

He went back upstairs to change his shoes. He put on the new pair he recently bought and decided to change back into his old pair. No need to have his neck and feet both hurting at the end of the day.

He turned on the closet light to find the shoes and noticed his shadow on the back wall. It looked like there was a lump sticking out on the back of his neck. He reached up and didn't feel anything where his hand met the shadow.

He stepped out of the closet to check the mirror. Nothing was there. Probably just a trick of the lighting. He got his old shoes, swapped them on his feet, and headed off to work.

Victoria texted him around 2 p.m. Neither Scott nor Wendy could fit him in for a massage, but they had a new girl, Stephanie, who was open. She booked him for 7 p.m. By 3 p.m., Franklin decided he would be fine with the Boston Strangler giving him a massage. Odd that that was what came to mind. It felt like something was wrapped around his neck.

He started the workday by ordering his new computer. It would take about a week to have it built and sent to him and another week or so to transfer or download everything he needed to the new drive. He recalled a time when he would get excited by the prospect of computer upgrades and the added capabilities. After his third or fourth computer, the ass-pain seemed far worse than any slight improvements in speed or capability.

It was a slow day, and he was finished with everything he could get done by around 5:30 p.m. He never saw Aziz once. That was great because Aziz didn't work on Fridays. Franklin would get a full four days away from the tiny tyrant. Small triumphs were better than none, and he was looking forward to getting a massage.

He parked his car on the street as the meters didn't charge after 6 p.m. He was only about eight or nine spaces away from the spa. The sun warmed his back as he got out of his car and walked to the door. He stopped, turned, and tilted his head back for a moment to feel the pleasant heat of the sun on his face. He loved the longer, warmer days of summer.

When he got to the door of the spa and opened it, he had to turn to his right to enter. He noticed that his lengthened shadow on the sidewalk looked odd near his head. It looked like a lump sticking out of his neck again. He paused for a moment with the door opened and moved back and forth to see if the shadow changed.

"Franklin? Is that you?" asked the receptionist, startling him out of his head bobbing.

He turned toward her and walked in, forgetting about the shadow as he said, "Oh, ah, yes. Hi, Becky. I think Victoria booked me for a 7 p.m. appointment. I know I'm early."

"Yes," she said politely, "with Stephy. She's new but really good. I could barely recognize you. You look all hunched over…and the sun is kind of in my face."

"Oh, yeah," he replied as he walked over to the front desk, "my neck has been killing me all day. I feel like I must have pulled something." He looked down into her squinting face as the sun angled in, making it tough for her to see. He said, "You should get a blind or something in here. That's got to be tough on your eyes."

Becky said, "Yeah, I told them we need something for the late afternoon on these sunny days. Scott thinks we should move the display shelves in front of the window, but I don't like the idea of not being able to see outside the rest of the day. I love watching all the people walk by. Plus, all the products would be sitting in the hot sun. So, your neck is bothering you?"

"Well, you said it yourself. I look all hunched over. I don't even notice that. I'm just super uncomfortable," he replied.

"Ok. Let's see if Stephy can get you straightened out. You're all checked in. Why don't you head into the relaxation room and have a seat. We have heated neck wraps if you want one while you wait?"

"Sure," Franklin agreed, "that sounds good to me."

"Hang on a sec. I have them right over here," she said as she got up and went over to what looked like a mini fridge. She opened it and brought out something that looked like a tube-shaped bean bag about eighteen inches long. She handed it over and said, "Here ya go. Hope this helps. Stephy has a lot of experience, so I think she can definitely help you."

"Thanks, Becky," Franklin said as he took the hot neck wrap and went to the door of the relaxation room.

The room was plush, pie-shaped, and dimly lit. The light seemed to come from behind the furniture and up the walls. The wider part fit several comfortable leather chairs with the narrow wall featuring a stone waterfall that gave off the relaxing sound of flowing water. Not an overwhelming or deafening sound, it effectively provided a soothing atmosphere.

Franklin sank into one of the chairs and placed the wrap around his neck. It was wonderfully warm, and he felt tension release from his shoulders immediately. He closed his eyes, took a deep breath, and let it out.

CHAPTER 3

THE MASSAGE

A WARM HAND ON HIS FOREARM gently shook him as a voice said, "Excuse me, sir. Excuse me."

Franklin turned to his right to face the voice. The left side of his neck screamed in protest.

As his face twisted in pain, the voice said, "Oh, I am so sorry I startled you. I think you were sleeping. Also, sorry that I'm a little late. My name is Stephy."

He looked up into the plain but pretty face of a woman who he guessed was in her 50s, but it was difficult to tell at first glance in a dim light. His mental image of Stephy was a young girl with unnaturally colored hair who said "like" and "ya know" far too often.

Bewildered, Franklin said, "Late? No, I was early. It's okay. What time is it?" as he pushed himself upright to stand.

"It's about five past seven. When did you get here?" she asked.

"Oh wow! I got in here about six thirty. I must have really been out. I hope I wasn't snoring or anything."

"No," she said, "at least not when I came in. Do you want some water or need to use the restroom?"

"Actually, I would like some water," he said, walking over to the cucumber water spigot next to the door. He used one of the supplied paper cups to take a drink. He downed three small cups as he said, "Sorry, I guess I was thirsty," pouring himself a fourth cup and sipping it as he rinsed his mouth.

Stephy led him to the back room and held the door for him as he entered an even more dimly lit massage room. She started the conversation quickly and professionally by saying, "Aside from your neck, which clearly seems to be bothering you, is there anything else you would like me to work on?"

"No," glad now that he wore his old shoes today, "it's mostly my neck."

"What seems to be wrong and where's it hurting," she probed.

Franklin began, "I woke up this morning and my whole neck on both sides was stiff, more so on the left side. My wife said I was spazzing in my sleep or something. I didn't wake up or anything. Now it feels like there's a weight tied to my head pulling me down or like something is pushing my head forward," as he motioned with both hands around the sides of his neck, "I've been uncomfortable all day."

She came back, "Anything causing tension or stress?"

"Yes," he continued, "usual work stuff. Well, I guess a lot more than usual, but not the worst I've ever experienced either. I've had pain like this a few times before, but not this bad."

"Okay," she said, "Do you have any dizziness, fatigue, nausea, or anything out of the ordinary that I should know about?"

Franklin thought about it for a moment, realizing that he almost said something about how his shadow looked wrong. That would have certainly set her first impression to *crazy*. So he said, "No…no. Nothing that I can think of. Just the stress of fighting with my boss."

"Okay," she said, "I know how that can be. I'll step out of the room and you can get undressed to your level of comfort and under the cover facing down, with your face in the cradle. Do you want the heat on in the bed?"

"No, thank you," he said, "it's only nice at first, then it makes me sweat. Oh, by the way, would you mind adding aromatherapy to the session?"

"I'm sorry, Franklin. I thought they told people up front. I have allergies to some of the oils they use in the aromatherapy. I can't use them. Is that going to be a problem?" she asked, seeming genuinely disappointed.

"Oh, no, no…not at all," Franklin said. "I like the smell, and I always thought that most therapists preferred using the pleasant scents."

"Oh, good," she sounded relieved. "I hate to put a damper on any-one's experience. I'll step out now and give you a few minutes."

After she left, Franklin got undressed and under the cover facing down. He played with the face cradle to get comfortable when a light knock came to the door.

"Come in," he responded.

Stephy came in and turned the lights even lower, then adjusted the covers to expose his back. She began at the base of his back and worked her way up. After about six or seven minutes, she started on his neck. It felt good to have the muscles massaged, but it didn't cause any pain that he usually experienced when there were knots being released. Within about a minute, Stephy abruptly pulled her hands away.

It was another full minute before she began working again. Cold hands started at the top of his head and gently moved down the sides and back of his head toward the base of his skull. This time, when Stephy got to his neck, only thirty seconds passed before she quickly pulled her hands away.

It sounded as if she were furiously shaking her hands, so Franklin asked, "Is everything okay?"

"Yes," she said, sounding skeptical. "It's just that both of my hands went numb at the same time. It's really odd. I've never had that happen before. Could you please give me a moment."

"Sure," he said.

She left the room and came back in a couple minutes with a few towels. She said, "I have some hot towels I would like to try if that's okay with you?"

"Of course," he said, knowing they usually charged extra for hot towels.

She said, "Okay, let me know if this is too hot," as she laid the towel over his neck and upper back. It wasn't too hot. It felt great. She began to rub his neck through the towel and only made it about a minute before pulling her hands back and shaking them again. The towel on his neck now felt cold. She took the towel away and added another hot towel to his neck and shoulders. She rubbed his shoulders and made her way toward his neck again. It was, maybe, twenty seconds before her hands flew away and the towel felt cold again.

"I'm sorry," she said. Then began to hesitantly add, "Th…this really…never happened to me before. It's like…I don't know…I can't feel my hands at all."

"Oh God," Franklin said. "Are you okay?" he asked, sounding concerned.

"Yes, I'm sure it's fine," she assured, though something in her tone suggested otherwise, "I'm just…ummm. Please, relax. I'll be fine in a moment."

He could hear her rubbing her hands together, and after about a minute, she removed the towel from his neck, quickly dried the area and covered his back with the blanket. She then moved to his feet, lifted the blanket, and began working on his right foot. Her grip was strong as she worked her way up his ankle and over his calf. She was quite good, but this wasn't the area that was hurting him.

He didn't say anything as she continued to work on his legs. Soon, she had him flip onto his back as she held the blanket and then began to work on his feet, shins, arms, and shoulders. As the session was drawing to a close, she walked to his head and began the last part where she massaged his face and neck. Starting with her fingertips on the sides of his crown, she worked down toward his neck. She slid her hands and forearms under his head, just past the trapezius muscles, and began to rub up toward his neck.

Suddenly, she yelped like a dog, startling Franklin as she threw her whole body back against the wall. It was a loud thump. He sat up quickly and turned to see if she was injured.

Stephy's face was contorted in a look of anguish as both of her arms hung at her sides, not moving. From just below the shoulder, the skin looked as white as bone. She began to sob as she spoke. "I'm so sorry, Franklin…something must be wrong with me. I can't feel my arms," she cried, rushing the words out. She sounded terrified.

The door flew open and Scott stood in the threshold, looking as if he was going to have to fight someone, his eyes darting between Stephy and Franklin. "What happened?" he shouted. "What did you do?"

"I…I didn't…nothing," Franklin stumbled. "She pulled her hands away like it was causing her pain. See if she's okay," he snapped to Scott as he gestured to Stephy.

Scott ran to Stephy and placed both of his hands on her upper arms as he faced her.

"OW," he barked as he pulled both hands back, shaking them like he got an electric shock.

"Scott, what's happening?" she cried. "What did I do to you?"

"It's okay, Stephy," Scott tried to sound calm. "Your arms are cold. That's all."

He reached out again like he was expecting pain and began to rub her upper arms, trying to get the blood flowing into them. If it was hurting him, he didn't react, he kept rubbing her arms.

Wendy then appeared at the door with Becky behind her, looking in like a nosy, traffic rubbernecker.

"What's going on?" Wendy said, turning the lights up and looking bitterly at Franklin like he did something violent.

Franklin ignored Wendy and Becky as he wrapped the blankets around his lower half and stood. He was worried about Stephy as he walked over behind Scott. His neck was hurting, but not as bad as when he came to the spa.

"Stephy, I'm…ahh," Franklin stopped himself from apologizing as he realized they were already thinking he was the bad guy here. Then he said, "What…what happened?"

"Franklin," Wendy said tersely, "I think you should step away from Stephy."

"No!" Stephy exclaimed through her tears. "He didn't do anything wrong, Wendy. My arms went numb. I can't feel them. Not at all. I think I need to see a doctor or something."

Wendy looked at Franklin and then said, "I'm sorry, Franklin. It's just…it looks like…"

Franklin, once again ignored her as he focused on Stephy. He asked, "Did it feel cold again? Your hands were cold after every time you pulled them away."

Stephy nodded and said, "It felt like a cold pain shot up my arms and then," she paused looking at both of her arms. Seeing them so white must have terrified her as she started to cry again.

Scott began to focus on her right arm, rubbing it from her shoulder down to her hand. Wendy came over and reached for her left hand.

When she touched her, she pulled back and exclaimed, "Jesus Christ! Your arm…it…it's cold, but…I don't know."

Scott looked sternly at Wendy and calmly but forcefully said, "Wendy, please take her left arm and help me. She'll be fine. I want to get the blood flowing into her hands. Come on."

Wendy did as she was told. She seemed distressed by having to touch Stephy again but soon took up similar actions to what Scott was doing.

Franklin turned to Becky and said, "Do you have any aspirin? Or can you get some?"

Wendy, getting where he was going chimed in, "Becky, I have some in my purse. It's in my locker, but it's open. In the center compartment, there is a bottle of aspirin. Please get them and bring some water for Stephy."

Becky looked stunned but nodded as she turned to run down the hall. She came back in a few minutes with a cup of water and a small, travel-size container of aspirin.

"Get two out and put them in Stephy's mouth," Wendy said.

"Here," Franklin said, using his one free hand to take the water out of her hand so she could open the childproof bottle.

As Becky put the two aspirin in Stephy's mouth, Franklin thought that some color was beginning to come back into her hands. He handed Becky the water, and she gingerly helped Stephy drink it.

"Call 911, Becky," Scott said.

"No!" Stephy protested, "I don't want all this attention! Besides, I don't have…" she looked down as she muttered, "insurance."

"Just do it, Becky. Now!" Scott said forcefully enough that Becky turned and ran down the hallway again. "Don't worry about that. This happened at work. We'll take care of the bills, Stephy. This is important."

Stephy began to cry again, but this time it seemed more because she was touched by his concern for her well-being as she said, "Thank you, Scott. People are not usually that…" she paused getting choked up, "kind to me," she managed to say.

They walked Stephy out of the room into the hallway so that Franklin could get dressed. He shut the door, dropped the blankets, and got dressed as quickly as possible.

It was about two minutes later that he emerged from the room into an empty hallway. He ran out into the lobby and was relieved to see that Stephy was now able to bend her arms and start to move her fingers.

Shortly after that, the ambulance arrived with as much noise and fanfare as one could possibly expect. Franklin thought, *Why don't they have a damn parade and fireworks to advertise more.*

Two large men and one petite woman came out of the ambulance. One of the men carried a large black case. The men immediately set about assessing Stephy's condition as the woman began to ask Wendy questions. Franklin realized that he had to urinate badly. He slipped back into the hallway he was in and went into the bathroom.

The lighting was on his right side. As he relieved himself, he noticed his shadow on the wall. It looked like he had a small child riding horseback on his shoulders. He stood in shock as he observed his shadow. It was moving and blending in with the shadow of his head. It was getting smaller like it knew he could see it. His left ear began to ring loudly. He reached up, but nothing was there.

He zipped up and went to the mirror, turning one way and then another trying to see something. Nothing was there. He noticed then that the middle bulb of the bathroom light bar was flickering. That must have been what he was seeing. He couldn't have possibly seen anything like that. Probably everything the last few days, and now this. He thought, *Great, now I'm seeing shit. Maybe I'm the one who needs to go to the doctor,* as he washed his hands.

He went back into the lobby, and they were taking Stephy's blood pressure since both arms now looked normal again. The woman from the ambulance came over to him and said, "Hello, sir, my name is Dr. Sampson. Good thinking getting the aspirin. I would have suggested the same thing."

Franklin said, "I couldn't think of anything else to do. Do you know what this could have been?"

"I have a few ideas," she said, and then, almost in a whisper, "but honestly, no. If it was one arm, maybe. But both arms at the same time," she shook her head, "this is a new one for me. Did you happen to notice anything odd?"

"Well, twice she pulled her hands away from my neck when she was massaging it. She said she couldn't feel her hands. I came in today because my neck has been stiff and sore all day. It was weird that it only seemed to happen when she was working on my neck," he replied.

Franklin then asked, "Is it common to have doctors riding in the ambulance?"

"Not really," she said. "I volunteered for this. I'm doing ride-alongs with the paramedics and EMTs. It helps with my internship. I've seen a lot of weird stuff doing this, so this isn't all that bad. But still…" She shrugged, then said, "Have you seen a doctor about your neck?"

"No, I just woke up today and it was stiff and sore. I've been pretty stressed at work lately. I'm sure it will pass," he said, having a flash of memory seeing his shadow move.

"Do you want me to have a look? You may have some swollen glands or something else. I could check. It would only take a moment," she said.

"No. No, I don't think this is the right place. I don't want people seeing a medical professional looking at my neck like *they* did something wrong." He nodded toward Becky who was now back behind the desk answering a phone call.

"Fair point," she said, "but if it's still bothering you tomorrow, you may want to get it checked out."

"Thank you, Dr. Sampson," he said.

"Rita," she said, smiling brightly at him. The smile made her look far too young to be a doctor, and he also realized that she was quite attractive. He supposed he wasn't used to seeing very many girls these days without their hair and makeup done. Rita Sampson looked like she woke up, splashed water on her face, and was off to work. Then she added, "I work most days at the Brigham and Women's ER. You can always stop by there if you want someone to look at it."

Franklin smiled back and said, "Thanks, but I'll make an appointment with my regular doctor."

Her face turned red as she shrugged and said, "Of course. I'm sure you have a primary care doctor. I'm just," she paused looking awkward, "I'm new at this doctor thing, and I just want to help people."

"I understand," he said as he began to feel awkward as well, then burst out, "Aftershave!"

Rita's face quickly transitioned into a puzzled look as he continued, "I wonder. Stephy said she was allergic to a lot of the aromatherapy oils. Maybe my aftershave or cologne may have caused a reaction?"

"I suppose that's as good as anything I can think of right now," Rita said. "Would you mind if I got the brand names from you? That way if Stephy decides to follow up, maybe we can test her for allergens."

"Sure," he said, "I can write them down for you. I also recently switched to a glycerin soap. I think it's scented plumeria. It's like a purple color. Who knows. Maybe it's something weird that I use, or some combination."

"I like plumeria soap. Bath and Body Works?" she asked.

"Probably," he said. "My wife gets it, so I'm not entirely sure."

"Oh," Rita said, seeming a bit deflated. "Yeah, that's…that's probably where she gets it. Um…thanks for your help, and again, good thinking with the aspirin. If you can write those down, that would be great." She turned toward Stephy and walked away.

Was this young doctor trying to flirt with me? Maybe. He never was good at reading signals from women. He went to the desk and asked Becky for some paper. She gave him a Post-it. He used one of the pens in a cup at the front desk to write down the brands of shaving cream, aftershave, soap, even toothpaste…just in case it could help. He walked over to Rita with the paper held out and said, "Excuse me, Rita. Here's what I used today."

She took the paper and professionally said, "Thank you, Mr. Germane."

Franklin said, "My wife is actually an ER doctor at Beth Israel. That's pretty close to B and W. Maybe you know her. Victoria Germane."

"No. I don't know her. The hospitals around there are like a city within the city," she said. "You have a good evening, sir."

She turned from him as if to say, "You're dismissed."

Oh well, he thought, *some people seem to get offended by the simplest things…like being married.*

He smiled, laughing to himself as he went back to Becky to make the payment. He, of course, gave Stephy a huge tip.

Wait until Victoria hears this story, he thought.

CHAPTER 4

CORRINA

CORRINA WOKE UP AT FIVE thirty in the morning as she had every day since 2002. She turned on the coffee maker and trudged down to the basement of the split-level ranch she had been living in since 1992. It was more like the first floor of the home than a true basement. It had light-colored laminate flooring, a small guest bedroom, a full bath, furnishings, and her small personal gym. The back door led to the rear patio where she would sit in the sun and read her books or work on cultivating herbs and flowers.

Each morning, she diligently performed three circuits of her exercise routine and twenty minutes of yoga. This took a little less than an hour. Then she would have her coffee as she got ready for work at the local grocery store. To people who asked how she managed this each day, she would explain that it was the key to her health.

In 2001, she was diagnosed with colon cancer. As she was only in her thirties, the diagnosis came much later than her doctors would have liked. Without insurance at the time of her diagnosis, her funds were seriously depleted by the treatment.

Following surgery, where part of her bowel was removed, then four months of chemotherapy and radiation, she was left weakened and needing significant daily care.

Her fourteen-year-old son, Franklin, stepped up to the task. Always a clever and thoughtful young boy, he diligently cared for his mother. A wiz on nearly every computer or device he touched, Franklin could hook up a telephone to a modem and use the internet since he was six years old. He even earned money on the weekends by helping people with their computer or network problems.

Franklin began by searching for anticancer diets and lifestyles. Then his grandmother, Abigail, would take him to the various stores he needed to get the specific groceries he wanted.

Franklin insisted on buying the expensive organic foods to make her meals. He subsidized the money Corrina gave him with his own money he earned from his summer and weekend jobs. Then he would spend time on the weekends preparing a full weeks' worth of meals that could be quickly heated for breakfast and lunch. He would often come home at lunch to feed her and care for anything she needed.

After school, Franklin cooked healthy dinners from recipes he found online. Then, he did his schoolwork and exercised on his old weight set in the basement.

Of course, Abigail and her husband Hector (when he was around) would help. But day to day, it was Franklin who carried the bulk of the efforts.

Once her cancer was in remission, the prognosis was not optimistic. The doctors speculated that there was a high probability of recurrence. If it did recur, she decided that she was not going to go through another round of treatment.

Franklin pushed her to start the morning exercise routine. She hated getting up early, when it was still dark, before Franklin had to go to school. He would practically drag her into the basement and push her to start the routine. He made her drink loads of water all the time. It was torture, and it all seemed like a waste of time to her.

Corrina was bitter and certain that she was not long for this world. Although she fought him at every turn, Franklin never let her quit.

One day, something strange happened while Franklin was at school. She could never forget the sensation—the feeling of being touched by God. And that touch was *not* gentle.

As she sat in her kitchen feeling sorry for herself and cursing the day she was born, a shock of pain, nausea, and weakness passed through her body. It grabbed her like the hand of death, squeezing the life from her. Torturous agony shot through her midsection. The end was upon her.

A bright light burst through the skylights, filling the room with glorious, warm sunlight. The worst pain she had ever experienced racked her body from the left side of her jaw to the bottom of her spine. A flash of memory hit her so hard that she let out a groan.

Calmness.

She stood upon a strange road. The warmth of the sun washed away the horror she survived, filling her with hope.

It was the worst day of her life…and the best day of her life. The day she met Charles.

Another wave of pain struck her. She cried out.

Her teenage son worked tirelessly to keep his mother alive and healthy. He was being repaid with nothing but complaints and cynicism.

Corrina gasped deeply from the pain as she admonished herself for her terrible attitude. No matter how awful she felt, she owed it to Franklin to meet him halfway.

Another bolt of pain—exponentially worse than anything she could imagine—slammed into her body. She screamed and fell to her knees.

An image of her son coming into manhood, sad and alone, flashed before her. He was kneeling before something evil…something that looked like…a bride.

An immense strength and power flooded into her body.

The light in the room faded. But Corrina emerged from this experience with a new, iron-like strength fueling her determination.

She stood from the floor that day and never complained again.

The next day, she was down in the basement exercising before Franklin even woke. She put the negative words of the doctors out of her mind.

In short time, she was stronger than she was before her cancer. And she was never sick again…not even a cold.

Her son was the inspiration that kept her alive.

Sweat beaded on her skin as Corrina came up the stairs to have her coffee. It was Thursday, her day off, so she could relax and have a leisurely breakfast. After eating, she enjoyed a second cup of coffee while sorting through her mail.

During the week, she put all the mail on the table and went through the whole pile on Thursday morning.

Things had been deteriorating in the United States over the last several years following the pandemic. It seemed the only things that ever came out of her mailbox recently were more and more hands reaching for money. Whether it was a bill that was increasing or the IRS demanding more without explanation, a trip to the mailbox was no longer a harbinger of good tidings.

She flipped through the advertisements and separated out the bills.

One letter appeared to be handwritten. There was no return address on the envelope. It looked like a child printed her name and address neatly across the front of the envelope. It was made out to Corrina Alemayehu.

Her hands began to tremble.

How did they find me? she thought.

Alemayehu was her maiden name. A name Corrina buried decades ago.

Corrina's family—and her maiden name—was from Ethiopia. In 1974, her family was able to escape from Mengistu and the Derg in the turmoil of revolution. They made a harrowing escape through Eritrea and onto a ship transporting coffee beans up the Red Sea, through the Suez Canal to Italy. Although it cost her parents everything they owned, they managed to get to America where they were granted asylum. Corrina only vaguely remembered the terrifying voyage as she was just a toddler.

Although highly educated, her father, Aaron, took work in the steel mills of Pittsburgh as a laborer. This paid well, and her mother, Abigail, was a wizard at stretching money. Corrina and her parents became US citizens in 1980. Her father later moved up to a machinist and then supervisor.

Aaron was a strong and willful man who invariably did what was right by his family. He always helped those in need and stood up for people who could not stand up for themselves.

Corrina grew up learning of the inequities she and her parents experienced in Ethiopia and other countries during their escape. She felt that, while the US may not be perfect, there was no other country with as much freedom and opportunity for people willing to work. Neither she nor her mother would tolerate any person who spoke badly of the United States.

She remembered Franklin being mortified after Abigail nearly got into a fist fight with one of his Brown University professors who called America a racist country built on slavery. Abigail called the man an ignorant snake oil salesman who never tasted food off anything but a silver spoon in his whole life.

Aaron died suddenly of a heart attack when Corrina was fifteen years old. This was devastating to both her and her mother. It was bad enough that she lost the man she remembered being a hero, but they could no longer afford to live in the house in which she was raised. They moved east of Pittsburgh to the town of Greensburg where her mother found work as a legal secretary.

Two years later, fate would, once again, forever alter the lives of Corrina and her mother.

Corrina went to a high school party with some friends. She could never fully recall all the events leading up to this ordeal, but she remembered the big house with a swimming pool. She and her friends had been given drinks and were having fun dancing to music. There were a lot of people there, drinking, smoking pot, and…*was she swimming?* The next thing she remembered was jumping up and running through the woods in the dark. There was blood on her legs and face. Her clothes were torn and her body hurt everywhere. She fell in the woods and woke under a pile of leaves near a road she didn't recognize. She remembered being so upset that her clothes were ripped apart as she walked down the road, beaten and crying.

A white man named Charles Germane drove past and saw her. He stopped his car and ran up to her from behind. She couldn't bring herself to look him in the eyes. He took her to his home and cared for her wounds, covered her in blankets, and insisted that she rest on his sofa. Charles told Corrina to sleep while he went out to speak with the police.

She would soon understand why he didn't just call the police.

She was wakened by the sounds of Charles systematically grabbing items and putting them in a bag. His demeanor shifted to one of unsettling concern as he gently but urgently got her back into his truck.

He drove Corrina to her home. When they arrived, Abigail ran to her daughter and began to berate Charles with threats of calling the cops. She had already contacted the police and hospitals looking for her daughter. Corrina defended Charles to her mother, explaining that he found her on the side of the road.

Corrina recalled the shame of having to tell her mother that she had been raped. Furious, Abigail picked up the phone to call the police.

Charles stopped Abigail from making that call. He quickly explained to them that the man who raped Corrina was very bad and very powerful. The police would not help her. This man would, and easily could, have Corrina and her mother killed rather than face *any* allegations. Worse yet, Charles said that the man who did it was already looking for Corrina. If she hadn't escaped the night before, she would already be… gone. Her friend, Carol, was now reported missing.

The three of them sat at the old kitchen table in their Greensburg home as Charles told them they needed to leave town immediately. Angry and having no place to go, Abigail refused. She wanted retribution for what was done to her daughter.

Charles patiently and effectively convinced them that *all* their lives, including his, were in great danger. They would kill him simply for helping Corrina.

Something in the way Charles spoke made Abigail understand the gravity of what he was saying. She had experienced many atrocities on her flight from Ethiopia and knew well the evil deeds performed by those wielding power. But still, they had no place to go.

Charles explained that he owned a large, secluded cabin several hours drive east of Greensburg in a small town called Gordon, Pennsylvania. He lived there alone when he wasn't in Greensburg for work. The tiny town was near the Schuylkill airstrip that Charles used to fly a small, twin-engine Cessna back and forth to the Latrobe airport as part of his job.

They packed what they could, and Charles drove them to the cabin that afternoon. He got them settled in with assurances that nobody could find them there. He had to drive back that night to be at work the next morning so that no one became suspicious of his leaving town.

The cabin was large and clean with three bedrooms and two bathrooms. It seemed that Charles or his family had money. He left them with an envelope containing two thousand dollars in cash, keys to the home, and keys to an old Chevelle that he was fixing up in a detached garage. The car, he told them, ran just fine, and they could take it into town if they needed anything. Or, if they didn't trust him, they could take the car and leave. But he kindly told them that they could stay as long as they liked.

He urged them to try to be as inconspicuous as possible if they went into Gordon as it was a small town with few, if any, African American residents.

Abigail's senses were on high alert, suspecting something nefarious from this complete stranger. After Charles left, she and Corrina talked about what they should do next. They didn't know Charles and couldn't imagine why he would risk his own life to help them. Corrina defended him by deducing that he had helped them this far, so why would he want to harm them? Perhaps it was the recollection of him gently treating her wounds. His unexpected kindness made her feel…a strange softness and warmth toward this man.

In the morning, Abigail used the phone and called her friend from work. It was Monday and she would have been expected to be in the office. Her friend's voice dropped to a whispered when Abigail called. She informed Abigail that some legally well-insulated thugs came to speak with her. Her friend tacitly confirmed everything Charles said. Some bad people were looking for her daughter…and her.

A week went by before Charles showed up again. He told them what he believed probably happened to Corrina. These people were looking for them locally but would not know to venture this far away in their search. If they stayed clear of that area, Charles figured they would probably be safe. He produced another envelope containing ten thousand dollars in cash. He told them they could take the money and leave if they wanted. Alternatively, they could stay with him as long as they wished.

Abigail was torn. She had never experienced such kindness and compassion from any stranger.

Corrina thought back to that conversation in the cozy den of the cabin.

"Why would you do such a thing for us?" Abigail asked in her strong accent. "You risk your life for us, yet we are not your family. You owe us nothing. So, I ask you again, Charles, why would you put yourself at such great risk for us?"

Charles began hesitantly, "The people I work for, they are not simply bad people, they are evil. I mean evil to the core. You hear horror stories about the Mafia and their ruthless hitmen. You know stories about serial killers and crazed, murderous people. But these people are beyond that. Normal people do not possess the understanding about the nature of *true* evil. You couldn't think of something horrible enough that these people wouldn't do. Nothing."

"Then why do you work for them? Does this not make you evil as well?" Abigail asked.

"You asked me why I would do this for you?" Charles said, looking at Corrina. "Anything I can do for you…or any victim of these people… would be but a minor penance for the sins I am committing each time I work for them. These…fucking demons!"

"Why don't you simply quit, then? Nobody is forcing you at gun-point to work for them," Abigail said.

Charles laughed and said, "As it stands, that's *exactly* what is happening. I cannot leave them, ma'am. You see, they won't just kill *me* if I leave. They've already explained very clearly that they intend to kill one member of my family for any task that I refuse to perform. You don't understand…" Charles put his head in his hands. "My everlasting soul is lost forever. I didn't know when I started working for them. It was good money, and I was young. I'm trapped." He looked up with tears in his eyes.

Corrina's mother went to Charles and put her arms around him. She said, "Your soul belongs to you, Charles. They can never take that from you. And you have a good soul."

He hugged Abigail back as he cried in her arms.

She recalled the memory of this exchange so clearly. He was the kindest man she ever knew and this was the moment that she fell in love with Charles Germane.

Charles was eight years older than Corrina. His family was from the Pittsburgh area, and he claimed to be of Italian descent. He was not exactly wealthy, but he was financially well off. Abigail became like an adopted mother to him, and he treated them both with great respect.

The three of them lived in the cabin, with Charles staying there on the weekends and sometimes two or three nights a week. Corrina recalled the feelings of happiness when he would arrive home. She remembered her subtle touches on his arms, him cupping the side of her face, the shared glances, the walks in the woods. The sun shone through the trees as they stood next to a pond when he first kissed her. Charles on his knee next to Abigail as he asked her permission to marry Corrina.

Corrina learned that she was pregnant long before they ever consummated their relationship. Although this was a child from rape, she refused to consider abortion. Charles supported her decision. They agreed that the child would know only him as the father. To avoid any Pennsylvania state records coming to light, he took them to Las Vegas where they were married in 1988, before the child was born. She was eighteen at the time.

Corrina and Abigail Alemayehu simply disappeared from Western Pennsylvania.

Later that year, Franklin Charles Germane was born. The vile assault became a distant memory as she looked upon the beautiful baby boy that she brought into the world. His bright eyes and handsome features could melt even the hardest of hearts. Abigail loved the child instantly.

Franklin quickly grew to a large toddler. The four of them lived peacefully for two years in the cozy home Charles provided for them. Corrina remembered that time as the happiest days of her life.

Tragically, Charles developed a rare and aggressive cancer before Franklin was old enough to remember him. As he was dying, he warned Corrina to take Franklin away from Gordon, Pennsylvania, as soon as possible and don't let anyone in town know where they were going. He explained that their lives would once again be in great danger if they did not leave within a week of his death. He told them his employers would come for the airplane and they would thoroughly search his home. He told them that if they learned Franklin was born, they would certainly kill him.

Although confused as to why anyone would ever want to harm her amazing son, two days after Charles died, Corrina packed Franklin and Abigail into their Chevy Tahoe and began to drive east in the middle of the night.

Before leaving, they triggered something in the cabin that Charles had put in place years earlier. The timer gave them eight hours before it would start a fire that would consume the contents of the cabin without causing a massive forest fire.

Corrina's heart was broken. The love of her life was gone.

Charles had given her a cash-filled suitcase, two handguns, a shotgun, and plenty of ammunition. They drove toward New England, staying in one hotel or another until finally settling in East Providence, Rhode Island. Here, she purchased the comfortable split-ranch home for the three of them to live.

Franklin was raised in a neighborhood with predominantly Portuguese people who were accepting and welcoming to him and his family. He grew to be a large, strong, and good-looking man.

The home and neighborhood were perfect for Abigail to grow old with her family. She eventually began to date a local ferry-boat captain named Hector from Seekonk, Massachusetts, right over the Rhode Island border. They got married in 1999. Abigail passed away at the end of 2019 from complications related to an unknown respiratory virus.

Abigail's funeral was the last time Corrina had seen her son. This broke her heart nearly as much as losing Charles. Franklin came over and hugged her when the services were over and then left with his asshole wife, Victoria, saying only, "I love you, Mom." She cried for two straight days after that.

Franklin got together with that woman in 2015. Victoria soon drove a wedge between them. *How could her son not see that this woman was not for him?* She was fifteen or more years older than him. She didn't want children or a family. She only cared about keeping her ass looking good so Franklin wouldn't leave her. He couldn't or wouldn't see how her hooks were in him. *How could he let this happen?*

Thinking of Franklin brought a tear to her eye. Much of the old fear she felt years ago, since Charles passed, had subsided to nothing. She lived here for over thirty years without a peep from anyone in Pennsylvania.

Nothing until now. A cold chill went up her spine as she opened the envelop and pulled out the neatly folded paper and began to read.

The letter fell from her hands as she began to cry.

CHAPTER 5

VICTORIA'S KINDNESS

"DOCTOR RITA SAMPSON, HUH?" VICTORIA said in a teasing voice. "Did she want to give you a physical? Or maybe a prostate exam?" She smiled wiggling a finger in the air.

"Could you focus on the story I told you and not the young doctor? I think Stephy was seriously injured!"

"Oh, so she's a *young* doctor. Is she hot too?" Victoria asked, in a playful manner that had underlying inflections of jealousy.

Franklin looked at her sideways and said, "I'm not going to tell you these types of things if you're going to get jealous," then quickly added, "and don't try to tell me that's not a tone in your voice. I've known you way too long for you to get that by me."

"Alright," she said, as her brow furrowed to a look of annoyance, "maybe a little. But why shouldn't I be? My husband is a gorgeous hunk and some hot, young doctor throws herself at you…and you're not even sure that's what's happening. You're kind of a doofus."

"Wait, now *I'm* a doofus?" he asked. "How is it that I am the doofus. I told you the whole story. And she wasn't *hot*. She was just cute." Then he added, "If she was hot, I would have been telling you about the ancient hag with hairy warts who showed up in the ambulance." He gave her an ingratiating smile.

"Dickhead. Larry David suggested that there are only two ways to get a stiff neck…and I know you didn't wreck the car!" she said.

This produced a laugh out of Franklin as he said, "Wow. My status keeps sinking in this discussion. First, I'm dashing, then a doofus, now a dickhead. And a cheating dickhead at that."

"Nobody ever said you were dashing!" She flashed his ingratiating smile back to him.

"Can you please quit? My neck is still hurting, and I have to work tomorrow. I don't know if I'm going to be able to sleep tonight," he whined.

It must have been an effective whine because Victoria came back with, "I'm sorry, baby. I was only teasing. And…yeah, I may get a little jelly, but that's just because *you're* so hot," she smiled for real.

"Oh, yeah! I suppose if I was at the Notre-Dame cathedral helping the short guy ringing the bells, *I* would be the 'hot' one." He chuckled.

Victoria laughed too as she said, "I'll be your Esmerelda, my love!"

"Maybe not. Then *you'd* be the one with the sore neck," he chortled, making a hanging gesture. "Not the Disney version."

"Here, sit on the end of the bed. I'll rub your neck for you," she said.

The thought of the last time she tried to massage him made him cringe. Nails poking in, hands like two little vices, and more pain than when she started. He said, "We have that back massager somewhere. The one that heats up. You know, the one with the two balls that move in and out. Where is that thing?"

"Oh, I put that under the seat of my car to make the ride more enjoyable." She laughed.

"Classy," he said.

"Hey, you knew what you were getting when you married me!" She laughed. "Sit on the bed. I'll go easy. I know you can be a bit of a pussy when it comes to massages."

"I don't think I'm a pussy, you rubbed my neck like you were tightening plumbing fixtures. I don't know how a vertebra didn't snap!" he said.

"It wasn't that bad!" she said. "It's supposed to hurt a little. You gotta loosen up those knots. You're just not good with pain."

"Tell me something," he said, "who the hell is *good* with pain?"

"Well, there was this one guy in college—" she started to say.

"Okay! That's okay! Sorry I asked," he interrupted.

"Oh, I'm only kidding," she paused. "He was a pussy too." She laughed.

He shook his head, sighed, and said, "Sorry if I'm not finding things too funny right now. I'm in a shitty mood, in pain, and fighting off a very high level of aggravation. So please…"

"Okay, okay, okay. I'm sorry. Please. Let me help. Just sit on the bed. If I'm doing something wrong, just say so. I can go easier," she said, sounding sympathetic.

He looked at her and nodded saying, "Okay. Thanks V. I'm sorry if I'm being a dick. I'm in a mood where everything seems to be annoying me."

He sat on the edge of the bed and Victoria got behind him with her legs around his hips. She dug her thumbs into his lower back causing him to jump in pain. "Christ, Victoria! Where did you learn to massage? The Spanish Inquisition?"

She broke into a fit of laughter and said, "Is that too hard?"

"Hell yes. Take it down about five to ten notches. And it wasn't that funny," he said.

"Oh yes. It's funnier than you think. Okay. How's this?" she asked as she lightened up and moved her thumbs in small circles up his back.

"Much better," he said, though her nails were scratching him more that he would like. For her, this was very gentle.

She moved up to his neck. When she got that high, she put her hands over his trap muscles and worked her thumbs up his neck. Then she abruptly pulled her hands away.

"What?" Franklin asked, concerned. "Is there something wrong with *me*? You know, I kept seeing this weird shadow…"

"No, no, no," she said as she got off the bed. "I want to turn the lights down and light the lavender candle. It'll help relax you."

She ran over to the dimmer switch and turned the light to low. Then she went into the bathroom and turned that light out as she set the candle on the bed stand. She quickly lit the candle and seated herself back where she was.

Victoria started gently and slowly onto his neck. It was much better than she had ever done it before. As she did this, she began to make a quiet purring noise.

"Interesting noise, kitty cat. Are you getting turned on?" he asked.

"Shhhh," she hushed him, "don't speak. You're supposed to be relaxing." She continued to make the purring noise. It was unusual as it had odd inflections, but he could feel the pain in his neck begin to diminish. The stress from the events of the day began to flow out of him and his eyelids got heavy.

Victoria continued this for about ten more minutes and then slowly and quietly stopped. She got up from behind him and stood in front of him. She grabbed the sides of his neck and kissed him on the lips and said, "Come on. Let's get you to bed before you fall asleep sitting up."

She helped him up as he said, "Thank you, honey. That was great. This is the best I felt all day."

"Okay. Shhh. Come on. Lay down," she said as she pulled the covers back.

He laid down and she helped him get his pants off. Then she covered him and kissed him on the forehead. He was sleeping before she blew out the candle.

CHAPTER 6

UNINVITED STRANGER

FRANKLIN WOKE TEN MINUTES BEFORE his alarm clock. He was a strong believer in patterns and looked for them in nearly all things. In his mind, waking up before the alarm clock signified a good day was ahead. His neck still ached, but nothing like the day before. This barely registered as pain.

He got ready for work and went downstairs. The protein shake Victoria made for him sat in the refrigerator with a note under it.

"Good morning! Happy Friday! I hope your neck feels better. Don't forget Ariel's shower is this weekend. I'll be driving there tomorrow morning and staying until Sunday night. See you tonight, babe! Have a great day!"

Franklin let out a sigh of relief. Thank God he was able to get out of that shit show. Ariel was a sweet young lady who simply made terrible decisions, *particularly* when it came to men. How an intelligent, attractive, and successful girl like her could keep getting involved with losers remained one of life's great mysteries to him. This was the third "Mister Right" to put a ring on her finger. In each case, she ended up paying for the ring. And *somehow*, these dickheads all managed to keep the rings when they walked!

Franklin thought, *She is so damned lucky that Victoria is always there for her.* He may have to go to Ariel's wedding, but he would not support any activities that promoted her nuptials. Besides, based on her history, there was statistically no chance that the event would ever take place. Maybe Ariel sought out men like this because her own father left her when she was young.

He put Ariel out of his mind as he drank his breakfast and searched his phone for the latest headlines. Typical depressing shit. It seemed like each headline was crafted to suck the joy out of life and cause fear for the future.

He put his phone down and made himself a coffee in his thermal to-go cup. He enjoyed the small comfort of his hot coffee as he drove to work listening to an audiobook. He liked to listen to fiction stories that provoked thought through fantasy or science-fiction tales. He was halfway through *Old Man's War* by John Scalzi.

Such a great concept. As someone who studied the hard sciences, it seemed that the possibilities in Scalzi's book were things that shouldn't be that far into the future. It made him start thinking about the direction of his own life and the prospects of getting older.

This led him to think about his career. The patterns that cycled so many times. Things start to go well and his research would make progress. Then, new management takes over, changes direction, halts projects…and inevitably, digression ensues at the hands of some inept director. The last major reorganization left him out on the street, despite being the best and most productive researcher in their organization.

The fact that losing his job devastated him nearly as much as the death of his grandmother led him to reconsider his priorities. He knew his work had become a defining aspect of his life…maybe even more so than Victoria. Maybe he had become an obedient slave to a large corporation to make money and pay exorbitant taxes on…every…single… thing in life.

Franklin considered the work he did real research with actual data. The direction Abbadon ventured into focused more on computer modeling designed to meet a chosen outcome.

Soon after letting Franklin go, Abbadon management realized that their predictive models required *true* data to function properly. They offered him his job back only four months after dismissing him. He hated the fact that he eagerly jumped at the opportunity. He should have left and started his own business to sell the data to Abbadon at twenty times what they paid him. But that took a lot of money and the economy was extremely volatile, especially in his field.

Recently, the urgency and pressure to use machine learning and AI models required his colleagues and him to overlook serious fundamental flaws in the way the coding was assembled. Management countered dissent with reprimands, insisting employees find comfort with ambiguity. *I bet our patients would love to hear that*, he thought.

He supposed he was helping to create new and safer drug products, even if it was for a large company. He considered what life would be like without large companies and corporations running the world. He imagined a life without every luxury currently available, a life without all the excess and greed.

What if mankind was dropped back into raw nature? He supposed it would be considered a much harder form of *work* if you had to go out and find food and water.

Maybe he was only a slave to his own need to breathe air, drink water, eat food, and procreate. Maybe his own desire for excess was to live in comfort and show that he could provide and protect. Maybe this was all done so he could attract a desirable mate like Victoria. Maybe humans were all just animals that…

This is way too deep for a Friday morning, he thought as he pulled into the parking garage. He would need to rewind the book later to hear what he missed as his mind wandered. He pulled into his parking spot and shut off the car. He downed the rest of his coffee, put his cup back in the holder, grabbed his backpack with his laptop, and headed into work.

It was a gray and dreary day. He was glad he didn't have to see his shadow as he walked from the parking garage to his building. That thought sent a twinge of pain into his neck.

Friday proved to be a calm and beautiful day at work without Aziz. Although he did send an email the night before with some additional requests for the software installation, it would be weeks before Franklin would have to deal with that. *Anything could happen between then and now,* he thought.

Sitting in traffic on his way home, relistening to the chapter his mind drifted through, his phone began to ring. He touched the thumb pad on the steering wheel to answer the call. A woman's voice roared a harsh and distorted, "Hello," over the speakers.

Franklin winced as he realized he had to volume too high for the phone. He turned the speakers down and said, "Hello? Who is this?"

"Franklin, it's me, Victoria. Where are you now?"

"Where do you think I am at 4:55 around Boston on a Friday before Memorial Day? I'm drag racing on Storrow, of course."

"So, you're on your way home? And in a good mood, I presume," she added.

"Yes. I should have taken the train today. It's always worse on a Friday before a holiday. Where are you?"

"I'm on my way to New Hampshire. I'm going up to see Ariel tonight," she said.

"Why are you leaving tonight? I thought you were going tomorrow?"

"I was. But she got into a fight with fucking Cletus and asked if I could come up early." She sounded exasperated.

"Who the hell is Cletus?" Franklin asked.

"Jeff. Her stupid, slack-jawed fiancé. I guess he got shit-faced and punched a hole in the wall and slapped her."

"He fucking *hit* her? Victoria, you have to get her away from this loser. They're not even married yet and he's beating her up?"

"He didn't beat her up. He slapped her. But I guess she slapped him first. I don't know. It's a whole big clusterfuck. I'm going to go up and help her…again! But there may not be a wedding shower this weekend."

"Yeah, no surprise there. I was wondering—Hey! Dipshit!" he yelled. "Keep your damn car in your own fuckin' lane!"

"Christ, Franklin. Why the hell are you yelling at me?"

"I'm not yelling at you. It's this asshole next to me texting and driving. He almost hit me. These numbnuts need to go to prison. I swear it's worse than drinking and—"

"Stop. All I hear is *you* yelling at *me*. You need to chill out when you're driving. You're going to end up in a road rage incident."

"Not me. I'm as cool as a cucumber. And by the way, you yell at people on the road more than I do!"

"Do you really wanna tit for tat with me right now? Seriously. You want to argue with me *right now*…as I'm going up to help Ariel after her boyfriend just beat her up?"

"You said he only slapped her! What the fuck, Victoria? Are you leaving something out of this whole story?"

"No. I'm not leaving anything out! I'm telling you not to start arguing with me now. I'm not happy about this at all. I had to cancel my hair appointment tomorrow morning and scramble to get packed tonight. And I probably won't get there until it's dark…way out in the sticks… and it's going to be raining. I'm pissed off."

"Alright, alright, I'm sorry. I don't want to fight with you. I know this sucks," he turned the subject back to her predicament. "What time do you think you'll get there?"

"Probably nine or so. That's what the GPS says now with all the traffic. I'll have to see how busy Route 3 is past Billerica. Who knows. Like you said, weekend before a holiday."

It was a two-hour drive on a good day, without traffic. Today could easily be four hours.

"Well, when do you think you'll be home? Are you staying with her or in a hotel tonight?"

"Sunday. I will be home on Sunday. I don't care what happens. If she puts up with this shit one more time, it'll be *me* who beats her ass. This may be the straw that breaks the camel's back with this bitch. She's a grown-ass woman getting played by these idiots. And I'm sick of being her shoulder to cry on." Victoria sounded like she was on the verge of tears. This was very unlike her.

Franklin felt a stab of sorrow for Victoria and the weekend she would surely endure with Ariel and Jeff. "I'm staying at her place tonight because my reservation at the hotel is for tomorrow. I forgot to call to see if they have any vacancies for tonight. I don't know. She has another bedroom, but if Jeff is there and they're fighting…I don't know."

"Do you want me to call the hotel when I get home and see if they have an open room for tonight?" he asked.

"I would love you to death if you could do that," she said.

"Okay. Just focus on driving. I will text you if they can take you tonight. But call me when you get there so I know you made it."

"I will. I promise. I'm sorry I didn't get anything for dinner."

"Fear not. Mazzoli's delivers! Even in the rain."

"Oh, you dick! You're going to get the triple-double supreme, without me!"

"With extra olives and pepperoni!" he added exuberantly.

"I can hear the stupid smile on your face." She laughed.

"Don't worry. I won't eat it all. There will be plenty left by Sunday."

"Oh sure. Eat that for two nights in a row. Good thing I bought you those stretchy jeans!" She laughed again.

"Good point. I'll order their Ultra Chop Salad too. That way I get something that grew out of the ground and not an aluminum can."

"I don't think that thing counts as a salad. Now I really am jealous. I'll be lucky if Burger King is open. Everything closes by 7 p.m. up there."

There was no response. "Hello? Franklin? Hello?"

Her phone buzzed as the text came in. "Sorry. Call dropped. Call you later. And I'm not texting and driving. I'm in gridlock. (heart emoji) you!"

She sighed and turned the music up as she aggressively but skillfully weaved through the slow-moving traffic.

It was downpouring when Franklin got home. He pulled his car into the driveway and ran up the curved walkway to the cover of the porch. He and Victoria purchased a split-ranch home, much like the one in which he grew up. This home had a back walk-out patio on the top floor as it was built into a hill. There were also doors leading out from the ground level on the left as you faced the structure.

He entered the code to the front door and heard the whirring noise as the lock opened.

The house was dimly lit, with only a few counter lights on in the kitchen upstairs. Down the split stairs, a hallway to the left led to a small basement area and a one-car garage. To the right was a full bathroom and a cozy den (which could be made into a bedroom). The garage was too full of boxes from the last time they moved to hold a car.

He set his bag on the floor under the coat rack and threw his keys and wallet into the bowl on the table next to a stack of mail.

He left his damp jacket on as he walked up the steps. The top of the stairs led directly into the open kitchen/dining room area. A dark hallway to the left led to another bathroom and two bedrooms. The living room was on his right and slightly behind him.

Franklin jumped as he saw the shadowed figure of a woman standing at the kitchen counter.

"Ahhh! Who the fuck are you?" Franklin yelled.

"Easy, Franklin," came the familiar voice. "And why do you have to swear like that? You have an Ivy League education and you talk like *that*?" said Corrina.

"*Mom?* What are you doing here?" he asked.

"Franklin, it's time we had a talk. Where is Victoria?" Corrina asked.

"She's away for the weekend. Is everything okay, Mom? Why are you here?"

"Everything is fine. It's good that she's away," she said. "I need your help. First let me introduce you to an old…acquaintance," Corrina said.

"What? What are you talking about?" Franklin asked.

"Hello, Franklin," came the deep male voice of a man sitting in the shadows at the dining room table.

Startled again, Franklin yelled, "Ahhh! Who are you?" His neck screamed with pain and he cringed, nearly falling to one knee.

"You look like you are in pain. Why don't you have a seat?" came the male voice. Then, in a jovial tone, "You were right, Corrina. He was surprised to see you!"

Franklin's eyes adjusted to the dark room, and he could see a man sitting at the kitchen table. He was large, about his mother's age or older with a bald head. But most strikingly, he wore a black eyepatch over his right eye.

Franklin grabbed a small statue off a shelf with other knickknacks and held it out defensively as he yelled, "Who the hell are you? What are you doing with my mother?"

Corrina and the man looked at each other and broke into laughter. Franklin looked back and forth between the two and realized there seemed to be no threat. He relaxed and placed the statue back on the shelf.

"I don't see what's so funny," Franklin said. "How would you feel walking into your home with an uninvited stranger sitting in your kitchen."

The man spoke first. "I apologize, Franklin. But you should see yourself. You're a big man, cringed over, holding a ceramic kitten, and looking about as menacing as a terrified teddy bear."

Franklin put a hand on his neck and stretched it in circles as he said, "Well, who are you?"

Corrina spoke, "Franklin, this is a man who used to go to the same high school as me. His name is Cassian."

Cassian got to his feet, held out his hand, and said, "It's very nice to meet you, Franklin."

Franklin cast a sideways look at his mother, walked closer, and shook the man's hand. "Charmed," he said, giving a quick, sarcastic smile that produced a chuckle from the man.

Cassian said, "How's your neck feeling? I can't image it feels too good with that thing on you."

"*What?!* What thing? There's something on me?" Franklin swatted his head and neck.

Cassian said, "Oh yeah, that's it. That'll knock it off," as he laughed.

"Seriously! Is there something on me?" Franklin looked around, trying to see if something was crawling on him.

"It's not anything like what you're thinking. You can't see it. But I bet you've felt it. Haven't you? How long has it been going on?" Cassian asked.

"My neck started to hurt yesterday morning. I just slept on it wrong," Franklin said, not even convincing himself.

"Did you get into a car wreck or something?" Cass said with a big, knowing smile.

"Oh. Ha ha ha," Franklin said. "Victoria already made that joke, Cassian."

"Let's have a seat so we can talk. Please, call me Cass," he gestured to one of the four chairs at the kitchen table.

"Can I get you some tea or coffee, sweetheart?" Corrina said.

"No, thank you, dear," Cass responded.

Corrina laughed and said, "I wasn't talking to you, you old wind bag! Let me help you with your jacket. You're all wet." She walked behind Franklin and helped him take his light coat off.

"Mind his neck, now, Corrina. Try not to touch it," Cass said.

"What are you talking about, Cass? What's wrong with my neck?" Franklin asked as Corrina slid his coat off.

"Can I get you something, dear?" Corrina asked her son.

"No. But I've been sitting in traffic, and I've got to pee really bad," he said.

"Don't let us stop you," Cassian said.

Franklin ran into the bathroom, flicked on the lights over the sink, and rushed to the toilet. As he washed his hands, he looked in the mirror to see if he could see something. Then he turned on the overhead light. For a brief second, it looked like his shadow jumped around his head as his neck spasmed with pain.

He walked back out into the kitchen to find his mother and Cass sitting at the table talking.

"Alright. Do you want to tell me what this is all about?" Franklin asked.

"I'm here to help you, Franklin," Cass said. "And to ask for your help in return."

"If you can help me with my neck, I would really appreciate that. But I don't know how I could help you. I'm just a research scientist in a rather obscure field," Franklin said.

"I know exactly what kind of work you do. And that is one way in which I need your help. But I need to tell you a story first. It's a rather long story that involves you, your mother…and the future of this world."

Franklin barked a quick laugh, looked at his mother, and said, "Let me guess. A once-in-a-lifetime investment opportunity? You're going to be disappointed when you see my portfolio. It's really good to see you, Mom."

"It's so good to see you, honey," she said, getting up and hugging her son.

Franklin hugged her back and said, "So, why did you bring a crazy man to my home?"

"Crazy man?" Cass said with a smile. "Oh my. How I wish I were crazy." He looked out the window as the smile faded from his face. "In retrospect, crazy would have been so much easier. I really don't know if it would be better or not, but I wish I didn't know what I know."

In a sudden movement, Cassian jumped to his feet with arms flung wide. He stared down menacingly at the two of them. They jumped back in fear as the man before them seemed dreadful and much larger than before. Power exuded from him as his one eye glared with intensity. Franklin felt like something on his neck was shaking as it moved around his head, trying to avoid the immense figure standing before him.

Within a moment, Cassian looked like a man standing in front of them with his arms held wide. There was no fear. No dread. Nothing special. In fact, he looked rather silly. Cassian began to nod as he sat back in the chair.

"I can get that thing off your neck," Cass said. "Well, I should say, I can tell you *how* to get that thing off your neck. But I do need your help."

"What kind of help? I mean, really? What can I possibly do for you? I'm not a psychiatrist," Franklin said.

"Very good," Cass smiled easily. "I remember when I was a kid, I hated the cold," he said as he looked off to nothing in particular. "The scientists at the time told us we were heading into a new Ice Age. I was terrified. I hate the cold and couldn't imagine a world of nothing but ice."

Franklin was looking around the room like he missed something and said, "Dude, what the hell are you talking about?"

Cass looked at Franklin and said, "It was years later when I learned that they were full of shit. We were fed news about alarming data generated to get more funding from the government. And the fools in government leveraged that bullshit data to raise taxes. The scientists were incentivized with a steady increase of ten to fifteen percent in funding to keep generating that crap. The money grew government wealth exponentially from the people they frightened into willingly giving up the money. The masses of people believed what they were told. No questions asked." Cass chuckled as he shook his head.

"First, I will help you with your neck," Cass said. "Then I need you to listen to my story. After that, you can decide for yourself if you will help me."

Cass paused, looked at Corrina, then Franklin, and said, "Knowledge is such an interesting thing. You can live your whole life in happiness not knowing something and then—boom—you learn that thing you can't unlearn. And life changes forever."

"Yeah, they even have a far more concise saying for that," Franklin said flatly. "Ignorance is bliss. Your long-winded philosophy isn't new."

Cass gave a winning smile and said, "I remember learning about quantum mechanics and all the theories about wave-particle duality. So much effort spent trying to wrap my head around this abstract concept," Cass shook his head, "then I find out that it's mostly wrong…like so many things we *think* we know.

"No matter what you decide to do tonight, Franklin, your life, as you know it, is about to change forever."

"Is that some kind of threat?" Franklin said angrily.

"No. It is not a threat, Franklin. But once you know something, it's impossible to unknow it," Cass said.

"What if I told you to leave now or I'll call the police!" Franklin stood as he said it.

Cass looked at Corrina with sympathy. Corrina said, "Son, you need to listen to what this man has to say. He's not lying about the Ice Age stuff. That really happened. I don't think he is here to harm you or anyone else. He seems to want to genuinely help. And I don't trust people easily."

Franklin looked down, then nodded as he slowly sat across from Cass.

"Alright, Cassian," Franklin said, "I don't see how listening to your story can hurt. We'll see if it changes anything. So, what's with the eye-patch? Did you lose your eye or something?"

Cass looked down at his black shirt and said, "I wear the eyepatch to accessorize."

Franklin smiled and said, "No, really. How'd you lose your eye?"

"Years ago," Cass began seriously, "I was in a terrible plane accident."

Franklin looked surprised and said, "A *plane* wreck? Whoa! Dude, you're *damn* lucky to be alive if you survived a plane crash."

"Well…it was a paper plane," Cass said.

Corrina laughed. A moment later, Franklin started to laugh as well.

CHAPTER 7

THE FATHER

C ASSIAN BEGAN, "I MUST FIRST talk to you about your father." He cast a glance at Corrina. She looked down at her hands on the table and gave a small nod.

"What about my father?" Franklin asked defensively.

"I need to tell you about your father. Your real father. Not Charles Germane," Cass said.

Franklin looked at his mother. Her eyes were wet as she gazed into his and she said, "I'm so sorry, baby. I made a promise to your father. I never think about it anymore. In my mind, your father is a great man named Charles Germane," she wiped her eyes. "You see, I don't want to remember that night. I put it out of my mind the second you were born… my amazing son."

Cassian spoke gently, "Your biological father, Franklin, was a man named Barry Bosco. Many would consider him a serial killer, but that's not entirely true. He didn't randomly kill people. He was just a murderous individual to anyone who stepped in his way. Your mother and you are miraculously alive today through her courageous actions and those of the man you consider to be your father. Had Barry found you, he would likely have killed you both."

"My real father was a…a murderer? Mom? What happened? Where is he now?" Franklin snapped.

Corrina looked up and said, "I don't know what happened that night. Your father told me rumors about how those people drugged and raped girls. It seems they were not merely rumors. As it turns out, every one of those girls ended up missing…or dead. I got away. I ran through the woods…in the dark. The next day, your father…Charles found me and took us away from that area."

"How did Dad…I mean Charles, know to take you away. Why didn't he call the police and have this," he looked at Cass and spat, "Barry bastard put in jail?"

"He worked for the Bosco family. Not by choice, mind you. They threatened him and his relatives if he tried to quit. The Bosco family was powerful and controlled the police, the town officials, government agencies—practically the whole town. Charles knew that they would kill us. And they would easily get away with it too. Your father risked his own life to get us to safety," Corrina said.

"Where is this piece of shit now?" Franklin demanded. "He's either going to jail or I'm going to fucking kill him!"

Cass had a grim look on his face as he said, "That's exactly how I felt…right before I killed him…and his whole family. They couldn't suffer enough for what they took from me."

Franklin stood, walked to his mother and hugged her. "I'm so sorry, Mom. I never knew." Tears formed in his eyes as he held his mother.

"Don't worry about that, Franklin. That was a million years ago. And I had you," she put her hands on his arms and straightened them so she could look at him, "you marvelous boy. I need your help too. I need you to listen to Cassian. And you are going to have to open your mind to things that you are not going to believe. I'm asking you to both trust and doubt every word he says. I need your brilliant mind to find the truth," Corrina said.

"That's the spirit, Corrina!" Cass said. "Speaking of contradictory advice, I'll have to introduce you to my friend later. That seems to be the pillar of *her* counsel," Cass smiled and then grimaced and jerked to the left as if something prodded him in the side.

"Are you okay?" Franklin asked. "You're not having a heart attack or anything, are you?"

"No. I'm fine. Some essences can't take a joke."

"You're a strange dude, Cass. I don't know if you're serious or joking with me. If you're putting us on, this shit isn't funny anymore," Franklin said.

"I assure you, Franklin, I am not joking with you…well, not about everything. The eye story was a joke," Cass said.

"So how did you lose your eye?" he asked.

"If you must know, it was a knife fight," Cass said.

"Really? So, what? Are you like a legit badass or something?"

"Damn straight. But I blame it on cheap, plastic silverware. I wasn't letting my brother get that last slice of butter. We both went for it and my knife snapped. Fucking piece of plastic went *right* in my eye," Cass said.

"You're kind of an asshole, aren't you?" Franklin said without inflection as Corrina laughed.

Cass shrugged and said, "The answers to your questions will lie within my story. Then the real questions will begin.

"I work as a scientific representative for a small pharmaceutical company. I have a degree in chemistry, and I focus mostly on talent recruitment," Cass said.

"Scientific representative? So, you don't do any real science," Franklin said.

Cass ignored the comment and said, "I understand that you are quite an intelligent and accomplished scientist. You now work in the proteomics laboratory under Dr. Winthrop Dodge at the prestigious Tzitzi Institute of Abbadon Pharmaceuticals. And you have the knowledge to determine primary, secondary, and tertiary protein structures. Am I correct?"

"Quaternary structures too, if needed." Franklin looked at his mother. "Did you tell him everything about me?"

Corrina looked offended and said, "He told *me* about you. Not the other way around. Please don't think so harshly of me, Franklin. I'm your mother. I would kill or die for you. No matter what."

"I'm sorry, Mom. I never know anymore…who I can trust," Franklin said.

"Color me surprised," Cass said.

"What's that supposed to mean?" Franklin shot back harshly.

"You are still quite naïve, Franklin. It is not uncommon for one to be highly educated, intelligent, and yet still very naïve. I mean no offense by this. But by the time I am finished speaking, you will be…less naïve.

"I need you to keep this in mind. When something is taken from you, you are always given something to replace that loss. Like a man losing his vision…or even part of his vision…and gaining other senses." He pointed to his own nose. "Some call that God. Some call it Fate. Scientists would probably argue that it's just the sharpening of other senses due to the loss of a primary sense, and it's the way things work naturally. But the old axiom of 'when one door closes, another will open' is not historically baseless."

"Are you here to lecture me?" Franklin asked. "I got it the first time. Yeah, people debate. So what?"

Cass continued, "Maybe it's optimism versus pessimism, because it is entirely up to you to find what you may have gained after a loss. You may never see it until you truly look. Seeing yourself is one of the most difficult things in the world to do, Franklin. This leads to every problem from poor self-image to the Dunning–Kruger effect."

"The what?" he asked.

"The Dunning–Kruger effect? Have you not heard of this?"

"No. What is it?" Franklin asked impatiently.

"See? There's always something new to learn.

"It is a cognitive bias that is simple to understand. Everybody experiences this in life. It is a descriptive explanation of overconfidence in the presence of ineptitude. It can be graphically plotted as *perceived* confidence in a skill versus *true* competence in a skill. In my opinion, this has a negative slope over your life, but it does tend to level off in the mid to late twenties. It may even get a positive slope if your mind is open.

"Imagine a man with little or no knowledge in…say, building a shed. He decides that he wants to build one on his own. He looks at his neighbors shed, takes some measurements, goes to the lumber yard, and buys the wood and materials he needs. How hard can it be, right? Build a frame, nail up the plywood, and shingle the roof.

"As he's building it, he realizes that nothing is lining up because he didn't level the ground properly. Now, the doors won't quite close, but he shaves off the edges to make it work. Then it rains and the bottom of the shed is sitting in water because he didn't consider drainage.

"Later, when his neighbor places a call to the town building inspector because the shed is built too close to his property and the water is attracting mosquitos, the town tells him that he must tear down the whole thing because he was supposed to pull a permit.

"A complete lack of self-awareness can lead a person to be confident in knowledge they simple do not possess."

Franklin nodded and said, "I know a dude like that at work. Guy's a mall ninja. Constantly playing video games like *Call of Duty* and watches war movies with guns and explosions. Rambo shit like *Commando* and *Hurt Locker*. I don't know. I don't care about that crap, but he's always bragging about this gun or that gun. He acts like he has some deep esoteric knowledge about the names of guns, the power, the bullets…everything. The way he talks, you would think he lives at the shooting range."

Franklin laughed as he said, "I know he's full of shit because we went to a range together once and this dumbass nearly shot his foot off. The rangemaster literally took his gun off him and told him not to come back. Dude doesn't know *shit* about guns."

Cassian looked a Franklin flatly and said, "Yeah, it's something like that." The sound of Ex laughing in his head was almost deafening. Cass said, "Shut the fuck up!"

"What? What did I say?" Franklin asked, looking perplexed.

"Not you. Someone else," Cass said.

Franklin looked around, confused, and said, "It's only the three of us in this room."

"Not so much, Franklin. You have no idea. Ignorance, willful or not, can exemplify the Dunning–Kruger effect. There are more of us in this room right now than you think. Off hand, there's you, me, your mother, and an angel named Ex," Cass said.

A smile spread across the face of Franklin. His dark skin with his green eyes made him a model of charm. He said, "So, what are you, like a Mormon or a Jehovah's Witness or something? Mom, you didn't give this guy a whole bunch of money or anything, did you?"

Cassian began to laugh. Corrina said, "I'm afraid it's true, Franklin. Cassian came to my home three days ago. He showed me. What he says about this…it's all true. Show him, Cassian!"

"I cannot, Corrina," Cass said. "At least not yet. And I will explain why. There is something special about your son. Ex suspected this, and I now believe she is right."

"The angel is a *she*?" Franklin asked, nodding with a patronizing look on his face.

"Try not to think of genders with angels and demons. But using a pronoun makes it easier than saying Ex constantly…and she *prefers* that.

"Unlike what is written in ancient texts like the Book of Enoch," Cass looked at Corrina, "the angels did not lust after the daughters of men. But men who were possessed or shrouded by their kind had much power. *Those* men found the women irresistible. And often, they abused their power to take what they desired. The children born of these women gave rise to a different kind of human. They were born with a human soul and the essence of a Seraphim. Seraphim are the demons and angels. The offspring of Seraphim are known as Nephilim."

Corrina gasped, "You told me when we met that Barry Bosco was possessed by a demon. Are you suggesting that my *son* is a Nephilim?" she asked incredulously.

Cassian answered, "I'm not suggesting it, Corrina. Your son *is* a Nephilim."

CHAPTER 8

NEPHILIM

"**I**'**VE HEARD OF THE NEPHILIM**," Corrina said. "The Ethiopian Bible includes the Book of Enoch. They are supposed to be giant warriors who bathed in the blood of mankind. They were wiped out by God in the Great Flood. How could Franklin be one of these monsters?"

Cassian tilted his head from side to side and said, "You are partially correct. God did destroy life on the planet in the Great Flood. And I think it was mostly because of the Nephilim. Human text and ancient text explain very little about these colossal men."

"Human *and* ancient text?" Franklin asked incredulously. "That suggests you believe *non*humans wrote our ancient texts."

"I don't doubt *that* for a minute," Cass said. "What do we really know about this world. Maybe it was stewards or angels or…other civilizations," Cass said with a shrug as he nodded skyward.

"It also appears that Nephilim *are* exclusively males. Perhaps the Seraphim essence attaches to the Y chromosome or something. I try to explain things as close to what make sense scientifically as possible.

"There is great debate among the Spurious theologians claiming Nephilim were giants, warriors, fallen angels…anything to steer humankind from the truth.

"The stewards, however, knew much about them. Great detail of the Nephilim and their powers are known by the stewards."

"Seraphim? Stewards? What the hell are stewards? What are you talking about?" Franklin asked.

Cassian said, "I believe the stewards are what some religions called the Watchers. Not the fallen angels called Watchers as in the Book of Enoch. That's a red herring. The Watchers are the scholars of existence. It makes sense as they are the ones *watching* events unfold! And, of course, recording these events. Their ranks consist of Godly souls who were either formerly shrouded or deemed worthy to enter into one of their open positions.

"I have met one of them three times in my life. He calls himself Stu. We are resonant, so he is…permitted…I don't know if that's the right word. But he is allowed to talk with me. He has vast stores of knowledge and struggles to withhold any of that information in the limited times I've had to speak with him. To that end, I actually know very little about them. But you could imagine their perpetuation like a form of universal academia…with politics and guile thriving among the leaders."

Franklin interrupted, "You said they have so much information. If you talked to this Stu fellow, why don't you know more about them?"

"The first time I met Stu was a whirlwind. Information came at me so fast…and he is funny, too; but I didn't realize that until years later. It was overwhelming. I probably got about ten percent of what he said. And that was still a lot. I had no idea how much he was holding back.

"The third time I met him," Cassian shook his head, "it was like downloading the internet. The entire internet…all at once. I'm a highly educated man, but I felt like a preschooler. He was talking about complex nonlinear thermodynamics, an antimatter universe, sub-subatomic particles held together by forces we only hypothesize as gravitons…I mean, shit that would have made Einstein or Tesla feel inept. I only recall the stuff that was important to me at the time.

"But let us not stray from the topic. I will tell you more about the stewards later, when I tell you about my second meeting with Stu.

"The Nephilim were a seemingly unexpected creation when human souls were born into vessels imbued with an essence of a Seraphim… that's an angel or demon. That essence is not something that is distinguishable between angel and demon because of the shared ancestry of their races. So, a Nephilim originated from either angel or demon is not inherently good or evil based on their source.

"The placating look on your face, Franklin, suggests that you are not buying what I'm laying down. I know the feeling.

"I will give you some advice that was frequently given to me. Your understanding of God, angels, and demons is all framed within your own dogma of *terminology*. Having great mental flexibility will help you to understand what I am going to tell you."

"No shit," Franklin said, looking annoyed. "Are you getting to a point soon? This sounds like a bunch of bullshit to me."

Cass said, "Please, Franklin. Be patient. It is worth the wait. I promise.

"As for the terminology, try *not* to think of angels, demons, and God in the ancient, religious images that have been implanted in your head. They are *actual* living beings who have been among us since time began. Even now. *Especially* now.

"There are also creatures called Spurs. They are human souls that have sided with the forces of Hell. They are the ones that prey upon desperate living souls from within the Dream World…that is what you would call Limbo. Their ranks have flourished in recent years, particularly since the pandemic. The lockdowns drove so many into despair and depression. There are so many now. Where once you may have met a single Spur in a month, you now probably meet one of them daily. Quite a successful plan for their side."

Corrina said, "You said you wanted to stay on topic with the Nephilim. Why are you switching to these Spur things?"

Cass continued, "This is relevant to all of us, particularly Franklin. Allow me to explain why.

"The power I am given by the angel is the manifestation of one of the seven deadly sins…envy. When I invoke the power of Ex, I leave my body and inhabit the body of any person of my choosing. I *possess* them. I can do this for any reason I like. If I wish to be beautiful or wealthy or…whatever, I simply push my mind into them and there I am.

"Any and every time I ever did this for self-interest, disaster and death followed. But, doing this against any person possessed by a Spur instantly banishes the Spuric soul back to Hell and the world seems to be a better place. But when I do this, I free the tortured soul that was trapped by the Spur. I am granted the ability to help those souls by—"

Franklin sighed heavily and said, "Cass, I mean this sincerely. I think that what you need is professional help. You seem intelligent and well spoken, but what you are describing sounds like a mental disorder of delusion. And your delusions are very convincing…enough so that you've managed to convince my mother…"

"Stop, Franklin," Corrina scolded, "I'm not out of my mind. Not even a little. Cassian showed me. He possessed me. I couldn't control my body. He could shove me in the dark, let me watch what he did, let me speak or stopped me in mid-sentence. I wouldn't be here right now if it wasn't true!" her voice increased in volume until she finished.

Cass said, "Stay calm, Corrina. You also did not believe me until you could see for yourself. The time for show and tell with Franklin is soon approaching. But he must first understand his *own* power."

"Power? What power?" Franklin said angrily. "I know that I am a strong man, and I could probably kick your ass up and down the street; but I would never do that because we live in a civilized society.

"However, since it seems you've drugged my mother into believing she was possessed by you, we are going to stop right here. I am going to call the police and have charges pressed against you. Then you will be escorted to a mental institution so that you can get the help you clearly need."

Cassian gave Franklin a hard stare for a moment and said, "I did not drug your mother. Give me ten more minutes, Franklin. In ten minutes time, if I have not convinced you, I will leave without the need for police or men with nets and little white coats that buckle in the back. And in that time, the pain in your neck will be gone."

When Cassian said the last line, Franklin screamed in pain and fell off his chair grabbing his neck. Corrina jumped to her feet and ran to his side to help him.

Cass said, "Well, at least now I know it can hear me."

"What do you want?!" Franklin roared. "What in the hell do you want from me? What are you seeing on my neck?"

"I don't know how I'm able to see it. Perhaps it's the way you're holding it. Maybe we can figure it out later."

"Holding what?!" Franklin asked.

"What I see is a reddish-black aura moving around your neck. I assume it's a Spur. You must have trapped it while you slept," Cass said. "It's afraid right now."

"Ahhh," Franklin yelled in agony as Cass said the last line. "Can you make this pain stop or not? If you can help, why would you wait? Why not just help me now?!"

"Ahh…now you want the help of a crazy man. Assurances, Franklin. I need an assurance that you will let me go," Cass said.

"Let you go? What are you talking about? You can leave whenever you want," he said, getting up from the floor. His eyes were watering from the pain as he began to pace back and forth.

"Being a Nephilim, your power, as I was attempting to explain, is this—any soul or entity that attempts to possess a Nephilim becomes trapped. And not only that, the Nephilim has full control. The pain you are feeling in your neck is a Spur that has latched on to you and is trying to escape. At least, I think it's a Spur. It's quite big. Can you see it? Maybe in the light and shadows or some other way. Maybe you feel it numbing your nerves…or a ringing in your ears."

Franklin stopped, then said, "I have seen something. I've been thinking it was my eyes playing tricks. But I have seen something around my head…I've seen it moving."

Cass said, "If you had any idea how to control your power, you would not be in pain. And that Spur would be trapped in the dark… exactly as it had planned to do to you. I can banish the Spur and send it back to Hell…if you choose to let it go, that is.

"Our problem is this. Once I do that, you will then be trapping *me*. And that is not something I really want to experience again. Do you understand?"

"No! No, not at all," Franklin said, his voice rising in pitch as he started pacing again. "Something is on my fucking neck, and I'm freaking out right now!"

Corrina jumped before her son and grabbed both his arms with her hands as she looked him in the eyes. She said, "Franklin, I need you to calm down." Her voice got softer. "I am here. Please. I need you to be calm."

Franklin took a few deep breaths and began to visibly relax. He nodded and sat back down at the table.

Cassian smiled and said, "There is nothing so powerful as the touch and sound of one's mother. It is beautiful. I wish that you could see what I see."

Franklin, still on the verge of snapping, said, "I understand not wanting to be trapped, but I still don't know how *I* would be trapping *you*. How am I supposed to let you go if I don't know how I would be holding you?"

Then, matching the quiet of Corrina, Cass said, "I don't know how you will release me yet. Ex tells me that it should be as simple as you allowing it. I only did this one other time, and I really don't know what I did. I will be taking a great chance here. I hope you can appreciate that. Once I do this, Ex will be speaking from my body.

"I am not sure what will happen with me. I think I can speak to you within your mind, but I don't know. It seemed to work last time. You will have all the control over that. Will you promise to release me?"

Franklin screamed again as his head was involuntarily jerking to the left and right, "Yes! I promise!"

"Oh well," Cass said. "And now for something completely different!"

The shift in perspective placed Cass high above the room descending rapidly on the thing attached to Franklin. The white sword swung down on Franklin's neck. The room flashed with white light and several low booms shook the whole structure.

Cassian found himself inside of an odd bubble. He could reach out and push against the walls of the bubble. There was no true sense of feeling, but the walls were soft. His feet were not bound, but walking did not move him. To his left, he looked through a distorted perspective to see a bunch of other bubbles.

Suddenly, the bubble next to him slammed into his, and a flaming red beast was biting and clawing at the barrier between them. This was no Spur! Franklin had trapped a *demon*! The other little bubbles were Spurs, still trapped to Franklin. Cass smiled and flipped his middle finger at the demon.

Cassian relaxed in an attempt to bring himself back home. Nothing happened. He was cut off from Ex. He seated himself in the bubble and began to focus his mind. Then he felt it…the core resonances of Franklin. It wasn't really speaking that Cass did, but he could fluctuate one of the resonances he felt within Franklin to communicate.

Cass said, "Franklin, can you hear me?"

"Yes." The voice of Franklin sounded like it was coming from the far end of a tunnel. "Tell me what to do now."

Cass communicated, "You have a demon trapped. And it's still attached to you. You also have a bunch of Spurs. Ex has banished all the attached entities, but you need to let them go."

"My pain stopped immediately when you did whatever you did. Are you sure anything is still attached to me?" Franklin asked.

Cass heard another voice speaking. It was faint, but clearly his own voice, coming from Ex, "Franklin, if you do not let go of that demon, you will draw unwanted attention to yourself. You must let it go."

"How?" asked Franklin.

"Sit down and close your eyes," Cass said. "I am going to help you to feel your own power."

Cass could sense Franklin's energy change. The lighting of the bubble holding him began to turn a cool blue color. Cass began to see dim, faint shapes of Corrina and himself in the room. He began to search and change his own vibrations and soon found what he was looking for. "Franklin, can you feel this," he said as he struck a chord connecting his bubble to the neck of Franklin.

Franklin chuckled as he said, "Yes. That felt really neat. What did you do?"

"Don't think about the feeling, but *where* you felt it," Cass communicated. "Then you will feel us all connected there. You will be able to tell which is which. The demon is violently red and angry. The bubbles of the Spurs are all a purple-black with fear. I am calm, light blue. Can you feel it?"

"Do that thing again," Franklin said.

Cass struck the chord. A few moments later the screaming bubble of the demon popped, and a silent vibration shook the room. All the other bubbles were gone too.

"I think I did it," said Franklin. "My neck feels great! I even feel like my mood is better."

"Yeah, wonderful," Cass said. "Now release me, please."

"What would happen if I did not let you go, Cassian? What if I held you?" Franklin asked.

"Don't you dare break your word, Franklin Charles Germane!" Cass heard Corrina yell.

"I just want to know what would happen, Mom. Will his angel do something? Or is he completely powerless?" Franklin asked.

"Ex can and will do nothing to you, Franklin. This is another power the Nephilim have. Do you recall when I jumped up and held my arms out? What did you feel when I did that?"

"I guess I felt fear…at first. Then it faded and it was just you standing there with your arms out. Why?" Franklin asked.

"This is how I knew you were a Nephilim. I stood before you with the power of Ex flowing through me. Your fear was an authentic reaction to seeing the fury of an angel standing before you. But you were able to siphon away the power as quickly as pouring water from a glass. Had you so much as slapped the table then, you likely would have shattered it to pieces. Do you now believe me and what I have been telling you?" Cassian asked.

"Yes. I believe you. But how is any of this possible? And if I siphoned off your power, how were you still able to get rid of the demon and the Spurs on my neck?"

"Release me and I will tell you more."

"Tell me more, and I will release you," Franklin said.

"Please, Franklin. Do not test me. I am not an angel or some Spur to be toyed with. There are things about me you do not know," Cass warned him.

"Cassian, I don't see you having much choice right now. You're not in any position to threaten me," Franklin said.

"Very well," Cass said. "Today is a day of teaching."

"I'm not threatening you, Cass. I said I would let you go, and I w… Agggggg!" Franklin screamed. He fell to the floor and began to vomit again and again. His hands were shaking and pain rocked through his midsection. He immediately released Cassian.

As Franklin lay on the floor trembling from the experience, Cass lean over him and said, "I never said I was helpless. I merely said I was trapped."

Cass reached down and began to help Franklin to his feet.

"What did you do to me?" Franklin asked.

"Those were two of your core resonances that I created a destructive interference with. I imagine it was unpleasant. Was it similar to being electrocuted?"

"Fuck, man. Whatever you did, I never want to feel that again."

"That was God punishing you for breaking your promise. And probably for swearing like that too," Corrina said. "And after Cass helped you with your neck."

"I was going to let him go, Mom. Really. I was. I was only trying to see what would happen. I was…today-years-old…when I found out my mother was raped by a demon and that I'm a damned Nephilim. That was *not* something I expected when I woke up this morning…*before* my alarm went off," he said, sitting down at the table, holding his stomach, and looking miserable.

Franklin's phone gave a loud, long buzz from the table he set it on to charge. "That's Victoria. She was going to text me when she got to Ariel's. I need to tell her about this."

"Do you love your wife, Franklin?" Cassian asked.

"Of course I love my wife. Why do you think I married her?" he said.

"If you tell her any of this, you will never see her again. Not ever," Cass said.

"Is that a threat? Are you threatening *Victoria*?" Franklin snapped.

"I am not suggesting any such thing. She will not be harmed. And I am not threatening her or you, Franklin. I am only—"

"Don't tell her, Franklin," Corrina said, "Don't do it. She'll only get angry with *you*. Then she'll probably come running home in the dark, thinking you're in trouble. Don't tell her. You can tell her when she gets home and we're long gone."

Franklin thought about it a moment, then nodded his head. "Okay. I won't tell her now. I'll tell her face to face when she gets home on Sunday. But I got to make a call first. I need to see if I can get her a hotel room tonight," he said.

"Yes. Please. Go ahead and tend to the needs of your wife. Does anywhere around here deliver pizza? I'm starving. My treat!" Cass said.

Franklin had to laugh.

CHAPTER 9

CENTRALIA

MALCOM PASEO DROVE HIS CAR up the dark and deserted road leading to Centralia, Pennsylvania. He had been in many creepy places with Cassian over the years, but he couldn't imagine any place creepier than this.

The story Malcom heard was that in May of 1962, the town began a trash fire that ignited a vein of coal. This began a series of underground fires that the town and state were unable to extinguish. There were supposedly toxic levels of carbon dioxide coming from the ground as the burning continues to this day and is expected to burn for another two hundred years or so.

The residents were evacuated and the government paid them for their land. The town had been abandoned for decades, with only a few residents refusing to leave.

The story sounds fishy to Malcom. Not the fire and the efforts to stop it. That's clearly a matter of public record. It's the removal of all residents, and potential witnesses, that looks suspicious.

The coordinates Cassian gave Malcom for each retrieval told him nothing about what to expect. It contained only a global position and a time: 40.806097, -76.344145, 1:17 a.m. This would be the sixth message Malcom helped Cass to retrieve. He was alone this time, but usually they were together. Cassian had to travel to Boston on an errand that he hoped would help him to solve the encryption.

They had to be careful when the portals opened. Stu explained that there was a unique metallic element called Desemilnoct, or Dese, for short. It is something that the stewards and other advanced civilizations used for all types of things, including opening portals between realms. But to do that, it had to be in a powdered form and, according to Stu, pulverizing the metal was next to impossible. While the metal was rare, this finely granulated form was, by any practical means, nonexistent.

The supplies Malcom carried never changed as he had to be prepared for all inevitabilities. He brought five kilograms of dry ice, three liters of mineral oil, flame retardant gloves, a fire suppressant device, and a respirator. They always wore the gloves and the respirators when the time came.

They were warned that there could be unreacted Dese flying around after generating a portal. Any ingestion in the aerosolized form, especially breathing it in, would lead to intense, rip-the-skin-off-your-face insanity if the metal were not purged from the cerebrospinal fluid. Currently, there was no medicine on Earth capable of performing that medical miracle.

In an action that was not sanctioned by the stewards, Stu provided Cassian the sets of coordinates nineteen years earlier in 2006. They were fairly accurate (within twenty feet and ten minutes) and easy enough to spot. They were also destructive as he found out when one occurred on the front fender of his car leaving molten metal dripping down onto the rubber of the tire. This is why the fire extinguisher was needed.

What he found in these *messages* was nothing remarkable at all. Twice it was some kind of meat. One found in Azerbaijan and the other in New Guinea. Once it was a sugary plant they recovered in Wales. Another time, in northern Canada, it was some type of salt lick. The one in Africa was a live mouse. How it survived the portal was anyone's guess, but it wasn't meant to live for long. This was the last set of coordinates Stu supplied. Creepy Centralia at one in the morning.

Cassian told him that the *messages* were something called prions transferred by a civilization far more advanced than us. They were sent in a form meant to be ingested by a specific type of animal. Once eaten, the prion would force neurological proteins to fold in a similar fashion and cause a sickness within that species. This was done to get the attention of scientists who studied proteins. The messages were encrypted in the prion sequence. But deciphering the messages was still a great mystery.

Three of the messages sat in a -70°C freezer and two others sat in a bath of mineral oil. Stu said that the demons knew about messages being sent in the prions. They began to have Spurs alter the information sent from earlier prion sequences so that the encryption process would translate into nonsense. When they did this, those prions would also transfer into humans and become deadly. Cass couldn't be sure what sequence would make sense since nobody had been able to decode any of them yet.

Pennico Pharmaceuticals was a generic over-the-counter company in Durham, North Carolina, that was established as a front to hide their research into the proteins. There was also Pennico Contract Labs (PCL) in Pittsburgh, Pennsylvania, that performed high-quality, protocoled in vitro testing for other companies.

Both arms of Pennico hired Mollosk Security Group to provide overall security for the company. Malcom Paseo formed the Mollosk Security Group, headquartered in Las Vegas, Nevada, in 1995. In addition to the considerable funds they generated through private security and their Pennico contracts, they were supplemented by anonymous endowments.

The chance that dark forces might be lurking about Centralia were low, even though Spurs were known to keep watch over the area. But they had no knowledge of the specific coordinates.

Spurs weren't so much of a problem anymore since Mollosk Security had Puriel Armaments develop a small, wearable, 360-degree camera capable of live streaming through its own dedicated satellite.

Puriel Armaments, located in Norfolk, Virginia, was established in 1993 by Darren and Tony Wagner. They designed and produced customized lethal and nonlethal weapons, including modified vehicles.

Mollosk Security Group had their central operations located on the outskirts of Gettysburg, Pennsylvania. Malcom kept at least eleven trusted employees monitoring his 360-camera when he activated the live stream.

The camera delay could get him killed, but so far, no Spur was able to touch him. Their desire to gloat and toy with people before they struck bought them their one-way ticket back to Hell. In each of the three times this happened to Malcom, a confused and terrified person was left in the wake. And each time, Malcom had to kill that person.

Cass explained that it would be a compassionate and merciful death without Ex there to help heal their mind. After watching Cass and Ex help Jimmy once they freed him, he never doubted that.

But Malcom did not treat the newly released soul to a compassionate or merciful death. He shut off the live stream, bound the person's hands and feet, covered them in gasoline, and lit them ablaze. A profound peace came over him as they screamed.

After Jimmy died those many years ago, something awoke within Malcom. Something dark. He remembered breaking it off with the girl he was dating. Molly was her name.

They were parked in the woods one evening. After having sex, Molly said something about going to her prom. Malcom gently put his hands on her neck and kissed her tenderly on the lips. Then his powerful hands began to tighten. At first, Molly thought it was playful. Malcom remembered feeling no remorse as her expression turned to panic. She fought back, punching and kicking. But this had no effect on Malcom. He enjoyed the pain she inflicted upon him before the life drained from her body and she went limp.

Malcom drove around with her lifeless body in the passenger seat. He went to a hardware store, bought a shovel, and took her to an orchard with soft, fertile ground. He had been here with her before. She really like it there, and the memory of that day felt warm and happy. He dug a deep hole and placed her in it face down so she couldn't look at him as he buried her.

He went home afterward and cried for what he had done. Not because he felt bad, but because Molly was no longer with him. He was really going to miss her.

Malcom realized that he had a problem and it was getting worse. There was no way to keep this from Cassian. So he told Cass about Molly and a few others he murdered, admitting his growing desire to kill people in the most horrific ways. It was a difficult subject to broach.

After jumping into him to make sure no possession occurred, Cassian appeared unfazed. Hearing about Malcom's strange compulsions came as no surprise to him. In fact, he confessed to Malcom about his own killing spree where he dispatched the remaining Bosco family members after they escaped that evening years ago.

Many long discussions ensued about who Malcom could or could not kill. But the two of them never told another person involved in their business. Cassian explained that Malcom's desires could, in fact, be leveraged to help with their ultimate goal. Cass did not like killing people. It was only done out of necessity. Some people deserved to be put down. And if Cass and Malcom deemed the crimes bad enough, Malcom was let loose. Cassian would ask Ex what she thought, but Ex would rarely interfere with those decisions.

When it came to demons, they were another problem. Malcom had yet to encounter one since Barry Bosco. But Cass gave him something he called a modified Tolaxnarm configuration. It was based off the design of something called a Tolaxnarm device. This was the device that held Cassian and Ex in Eric Bosco's murder shed. The wearable form was called the Tolaxnarm configuration.

Cass said that this *modified* Tolaxnarm configuration would be far less effective against demons than the original device was against angels. But it would provide a brief window of time to stop a demon.

Malcom was loath to use it for two reasons. First, it involved getting covered in pigs' blood, which smelled like shit. Some protein that worked against demons was produced by pigs. The original device used against angels had the blood of a young lamb…not that that would smell any better. Also, the device itself looked remarkably and utterly ridiculous. It was a pink vest with a fluffy pink ring circling his midsection that hung down from the shoulders. It looked like a little girl's lacy princess costume enlarged to fit an adult.

Cass showed him how he could quickly put it on and puncture the blood packets. If the demon attacked, it would separate the power from the possessed long enough for Malcom to kill the person with his gun. But he had precious little time.

When asked why it had to look so stupid, Cass told him that the power of the demon was greatly reduced when the one they possessed consciously (or subconsciously for the demon) reacted to humor. Seeing this large, serious man with a gun wearing a fluffy pink dress was… unexpected.

Malcom considered that this explanation could be bullshit. Cass and Tony may just want to see if he would wear it. Over the years, precedent was set by them messing with him in such ways.

He couldn't wait to get back to the hotel off Route 81 on the other side of Ashland and Gordon. Bouts of heat lightning created glimpses of the low-hanging clouds making the whole scene feel oppressive. He turned left down the unmarked road that the map called Laurel Street and cut his speed to a crawl.

The time was 1:12 a.m. It wouldn't be much longer. He sat in his car waiting, at least one hundred feet from the coordinates. By 1:30, nothing came. He continued to wait. It was nearly 2 a.m. It had never been this late before.

At 2:12 a.m., just as Malcom was getting ready to leave, a blinding flash occurred in front of him. Something large flew through the opening that appeared about three feet from the ground. All the plants encompassed by the circle were singed or burning slightly. Then, something unexpected happened.

A tall, thin man stood.

CHAPTER 10

CASSIAN BEGINS

"CALM DOWN, VICTORIA," FRANKLIN SAID into the phone, "I paid $250 to get you in at the Coppertoppe. Take Ariel and stay there. The room is a suite that's big enough for both of you. Figure out what you're doing tonight or tomorrow morning. The Bristol House of Pizza is on your way there and it's open until 9 p.m. Get what you want, grab that dumb bitch, and go to the hotel," Franklin said.

Audible yelling from the phone could be heard by Cass and Corrina as they exchanged knowing glances.

"Okay. I'm sorry. I only called her a dumb bitch because you did!" Franklin said.

More audible yelling.

"I understand that you are having a bad night, but don't take it out on me. I'm trying to help you!" Franklin paused. The yelling stopped.

"Good. I'm glad," Franklin said. "Are you going to be alright?"

"Okay. Call me if you need anything. I love you."

After a moment, Franklin pulled the phone from his face and hit the end call button.

"Let me guess," Corrina said, "you're not allowed to have the last word. Am I right?"

"Please, Mom. Can we *not* do this again? Victoria is the woman I love. I wish you could understand that. She is very loving and sweet to me. All you can ever see is how bad she is," Franklin said.

"Oh yeah! As long as you're under her thumb, you're the cat's ass! Once you try to—"

"Corrina!" Cass said. "Remember what we discussed." He gave her a stern look that made her stop talking and nod.

"What do you mean?" Franklin asked. "What did you talk about? Were you talking about Victoria?"

Cassian looked at Franklin and sighed. Then he said, "Did I not tell you, Franklin, that your life, as you know it, would forever change today? That is not to say you will not have your job or will not continue living your life. It will just never be the same as it was."

"Well, no fucking shit, Sherlock," Franklin shot back.

"What did I tell you about that cursing?" Corrina yelled at him. "At least you could have some respect for me when I'm around."

"I'm sorry, Mom. I know I swear a lot. I don't mean any disrespect," Franklin said.

Cass spoke again, "When I am done telling you my story, I am going to ask you for a favor. It's not a 'can-I-borrow-five-bucks' favor. It's even bigger than a 'can-you-drive-me-to-Logan-Airport' favor. It's a 'this-will-change-your-life-forever' favor. That's why I need to tell you the story first. If you agree to help me, I would be in your debt. If you say no, then I will leave you pretty much as I found you…with one minor change."

"What kind of change?" He asked.

"Well, 'minor' is a relative term at this point. What time is that pizza going to get here? Didn't you call them like an hour ago?" Cassian asked.

"That was barely fifteen minutes ago! It's Friday night. They said forty-five minutes to an hour. That means like an hour and a half for them. Are you that hungry? I have some cheese and crackers if you can't wait," Franklin said.

"No, no, no! Don't trouble yourself. I'll wait for the pizza. But it's a long story, and I didn't want to start the story on an empty stomach. When will Victoria be coming home?" Cassian asked.

"She's not getting back until Sunday."

"I have a feeling that your wife is going to be home tomorrow," Cass said.

"So, you're psychic too?" Franklin asked.

"No. Don't be ridiculous. Nobody has psychic powers, Franklin. That would give one access to your mind. That is simply not possible," Cass said.

"Yeah. That would be ridiculous, right? A guy who says he's an angel, possessing people, and trapped by a Nephilim…you know…like me. Sure. Psychic powers *do* seem a little ridiculous!" Franklin gave a fake laugh.

"I never said I was an angel, Franklin. I am *shrouded* by an angel," Cassian said with a big smile.

"What the fu…whatever man! I'm just saying," Franklin shrugged.

Cass nodded and said, "It is important you recognize that your mind is yours and yours alone…except for God. And that's only because your mind is a piece of God. Nobody, and *I mean nobody*, has access to your mind.

"As for me, I see things in my dreams. Some dreams are visions into other realms that may be ours or may be similar to ours. I don't really know anymore. The various realms have something to do with the three aspects of light. Each aspect that splits off creates another realm where the radiant light of that realm is composed of the other two aspects. It's kind of some deep stuff.

"I seem to be able to slip into the Dream World and travel around when I sleep. It's one of several theories I was told about. After all these years, it has stretched my understanding of the word *real*. Sometimes I'm *crazy*, spot-on with my predictions, and other times," he sighed, "well… I'm so far off that I *look* crazy. That's the kind of thing that makes you question yourself. You know?"

"Yeah. I know," Franklin said sarcastically. "Why don't you go ahead and start your story. The food is coming. We can take a break when it gets here."

"You told them no olives, right?" Cass said.

Franklin gave him a look of mock surprise and said, "Yes. I told them *no olives* on *half* the pizza! I like olives."

"Alright. But if I get even one olive in a bite, I'm going to be pissed," Cassian said seriously.

"Olives," Franklin scoffed. "Are you for real? Worrying about pizza toppings right now? What the fuck is wrong with you, dude?"

"Look, Franklin. We must embrace the small pleasures in life. Wonderful music. A fine wine. A relaxing massage. Eating a delicious slice of pizza with pepperoni and mushrooms. That last one is something I genuinely love in life. And nothing can fuck *that* up like a gross-ass, slug-textured, shit-tasting olive hidden underneath a slice of pepperoni, like a land mine for your tongue!" Cass turned to Corrina, "My apologies for swearing, Corrina."

She started to laugh.

Franklin shook his head and said, "I think you might be on the spectrum, guy. If you get a widdle olive on your widdle tongue," he mocked a child's speech. "I'll call them and order you another pizza. Okay?"

"Well," Cass tsked. "That would just be wasteful. I can pick them off. But if they cut them up real small, thinking all people *like* a tapenade…" He shook his head.

Franklin looked at him blankly and said, "Get on with your story, you psycho, so we can get this over with."

"Psycho? Franklin, we are going to be great friends soon. Have you heard the saying 'brevity is the soul of wit?'"

Franklin nodded.

Cassian said with a brilliant smile, "Well, I am *not* very witty."

"Oh, fuck!" Franklin mumbled, shaking his head.

———————————

Cassian's story began two years after Corrina had disappeared. Cass had seen her in school, but they did not know each other. Corrina was two years ahead of him, and he only moved to her school a few months before she vanished. He never heard a rumor about her. He figured she moved. As she was one of only five African American students in the school, he did notice.

Cass gave an abbreviated version of the events of 1990 into 1991. First the story of Lynn and his fateful car crash, explaining how an angel named Ex came into his life…and, like a dick, made him wait seven months before speaking to him. That comment was followed by another flinch and sharp intake of air, but also made Cassian laugh.

He told them of stewards, Spurs and demons, and touched upon the Dream World. He explained his own power and the consequences of its use and abuse. To preserve their trust, he even told them about his appalling treatment of Miss Jennifer Turnbull.

Corrina looked mortified by this. He explained that there was not a day that went by where he didn't feel haunted by his actions. She seemed to understand, but her demeanor was more tense after that revelation. It didn't get any better when he explained that he began dating Lynn's younger sister, Mary.

Cass told about what happened with Lynn's older sister, Beth, and how he left her at one of the Bosco family parties. After telling this part, Corrina probably sympathized with Beth's distaste for Cassian.

He went on about how Lynn and her son, Samuel, were killed by his step-grandfather, Bill. He told them how his grandmother and Bill were involved with the Bosco family. Then he told the tale of how he released his grandmother from a Spur and her revenge against Bill.

Cass told them about the attack on his family and his escape, relaying the death of Doug Bosco at the hands of Mary and her allied Spur, Khalima. He talked about the torture he experienced at the hands of Eric Bosco and described how his friends risked their lives to save him. Tearfully, he relayed the sacrifice of Jimmy Adams to save their lives.

Finally, he explained the fight with Mitch Bosco where Mary saved his life. Then how Mary was brutally killed by Barry Bosco. He made sure to detail how Barry died.

Cass touched upon the aftermath of these events and how he and Ex went about exterminating the remaining members of the Bosco family.

Cass didn't notice at the time, but while he was doing that, the military came in and removed all evidence of the Bosco family existence. Even their property was enclosed with high voltage electrical fencing. Armed guards are still stationed there, nearly thirty-five years later.

Many years passed before Cass realized his destruction of their family was a huge favor to many three-letter agencies.

Cassian said, "Ex was convinced that there was something much, much bigger going on. Something that would change the world for the worse. At that time, I was young and naïve." Cass looked down and to the right for a second and said, "Yeah, I was stupid. I exemplified the Dunning–Kruger effect. Are you happy?"

"Happy about what?" Corrina asked.

"Not you. Ex. She speaks to me…and never forgets anything I do…ever," Cass smiled.

The doorbell rang. Cassian practically jumped from the table and ran to the door. He tipped the driver $25 on a $65 bill that already included the delivery fee.

Franklin came to the door to help carry the food inside. When he saw the tip he said, "Jeez. Thanks, man. I'm gonna get good service from them for a while."

"It is important to be generous with *any* person who is willing to work for a living these days, especially in food service. You place a great deal of trust in these folks. That man had to come out in this driving rain, spend his own gas money, risk his life on the road just to bring us nourishment.

"I recognize the value of that. What do you think he would get if he got injured? Zippity-do-da! That's what. Small, family businesses, with thin profit margins, have to forgo employee healthcare benefits. That's so they can afford their quarterly donations to our insolvent, drunk Uncle Sam who likes to start foreign wars that enrich those in control while pissing on those who do the funding.

"Ahhh, but I digress," Cass said.

"Are you some kind of fringe, anti-government guy who likes to stir shit up from your soapbox?" Franklin asked.

"Yes. Unfortunately, that has become necessary. Too many decisions being made by the Spurs going unrecognized by the increasingly disinterested or disenfranchised masses. I'm not public enemy number one on any list you will ever find. But if they knew about my fact-finding campaign, I don't think I would last too long.

"And, I'm sorry to be the one to tell you this, but I'm certain they would want you dead too," Cass said.

"Me? *What?*" Franklin asked surprised.

"If the political and economic powers that be found out *what* you were, the contract on your life would be signed faster than I could eat a slice of this pizza," Cass said casually.

"What?" Franklin exclaimed. "What do you mean? People would try to *kill me*?!"

"Yes. Of course. You are a Nephilim, Franklin. Most of the forces in Heaven *and* Hell seem to want your kind eliminated. Not me, though. I value all life and think the Nephilim have as much right as any other species to survive. You are something of an anomaly. Something nobody can control.

"Right and wrong have become such blurry concepts as I live my life. Perhaps Shakespeare is correct. Only thinking makes it so. You know, there are a billion shades of gray between black and white," Cass said.

Franklin threw the box of pizza on the table and sat down heavily. The implication of this came as quite a shock.

"Hey, easy with the food. I don't want one of your nasty-ass olives jumping onto my side of the pie," Cass said.

"How can you be so fucking glib about this!" Franklin roared at Cassian. "You just told me my life could be snuffed out because of who my father is! Maybe if you are the only person who knows about it, I should just snuff *you* out! Then I don't have to worry about it anymore!" he yelled.

"Franklin!" Corrina yelled back. "Did you suggest that you would *kill* this man? How could you say such a thing?!"

"No, no, no! He's catching on fast, Corrina," Cassian said. "You have to understand. This is exactly how it happens. Once you see the danger to your life and that of your family, your perspective *will* change. The unthinkable becomes quite reasonable. This is a good thing."

"I don't want my son entertaining ideas of *murder*, Cassian! You never said anything about that!"

"It is not murder, Corrina. It is self-preservation. What would happen if someone else found out that Barry Bosco was Franklin's father? Do you think they would throw him a party? Or do you think they would try to kill him without any warning? Shouldn't he know how and when to protect himself?" Cassian fired back without a bit of his previous nonchalance.

Corrina stared at Cassian for a long moment, then relented, "Keep my son alive, Cassian. That's all I want."

"I think I can do that, Corrina. Especially if he is willing to help. At the very least, I will leave him with the knowledge of *how* to defend himself and what to look for from those wishing to do him harm." He gave her a hard stare back.

Corrina nodded.

Franklin looked between the two of them and said, "What's going on here? What are you not telling me?"

Cassian turned to him and said, "When I am done, you will have all the information I have. My hope is that you will be able to ask better questions than I did."

Franklin shook his head. "Maybe you're some fucking nutjob, man. I don't know what to think right now."

"Do you doubt what happened less than an hour ago…with your neck?" Cassian asked.

Franklin looked around the room, like he wanted to run away…just escape. He knew he couldn't. He looked at Cass and said, "Fine. I'll decide whether or not I believe you. But you better hope I believe you, Cassian," he said with menace in his voice.

"Fair enough," Cass said with a brilliant smile as he opened the box holding the pizza.

CHAPTER 11

LINES IN THE SAND

"H E OPENED A PORTAL?" ILLOC exclaimed, in mock outrage in the room full of Acera and Bilved stewards. "Who sanctioned this? And to where did the portal lead?"

"Tidorey claims that this information cannot be determined," Lanilti said, feigning indignation to go along with the show.

"It is forbidden to interfere directly with the split realms. What was sent through this portal and who was the recipient?" Illoc yelled.

"Why are you concerning yourself with what transpires on the split realms, Illoc? What business is this of yours?" said Doti almost playfully from across the room. "Portals are sanctioned by the Grad stewards. Why don't you ask them?" he asked as he walked closer to Illoc.

"Indeed, I will, Doti," Illoc said. "I am certain this was Tinilfasela sending something to his resonant. Direct interference with a pathway to aid either cause is not permitted. This could be construed as an act of war by the demons."

Doti said, "Our purpose is to record and learn from what we see and help creation where we can. Was Tinilfasela not the epitome of this aspiration? Our purpose is not to dictate what is done. If the act was sanctioned, there was a reason. A reason that doesn't involve you. Or does it? Why do you feel this intense need to control events? Or is it the outcome you wish to control?"

"What power does this angel or soul possess to permit such favoritism?" Illoc continued, "I am not trying to control events, but this could threaten our existence. We maintain a tenuous peace with the demons, but neither side is to benefit from our knowledge. This action clearly benefits one side! The demons could see this as a betrayal by the stewards. Providing such knowledge to those it is not meant for is how the original thirteen named angels got into so much trouble in the beginning. Do you not recall the stories about the sharing of antimony and other such metals?" Illoc said in a patronizing tone.

"That is *not* how it transpired…not as you describe it, Illoc. Are you beginning to believe the very text *you* helped to create? You associate the crimes of the Matriarch Era with the angels while justifying the vast overcorrection of the established Patriarchy. The power was meant to be equal between men and women. Distorting the text with your rendition of the truth ushered in a belief that the male dominance on Earth was sanctioned by God. What you say is not factual, and *you know it*," Doti said.

"I make no claims of malfeasance by the angels. But it was their teachings that brought about the Matriarchy. That was an evil time in their history, Doti. Women rode on the backs of Nephilim and claimed billions of lives. They brought the wrath of the Builders by using a power they had no right to use. Recurrence of those actions *had* to be prevented in the future," Illoc said.

"Not in the way you did it. You want to sway the next generations to garner support for your ideology. The thirteen angels you speak of were punished for teaching forbidden knowledge," Doti said loudly, looking around the room. "The rest were offered a choice to defend what they felt more appropriate to their own beliefs. They were never slaves. Some Seraphim did not agree with chaos *and* order to generate conflict. God wanted and *needed* angels who would be the parchment to the pen. They were the ones who openly opposed God to become demons.

"They were not all contentious…especially in the beginning. Many knew and understood their purpose. The real contention began when the thirteen named *fallen* angels of chaos, with Azazel at their helm, *betrayed* the side they claimed to support.

"You, Illoc, fuel the fires of that contention. You would make *all* demons seem horrible…but many were brave. Demons had to walk away from the existence they built…outcast in the eyes of humans and

Seraphim alike. Many *are* bitter, spiteful, and hate humankind. But there are others that are benevolent.

"We also know there are angels as treacherous as some of the worst demons. They despise the humans as well. You pretend to want the ear of the angels to help with their cause. I believe what you really wish to do is add to that hatred.

"Things have changed dramatically since that time and most Seraphim have lost sight of their purpose. But stop acting like what *you* wrote has transformed into law! These are merely *rules* that we have accepted for guidance. They are as meaningless as the peacocking of fools or the woes of the wealthy."

Illoc looked furiously at Doti and said, "I do not need a lecture from you. Lanilti, find Tinilfasela. I want to speak with him. Who is his Karma steward?"

Lanilti said, "He was placed under Tidorey after the shrouding of his resonant."

"Is it true that Tinilfasela is slated to move directly into a Bilved level when his shrouding ends? They will allow him to skip over Karma level? This is not how we operate," Illoc said.

Doti said, "That has not been confirmed, Illoc. But you are free to question IllGrad about this type of promotion. Would you like to question *his* resolve?"

Illoc looked around nervously then said, "Lanilti, bring Tinilfasela. I will get to the bottom of this portal business personally," regaining his composure and his slick politician facade.

"This is good. I have been anticipating your confrontation with this young steward," said Doti with a genuine smile, "I think that you will find this one rather…interesting. You should prepare yourself if you wish to be steadfast on protocol. Perhaps you should consult with IllGrad first. Tinilfasela is one of the most—" Doti stopped short and said, "I want you to see for yourself. Particularly with your ramblings of control…"

"I am not trying to control anything!" Illoc shouted.

Doti ignored Illoc as if nothing were said. "But I will give you no more information, only advice. Tread carefully with Tinilfasela, for he may well be one of the next Grad stewards, if not the next NilGradMa."

"What are you talking about? Tinilfasela is nothing more than a formerly shrouded soul like the rest of us. He just happened to be resonating with the comatose body of the Chosen when the shrouding occurred. Tinilfasela can now speak directly with the angels. We should be leveraging that for our needs. I care not about—"

"Yes, you do!" Doti said. "Why else were you trying to find the soul *before* the shrouding? You knew this one would give you direct communication with an angel. You wanted a steward you could control to be the resonant. What is it you have been so adamant to get? The ear of God? Or perhaps it's the attention of the demons you seek?"

"I want nothing of the sort," Illoc defended. "I have been in study for well over three thousand of that planet's years and even more in the magnetic realm," Illoc said. "Do you believe that you can threaten me with vague accusations or some presumed knowledge about this resonant steward?"

Doti laughed. "It is your motives that are vague. If you controlled the resonant steward, you could feed information to the angel. What that information would be, I am yet uncertain.

"Now you want to meet with Tinilfasela. Why? To feed him information? To bend him to your will? Could you trust that any soul does not have its own motivations? You *do* know the souls of a steward may come from *any* realm and may have existed for centuries before arriving here, don't you?"

"I am not stupid, Doti! And I am *not* trying—"

"Then why do you act so!" Doti interrupted, the calm, playful demeanor now absent. "Your ignorance and lack of respect make you sound like one of the fools from Sjoshjain before their destruction. I see through your plotting. I see the way you behave, and it makes me sick. You will *never* be a Grad as long as I am here. You are the epitome of what is wrong with the stewards. I can no longer hide my contempt for you and your allies," Doti said, looking at Lanilti. "I will not see you do to Tinilfasela what was done to him when…" Doti cut short.

"What are you saying, Doti? The nature of your accusations places my life among the stewards in great danger. Are you…threatening me?" Illoc asked.

"Yes, I am! I will threaten you until the day of *my* dismissal or *yours*. I will not hide my feelings toward you. I lack the proof that you defy our cause. But I think you are the one who provided the demons with the information they needed to capture the shrouded—the directions for a Tolaxnarm device. I think you are the one who tricks the Grads and stewards into believing your myths. I would sooner trust the words of the serpent than the foulness from your tongue." Doti stared at Illoc in defiance.

A smile spread across the face of Illoc. "My friend, I think you have greatly mistaken my stance on these issues."

"Please, Illoc, do not call me friend. We are not. We never have been. And we never will be," Doti said curtly.

Illoc ignored this and continued, "I am sworn to serve the angels and the side of chaos to promote creation. I do apologize if some of that lawful venom seems to creep into my actions. But do we not all agree that *some* order must be maintained?" Illoc asked politely.

"Order and control are two different things, Illoc. You conflate the two in a manner suggesting that only *your* way is correct. I do not agree with you. I believe that you want nothing more than power and absolute control. Having you in the Grad stewards would be lending an ear to Satan himself.

"Let me ask you something, and your answer may well change how I feel about you. What would you do if you were made NilGradMa in the next span?"

"I would change nothing…at first," said Illoc in a relaxed voice. "Then, I would stop this dissent from the lower stewards who have been corrupted with these false alternate histories. There must also be respect, Doti. You have to agree on *that*!"

Doti smiled, but did not nod.

"Then, I would leverage the shrouded resonant. They could be the conduit we require to better understand the shrouding process and when it will occur. This would greatly improve our ability to communicate directly with God and assist the angels. This is what we *need*! There is no reason to secure that information from allies like us. Why is this such an important—"

"Let me stop you there," Doti said loudly, "before you make a bigger fool of yourself. This is not something held secret by the angels. It is held in confidence by God. You are…you really are…an asshole!" Doti said.

Murmurs of disbelief swarmed among the stewards as profanity of this sort had not been spoken openly in many generations.

"A filthy, feces-covered asshole," Doti said loudly, to accentuate his disgust. "I do not say this lightly. What we are witnessing is a steward who is attempting to overthrow our cause!"

Loud gasps of shock occurred throughout the room.

"Doti!" came the commanding voice of the NilGradMa. "A word with you."

Doti put his head down and began to walk toward his leader. Illoc wore a satisfied smile. As Doti walked past Illoc, his eyes shifted to his adversary and he whispered, "Kebra."

The smile vanished from the face of Illoc.

CHAPTER 12

COLLEGE

"I STARTED COLLEGE IN SEPTEMBER OF 1991," Cassian said. "It would be five years before I would again speak with Stu, but fifteen years before we were meant to speak. You will understand what I mean by that later.

"This was a tumultuous time in my life. My mother had to move from where we lived for the past five years. My grandmother went to live with my aunt Susan, who had come to a change of heart in the month or so following the events I told you about.

"I still don't understand how this works, but something lifted from my two aunts and my mother once Grandma Betty was freed from her Spur. Very similar to Malcom and his mother, Maureen.

"To make matters worse, I had to move into the dorms at the University of Pittsburgh. Have you ever lived in a dormitory, Franklin? It kind of sucks in a lot of ways. You don't often get choices, especially as a freshman.

"Mind you, this was only weeks after I had just had the worst day of my life. The demons would certainly have killed me or tortured me for months if my friends had not helped me escaped. I was angry enough at the time to vengefully deal with the rest of the Bosco family…in an appropriate manner. At least on my free weekends.

"But I want to tell you about my college roommates…"

Cassian got off the elevator on the sixth floor, carrying his large duffle bag full of clothes. Room 602 was directly in front of the elevator. He keyed the lock and opened the door to the dormitory. Two large windows with sheer curtains lit the neat room. The dark blue, Berber-carpeted floor had duplicates of each piece of furniture: simple wood-framed beds with mattresses, wooden desks, each with two drawers, and matching chest-high bureaus, each with five drawers. The beds were stacked like bunk beds to save space, but it was clear they could be separated to single beds.

Someone else had already claimed the lower bed that was made with a light-brown blanket and two blue and gold Pitt throw pillows on top.

Mike pushed past Cass with a lamp and a few bags hanging from his arms. "Don't just stand there, dumbass. There's still a ton of stuff to bring up. I can't stay parked there all day."

"Sorry, Mike," Cass said, "I didn't expect it to be so—"

"Craptacular is the word you're looking for. Yeah. It's a dorm, not the Ritz. You'll be okay," Mike said, looking around the room. "But you can't be on the top bunk, not with your foot. Here, help me separate these."

He and Cass went about the task of taking the top bed down and moving one of the desks and bureaus to create space for the other bed. It made the room more crowded, but there was still plenty of room to move around.

"God, it's kind of small," Cass said.

"Are you kidding me? This room is massive compared to the Towers. Don't you remember that little pie-shaped room I had my first year?"

"Oh yeah. That was a matchbox. I don't know *how* you did that," Cass said.

"Yeah. And you get your own bathroom with a shower. I had to share a bathroom…and athlete's foot…with the whole damn floor. That really sucked. You're so lucky to be getting into McCormick Hall and not the Towers. Sure, these buildings pre-date the arrival of Columbus, but you have an actual room!" Mike said.

"It's comforting to know that the elevators were probably once powered by horses and donkeys," Cass said. "I wonder who my roommate is?"

"That's kind of an important thing to know. Hopefully he's not some dickhead like that dingus, Chansky, I had my second year. What a fuck-tard he was. Did you know he's in prison now?"

"Really?! What for?" Cassian asked as they both went about getting his room set up.

"You know he was a juicehead. I guess in a roid rage, he beat up his girlfriend and this guy she was talking to in CJ's. He just went over, right in the bar, and started beating the shit out of them both. He fucked her up good too. Fortunately, the cops were right there on the corner. They tazed him two or three times, cuffed him, and took him away. That asshole should be locked up in a cage," Mike said.

"Holy shit! I didn't know that. When did that happen?"

"About a year ago. You were a little preoccupied at the time, what with the whole hanging-on-to-life thing. I'm sure I never thought to tell you about it. I mean, who cares about that piece of shit. Not me. I hope the fuckin' guy is getting raped on a daily basis," Mike spat. "What drawer do you want these in?" he asked, holding up some empty note-books.

"Oh, um, top drawer, I guess," Cass said. "I'm not too worried about that. I might change it later. As long as it's all put away."

"Anyway," Mike continued, "he used to make me stay out of the room until like two in the morning while he banged that useless bimbo of his. She finally got a dose of what everyone else around him tolerated. He literally rearranged her face. Her nose and left cheek are crooked now."

"Wow. I had no idea. How long did you have to live with him?" Cassian asked.

"Only one semester. He flunked out. I didn't see him with a single book or ever going to a single class. He played Sega any time he wasn't in the gym and smoked so much weed that I used to get contact highs from his clothes. I genuinely hate this guy. Let's hope you get a good roommate."

As if calling for him, a medium-build guy, a little shorter than Cass, with long hair and handsome features walked into the room. He was casual and relaxed as he said, "Hey. How's it going, man. My name's Clay. You must be Cassian," he said to Mike.

"Not me. That's your man right there," Mike said, stepping aside and pointing to Cass.

Cass walked over and held out his hand, "Hey, Clay. Nice to meet you. This is my brother, Mike. He's a senior."

Clay and Mike shook hands. Mike asked, "When did you get in?"

"I got here yesterday. I did a year in the Towers, but this year a group of us managed to get into McCormick. We got to move in a day earlier."

"I did two years in the shitty Towers. Then I got an apartment down on Bouquet," Mike said.

"That's a good location. Close to everything. How do you like it?" Clay asked.

"Well, the place got broken into last year. They took my entire stereo and my computer. As long as you don't keep anything valuable, it's great," Mike said sarcastically.

Clay nodded and said, "That sucks, man. I know a bunch of guys in South Oakland that had similar problems. I might have given up on the dorms if I had to do another year in the Towers. I have some friends that are still stuck there this year." He turned to Cass and said, "I took the bottom bunk. I wasn't sure what you might want. I'm guessing you didn't want the top bunk either," Clay said, gesturing to the other bed, now set up across the room.

"I don't know if jumping out of bed is going to be an option for me," Cass said.

"What's up with the eyepatch? Did you get some kind of Lasik surgery? I've been reading about that lately. They can, like, fix somebody's vision using lasers and stuff," Clay rambled.

"No. I don't think a laser is going to fix this," Cass said, lifting the eyepatch and tapping the prosthetic eye with a fingernail, making a light clicking noise.

"Oh fuck! Wicked dude! So that thing is like legit, man. This is cool. My roommate's a fuckin' pirate! You can be my room-matey! Arrrr!" Clay said jovially.

Cass and Mike both laughed. Cass said, "That's only half of it. I got the peg leg too." Cass pulled up his left pant leg.

"Get the fuck out of here! Really? My-man, we are getting a parrot and painting this room to look like the Caribbean!" Clay held the palm of his hand up in the air. Cass smiled and obliged by attempting to slap his hand…and completely missed. Mike burst out laughing.

"What was that, dude?" Clay asked with a surprised and concerned look, "Don't you know how to high-five someone?"

Cass leaned in conspiratorially and said in a pirate voice, "Thar's a little-known secret about us real pirates. We don't know how to high-five…or catch shit."

Clay wore a puzzled look. Cass laughed and said, "I have no depth perception. I'm not so good at high-fives, catching shit, Ping-Pong, threading needles…you know. Stuff like that."

"Oh man. That sucks. Sorry, dude. A least you can laugh about. I'm glad you're not all depressed and shit. That kind of energy brings me down. Hey, you don't smoke or nothing do you?" Clay switched subjects instantly.

"Uh, no. Why? Do you?" Cassian asked.

"Oh. No way, man. I'm allergic to cigarette smoke is all. You seem like a pretty cool guy. I didn't want to have to move if you were a smoker. Did you meet any of the other guys?"

"There's more than you and me?" Cassian asked.

"Dude, this is a suite. There are three bedrooms here, and the rooms are set up by some fucking idiot. Check it out. Bathroom is the first door on the left down that hall," Clay pointed to the right of the room entrance. "At the end of the hall is Zab and Clark. We all have to share the bathroom."

"Did you say, 'Zab?'" Cassian asked.

"Yep. That's Cory Zabrus. He's a really cool guy, but whatever you do, don't *ever* touch his Ruffles and French onion dip. You'd be safer sticking your finger in his girlfriend than his bag of Ruffles. If he invites you to have some, that means he likes you. But don't even think about it if he doesn't make the offer."

Cass and Mike were laughing as Cass said, "He comes with rules? How cool can he be?"

"You'll see. He's totally laid back and loves pranks and practical jokes, but seriously…don't touch his chips. That's the only rule.

"A bunch of us got together last year and fought to get into this building. Being a freshman, don't be too surprised if they fuck with you a bit.

That'll come mostly from Keith and Zab…and me, but I'm not going to fuck with you. I don't want you taking your leg off and beating the shit out of me in my sleep!" Clay laughed.

"He can't do that," Mike said, "you'll hear him hopping before he can get to you."

"I hop in my socks. You won't hear shit." Cass laughed. "Who's Keith?"

"Keith and Dave live down that hallway," Clay pointed to the left of the entrance, "They have their own entrance through the kitchen, but have to go through our room to use the bathroom. Here's the bad news. You're new, so you didn't get a choice. But I drew the short straw. Our bedroom was probably a living room for what must have been a hotel years ago. Zab and Clark have to come in and out right through our bedroom. That part really sucks. Fortunately, they are both pretty considerate guys and hopefully won't abuse it.

"Keith, on the other hand, can be a bit of a bull in a China shop. He'll take a shit with the door open while you and your girlfriend are eating at your desk. Guy's an animal. But he's funny as hell, and we all got along well last year in the Towers. We're petitioning to get a better room next year. They're not all set up this stupid."

"Oh, that…really kinda sucks," Cass said.

"Usually, first-years go straight to the Towers. How'd you manage to get in here?" Clay asked.

"I guess I'm just lucky," Cass said flatly.

Clay burst out laughing, "Dude, I am so glad you have a sense of humor. The guy you're replacing…his name was Ted. He took everything so literal. Couldn't joke. Couldn't understand a joke. Hated pranks. He was friends with Keith, so we all agreed to have him join us. But he suddenly dropped out last week. Probably for the best. I thought he and Zab were going to come to blows a few times. Zab won't back down from shit either. Ted ran to the RA and tried to get Zab thrown out last year for pennying his door."

"What's an RA and what's pennying a door," Cassian asked.

Mike said, "You didn't read any of the shit you were supposed to read, did you?"

Cass shrugged as Mike shook his head and continued, "RA is the resident assistant. They're like the police of the floor. Pennying is when someone sticks pennies in the door frame so you can't open the door. It's a stupid prank, but no reason to run to the RA. You better find out the rules on bringing in beer and stuff. You can get in a lot of trouble if you do it wrong or, in your case, happen to be underage."

"What happened to Ted to make him drop out?" Cassian asked.

"I don't know," Clay said, "but he ain't in this suite—"

<hr>

"Excuse me, Cassian," Franklin interrupted. "This is a nice story, and you tell it very well, but I honestly don't give a fuck about your first dorm and your room-*mateys*. Are you going somewhere with this story? I mean, I have a life I'd like to get back to."

"Don't be rude, Franklin," Corrina scolded. Then to Cass, "But I have to agree, Cassian. Is there a reason we need to know any of this?"

Cass sighed. "I don't know, Corrina. I'm telling my story to both of you…warts and all. I'm not going to lie and pretend I've been some kind of saint. I have not. I have killed many people and done things I am not proud of doing. I'm telling you this so that you know who I am. Then you can decide if you will help me. And maybe Franklin will pick something up in my story that helps. You know…an outside perspective."

"Help with what, Cassian? What is your goal? I mean, what exactly are you trying to do and why did you ever come to me?" Franklin asked.

"First of all, I have some items in which protein structural information is required. I don't know to what degree these must be interpreted. You can do that, can't you? I mean, with the proper instrumentation, right?"

"Yes. It's not always easy, but I can do that if I have enough sample. I have a good bit of freedom to operate, for the most part. It's not as easy to hide anything that requires the crystallography instruments for secondary, tertiary, or quaternary structures, but I can still manage some discretion."

"But you can interpret the data properly?" Cassian asked.

"Yes, I can. But I don't think that you're telling me incriminating stories about you killing people to get my help with protein structures," Franklin said.

Cass nodded and gestured toward Franklin with an open hand and said, "See. This is why I'm here. You're a sharp one, for sure. I'm also here because you are a Nephilim. There is another, very powerful Nephilim who is coming for me, and I was hoping you may be able to level the playing field."

"Who is coming for you, Cassian?" Corrina asked.

"My son, Samuel."

CHAPTER 13

THE SON

"No, Lynn. I'm not going to listen to this again," Samuel said, reaching into a loose pile of 9mm bullets on the table and loading them into one of the six empty magazines. The bullets looked like tiny pills in his huge hands. "I know you have a soft spot for this guy, but I don't see why. This asshole hooked up with your sister after getting *you* pregnant and then later tries to kill me. He was there when Mary died…under extremely questionable circumstances. You do know that they're still investigating the shit that happened at the Bosco house. I've been wondering if Cassian had something to do with Aunt Beth killing herself," Samuel said. "I hold no such feelings for the man. I want him locked up or dead."

"Don't say such things. Aunt Beth was sick. He was nowhere around when she died, and he did *not* try to kill you. He's your father, after all," Lynn said, gently placing a hand on his shoulder as he sat at the kitchen table, deftly working the ammo into place. Though Lynn stood next to him, she had to reach up to put a hand on his shoulder.

Samuel was a massive person, standing at six feet nine inches tall with about three hundred pounds of dense muscle over his frame. His deep-set, hazel eyes always reminded Lynn of Cassian. And while Samuel had smooth, tanned, and handsome features, he radiated a frightful demeanor that was off-putting to most people. It wasn't just his size. The feeling of true threat exuded from his sharp, callous nature and complete lack of fear. Other agents at the FBI felt an uncomfortable apprehension in his presence.

"I know that's what you say. He's my father. Maybe we should get a DNA test. I don't think you really know for certain though, do you? That's what Grandma Sarah told me all the time.

"Think about that. Your own mother…telling her only grandson about *his* mother being a whore. Ahhh, good memories," Samuel said, shaking his head and chuckling without humor.

Lynn scowled at him. She hid the deep pain his comment caused and said, "Do you know that you sound exactly like your father? Particularly when you fight with me. I was *not* a whore. I was—" she stopped herself. "Your grandparents are just…extreme."

"Extreme?" he said with an uptick in pitch. Then his tone took on a placating calmness, "Mother, your parents are fucking religious psychotics. I don't have a relationship with them and I don't want one. They treated me like the bastard child that *they* were stuck with…and I guess that part was true. And as far as I am concerned, they are complete strangers to me. They called in the Catholic church to perform an exorcism on me. A fucking *exorcism* in the twenty-first century! What the fuck is wrong with them.

"Then, when I was 'too much to handle' they call Cassian to come and get me! Because they couldn't find *you*! And that asshole—well, he should pray I don't get my hands on him. But all the praying in the world isn't going to stop me. His friends can't hide him forever. I *will* catch him," Samuel said.

"I am begging you to stop. Nothing good is going to come of it. I feel it. Do you really *need* to do this? What do you think you will achieve by locking him away? Do you think this will somehow make you whole or make you feel better?" Lynn asked.

"You know, there is another option to locking him away? One that I'm partial to. Dead works just fine with me," Samuel said with a sardonic grin.

"Why would you say something like that? Don't be this way. Why don't you try calling him and talking to him first?"

"The time for talk is over. He had his chance. He's wanted for questioning, and I am an expert at asking questions…face to face."

"When was the last time you spoke with him? When you were eleven or twelve? You would never speak to him when he called for you. How is it that your hatred of him has grown like this and you barely know him?" Lynn asked.

Samuel silently placed bullets into the magazines as he looked at his mother under his brow.

She continued, "You shouldn't cast so much blame on him. For the first four or five years of your life, he didn't even know you were alive. Not until Aunt Beth told him about you. That was partly my fault. I never told him we were still alive after..." she trailed off.

"Partly? It was *completely* your fault," Samuel said.

"No. It wasn't *all* my fault. Eric Bosco made it look like we were dead. Killed by Cassian's gross, drunk step-grandfather. Ooooh, do I hate that fucking guy. If he wasn't dead, I would murder him in a heartbeat. But our phony death was all over the news. I can show you the tapes! Even *my* family thought we were dead," Lynn said.

"I've seen the tapes. I probably know more about what happened than you do. But I'm glad you kept me away from Cassian. When he first met me, he tried to kill me or whatever he did. No. Fuck him. I don't want to see him again unless it's through bars or a clear body bag.

"And why is it you want me to have a relationship with him? Doesn't Phil take issue with him too?" Samuel asked.

"You don't know half of what you think you know. But, yes, Phil takes issue with Cassian...and everyone else, for that matter. You know how he is. He doesn't like me talking about Cass, and he would flip out if he knew I ever spoke with him again," Lynn said, taking a seat across from Samuel. "But Cassian didn't try to kill you. He was trying to help you...with the voices. And he was trying to tell you about yourself and what—"

"What do you care? You only give a shit about yourself and what affects your little world. You don't really give a shit about Cassian or me. Why are you bothering with any of this. It's so unlike you, Lynn. Caring, I mean," Samuel said harshly.

Tears welled up in her eyes as she said, "Please, Samuel. Don't be so angry with me. I have always loved you. I just don't know how to help you. You have no idea what I did. You don't know everything I—"

"You can stop with the crocodile tears. That shit won't work on me anymore. That's one thing I have in common with my dad. I see through your fake shit. You cry now to get your way and then go about doing whatever you want, no matter who it hurts. You dumped me with those…I can't stand to think about it. You bailed on me when I was nine so you could run off to California with Chip or Biff or whatever the fuck his name was. And you left me in Utah with two insane cult members. I mean, what the actual fuck, Mom!"

"I was young, Samuel. I know I was doing stupid and selfish things. I was messed up from what I went through. And you were different from other kids. You started acting—" She stopped and said, "There were just some little things that I had to do for myself. I thought you would be better off with your grandparents," Lynn said.

"*Little things*. It's endearing how you try to minimize coke and cock by calling them *little things* for *yourself*. Maybe Cassian was lucky that he found out who you really are before you could fuck with his head and his life any more than you already did."

Lynn slapped his face…hard. His head didn't move. Not even a tiny bit. She pulled her hand back in pain as he sat, smiling at her.

She yelled, "I didn't do anything to deserve that! Not from you! Not from your grandparents! And certainly not from him! I was seventeen years old! He would have been happy to get married before we finished high school. I didn't want that! I didn't want—" She cut herself short. Then, calmly, "I didn't want to be his possession or some boring house-wife.

"Maybe it was all those stupid fucking movies we watched back then. Strong, independent women…*my ass*! What a bunch of *bullshit*!" she yelled. "I thought I was going to end up rich or famous or at least have rich men falling all over me. *None* of that happened! I was young and stupid. Can you please try to forgive me?! Even a little?"

"Forgive you for what?" Samuel said calmly. "That's like faulting the rain for getting me wet. Your behavior is like any other force of nature. You leave disaster in your wake. Do you think that because you apologize for doing it you're all good? It would be one thing if you changed your behavior after you apologized. But not you. You turn around and do it all over again.

"There's nothing to forgive, Mom. You did it before and you will continue to do it again and again and again. As soon as you walk out of the room, you forget everything you said or agreed to in a conversation. But I can minimize the damage you do by simply not participating in your crazy cycles."

"Fine. Go ahead and be that way. But you *are* going to regret it one day. Treating me like this…and going after your father. I recommend you stop your investigation into him.

"You're right. I think he had something to do with Mary dying. But I don't think he killed her…or Beth. And I don't think you fully understand what he is capable of doing. He may not look like much to someone like you, but there is something about him. He's dangerous. I don't want you getting hurt," Lynn said.

"He's troublesome. *I'm* dangerous. Don't worry about *me* getting hurt. He's not going to get a chance to do that again. And I'm not some eleven-year-old kid now. I will *fuck* him up. And besides, it's not up to me anymore. The case has already been assigned to me, so it's my job. And I intend to accept this task with great vigor!" he said through clenched teeth.

"Phil and I have a flight to Tampa at 2 p.m. Are you still coming down in August? You know you're welcome to stay with us." Lynn said.

"I'll be down in August. I have my room booked at the Fenway Hotel. It's a nice place. This is strictly business," Samuel softened a tiny bit and said, "You're welcomed to come visit…but leave your dickhead at home. I know Phil can't stand me. If I even see him look at me funny, I might drown him in the fucking bay."

Lynn stood and put on her light jacket as she moved to leave. She opened the door, turned slightly, and said, "I warned you. I don't see anything good coming from this." She nodded and added, "Please take care of yourself," as she stepped out onto the damp porch.

"You take care too, Lynn!" Samuel said cheerily as she closed the door behind her. "And don't let the door hit you on the ass on the way out," he mumbled.

He took the six full magazines in his hand and stood from the table, bumping his head on the overhead light. He ignored it as he said, aloud, "Yo, Semen-jizz. Wake up!"

"You piece-of-shit mortal. My name is Semjaza and you know it. What is it you want?" came the voice in his head.

"How'd you like a shot at one of the angels?" Samuel asked.

Laughter came in his head. "Oh. So, you believe you know who one of the shrouded is, do you?" Semjaza asked with clear arrogance coming from the grating voice.

"Well, yes, oh demonic one who doth know-eth so much. I think-eth thou might-eth be-eth interested in what I-eth know-eth" Samuel said jeeringly.

"Don't mock me you bastard child. You are nothing but an advanced form of bacteria made from the cum and cells of that petri dish you call a mother," Semjaza said venomously.

"A bacteria that has your ass in chains. Right? I'm offering you a chance at freedom. Are you going to sit there and insult me now?" Samuel asked.

Silence lasted for a full minute. Samuel waited without saying anything. He had become quite happy with uncomfortable silences, particularly between himself and the demon he let up to speak with him.

Finally, Semjaza said, "What is it you wish to know now? And what assurances do I have that you won't betray me again?"

"Oh, Ad-mir-al," Samuel said in his best Ricardo Montalban impersonation, "I have given you no word. In fact, in my judgment, you simply have no alternative!"

"How clever you are. Words spoken just before vengeance was exacted upon Khan in the movie. You fool. How you ever got the best of me I will never know."

"Oh, you know damn well why, Jizzy. You have no more self-control than those you hold in such contempt. Why don't you tell me some more about these shrouded. Maybe we can work something out. I know that you are not stupid enough to think that I would let you have him...or her...but that doesn't mean we can't bargain for your release. I could be persuaded into letting you go. But I do have one condition to that. You have to give me another. The one who can tell me about metals. You know what I want," Samuel said.

"Azazel," Semjaza said.

"Bingo!" Samuel said.

CHAPTER 14

UNEXPECTED STRANGER

S LIGHTLY SINGED, GRAY-BEIGE CLOTHING IN a strange, layered fashion hung from the thin, tall man. He initially looked left and right, as if he might run. But he then stood straight and began to walk toward the light Malcom had fixed on him.

"Hallo, welk jaar is het?" asked the man. Then quickly added, *"Welches jahr ist es? Zdravstvuyte kakoy seychas God?"*

"What?" Malcom asked.

"Ah, English," he said. "Hello. Can you tell me what year is it?"

Malcom took off the respirator he was wearing and said, "Holy fuck, man! Are you like a terminator or something?"

At a frantic rate, the man said, "No. I simply wish to know what year it is in your realm. I mean to say, we believe we have been accurate with our dates and locations, but truthfully, we don't know. Who are you?"

"Whoa, slow down there, pard," said Malcom. "My world. I get to ask the questions. Who the hell are you, and where the fuck did you come from?"

"The…fuck…did I what?" asked the man quickly. "You keep using that word. I know not what you mean. Was there a sexual encounter that occurred? If so, I meant no disrespect to your species or your culture."

Malcom laughed and said, "No, there was no sexual encounter. It's just a term we throw around. Where did you come from?"

The man frantically reached into what looked like a pocket on his pant leg and pulled something out. He threw it into his mouth and chewed quickly. Then he said, "I come from another gravitational realm such as yours. We have…progressed. We have been trying to send messages to you to help. Have you received any of our messages?" came the rapid response. Then, "Are you a demon? A Spur? I have read about Spurs. If you are…do you know what they are? You would not tell me if you are one, though. How can I know? Am I…fuck…as you say? Could you please lower the light source from my face?"

"Relax a little," Malcom said, lowering the light to the ground. He opened the car door so the light was more diffuse and comfortable for the stranger. "You are speaking *very* fast. You are not 'fuck,' as you say. It just so happens that I *do* know about demons and Spurs. I am neither of those. I can assure you.

"I have been tasked with getting your messages," Malcom said. "But this is the first time a live person came through the…portal."

The man looked impatient and started rolling his hand as Malcom spoke. "Look, am I annoying you in some way?"

"Why do you speak so slowly? Do you think I cannot understand? I know your language well. Your slow descriptions are unnecessary."

"Jesus Christ," Malcom mumbled, "what the hell is going on here?"

Rapidly, the visitor said, "You speak freely about your representative. Is it common to disregard their sacrifice? And Hell. Let us not speak of that place. It makes my skin prickle. I am susceptible to visions now and wish to have none from *that* place occur."

"Dude," Malcom said, "you think I'm speaking slowly? I think you are talking like a recorded message on fast-forward. Can you please… take a breath and speak at a pace where I can understand you?" Malcom asked.

The man looked down and took a deep breath. When he looked up and spoke, it was almost like a different person was speaking. The cadence was deliberately slowed.

"I apologize. My realm exists in a slightly different time scale from yours. It is not so different that I cannot adjust, and it seems that it is not as difficult as I had anticipated it would be during my adjustment. I come from an alternate gravitational realm, tangential to your realm at points. We have evolved beyond your world. Consider a fraction of a second faster over billions of years and you can see that we are a millennium or more ahead of you.

"We have observed a similarity in the pitfalls encountered in your past that makes us confident that we can help you. We were given similar help from an advanced realm. I think it is important that we all work together. When our society obtained more *understanding*, we realized that downturns in adjacent realms had strong effects on our world. We also felt it ethical to lend aid to slower gravitational realms such as yours. Do you comprehend what I am saying?"

Malcom replied in a slow manner with a deep voice, matching the strangers, "Yes, I get it. The way you are speaking now makes me think *you* believe that *I* am stupid. I am not stupid. I was expecting a piece of meat or a salt lick or something else; but I wasn't expecting *you*!"

"I am sorry, but I need to adjust to your time scale. As to your point, here is the message," he touched a thin bracelet on his wrist, then reached into another pant pocket and held out a piece of cloth with frayed ends.

"What is this? The message?" Malcom asked.

"It is a prion message that will develop in insects. The insects will become extremely aggressive. The messages have to be obvious. We want you to find the message without destroying the population of the species it is meant to propagate within. But it must be advanced enough so that only your scientists could decode them. When you learn to read the sequences of subunits, you will have the first part of the encryption. I cannot tell you more," he said.

"How is it that *you* came through the portal?" Malcom asked as he gingerly placed the cloth into a small plastic bag and put it on the dry ice.

"It is not necessary to freeze that. It can be kept at room temperature or slightly warmer. It was meant to be eaten."

"You should have put that in your past messages," Malcom mumbled as he put the bag next to the bucket of dry ice and removed his own gloves. "What's your name, fella?"

"I am sorry, but it would be unwise to divulge my name. It could be used against my family in my world," he said.

Malcom shrugged and said, "How would you feel about me giving you a name? Just so I can call you something. Do you have something you would prefer?" Malcom asked.

"What is the name of your moon?" he asked.

"The moon," Malcom said.

"Yes. What do you call it?"

"That wasn't a question. That's what we call it. The moon."

"You call your moon 'the moon'?" he asked. "That is…lame. What is the name of your second planet?"

"Venus. If you want to be called by the planet that represents our females, I can do that," Malcom said with a smile.

"No. I want no representation of either the Matriarchy or the Patriarchy. Call me Friz. It is a nickname of a great man in my realm."

"Friz…it is," Malcom said with a smile as he rhymed the words.

"What is it that you are known by?" Friz asked.

"They call me Malcom."

"Malcom!" Friz exclaimed. He suddenly looked away for several seconds as he grabbed the side of the car to stabilize himself.

"Are you okay? You seem to know my name," Malcom said.

"Yes. I will be fine. It is a side effect of the…trip through the portal. I know nobody from your gravitational realm. We have only sent probes here to learn of your past. Very interesting how similar our worlds have progressed. At least up to this point in your time," Friz said, nodding.

"You keep saying 'gravitational realm.' What does that mean?" Malcom asked.

Friz said, "We believe True Light is composed of three, primary components: electric, magnetic, and gravitational waves," Friz said deliberately slow. "The True Light is thought to house the Watchers as it passes through the realm of Time. Time is the realm where it is be-lieved that the Seraphim…that would be what you term the angels and demons…exist.

"As I understand it, and this could be inaccurate, the True Light creates three types of existences. One realm of electricity where light is observed as gravitational-magnetic synchrons. A synchron is what you term a wave-particle at this time in your history. One realm of magnetism where light is observed as electro-gravitational synchrons. And our gravitational realms where we observe light as electromagnetic synchrons.

"As with all things in life, it is nearly impossible to study the primary facet of a realm in which you exist. Imagine being *on* a wave and trying to study that wave with no point of reference. This is why the phenomenon of gravity continues to remain enigmatic to my civilization…and I assume yours as well.”

“Okay. Wait a sec there, Friz. True Light? Are you saying that our entire existence is only a fraction of some kind of light? Not even our light as we know it is real?” Malcom asked.

“You are not stupid, Malcom. You seem to understand my explanation. That is the theory I believe,” Friz said. “But all existence is real enough. The light we observe is real and contains much energy.

“If the beams of True Light pass in parallel, you can begin to imagine the overlapping of realms. There is something known in your world as the Flower of Life that shows these realms as a two-dimensional cut of where the circles overlap. We believe that the nodes represent beams of True Light and the realms overlap in many places.

“Only life from a gravity realm can physically interact with life in another gravity realm. I do not believe we could interact with a lifeform from an electric or magnetic realm. Perhaps they exist as ghosts or spirits in our worlds.

“We think each realm of Time encompasses one beam of True Light and three split realms. It also could be that these nodes represent physical locations where communication between all realms is made possible. Does that help to explain it?”

“Well, in truth, Friz, not really,” Malcom said. “This seems like physics or something like that. Maybe Cassian’s friend Stu can understand it, but not me. So, how is it that you are in my realm. Like, how is it that *you* are physically here?”

“As I said, we have sent probes into your world in the past. We even sent small animals through. We were never sure if they survived, but I suppose I now know the answer to that mystery. Unless, of course, I died when passing through the portal and I am now in a new life,” Friz said, looking deep in thought.

“I don’t think so, buddy. I watched you appear through that spherical explosion.”

“I recall that I dove through the hole when it appeared,” Friz said. “I was being pursued by three demons. They like to work in threes. I should not be alive right now. And stopping me was a massive effort on their part.

"They had a high risk of exposure and may be preparing strategies for the eventuality that I survived. In my world, they could be in a panic mode. Do you know what the demons are capable of doing when they are like this? They will create a war between civilizations just to cover up my escape. They are *that* powerful even without Spurs," Friz said.

"You don't have Spurs in your world?" Malcom asked.

"We were able to eliminate Spurs. One of our great representatives sacrificed his life in our realm to destroy the Spurs in our world. It was an amazing time that shook the foundations of our world, ushering in a long period of peace. But there is no way to get rid of the demons. They continue to fight against us at every turn," Friz said, looking off into space again.

"I don't fully understand this whole demon, angel, and Spur thing," Malcom said. "I'm not sure what is right and what is wrong anymore. But I believe in Cassian, and I'm gonna help him in any way I can. What he did for me—" Malcom stopped himself as he realized he was getting too personal. Then he said, "But please, continue telling me how you got into our world."

"We had been compromised," Friz said. "I had the message. They could have intercepted that. Without knowing the encryption, it is useless. But if they caught me, they would have forced me to tell them the process we have been using. Knowing that, they would be able to figure out the encryption in only a few hundred years. So I jumped into the portal when it opened."

"A few hundred years," Malcom whispered incredulously. Then he said, "Dude, did you have any idea what would happen? Couldn't that have killed you?"

"Yes, of course. I was unsure if I could fit through the portal. It was small and only open a brief period of time. But even if portions of my body had been severed, it would have been preferable to the torture they would surely have practiced upon me. I don't ever want to experience that type of pain. I chose the prospect of death. I do not have the courage of a representative. But I did leave everything I ever had to deliver this message."

"Wow. That's impressive, dude. You sure deserve a beer for that one, later. But I think I need to bring you to meet my friend Cassian. Maybe he'll know what to do with you. Figures the one time he doesn't come, *this* happens," Malcom said.

"A beer? I feel as if you are belittling my sacrifice, Malcom. Perhaps that is the nature of your slow adaptation process," Friz said, sounding agitated.

"No, no…I am not belittling your sacrifice. I'm sure it was very dramatic. Can I do something for you? Is there someone you need to call or something?" Malcom asked with a callousness to his tone.

"No. I have no one in this world," Friz said, giving Malcom a calculating look.

"So, Friz. Are you hungry? You're lucky, I ordered a large pizza with sausage, mushrooms, and ricotta before I came here. There's a lot left over if you don't mind cold pizza."

"Yes, lucky is how I feel," he said with clear sarcasm. "I abandoned my whole world, including my family. I am about to travel with a man named Malcom. Forgive me if I am not feeling as if God has favored my actions at this moment. But I do have much information to relay to the one you call Cassian. So please do not kill me."

"Kill you?" Malcom said surprised. "Why would I want to kill you, Friz? You're a huge puzzle piece to us," Malcom said.

"I am not saying that anyone would wish me to die, Malcom. Information we have about this time in your history suggests that violence is common and many people are killed without justice or consequence."

"That's a bunch of nonsense. It's not the Wild West or anything." Then Malcom said with a slight western drawl, "We got strict rules o' law in these here parts."

"I appreciate the pacification in your inflection, but your analogy provides little comfort. I may prefer your Wild West era. The deterrence of normalized confrontations with armaments kept physical altercations and violence lower than currently reported in your world. It was a lack of antiseptics that challenged life in that time," Friz said.

Malcom shrugged and said, "Well…I am sure you will see that we are quite civilized. Why, we even wash our hands after we shit."

"Wonderful to know. What should we do next?" Friz asked.

"It's late. It's been fun chatting, but let's get out of here," Malcom tapped the car with his hand, "and get to the hotel. When we're driving, I'll call Cass and see if he's up," he said, pulling out his phone.

"Do not activate that thing near me, you fool!" Friz said, slipping back into his rapid speech. "I have surely ingested Shazo," Malcom looked confused. "What you call Desemilnoct. I took the purging formula, but I can feel the visions already!"

"I don't know what you are talking about. What's this have to do with my phone?"

Slower, Friz said, "Please. Turn it off. The right high frequency passing through me could trigger the metal to initiate…visions from unknown worlds. Even Hell. My mind is not strong enough. I would surely fall into madness."

Malcom shrugged and powered off his phone.

"Thank you. And I apologize for calling you a fool," Friz said. "You could not possibly know."

Malcom walked around the car, opened the passenger side door, and gestured for Friz to enter.

Friz walked over and stood by the door as Malcom walked around to the driver's side. Malcom gave Friz a smile and nodded. Friz returned the smile with a similar nod…and then his eyes widened, and he immediately sprinted off into the woods.

Malcom ran around the car and yelled, "Friz! Where are you going? Don't run. I can help. Really! Come back!"

It was too late to be chasing this nutjob. He had the message. He would tell Cass about Friz, but he had no intention of chasing this guy down at nearly 3 a.m. through the woods of Centralia. More than likely, Friz would turn up in some police station somewhere, and they could pick him up later.

He sighed then got in the car. He couldn't wait to get back to the room for some pizza…and sleep. As he drove, he thought about his strange conversation with Friz. What amazing revelations. But he remembered the look on his face when he said his name. Was that a look of fear? Did this guy know about his secret? Dammit. Maybe he should have killed him when he had the chance. But Cass would have been so pissed. No. No way could Friz know. *Nevertheless, I should probably start looking for him tomorrow*, Malcom thought.

CHAPTER 15

THE PIZZA CHRONICLES

"You said earlier that Lynn and Samuel were killed by your step-grandfather. Are you making this up as you go along?" Franklin asked.

"Well, I guess I spoiled that part of the story," Cass said. "I was trying to do this in a sequence, but I understand. Maybe you don't want to hear about my dormitory or my suitemates."

"No, not so much. You said you need help with your son. Why don't you start filling in some of the gaps in your story," Franklin said.

"Are you sure? Some of these stories are funny. Especially the times when Zab and I would get into our pranks. Like one time, after Zab got onto the cheerleading squad—"

"Your roommate was a cheerleader?" Franklin asked.

"That's kind of a long story. See, he was dating a girl who wanted to get on the cheerleading squad—"

"That's okay. I don't need to know. You had a cheerleading roommate. That's fine," Franklin said.

"Well, one night they had a pep rally down in the quad at 6 p.m. Zab fell asleep on the sofa after he ate a *huge* lunch.

"I set all the clocks two hours ahead. I got his girlfriend, our roommates, and all the other cheerleaders in on it. I even had television shows set up on the VCR playing from the day before. He woke up at 2 p.m. thinking it was 4 p.m. He had *no* clue.

"At 5 p.m., he made two big sandwiches for dinner and ate them! Of course, it was only 3 p.m., and he *just* ate a giant lunch two hours ago."

Cass started laughing and said, "After he ate, he started complaining about how *bloated* he felt!"

Franklin contained his laughter but had a strained smile on his face. It was hard because Cassian had a contagious laugh. Corrina started to laugh.

"Wait, it gets better. Zab was joking about how he missed two classes while he *thought* he slept for two and a half hours. After eating, he jumped in the shower and got dressed in his cheerleading outfit. He was on his way to the elevator to go out into the quad for the pep rally!"

"Please tell me you let him go to the empty quad!" Corrina said as she laughed.

"*I couldn't,*" Cass said. "I didn't have the heart to let him go. What was really funny was that it took half an hour to convince him it was a gag. *Everyone* he called was in on it! Even his girlfriend told him the wrong time!

"He was so pissed at me that he didn't speak to me for like three days.

"It wasn't until one day when we were riding up the elevator in silence that he started to laugh and said, 'You fucking got me. You got me so good, you bastard. I wish I would have thought of that.'

"After that, it was all fine. He did get me back later. It was something with a dead fish in my pillowcase. But I knew I had it coming!" Cass continued to laugh.

Franklin said, "That is funny. But, please, get on with your story," he said as he started laughing again. This caused Corrina to burst out laughing too.

"I think maybe you should leave in some these stories," Corrina said.

"Well, it's good to have the funny parts in there. A lot of the story is not so funny, so it helps. But a lot of my time at college was very routine.

"I went to class in the day and spent my evenings in the Hillman Library doing marathon study sessions, frequently with my suitemates. We snuck in hidden bottles of highly caffeinated soda in our bags since food and beverages were prohibited in the library; but we were rebels. Rebels who studied until midnight when the library closed. After that we would go to the Cathedral of Learning common room, which was open all night. We studied there until two to four in the morning, went back to the dorm, and slept until we had to get up for class. It was a lot of hard work, but we also had a lot of fun as we studied.

"That accounted for Saturday through Wednesday. A lot of the people went home on the weekends, so Friday and Saturday weren't the fun nights to go out. *Thursday* night was the party night. Bars had quarter draft nights where you could hardly move inside if you could even get in. If you got there too late, you waited in line around the corner. When the bars closed, we would each get a large pizza at the 'O.'

"The O was The Original Hot Dog Shop on the corner of Bouquet and Forbes. Sadly, it's now gone. But it was the best worst food you can imagine for super cheap prices. The large pizza was only $2.99! Can you imagine that today? This was no personal pan pizza. It was a delicious, sixteen-inch pizza for three bucks and change with tax. At two in the morning, after a big bunch of bargain-basement beer, it was the best food you ever tasted!"

Franklin said, "Big bunch of bargain-basement beer! Say that five times fast. I noticed you have quite a fondness for food. Particularly pizza. Maybe you could call your story *The Pizza Chronicles*?"

"I like that name. If I ever write a book about my college years, maybe that would be a good name. Of course, I'm not sure I could corner the market on pizza stories. There's a whole cartoon about pizza-obsessed turtles. Ahhh, but who could believe turtles might walk upright and eat pizza," Cass said.

"Yeah, who would believe anything that crazy," Franklin said mockingly.

Cass smiled and said, "I have been laying down a background so you know some of the characters. Now I will start to tell you some of the odd stories I want you to hear about. This was the latter part of my third year at school. We had gotten a room on the eighth floor where each pair of roommates had their own room, and Clay and I weren't stuck sleeping in the living room. But, since we got along well as suitemates, we continued to live together. One Saturday night, when I got in from studying kind of early and Clay had gone home for the weekend…"

Cass woke to a dark room. This room seemed unfamiliar, but it was his room. It was dark. The clock on the desk read 3:23 a.m. College. Yes. This was his dorm room. Some commotion was going on outside, in the hallway. He swung his foot over the side of the bed, feeling each spring as it dug into his legs. He sat up and looked at the door. It sounded like a crowd of people were outside of his room, whispering.

He put on his prosthetic foot—a good indicator this wasn't a dream— stood and walked out of his room into the living room. The whispering got louder and a sense of dread filled him.

An orange glow was coming from under the door to the hallway. The light didn't look anything like the usual fluorescent light that perpetually lit the central corridors.

"Ex? Are you there?" Cass whispered to an empty room.

"Of course. What is going on? I am sensing something is amiss," Ex said.

"I was just wondering if I'm dreaming. Am I dreaming?" Cassian asked.

"Have I ever spoken with you when you were dreaming before?" Ex asked.

"No," replied Cass.

"Then you are not dreaming," Ex said.

"Can you hear what I'm hearing…behind the door?"

"Yes. It feels wrong to me too. Be ready."

"Ready? Ready for what?" Cass whispered.

"Monsters," Ex said.

"What? Monsters? What monsters?" Cass said.

"Get ahold of yourself. There is no such thing as monsters," Ex said, chuckling. "At least not *much* worse than what you have already met. Open the door."

Cass reached out tentatively to grab the door handle. The sound in the hallway grew louder as the light under the door grew brighter. Cass mustered his courage and pulled the door open.

Silence and darkness.

The usual hallway lights were out. Off to his left, light from the end of the hallway, where the stairway door stood open, was filtering into the corridor. Cass turned right and a swirling black mass opened in the darkness of the hallway. He stepped into the hall and began to approach the mass. As he got closer, he thought he heard the anguished sound of many people lamenting in hushed tones.

"Ex," he whispered, "what is this?"

"I am not sure, Cass. I seem to recall seeing something like this before…many, many years ago. It could be a gateway," Ex said.

"What do you mean by a gateway? Gateway to what?" Cassian asked.

"To another realm. One that is close to yours. It is highly uncommon. I think it can happen when the veil between two realms is thin and they are overlapping. But something must *cause* this to happen. They are not spontaneous."

Cass began to reach out to the mass when Ex yelled in his mind, "Do not touch that, stupid!"

"Why not?" Cass replied, pulling his hand back.

"If it closes with your hand in it, your hand stays there!"

"You mean…" Cass said.

"As clean and quick as a guillotine. Your pirate ensemble will be complete with a hook to match your eyepatch and leg," Ex said.

"How is it here and what does it mean?" Cassian asked.

"I do not know. These are uncommon. But I seem to recall something bad came from the last one I saw. Someone from another realm has figured out how to breech the veil between worlds. It takes a tremendous amount of energy even when the veil is thin at certain nodes. It could be from your resonant steward. They are only supposed to be open for a moment. I do not know how it is remaining open this long. Perhaps the realm of its origin is currently very far away," Ex said.

Then a small flash in the center occurred and something small dropped to the floor. The gateway instantly vanished.

"Cass?" came the voice from behind him causing him to yelp in surprise.

He heard laughing as he turned to face his roommate, Clay. He whispered, "Christ, Clay! You scared the shit out of me. I thought you went home for the weekend."

"Yeah, I did. But I got into a fight with my mom. So, I came back. You didn't budge when I came in," he laughed. "You must have been wiped out, dude. I expected you to still be out at the bars when I got in. What's going on here? And why are the lights all off?"

"I don't know. The power is on. My clock is still working," Cass said.

The door at the end of the hall, opposite the stairwell opened and Chelsea was standing in the doorway looking absolutely beautiful, despite the robe and messy hair, "What the fuck is going on out here, Clay?" She demanded. "Why are the lights out?"

"Sorry, Chelsea," Cass said, "I don't know why the lights are out. Is there a switch somewhere for the hallway lights?"

"I don't know, Cass. It's three thirty in the fucking morning. I'm trying to sleep. All I can hear is Clay's voice. What are you yelling about?" She said in a bitchy tone that was unusual for her.

"I thought I heard something out here. I came out and the lights are all off. It's not the power. Clay startled me and I yelled. Sorry to wake you," Cass said.

Then the lights began to flicker and suddenly the hallway looked like daylight from the overhead fluorescent lights. They all squinted against the brightness. Chelsea turned and closed her door without another word.

"Why did she immediately think *I* had something to do with this?" Clay said, "I think she likes me." He had a big smile on his scruffy but handsome face. A lot of girls did like Clay, but Chelsea made it clear that she did not like him in the least. It was a phrenological dislike from the moment she met him.

Cass looked at him, nodding, and said, "Oh yeah. I think she's really warming up to you," then he laughed as they both went back into the room. Cass looked back in the hallway quickly to see if he could see what had fallen out of the dark mass. He saw a small, black stone sitting in the middle of the hallway.

He grabbed the stone and held it in the palm of his hand. The color seemed to shimmer to a greenish metallic color. As soon as he touched it, his head swooned and he felt an overwhelming reminiscence of Mary… and Khalima.

When the feeling passed he took notice of a small bug scampering toward the stairwell. That wasn't too alarming since that's where the trash was kept until it was picked up each week. But when he saw it, an image of spiders passed through his mind.

As much as he disliked insects, he realized that roaches thrived in the city. But spiders were something different. Cass hated spiders. They freaked him out. It didn't help that they seemed to have an affinity for him as well. He would frequently find spider bites on his skin.

He heard that the average person swallows about eight spiders per year, but he didn't believe that at all. There was a time at Boy Scout camp when he woke up with a spider in his mouth. It was an exceptionally disturbing experience that one doesn't forget. If it were happening eight times a year, people would be sleeping with scuba tanks and sealed helmets.

<hr>

"What the hell are you talking about?" Franklin interrupted. "You went from a black stone, to a roach, and then on to this tangent about spiders. Why are you telling us about how much you hate spiders? I don't like them either, but who gives a shit?"

Cass said, "I don't know, Franklin. I told you before, I don't know what all this means. I am telling you the story so maybe you will see something I missed.

"When I touched the stone, it made me think of spiders. I'm telling you what went through my head after I picked up that rock. And what I'm going to tell you now is what went through my head, what it reminded me of. I don't know. If I go off on a tangent, maybe that's my soul telling me what to do."

"Your soul? Or your ass-soul?" Franklin said.

"Please just listen. It does affect you too," Cass said. "Whatever the case may be, spiders do seem to flock to me…"

<hr>

None of his fellow Scouts would have a single bite over a weekend trip and Cass would have no less than three. Sometimes they got infected and once he got impetigo from a bite. That was much worse than the bite, and it took weeks and antibiotics to get rid of the itchy rash.

Several weeks earlier, when Cass was home helping his mother clean out the shed of her new home, he saw a wolf spider that was easily as large as his hand. He ran out of the shed screaming as Ex laughed uncontrollably in his head. It was then that Ex told Cass something that astounded him.

"Cassian, there is something you should know. Spiders are the defenders of human life by design. This is why you are never more than three feet from a spider at any time in your life. It is not as if they *like* humans or have any symbiosis other than the fact that humans tend to generate waste that attracts their food. They are no more aware that they are your defenders than you are aware that they are defending you."

"How is it defending me when they're always biting me? I think they hate me, Ex," Cass said.

"The Seraphim always draw spiders, Cass. A spider's vision transcends realms. What they are protecting you from is something you cannot see. Let us leave it at that. You do not want to know more," Ex said.

"You mean that I am going to attract even more spiders now that you are with me? You never said anything about that. Fuck. I didn't sign up for that. All this other shit seems minor now. Damn. Spiders!" Cass said.

"You did not sign up for anything, Cassian. You were chosen. And I told you before, I hate whining. Please stop," Ex said.

"I'll whine if I want to!" Cass said. "I hate spiders. Now you tell me that they are coming after me?"

Ex sang mockingly in his head, "You would whine too…if spiders came after you."

"Shut up, Ex. This isn't funny. I really hate spiders," Cass said.

"I know. You stated that. It makes it a little funnier to me," she said laughingly. "Do not be afraid, Cass. Fewer people die of spider bites than just about any other form of death, including crossing the path of a demon or a shrouded."

"Are you trying to say that I kill more people than spiders?" Cass asked.

"Statistically, yes. You kill far more people than all the spiders in your world combined," Ex said. "Be grateful you do not need to travel to Australia or live on a planet like Lavambigia where the spiders have wings."

Cass shuddered and said, "Flying spiders! That would be the worst thing I could ever imagine."

"Indeed, you are correct about that. God allowed them to destroy that world. They were the size of small dogs and could fly at tremendous speeds. They could both bite and sting as they were hybridized with a very dangerous Hymenoptera. The bite was painful but only used to hold their victim in order to sting them. Their venom was not more toxic than most of the species here on Earth, but with a much different mechanism of action. A single sting introduced enough venom to paralyze a person. But the venom also began the slow digestion of organs to feed their off-spring. Most were alive as the infant spiders ate the Lavambigian people from the inside.

"It was an uncommonly unpleasant way for a race of people to end, but they brought this fate upon themselves. They bred the species after being warned many times to stop playing with genetic modifications of that nature. That is a story where the Spurs and demons won. Maybe we can stop something like this from occurring on your world," Ex said.

"Yeah, okay. I'm all for stopping shit like that," Cass said, clearly rattled by the story.

"Wait," Franklin interrupted, "when did Ex tell you this, about the spiders?"

"I don't know. That was sometime after 1992, after my mother moved to the smaller home, closer to the university. It was still very rural and lots of creepy crawlies!" Cass said.

"Yeah, but I don't like spiders either, and I would swear they come after me too. I remember one time as a kid, my friends and I were playing in the woods. We lifted this piece of wood and a huge spider was sitting there. Its back was round and massive and looked like it was shifting shape. Suddenly, thousands of small spiders started scrambling off the back of the large spider. They all ran toward me. Not toward any of my friends. That was so long ago. I thought it was just a nightmare… until you told me that story," Franklin said.

"Ex said that makes a lot of sense. Your Seraphim pedigree gets you platinum access to the arachnid protection program, Franklin. Doesn't that make you feel better?" Cass said.

"Hell no!" Franklin said.

"Me either," Cass replied. "But I have learned to coexist with them. Sort of a trial by fire incident. Maybe we will have time to get to that later."

Corrina added, "You said you got bitten a lot when you were younger. According to your story, you weren't shrouded then. Maybe it's just something about you."

Cass sighed and said, "Yes, you are correct. I am starting to wonder about his whole shrouding thing and when it starts, Corrina."

Franklin said, "Yeah, I've been wondering about that too. You say Samuel is your son *and* he's a Nephilim. Your timing isn't making sense. You were in the hospital when you were shrouded. You didn't have sex with Lynn after that, did you?"

"No," Cass said. "In fact, it was maybe a month or more before Lynn and I were intimate. I asked Ex about this, but the angels are forbidden to discuss the shrouding process. I'll tell you more when I get to what happened with Samuel.

"But I'm getting off topic again. Where was I?"

"Black mass in the dark hall. A small black stone that changed color and reminded you of Mary and spider stories. Then you got distracted," Corrina said.

"Ah, yes! Thank you, Corrina," Cass said. "So, I went back in my room and went to sleep. The next day…"

CHAPTER 16

CHELSEA

Cassian woke at about nine in the morning and got dressed in sweats. He and Zab went to the Pitt weight room in Trees Hall at the top of what was known as Cardiac Hill. Just getting there was all the cardio work anyone would need.

Zab was one of those guys who worked out two or three times a week and ate potato chips and dip, french fries, pizza, Ho Hos, beer—whatever shitty food you could think of—and looked like he stepped off a muscle-magazine cover. He would talk about getting fat but seemed to be perpetually shredded. He was like a rich man crying poverty. Cass, on the other hand, would gain weight just smelling that food, so he had to work out and jog to stay in shape.

At the time, Zab was dating a girl named Leena who lived in the all-girls dorm, Brackenridge Hall. McCormick Hall was co-ed, so males and females lived on the same floor, but never the same room. Leena always went with them to the gym and then sidled up with the cheerleaders. She wanted to get on the squad and so placed her nose firmly up the ass of the cheerleading coach. This was the impetus to Zab becoming a Pitt cheerleader.

Cass and Zab grew to be good friends over the years. Practical jokes became something of an art form between the two. It couldn't be something as simple as shaking up a beer they were about to open. It had to be well thought out and have multiple levels. You couldn't just put petroleum jelly on the shower handles. You had to think about their next move. You had to figure out a way to put sand all over the back of the nearest towel, so the sand mixed with the petroleum jelly on your hands. Then when coming out of the bathroom to get another towel, a balloon with talcum powder would pop from above. Opening the drawer where more towels were kept would pop a glitter-filled balloon. Levels and layers became the game.

By his second year, Cass changed his major to the hardest subject in his curriculum—chemistry. He did this more to assure himself that his brain was still fully functional after slamming his head onto a dashboard at fifty to sixty miles per hour three years earlier. Zab, Clark, and Keith were all senior engineering majors, David was a communications major, and Clay was an economics major.

By his third year, they were living on the eighth floor of McCormick Hall. Cass and Clay and their four other suitemates were in room 802. Across the hall from them was room 801 with six girls living together. To the left of their room, at the end of the hallway next to the stairwell was another suite, 804, with four guys living together. At the right end of the hall was a double room, 803, which Chelsea had all to herself. This was because the girl she shared the room with dropped out and through some glitch or favoritism, she wasn't replaced.

Chelsea was the beautiful epitome of charm, on the outside. She appeared as an image of virtue and kindness to many people. Her enthusiastic participation in events that supported causes such as ending world hunger and cancer awareness always seemed to place her in the spotlight of some type of media. She joined the Tri Delta sorority (but she wasn't giving up her private room for any sorority house), ran for homecoming queen, ran for class president—all things that made her appear as a competent, caring leader of her community.

In truth, she privately mocked most of these causes. This was all done to place her pretty face in front of the cameras. She projected virtues that seemed ironically void from her true personality. It took some time before Cass saw the deeply unkind and self-centered nature of Chelsea. She seemed compelled to compete with everyone around her... even though nobody else knew it was a competition! Something dark drove her.

One of the girls in 801, Jennifer Salas, was an applied mathematics major. She and Cassian became good friends. She even joined the marathon study sessions with his other friends. Jen was pretty, blond, fun to be around, sharp as a whip, and had a huge crush on Daryl, the football player on the third floor.

Daryl had also become good friends with Cass and Clay. He was a huge African American guy from the Deep South with a strong accent. To Jennifer's disappointment, Daryl had a thing for more…voluptuous girls. While beautiful, Jen did not fit any aspect of that criteria.

After a while, Jen became like one of the guys. They would speak as freely around her as she did around them. She spent a lot of time in their dorm living room watching TV, studying, or just hanging out.

At one point, Jen got a job working at Hooters restaurant. She told Clay and Cass about her new employment as the three were watching TV on the sofa. Cass slowly leaned forward, turning his head to look in the direction of her not-so-ample chest. Without looking at him, Jen threw up one hand and said, "*Shut the fuck up, Cass*!" which made the three of them laugh.

"What?" Cass said. "The wings are fine, but I really like the legs!"

Clay said, "Come on, Cass, they have the *breast* wings around."

Jen laughed harder and said, "What are you talking about, Clay. I know you and Cass prefer the hot dog shop!"

"Before you say anything, Franklin," Cass said, "it was the 1990s. This was neither meant, nor perceived, as *harassment*. Clay and I both loved Jen…and not in any physical way. It took a long time to get to that level of comfort between us."

"Hey, I didn't say anything," Franklin said.

"Oh, I could see your face," Corrina said. "You were thinking it." She laughed.

"Yeah, well, I have annual trainings about this at work. That shit would never fly today," Franklin said.

Cass smiled and said, "I know. It sucks for people today.

"But we had fun together and enjoyed the kind of friendship people cherish forever. One thing that none of us noticed…"

This was making Chelsea extremely jealous. It wasn't that Chelsea liked any of the guys in Cassian's suite. She just didn't like Jen having the type of relationship they shared. So Chelsea began a private campaign to cause problems for Jen.

She started by befriending Jen's roommates. This was something easy for Chelsea to do. Why she didn't simply try to become friends with Cass and Clay is still a mystery. It seemed that she didn't really want what Jen had. She just didn't want *Jen* to have it.

On one rare occasion, Cass and his roommates snuck several cases of beer into the dorm for a party. Everyone on the floor was invited, but not everyone was over twenty-one years of age, including Chelsea. People were having a good time, drinking, talking, and generally blowing off steam.

Cass noticed Chelsea was tipsy when they both reached for the same beer and she almost fell over. After he helped her steady herself, they began a conversation that left Cass stunned.

"So, Cass, is there something going on with you and that Jen slut you and Clay hang around with?" Chelsea said, slurring a bit.

"Why would you call Jen a slut? Maybe you should get to know her. You'll get to see why everyone likes her," Cass said.

"I call her a slut because she's a slut. She gets around, Cass. I know," she said. Then added in an ominous tone that seemed like it should have been internal dialog, "I am going to beat her."

"What do you mean? You're going to fight her?" Cassian asked incredulously.

Chelsea looked surprised and said, "Oh. No. I mean I'm going to beat her—in life, you know. I'm going to win."

"Win what, Chelsea? Why would you need to beat someone who's not even competing with you. Unless you're into Daryl," Cass said.

"Pffft. I'm not into Black guys like *she* is. She probably did that whole room down on the third floor. She's a pig, and I don't like her. I hope she gets fat like her fat-ass roommates. A whole bunch of cows in that suite. I can hear them mooing at night while they graze on the O pizza and fries I always smell coming from their room." Chelsea laughed.

Cass looked up and saw Jennifer's suitemate, Monique. Compared to Chelsea or Jen, Monique was a big girl. But that, in no way, diminished her beauty or the warmth and kindness felt by those in her presence. The pain Cass saw register on her face made him feel sick.

Chelsea had been hanging around Monique and her roommate, Janice. She heard everything that Chelsea said.

Without a word, Monique turned and walked out of the party. Cass ran after her and caught up to her in the hallway.

"Monique, stop! Don't listen to that shit," Cass said.

"Why do you care, Cassian? Aren't you just tryin' to get in her pants too? You comin' out here to make sure the fat, Black girl is doing alright? Is that it? Don't you worry about me. Just go back to that spoiled little hoe. I should've never let that bitch get close to me," she said angrily, fighting back tears.

"I do care, Monique. I didn't know she was like that," Cass said as he walked closer to her.

"Why do people got to be like this?" Her voice trailed off as the tears began to form in her eyes.

Cass went to her and put his arms around her. He could see the white pulses of light offering her comfort from Ex. She hugged him back as she cried on his shoulder.

"Someone's got the jungle fever!" he heard Chelsea say from behind him as she laughed.

Cass turned his head and glared at her. Then he roared, "Get out of here!"

Monique shrunk away from him in fear and Chelsea fell backward onto her ass, spilling her drink all over herself. The whole party went quiet. In fact, it seemed like the whole building went quiet. Clay and Zab ran out in the hallway to see what happened.

Cass looked around as the four sets of eyes stared at him in shock. Cass said, "I'm sorry. I didn't mean to yell."

Someone was running down the steps. Chester, one of the RAs for the eighth, ninth, and tenth floor thrust his head into the hallway. "What the *hell* was that? Who's yelling?"

"What?" said Clay without missing a beat. "I didn't hear anything, Chester. What did you hear?"

"Somebody was fucking yelling down here. I know what I heard!" Chester yelled.

"The only one yelling is *you*, Chester," Zab said, following Clay's lead.

Chelsea was sitting up, about to get on her feet. She said, "Cass was the—"

Clay cut her off and said, "Cass was the one who noticed that Chelsea fell over. Maybe she yelled when she fell."

Chelsea started to protest when Zab helped her up and whispered in her ear, "If he finds out you're drunk, *you're* going to be the one in trouble."

"Step away from her, Cory" Chester said to Zab, using his first name. Only Chester called Zab by that name. "What were you going to say, Chelsea?"

"Oh," recognition registered on her face, "Cass was helping me up. I just fell."

"Are you inebriated, Chelsea?" Chester asked.

Clay went over to Chester with a winning smile and said, "Come on, Chester. We were just blowin' off a little steam. We been busting our asses studying. You see us. Have we caused you *any* problems this whole year?"

Clay had a way about him. Chester eased up and said, "Look, just keep it down. Whatever I heard…sounded like it shook the whole building. I can't have that kind of shit going on."

"Sorry, Chester," Clay said, "I promise it won't happen again."

Chester looked around, nodded, and then turned and went back up the stairs.

Clay turned to Cass and loudly whispered, "Next time, how about keeping it down to a college roar! Asshole."

This caused Monique to burst into laughter. Then Zab, Cass, and Clay all started to laugh. Chelsea turned and ran to her room without looking back.

Cass went to Monique and said, "I'm so sorry. I didn't mean to frighten you. I was just so…fucking mad at her."

"It's okay, Cassian. You made me feel about a million times better. Thank you for being so nice to me," Monique said. "I should have known when she was taking digs at Jen that she's not a nice person. I actually felt bad for Chelsea. You know…'cause she really doesn't have any good friends. That girl is cold inside."

"To hell with her. Don't even think about it again," Cass said.

"No, Cass. We need to pray for that poor girl. She's going to be alone a lot in her life," Monique said.

———————

"I was glad that the kindness I knew she possessed wasn't completely destroyed by that betrayal," Cass said to Franklin and Corrina. "I wish I could have been as forgiving as Monique. But I am not. It was this day that I decided to do something about Chelsea. Something that I will regret forever. But in so many ways, I would do it again in a heartbeat. Just…different…maybe.

"What I had in mind was devious, but, back then, I thought it was fitting for someone like Chelsea. And of course, two and half years of pranking back and forth with Zab created a master architect for shit like this. Now mind you, back then, in 1993 and 1994 there were not nearly as many Spurs. I could get away with more than I could today. But I was usually careful. It was a lot of work because I had to test everyone on that floor at one time or another."

"What do you mean by testing them?" Corrina asked.

"I had to be careful. Any Spur would be able to see the glow around me if I jumped into someone else. So, I managed to be alone with each person on the floor at some point. All I had to do was jump in them for a moment and come right back," Cass said.

"Get on to Chelsea," Franklin said, intrigued.

"Well, a couple days after the party I sat with Monique and the others from room 801 as they vented about being used by Chelsea. We laughed, tossing around various payback scenarios from lighthearted to really dark. It was when Monique teared up reliving the 'grazing' comments that I thought up this idea.

"So here's what I did…"

———————

Cassian carried the large bag of food into his room. It had dark circles of grease forming at several places. The marvelous aroma of fried onions brought a smile to his face. That bag must have weighed five pounds. The cost of the food wasn't too bad, since the cuisine intended to get people fat is always the cheapest shit.

He had a narrow window of time. This was going to be tricky to keep Chelsea from understanding what was happening.

Cassian worked out her schedule against his. On Monday, Wednesday, and Friday at around 6 p.m. she got back to her room. Those nights he came home with the food around 5:30. He would wait by the door to his room as Chelsea got off the elevator. As soon as she got her door open, he did his mental push.

He then had Ex carry the bag of junk food to Chelsea, which she gladly accepted. Then Chelsea/Cass ate the most calorically dense cuisine that the O and other fast-food restaurants had to offer.

The real trick he needed to work out was how to keep Chelsea from getting too suspicious. One night, after he smoked a joint with a friend he had in the Towers, it hit him while consuming his second bacon double-cheeseburger. Just a tiny hit of marijuana would make Chelsea feel hungry, while he wouldn't feel a thing when he flipped back.

So, he bought a bag of marijuana from his friend and a small pipe. In college, weed was easier to get than alcohol for a minor. After Chelsea/Cass ate, he opened her window and took a tiny drag or two from a little one-hitter pipe packed with a nice indica weed. He didn't want her to get stoned. He only wanted her to feel a little chilled out while still leaving her feeling the munchies…despite having eaten a ton of food.

When he was done, he and Ex cleaned the room, and Ex carried all the evidence back to his dorm. Chelsea/Cass brushed her teeth and took a couple antacid tablets to prevent bloating. Then he took Chelsea to the door entrance as if she just walked in and then flipped back into his body. He was careful not to let anyone see him going in and out of her room.

"Cassian," Corrina said, "I listened to the story you told us about Beth and your grandfather. Didn't you learn anything about addiction ruining people's lives?"

Cassian looked at her for a long moment and said, "At that time, I *did* ponder what I had done…for a long time. I knew what could happen with addictions, but I didn't think about food or weed being an addiction. There are always unintended consequences when you fail to consider everything. But I was a *stupid* kid.

"That *Super Friends* mentality is the type of influence that stunted the critical thinking skills of an entire generation. Sure, the message of being kind and honest with people is a good message. But I, unknowingly, caved to the more subtle social influences they pushed. The ones that taught kids that the villain must suffer.

"And Chelsea was the villain.

"Kids are very impressionable, and I was no different. Those cleverly crafted agendas were woven into our consciousness, teaching us *their* version of right and wrong.

"Don't get me started on John Hughes and Ivan Reitman and the rest of them. Let's just say that being raised by Hollywood—and, of course, their advertisers—could lead a person astray. Unfortunately, those shows and movies never mention the unintended consequences from the 'righteous' actions of their hero or heroine.

"It's quite possible that effective editing influenced the morality of an entire generation!

"I made a foolish decision and determined that what Chelsea had done to Monique warranted the *drastic* punishment that *I alone* would administer. I thought it would be funny to watch her get fat." Cass took a deep breath and sighed. "I also had this vision of me being some kind of hero for those who couldn't stand up for themselves.

"I was so naïve. People were *meant* to stand up for themselves and not to accept great injustice. It's sad that a once strong and self-reliant people have become a passive society of skilled television watchers swallowing carefully produced bullshit. I ought to know. I swallowed it for nearly thirty years.

"I also never considered that Chelsea might have had other problems. She must have lost a lot of weight at some point in her life because she gained it back *very* fast. Perhaps she was bulimic."

Franklin said, "If she was bulimic, why didn't she just puke up the food?"

"Bulimia is not just throwing up food. It is a mentality of binging and purging. The purging could be puking after a meal or, say, running ten miles for even the slightest binge, like eating *one* cookie. It's not a good or happy place to be, mentally. I didn't know it back then. Chelsea started purging without even *knowing* about her binge.

"It would be years before I realized why emotional judgments of this nature are not up to me or any other person. A true abuse of power…even when you feel, deep down, that *you* are wielding that power justly…is usually blind to the consequences," Cassian looked down in shame. "I was the one abusing the power. Something I *swore* to myself that I would never do. And there I was…doing it anyway without ratiocination.

"All because I was so confident. You don't know what you don't know. Oh, but once you see it…ignorance is not bliss…it is perilously corruptive.

"There is one good thing I can say about what I did…"

These were wonderful times for Cassian. He got to eat the best food and never gained an ounce of weight! He couldn't say the same for Chelsea. She began getting bigger and bigger each week. By the end of the first week, after she noticed she was packing on the pounds, she started with an exercise routine that would cause the strictest bodybuilder to cringe. She woke early in the morning and ran for several miles. She drank only water and ate next to nothing.

Cass had to give her a lot of credit. He had to eat an awful lot of food to keep up with her ability to purge through exercise. But after less than a week of that, she slowed down. The weight was still going on, and she felt tired all the time.

Though Chelsea ate practically nothing on Sunday, Tuesday, and Thursday, she ate enough for two grown men on Monday, Wednesday, Friday, and Saturday. She soon lost her ambition to keep up with that level of exercise. Cass didn't think the couple tiny hits of marijuana could do that. And then she started missing classes.

They all watched in amazement as Chelsea began to blow up like a tick. She had put on about fifteen pounds in only three weeks.

Ex finally confronted Cass and said, "I am not here to prevent you from your pathway to creation, Cassian. Each person must make their own road. But what you are doing is an *overcorrection* of justice for what this girl has done."

"You heard what she said, Ex. That was rotten. And Monique was so crushed. I don't know. This does feel wrong, though. Chelsea is starting to look like hell," Cass said.

"That girl is truly suffering. I believe she has stopped eating altogether…at least any meals that she knows about. You will drive her into despair," Ex said.

"Whoa, whoa, whoa," Franklin said, "How is this overcorrection? The racist bitch got what she deserved. I'm thinking this is hysterical!"

"No, it's not, Franklin," Corrina interjected. "It's mean. It's different for girls. You don't know. I want to know why it took Ex so long to say something to you? Your angel was physically complicit in this when she controlled your body at your request. Aren't angels sent from God to help people?"

Cassian looked at Corrina and said, "God may love all souls like a parent loves a child. But it's a tough love. Ex must help me and not interfere with my pathway. It has to do with each person making their own choices. I can ask Ex for advice, and she will provide her opinion. But only a few times has Ex ever intervened to sway my choices. This was one of those times.

"And Franklin, at the time I felt the same way you do now. But Ex was accurate in her radically simple assessment. My overcorrection of justice drove Chelsea to despair. I was exploiting an unknown mental disorder and it was cruel. Though not without exception, I have come to see that stealing the self-worth of a woman is akin to stripping a man of his dignity.

"As a fat kid who was teased in my youth, I thought I knew everything Chelsea would go through. It might be rough, but certainly justifiable. Right?"

"I think so," Franklin nodded.

"Ex showed me that I was steering Chelsea into despair. I was punching down, and it was awful. Grotesque hubris with Seraphic backing. I became an exceptionally powerful man who couldn't see the selfish reaction of the bullied child he once was. I had *become* the bully who overshadowed any notion of the 'good guy' defending Monique.

"Men don't understand the minds of women…not at all. No man should ever judge the emotions of a woman. Just as no woman should ever judge the threat of violence and danger that men face each day," Cass said.

"What the hell is that supposed to mean?" Franklin said, "Women face violence too…maybe more. And men can be every bit as tied up in their self-image as women."

Surprisingly, Corrina yelled, "Aww, *bullshit*, you fool! Cassian is absolutely right. You don't know what it's like to be a woman. You seem to have lived too long under the protection of your wife. Or maybe you don't see it because you are a big man and other men in these times *fear* you. Your father and grandfather knew it. Both of those men faced terrible people and terrible threats that you or I never knew about. And because of what your father did to protect us, we are still alive. Don't you dare dishonor him by thinking you ever faced the same threats. At least not as an adult. It is *hard* being a man…every bit as hard as it is being a woman. It's just different."

"I face threats all the time at work, Mom!" Franklin said. "And so does Victoria. I don't buy into that shit!"

"Franklin," Cassian said, "the threat is always different. Always. I think it is time to tell you a bit more about yourself and the Nephilim."

"Man! I don't know why you keep drifting away from your story. *You* said you wanted to tell this shit. I was hoping to have a peaceful Memorial Day weekend…alone!"

"Alone?" Cassian asked. "You want to be alone this weekend? You don't want your wife with you?"

"Of course, I want my wife with me!" Franklin said. "But I don't want you two here!" he yelled.

Corrina looked crushed. Cassian put a hand over hers and said, "It's okay, Corrina. He doesn't know yet."

She nodded, with a tear spilling from her eye.

"I'm sorry, Mom. I don't mean it like that," Franklin said. He looked at Cass and asked, "And what don't I know?!"

CHAPTER 17

THE MATRIARCHY

"What have you heard about the Great Flood that destroyed the world?" Cassian asked.

"Aside from what you said earlier? I know about the old fables of Noah and his ark and all the wild animals calmly filing in two by two. Whatever," Franklin said, dismissively.

Cass said, "Let us forget about Noah and the ark for the time being. But you have heard of the Great Flood?"

"Yes, of course," Franklin snapped. "It's getting late and I'm tired of this shit. Are you going to tell your story or not?"

"Patience, Franklin. You don't fully understand *why* you are so aggravated right now. Please let me explain," Cass said.

"Oh please, massa…please tell me why I's so annoyed," Franklin said, mocking LeVar Burton as Kunta Kinte in *Roots*.

"My God, Franklin! I am shocked that you would act like this!" Corrina reprimanded.

"It's okay, Corrina. I told you this would happen when I threatened his nature. Be strong," Cass said.

"Threatened what? You fuckhead!" Franklin yelled.

"After the creation of humankind…and, I now believe in some kind of combination between creation, evolution, and adaptation. Whatever brought us to this point—"

"Uhhh, it's called evolution. Duh," Franklin interrupted.

Cass continued, "We don't know half of what's going on. Evolution is a solid theory, but statistically impossible by all measures…"

"You're gonna deny evolution…" Franklin yelled.

"I never said *denied*, Franklin," Cass said. "It is simply that I don't believe that theory *as it stands*. Knowing about epigenetics as well as you do, you must be able to see the directionality of adaptation over random evolution. Please. We don't have time to get into a philosophical debate."

"Alright…whatever. But you are the one being the provocateur here. Get on with it," Franklin said, annoyed.

"You are right. I am being provocative, but not in the way you would understand," Cass said. "I don't know if you read the Bible or any other historical literature of that nature, but there is a long time missing from human history."

"I don't believe in any of that stuff, Cassian. I'm sorry, Mom. But modern religions never really hit home with me. There are too many parallels with all the other Greek and Roman myths," Franklin said.

"Try to think of these books as historical remnants rather than the image your mind creates when you hear the term 'religious scripture.' Christians have been told that the Bible is the only book by which we must live our lives," Cassian paused. "Other religions follow the Quran or the Torah. Books such as these have been corrupted by so many hands over the years that it is difficult to tell the truth from the Spuric lies."

"So, you admit…the Bible is a lie!" Franklin said.

"I did *not* say that! Not at all," Cassian said. "If you are a discerning and intelligent reader, you will find many truths within these texts. But read at face value, you may find these books harsh or deeply depressing and pessimistic. Let us not get into the Bible or any other literature. Let us consider what is *not* written."

"What is not written," Franklin said. "You're here to tell us what was *not* written?"

"Yes," Cassian said. "What you don't know is that the majority of human history, much more than is currently known as *recorded* human history, has been eliminated. Wiped clean from nearly every record found to date. In particular, the destruction of a time the stewards refer to as the Matriarchy. It was crucial for the demons, Spurs, *and* angels to obliterate this completely."

"You mean like women being in charge?" Franklin asked.

"Exactly," Cass said. "Destroying evidence of the Matriarchy was crucial so that they could install a Patriarchal society…which was established by all known religions or myths. The Bible, the Quran, and many other religious texts all support a Patriarchy. Think about Zeus or Odin or any of the other powerful male gods. Designed for Patriarchal control."

"How is it that you seem to know about this and nobody else in the whole world knows this?" Franklin asked. "Who told you?"

"You could say that it came to me in a dream," Cass said. "A dream in which…I was given access to the first book of the stewards!"

Cassian flinched as Ex yelled in his head, "What? You told me that your knowledge about the Matriarchy and Nephilim were conveyed by your resonant steward!"

"What's wrong, Cass?" Corrina asked, concerned.

"I'm getting a bunch of shit from Ex. She believed that what I am telling you came directly from Stu. She didn't know that I…accessed… the first book," Cass said. He looked down and to the right and said, "It was only a small portion of the first book. No others. And I didn't tell you for this very reason. I was warned that the angels wanted the location of the books and the knowledge that the stewards held in those books. I didn't want to muddy our relationship by having you ask me about the Library."

"So, *this* was the Library you wrote about all those years ago. You knew about it and never told me? This is a great betrayal of trust…" Ex said.

"It is not, Ex. I did not betray you. I kept it from you to *preserve* our relationship, which I have come to cherish greatly. Please don't be angry with me. I have my reasons. I wanted to tell you about it the night after I first discovered it, but something deep down inside me screamed not to do that," Cass said.

Silence for a moment. Then Ex said, "I understand why you did it. This is from your soul, and so it is the will of God. Perhaps it was wise of you to keep your own council on this. I apologize for my outburst. But we should talk about this more later."

"As long as you promise to never push me on the information in the book or where they are located. You will soon learn who provided me access," Cassian said.

A longer silence. Ex said, "I will agree to those terms. Though it leaves precious little to discuss."

Cassian laughed and said, "I'm sorry for that. But I must protect the wishes of those who helped me."

"You look like a crazy man over here," Franklin said. "What are you doing? Talking to your liver?"

Cass slowly looked up and said, "The Matriarchy was the time when the Nephilim came to great power. They were, in fact, so powerful that neither God nor Satan could control them. Any angel sent against them was rendered powerless. The same with any demon or Spur. They could trap any of these entities. And with their ability, they began to wield the power of both Heaven and Hell on Earth. The blood of humankind flowed like rivers as the Nephilim could not be contained."

"I thought you said that the Nephilim could only be males? If that's the case, why do they refer to this time as the Matriarchy?" Franklin asked.

"The Nephilim appear to have only two known liabilities. First, they are still mortal souls contained in a mortal body. They will age and they will die. Since it is the *body* of the Nephilim that contains their ability— and not the soul—when they physically die, their soul is like any other Godly soul. But the Seraphim essence is a dominant trait likely passed on the Y chromosome to the male progeny of Nephilim. So, they could propagate their line.

"The second liability—which relates to you, Franklin—is the reason this time is called the Matriarchy. The only people who have ever held absolute control over the Nephilim are those they chose as their female mate," Cass said.

Franklin snorted and said, "So, you're saying that I'm pussy-whipped," sounding offended.

"Please, Franklin," Corrina said.

"I'm sorry, Mom. But this guy is trying to say that I only listen to Victoria. That's bullshit!" Franklin said.

"Is it, though?" Corrina yelled. "Is it really so hard to believe? You turned your back on me and everyone else in your life the moment you met Victoria. *Everyone!*"

"No, I didn't! You didn't like her. The only way to keep you both happy was to keep the two of you separated," Franklin protested.

"Oh, so that's what you've been doing by never calling me on my birthday or Mother's Day or any other time? What about your friends? Do you speak with any of them? Do you still golf with Billy, Tyrese, or Scott? How about Randy? Forget about any female friends you had. I *know* you're not allowed to speak with them!" Corrina said. "And when Cass pushed this the tiniest bit, your whole demeanor changed. You got a huge bug up your ass. Look at how angry you are right now. Look at your own *hands*!"

Franklin gazed down and saw his clenched fists. He relaxed his grip as he looked between Cass and Corrina with a bewilderment on his face. His mind raced for an explanation.

Cass continued, "The mates of the Nephilim were sometimes Spurs and sometimes not, but it did not matter at that point. The select women controlling the Nephilim became *incredibly* powerful. And what inevitably follows great power is corruption.

"Queendoms were formed and men and women alike became slaves in servitude to the queens. They came to power over a two-thousand-year period, developing many advanced technologies. Things we don't understand today. I can tell you that they were the ones who built the pyramids and other such inexplicable structures around the world. Then they began their brutal, iron-fisted rule that lasted for another thousand years.

"There was only one way left to kill the Nephilim and end the power of the Matriarchy. This is why the planet and all terrestrial life was destroyed. After that, the shrouded and the demons were forbidden from allowing the survival of any offspring created while a Seraphim was occupying a human."

"Were there any Nephilim that didn't...you know...obey the women?" Franklin asked, uncertain of his own reality.

"There was no mention of this happening, Franklin. I am sorry. You should not feel badly. Many men fall into this type of control. Were it not for the power you have, it would never be an issue. But right now, whether she knows this or not, Victoria is one of the most powerful women on the planet…because of *your* faithfulness to her."

"Didn't other Nephilim challenge each other?" Corrina asked.

"Yes. The battles were savage," Cass said. "And any that stood in the way were killed. When a queen went to war with another queen, she would send her Nephilim to kill her opponent. The fighting could last for months as neither would back down. And once one of the Nephilim fell, the entire queendom was wiped from existence. It was a bloody and brutal world."

"Why is there no record of this?" Franklin asked.

"You will hear some references to the Nephilim and this time in the Book of Enoch. Even the Bible has a line or two about it. But all mention of the Matriarchal queendoms has been scoured from Earthly records. What followed next was the establishment of a Patriarchy. What was once meant to create equality between men and women was soon bastardized by the Spurs and Satan. Women were made into lesser beings, responsible for all the hardships of life. This became a dramatic overcorrection that men were easily swayed into following as the righteous word of God.

"But I don't know if that's the complete truth. I don't know what to believe after what I saw in that book," Cass said. "I wish I never knew those books existed."

"How do you know that I won't use the power against you if Victoria asks me to?" Franklin asked.

"I don't," Cassian said. "But you were raised by Corrina. And I feel strongly that you are a good person. Of course, I'm not always the best judge of character. At some point, I need to put my trust in someone."

"You are trying to get my boy to go to battle for you. Is that what this is all about? You need my son for protection against another Nephilim," Corrina said defensively.

"I need the help of your son for several reasons, Corrina. And yes, I need his protection. I believe Samuel holds several Spurs. I know that he found ways of summoning demons, so I have to assume he has trapped at least one. I am nearly powerless against him alone," Cass said.

"Well, couldn't you do to him what you did to me earlier?" Franklin asked.

"He would never let me get to him like that again. If I jumped into him, he could trap me, stuff me in the dark, destroy my body, and then release me into nothingness," Cass said.

"If I steal away your power, how is it you can still jump into people? Isn't that the power Ex gives you?" Franklin asked.

"That's a great question. And one I have no answer for. Perhaps it's the time delay it takes for you to siphon off the power. I jump before you can take it away. I don't think that's quite right, though. Maybe it's something to do with the intended use of the power.

"But, when Samuel used the power of a demon or the Spurs, I *didn't* see an aura around him. Maybe you pull the energy through another channel…one I can't see. I couldn't see anything attached to Samuel, like I could see that demon attached to you. It must have something to do with how you can hold them," Cass said.

"So, you must have been trapped by Samuel before. Is that right?" Franklin asked.

Cass sighed and said, "I'm getting ahead of the story, but you should know this. You see, years ago, after I learned that they were still alive, I tracked down Lynn. I assumed Samuel would be with her. He was not. She told me that she left him in Utah with his grandparents. I went to get him.

"When I showed up, Sarah and Toby, his grandparents, knew me and suspected that I was Samuel's father. To *my* great surprise, they were *relieved* to see me. They wanted to be rid of the 'demon child.' Crazy bastards were trying to perform an exorcism on the poor boy. He was only eleven at the time. It was terrible what they were doing to him.

"There were two priests and a few goons from their church in the house. I asked to see Samuel, and they took me into the basement. They had him chained to a chair. They must have been working on him for weeks if not months. He was malnourished and thirsty. He didn't know how to wield the power of the Spur or Spurs that he had trapped. If he had, he would have slaughtered them all.

"When I saw what they were doing to him, I was furious. Ex calmed me down because my first instinct was to kill them. So, I played along with their bullshit to see what I was up against. They took me back up-stairs, and I did what any father would do…I beat the shit out of them… including Mary's parents.

"Everything was going great until I went back into the basement and Samuel sucked all the power from me. Something must have awakened in him because he was able to break free from the chains instantly. I was still able to jump into him and found myself trapped with at least two other angry spirits around me.

"This was the first time I ever experienced anything like this, so I didn't know what I was seeing. Inadvertently, I banished everything attached to him. But we were all still trapped, and now Samuel knew how to access our power. He killed one of the priests before I could do anything. I was lucky that he didn't know who I was. I tried to talk to him, but the boy was on a rampage.

"That was when I did to him what I did to you, Franklin. Only, I didn't know what I was doing and I nearly killed him. Ironically, I was warned by…an unexpected source, that this might happen. But that was probably the only thing that saved my life, because he seemed ready to massacre everyone.

"This was my opportunity to kill him. Ex warned me about the dangers of keeping him alive. But I couldn't kill my son," Cass said.

"But you didn't know if he was your kid?" Corrina said. "You said he could have been the son of that Eric Bosco demon."

"I knew the moment I saw him. I could see my own mother's eyes in him. I knew he was my son. And I wouldn't let Ex or anyone else kill him," Cass said. He looked down and to the right. "I know, Ex."

There was a long pause before Franklin said, "Well, who knows, maybe he'll bite off your finger later and dive into a volcano to save the world."

Cass gave him a puzzled look and then burst into laughter. He laughed until tears came from his eyes. Corrina and Franklin also laughed, but Corrina was unsure what was so funny.

As Cass regained his composure, Franklin asked, "So what happened with this Chelsea bitch?"

"Yes, back to the story. Forgive me for straying into other tributaries, but I believe in crossing bridges when I get to them. I'll talk more about Samuel later.

"At this point, Chelsea was ballooning quickly, and I was going to end this abuse…"

<hr>

Cass couldn't tell Chelsea or anyone else what he had been doing. It wasn't as if he could say, "Hey, I'm shrouded by an angel and I've been possessing Chelsea the last few weeks to make her eat like a pig without knowing it."

The next day, he walked to Chelsea's room to check on her. He never wanted to hurt her. He only wanted to give her a taste of what she had done to others. But he and Zab became used to taking things so much further than other people that Cass lost sight of how far he let this go.

Cass knocked on her door.

Chelsea opened the door. Although she was only slightly plump, she looked heavier since her clothes were too tight. An amazing smile lit her face. She said, almost in disbelief, "Cassian! It's you!"

"Hi, Chelsea," Cass said, feeling awkward, "I wanted to come by and see how you're doing. It seems like you've been really frazzled lately."

"I cannot believe that you are here. Thank God!" she sounded so excited, "I prayed that I would find you and here you are…right in front of me!"

Cass said, "I've been worried about…wait. What? You prayed you would find *me*? I live right there," he pointed to his door.

"I don't know what you're thinking of doing, Cassian!" her voice dropped to a whisper, "But whatever you do, *don't* possess me, stupid."

The color drained from Cassian's face.

Chelsea said, "It's me, Cass! It's Mary!"

CHAPTER 18

ARIEL

"To hell with that asshole, Ariel. You don't owe him an explanation for what you do. This is a nice hotel. We have adjoining rooms…thanks to Franklin," Victoria said, smiling as she sipped a glass of white wine. "Now, you can do whatever you want, but I swear to God, if you invite that asshole *here*, I am fucking done—with *you*. Do you understand what I'm saying?"

"I know, Victoria. But what am I going to do? Just ignore the calls and texts?" Ariel said meekly. Ariel was a thin, red-headed girl of average height, large breasts, and a very pale complexion. She was pretty, but extremely insecure. Men fell all over her, but she was too mentally preoccupied with winning the approval of whatever guy she was with to notice.

"Yes. That's exactly what you're going to do. Okay?"

"Yes."

"Here, give me your phone. I'll block his fucking number right now!" Victoria said.

"No! I don't want to block his number. I only want to take a break. I'm *not* breaking it off with him, you know! I'm giving him some time to think about what he did. You're so right. He can't keep walking on me like that. If I want to have a bachelorette party in Boston, I should be able to!" Ariel said.

"That's what I'm saying. Fuck that bullshit. He's going to have a bachelor's party at the Elks Lodge. Why can't you have a bachelorette party?" Victoria said.

"Well, he was complaining about the cost, but I think he doesn't want me going into the city. It's like you said, he wants to control everything," she said, still sounding meek, but with more conviction.

"That's the spirit, Ariel! You're the Little Mermaid!" Victoria said, filling her glass with more wine.

"Yeah! Fuck him! I *am* the Little Mermaid! He should be wanting to live with *me* under the sea! Not the other way around." Ariel was slurring a little at this point.

"Alright. Finish that wine. I saw an Irish pub on the maps around here. We're going out!"

"Really?" Ariel said. "Where to?"

"I told you, dumbass. The Irish pub I saw on the map. I think I passed it on the way here. Let's Uber there," Victoria said.

Ariel laughed. "You want to get an Uber there? Where do you think you are?"

"Fine. I'll drive. It's not that far, and I'm not even close to being drunk," Victoria said. "What do you need to do to get ready? Pretend like this is your bachelorette party!"

"Yeah, right? Okay. Let me clean up these crying eyes. I look like a raccoon. I'll be ready in ten minutes. Let me just call…" Ariel looked at her phone.

"Give it here. I'm not going to block him. I'm going to shut it off so you can take a break from him. You can talk to him later, when you've had a little time to think," Victoria's mannerisms and tone were so subtle. She was a master at keeping Ariel from breaking down into tears again.

"Okay. You're right…as usual."

Twenty minutes later, Victoria and Ariel walked into the bar. It had quite a large crowd for a small town, but there were a few spots open at the bar. After a little asking and people shuffling, the two sat together at the counter. Ariel had a light beer and Victoria ordered a glass of white wine. It was a cheap sauvignon blanc, that had probably been opened for days, but she didn't care at that point. As long as it wasn't oxidized to piss yellow, she was fine.

"Now, Ariel," Victoria started, "what are you going to do about Jeff? Do you want to talk about it, or do you want to forget about it for now? Either way, we can't let you become his little lap doggie once you're married?"

"Fuck that," Ariel said, "I'm doing whatever I want when we get married. I run the show," she slurred and started to laugh as she drained the last of her beer.

The female bartender came over with two shot glasses and said, "Complements of the man at the end of the bar. What's your poison?"

Victoria said, "Tequila. And which guy? The fat, bald one or the normal looking guy next to him?"

The bartender burst into laughter and said, "The normal guy. The fat, bald guy is my husband."

"My God. I'm so sorry," Victoria backpedaled.

"Oh, don't worry about it. We both know he's fat and bald. But he's got everything I want in a man," she winked and looked down, "you know…a sense of humor!" she started laughing again. Victoria and Ariel joined in. Then she looked at Ariel and said, "How about you, dear? Tequila too?"

"Sure," Ariel said, shirking off her usual meek exterior, "Why don't you tell him to come down here and join us?"

The barkeep turned to the man and said, "Shep, you want in on this. They invited you to join them."

"Hell yeah!" Shep said, "What are we drinking, Margaret?"

"Tequila," Margaret said. "Lime and salt?"

"You bet!" He turned to his tall friend who was bent over one of the tables chatting up some potential prospects. "Let's go, Micky."

Micky turned and looked at Ariel and Victoria. A striking smile spread over his face as he saw the two women who looked like angels in the dark bar.

When he got over to them, Shep squeezed in to the bar close to Ariel and said, "Make it five, Margaret. You're joining us too, aren't you?"

"Hell, if you're buyin', I'm drinkin'." She laughed as she grabbed three more shot glasses and lined them up on the bar. She set out the saltshaker and put five lime wedges on a napkin.

Micky walked up behind Victoria and said, "Hey beautiful, what's your name?"

Victoria smiled and said, "Flattery will get you everywhere, honey. My name is Jessy. And this lovely little ginger is Fiona."

Ariel gave Victoria a surprised look then shrugged and gave Micky a smile.

"Jessy, huh? Well, that sure is a pretty name," Micky said.

Then Shep said, "Do you know what Fiona means?"

Ariel shook her head and said, "What's it mean?"

Shep said, "It means beautiful little angel."

Victoria said, "Fiona is Gaelic for fair…or *white*. It's been around since the turn of the twentieth century where it was mostly used in Scottland and then later began to spread out from there."

"So, you know about names?" Shep asked, "What does Shep mean?"

"You mean you don't know?" Victoria said, shaking her head. "Shep refers to men who like to fuck sheep."

"What?" Shep said, sounding angry.

"Come on now, Shep," Victoria stifled a giggle, "You should know it's a shortened name for the profession of shepherd. You know, like the guys who round up little…white…sheep. And then fuck them!" Victoria broke into laughter, which got Micky, Ariel, and Margaret laughing too.

Shep looked around and considered his options, then decided joining the laughter was his best option.

By now, Margaret had the shots ready. Shep slapped a fifty-dollar bill on the bar and started handing out the shots. Everyone got the salt on their hand and had the lime ready.

"What do we drink to?" Ariel said.

"I know!" Victoria said. She held up her shot, "Here's to men who fuck sheep!" She licked the salt, slammed the shot, and sucked the lime. They all started to laugh and then threw back their shots. Shep laughed too, but the look in his eyes didn't match the smile on his face.

CHAPTER 19

FRIZ KNOWS

Friz ran easily through the woods. The corneal modifications made seeing in the dark a simple task. He was unsure if they would adapt to this gravity realm, but everything seemed to be working…just as in his own realm. When he knew he was far enough away from Malcom, he slowed his pace and began to listen for pursuit.

He could have dispatched of Malcom but knew that doing so could alter the events on this world and possibly lead to the planet's destruction. Eradicating potential historical figures raised several moral issues for Friz. *Potential historical figure*, he thought, *aren't we all.*

This thought made him swoon with new visions. He shook his head to clear his mind. Once he found an opening in the woods that had a clear view of the sky, he took a small, thin, pencil-like device from a pocket within the inner left sleeve of his garment. He stuck one end in the ground and pointed the other at the moon. He touched the top of the device to activate it. He gave it several minutes to collect data. Once it was complete, the small clearing lit up with a 3D map that only he could see. He identified an old church within 135 kHz wavelength (about two thousand meters) of his location. A house of God might be a good place to rest…maybe.

He pulled the device from the ground, wiped off the dirt, and put it back in the proper pocket. Then he made his way through the dark woods. After about fifteen minutes, Friz walked out of the forest toward a white building with no lights on. He adjusted his view and saw the church had heat signatures of two occupants. His mind flashed an unpleasant image of horrible creatures living within the church.

The visions from the Shazo were intense, but he knew they may contain elements of truth. Another unfortunate prospect of entering this church. The drug he took to counter the effects and purge the metal from his system made him feel sluggish.

Walking around the building to the front, atop of a set of concrete steps, Friz began to knock on the double doors. He knocked three times, waited one minute and repeated the knocking. Within three rounds, he noticed that lights began to illuminate the left-most windows of the church.

Moments later, an elderly man holding a pistol in his hand threw open the door and said, "Who are you? And what the hell are you doing banging on the door at three in the damned morning?"

"I apologize to you, good man of the church. I come to you in great need. Might I find refuge within your holy sanctuary?" Friz said, quickly, but focusing on trying to speak slow and deliberate.

"Who is it, Davey?" asked a rugged, feminine voice from somewhere behind him.

"It's some weird, tall guy asking for *refuge* in our *sanctuary*," Davey said, speaking the last four words overdramatically.

"Well, let him in, you old badger. No point in runnin' a church if ya can't be charitable," she said, peaking her head around the door. "And put that damn gun away, Dirty Harry. Who you expecting out here at night? The Crips and the Bloods?"

"How the hell should I know? Who goes knocking on your door in the middle of nowhere at this time of night?" Davey said.

"Come on in, dear," the old woman said. "My name is Dierdra and you already met my sweet husband, David," she added sarcastically. "What's your name?"

"I am known by the name Friz, Dierdra. Thank you for inviting me in. Can I offer some form of payment to you? I have little that may be of value to you," he said politely.

"Well, now that you mention it—" Davey said.

"Oh, shut up you cheap, old bastard," Dierdra interrupted. "No, young man. We are all God's children and meant to help one another. Please come in."

Friz walked in and saw the small nave lined with pews on the left and right leading up to the altar. His mind flashed of horrid creatures crawling out from under the altar. He felt a rush of panic as he pushed the images aside. The old woman guided him off to the left and down a hallway that went to the back of the building where they lived. She went into the tiny kitchen and started making coffee.

"Well, what the fuck are you makin' coffee for at this damn hour, woman?" Davey said.

"Can you please not use that language. We live in the fucking house of God, and we have a visitor. The least you can do is show *him* some respect. Besides, you're not going to sleep anymore tonight. I probably won't either," she snapped.

"Well, that's a fair point," Davey acknowledged.

Friz wore a perplexed look as he said, "I am terribly sorry for disturbing your rest. Is it common for you to awake and then not sleep again?"

"You're not from around here, are you, son?" Davey asked.

"No, sir. I am not. I live in a large city known as New York," Friz said, recalling the proximity to the city from his map.

Dierdra and David shared a quick look.

"Would you like something to drink or maybe to eat?" Dierdra asked.

"I would prefer…what you normally would drink," Friz said. "Or water! Yes, water would be fine." He was thirsty.

Dierdra grabbed a glass out of the cabinet as David opened the fridge and pulled out the half-filled Brita container. As David carried the water pitcher over to the table, he slipped and nearly fell over, dropping the pitcher. Friz responded quickly by grabbing the water pitcher before too much had leaked out. It was cracked and water was going everywhere.

Diedra took the pitcher from Friz and brought it to the sink as she said, "Christ sakes, ya damned klutz. This is broken now, you know? You're going into town and getting a new one tomorrow," she stated like a demand. "I'm not drinking this shit water."

The two got into a small argument about the broken water filter.

They were clever, but as fast as they were, Friz saw what Diedra did to his glass. The small something she sprinkled in it. Could no person on this realm be trusted? He would patronize them for a bit and then make his escape. He saw the back door. It appeared to have multiple locks. *So much for the charity of the house of God here*, he thought.

"It's quite alright," Friz said, "I am not that thirsty. Perhaps we could talk for a bit?"

"Yes," David said, "I would like to know how you got out here in the middle of the night from New York? How about that puzzle piece?"

"Oh yes. I have a friend named Malcom. He was driving a car. The car had broken on the road near to this location. I explained that I would go to find assistance. He agreed to stay with the car. I became quite lost and had been searching for many hours for help. I saw your church and felt that this may be the best place to get assistance. I am so glad to find such nice and honest people to help." Friz said with a smile.

"Aww, fuck it," Diedra said, as her skin began to blanch, "I'm too tired to play nice."

"Already?" David complained, "We didn't get to toy with him none!" His tone took on a gravelly aspect.

Friz heard the pistol cock behind him as Dierdra's horrifying new face turned to him. The dead, white skin was contrasted by her huge black eyes and red lips. Rows of sharp white teeth glistened as she said, "Who the fuck are you?" the shrill voice screamed as the cold, black eyes bore into him.

The raspy, creepy voice of David said, "We're eating this one! I need meat. I don't give a fuck about who needs information. This dead-ass town sucks, and if we *have* to be here, we're going to start eatin' better!"

"Go ahead, Friz. You go on and fight if you want. It makes the meat taste better when you're filled with fear and adrenaline," Dierdra said. Blue veins patterned starkly against her flesh making the whole appearance surreal and gruesome.

Friz moved slowly to grab something in his right sleeve. Dierdra had his hand in her vice-like grip before he could reach the pocket.

"What do you got there?" she asked, moving her face right up to his. Her speckled tongue came out of her mouth and licked his lips. Friz cringed in revolt as he saw tiny maggots poking out of the white sores on her tongue.

"It's only a writing utensil," Friz said, spitting like he was trying to get a hair out of his mouth. "A…a pen is what you call it. I mean you no harm."

"Well, Friz, we mean you all kinds of *fucking* harm," David grated from behind him. Friz was terrified by the appearance of Dierdra. She changed so quickly. He started to wonder if this was another vision created by the Shazo.

"Slowly, Friz," Dierdra said. "Davey, you slow down. You don't need no gun anyway. He ain't got no answers if he's dead. I'm sure he's got plenty to tell us! You need some paper to write something down?"

Friz slowly pulled the thin metal rod from a small pocket in his left sleeve. He gave a hard blink and then pushed the top of the rod.

The frantic strobing light and sound that began to pulse from the rod inundated the room, making the dim kitchen light seem like darkness in comparison. David and Dierdra were frozen as Friz stood from the chair he was seated in, pushing away from Dierdra's grip and wiping his mouth.

"I have read about Spurs, but never actually met one. We have rid our society of your kind. You truly are what the ancients described in nightmares," Friz said, looking at the two dreadful statues that stood, shaking as if they were desperately trying to break free. The muscles of their bodies held them firmly in place.

"Forgive me. I am not one to gloat. I do apologize, but I will not take chances with you as stories about the dangers of your kind still haunt me from my youth," Friz said as he pulled a long, sharp rod from his right hip and jammed it into David's temple. When he pulled it out, a small puff of smoke came from the hole and the wound was instantly seared shut. Though it instantly killed Davey, his body stood still, held immobile by the rigid muscles.

He turned to Dierdra and said, "We have overcome your kind. May you do better in your next life…if you ever escape Hell."

Friz jammed the spear into her temple.

Friz stopped the strobing light and sound. Davey dropped to the ground as Dierdra slouched over and fell across the kitchen table.

He picked up the glass that Dierdra was going to give him. He blinked hard three times and then glared into the glass.

So, they were going to paralyze me, he thought. *Why?*

He went to the sink and filled a clean glass with water. He pulled a metallic-looking vial from another hidden pocket, opened the top, and sprinkled a dash of powder into the water before drinking it down. He repeated this action two more times before he began to investigate the church.

He opened each door he could find and searched the home thoroughly. He climbed into the loft where the church organ was located, then down into the small basement, which was only big enough to be the foundation of the living area. He looked everywhere and found nothing unusual. Then he went out into the church nave to looked around.

On the wall behind the altar was an image of a cross with Christ hanging from it wearing his thorny crown. Friz stood between the altar and the pulpit facing the mural. He crossed both hands over his chest, put his head down for a moment, and whispered, "Your pain in all realms rings throughout eternity."

Friz was about to leave when he had another powerful vision about nightmarish creatures pouring out from beneath the altar. He began to knock on the sides of the wood. It was, of course, hollow, but he heard something much different with his auditory enhancements. It was a deep echo.

He began to feel around and try to move the altar, but it was firmly in place. He took the rod from his sleeve again and pushed a few places on it. It began to vibrate and give off a high-pitched sound. He touched it to the top platform, and it began to shake until it slid to the right exposing stairs that led underground. He shook his head and thought, *Primitive, but effective enough that I nearly missed it.*

Blinking hard again, Friz descended the steps leading underground. He made sure to close the altar above him before going too far.

The stairs were carved into stone and spiraled in a tight circle that prevented seeing too far ahead or behind. From his visions, Friz feared he may be walking into a pit of demons.

He pulled up the map again. It took several minutes before a red sign in the upper right flashed "Signal Lost." But the map that was displayed was shocking. The spiral stairs through stone and earth went deep underground before the signal stopped. Perhaps this was the limit of the device on Earth. At least he knew how much farther he had to go. No life forms showed on the stairway. He shook his head.

After several breaks to rest his thighs during the long descent, a dull green light began to shine from beneath him. The device he carried could still not get an image of what lie below. Cautiously, he made his way down the last round of steps. When he looked around the corner, Friz said aloud, *"Jhamna scheah!"* (Holy fuck!)

CHAPTER 20

ABBADON AND DIOBALST

"Is this the Mary from high school?" Franklin asked. "Lynn's younger sister that you started *dating*? Wasn't she killed?"

"She *was* killed…at the hands of your father, no less. This is where the story starts to get weird. Well, weirder," Cass added. "This was something I wouldn't have expected in a million years. Mary had been gone for about three years at this point. I was only then starting to get over her loss."

"You were a young man in college," Corrina said with disbelief in her voice. "You must have been seeing other girls."

"Well, of course I was. Some people considered me to be kind of a womanizer of sorts," Cassian sighed. "I was not a womanizer. You see, I just *liked* women. I mean I still *do* like women. I like being around women. It's their unique perspective on…everything. They have insights on things I would never think of on my own. I believe this is why men and women were meant to work together.

"Even though I was awkward around them when I was younger, over time I developed this ability to speak comfortably with women. It was like I had this…I don't know…maybe I still have it…*unintentional* charm that comes to the surface. Maybe it was genuine interest or something I picked it up in college from hanging around with my one friend, Kellen Metzler. That guy had a true gift of gab. He was so smooth and always knew what to say to women to make them laugh and feel comfortable—"

"So could Ted Bundy!" Franklin interrupted, smiling.

Cass returned the smile with a nod and said, "I was far from being as good-looking as Mr. Bundy. But I managed to date a lot of great women…without murdering any of them. I dated a lot, but I didn't sleep around."

"Sure. You just took a girl out on a date, walked her back to her room by 10 p.m., and kissed her on the cheek? Come on, Cass. I knew guys like you in college. Don't try to sell the goody-two-shoes act to me," Franklin said.

"Those details will remain between me and them. Nevertheless, I remember each one, whether the connection lasted a day, a week, or a few months. Each inspired me in their own way. This may sound mawkish, but I hold them fondly in my heart…though some hated me at the end. I was far from perfect, especially back then. I mean, there were plenty of times when I was a huge asshole," Cass said.

"Oh, you still are," Franklin said, making the three of them laugh.

Cass looked off toward the window and said, "But when you have that one special person in your heart, they have a power to pull you back."

Franklin scoffed and said, "I don't buy that 'each one was special' talk, Cassian."

"I don't care if you believe what I say or not. I have a…kind of love…for each of these women. Their memory is special to me."

Cass looked at Franklin and said, "What I find funny is that a Nephilim might criticize *me* for having a soft spot for women."

Cass turned to Corrina with a knowing smile and said, "How many girlfriends did Franklin have once he got to high school?"

"Three," she said quickly. "He'd get with a girl and that was it. He was wrapped around her finger. The first two broke up with him. He married the third one. Each time he broke up, he was so crushed you would have thought his world ended."

"What the hell, Mom? Why are you telling him all this?" Franklin asked.

"Because it's true. You tell me how many girls you dated?" Corrina said.

"It's okay, Franklin," Cassian said. "You are a Nephilim. It is your nature."

"You're critical of me because I'm faithful to my wife?" Franklin asked. "That should be a virtue. It's not like you're some kind of all-knowing saint. You killed people. You're going to Hell with all the rest of us." Franklin chuckled.

Cassian's tone turned dark as he said, "Take my word on this, do not make jokes about Hell. People talk tough like it's a big joke. Believe me, it is not a fucking joke, and it is not a 'cool' place where all the 'cool' people go. It is an unimaginable, hate-filled place.

"I never said I was a saint. Not at all. And I am certainly not judging a commendable attribute like faithfulness to your wife. It's just that I had many accusations thrown at me in my life. Particularly from classmates and peers, envious because I could speak comfortably with women. Very few of my friends from college who survived what was about to happen ever spoke to me again. Of course, I brought them a lot of grief.

"But I'm getting ahead of the story. As an aside, I later made friends with a guy who was a Spur. I was stupid and never checked him out. I found it ironic that his name was Bart. That was the name of Williams's little brother who hated me. Before I took care of the Spur, he did much to tarnish my reputation. Of course, I played my own part in this, so I can't fully blame the Spur. But that's a story I'm not getting into today.

"Even though I banished his Spur, and many of the threads unraveled, the damage to my reputation was done. Amazing the depth of harm rumors can do to you. The people involved still associate *their* troubled times with me. I can't fault them for that.

"Bart, however, became extremely faithful to me for many years. Sadly, he was killed during the pandemic."

"Sorry to hear that," Franklin said. "Did he die from the virus?"

"He was murdered. He was a civil engineering major in college. He rose quite high in one of the federal agencies. He helped me gather much of the information I currently hold. He knew far too much, and they found out that he was betraying them. Fortunately, he never mentioned my name to anyone. That is, until Samuel got hold of him. When he was done, they injected him with the virus," Cassian said, shaking his head with a sad look on his face.

"Oh noooo! So, you think the government killed him? Hey, Mom. Are you going to sit here and let him talk shit about the USA? You and grandma nearly got *me* thrown out of Brown to support the American government," Franklin said jovially.

Corrina looked angry as she said, "Just listen to Cassian. He and I talked a long time about this. Something about what's going on right now is *wrong*.

"This country was founded on the bravery of bold men and women. People who left the safety of their civilized world to come here and try for a chance at freedom. Can *you* imagine doing that? They didn't just book a flight or sail on some comfortable cruise ship to America. It was a brutal voyage. And they were leaving everything behind on a gamble for a small chance of success…or death. Your grandfather did it…with your grandma and me in tow!

"He was a brave man. The foundation of American heritage is *bravery*! They were the bold and fearless people of the world. *You* come from that kind of bravery. The kind of bravery that leads to great things.

"Too many people—like your teachers—spoke badly about the colonists. Do you think your pompous professor would ever do something as daring as what the Founding Fathers of this country did? What *your* grandfather did?

"It was these same courageous people—farmers and pioneers—who stood against *royalty* for less than a five percent tax. Now we pay fifty percent or more of our income in taxes. For *what*? People who start war and pestilence so they can steal money from the public. That's what it comes down to. They're barely even hiding it anymore. All you have to do is open your eyes and look, Franklin.

"It's not the *government*. And it's not the *people* in the government. It's the people *controlling* the government. The lawyers, politicians, and the thieves getting rich as they destroy the honor of those who sacrificed *everything* to live free.

"The only word I have been able to describe what's happening is *evil*. It wasn't even Cass who first told me about this evil. It was your father, Charles Germane. He used the word 'demons'!"

Franklin fired back, "Everyone is a demon or a Spur now? Is that what you're saying? I thought Spurs didn't work together, Cass. Now they're all cooperating to control our government?"

"Franklin, your tone suggests that your mind isn't open right now. Are you willing to listen and maybe consider another perspective? If you are, I will try to explain," Cass said.

Franklin put out his hands, nodded, and said, "I'm fine. I will listen."

"Good," Cass said. "I used to believe that the Spurs didn't work together. I am nearly certain that they don't *know* other Spurs when they meet them. But there is something that feels coordinated when they occupy enough of a particular social class or industry.

"I now believe that once any group gets above a certain percentage of Spurs, a demon will enter that group to unite them. Then they act to influence that entire faction. These collective groups leverage their accumulated power to sway companies, governments, foundations, and unelected nongovernment organizations. This is how so few can amass control over so many.

"There are not enough demons that *all* these people could be under demonic possession. But that doesn't mean they are not under demonic *control*. They use several means to control people. Fear is their favorite. They can intimidate people with legal action, loss of wealth, public hatred…or just straight up violence.

"The other way is through bribery. They offer wealth or power. This can intoxicate many to the point where moral repercussions become a distant concern. The demons always provide twisted ethical justifications for turning a person to accept their will.

"But most often, it's a combination of the two methods. They offer wealth and power to an ambitious person. Bargains are accepted with considerations that there may be a few…shady or unscrupulous actions involved. Once a person performs that action, the trap is closed. The demons use fear of prosecution or persecution to hold them under their thumb.

"Today, Abbadon supplements nearly thirty percent of the federal scientific research budget. Do you think the people working in the government want to lose that money? Of course not. But to get that money, the agencies must look the other way on certain unethical practices. The demons set up key individuals in charge of writing policy to take the blame for any criminal activity.

"Once they have the evidence they need, the demons dictate policies to get full control over agencies. It doesn't take everyone. It only takes a *few* strategic positions to make it seem that the entire system is corrupted.

"Demoralization sets in as the masses feel they can't contend with such powerful entities like world governments or massive conglomerates. This leads to feelings of hopelessness and depression.

"The ancient levers of fear and shame are still being used by powerful hands. The two-week lockdown was supposed to stop the spread of the virus. This was not about the virus. It was about control and getting people to fall in line. But most importantly, the *massive* spike in despair increased the number of Spurs exponentially around the world.

"*Two years* of lockdowns drove up the suicide rate…as well as the *attempted* suicide rate. This opened millions of targets for the Spurs. And the nightmares they produce will drive people even deeper into depression. I can personally attest to that."

"The physical connection with another person generates a tremendous amount of energy. This power can heal, sooth, enlighten, or inspire. The demons stopped all forms of human contact. For many people, the isolation from lockdowns was nothing short of a death sentence. People with depression will suffer in silence," Cassian said.

Franklin looked down and shook his head. He said, "Are you an epidemiologist who knows about pandemics? You claim to have a degree in chemistry, but you sound like one of these anti-science people."

Cass said calmly, "Franklin, when you place a label like 'anti-science' on someone, you mentally categorize that person as someone who should not be listened to…should not be respected…and by virtue of your own semantic barrier…should be excluded from society and civility. You even called them '*these* anti-science people' as if they were an object to be ignored or eradicated.

"A common tactic the demons and Spurs use is to dehumanize entire groups of people so that great atrocities such as slavery, genocide, medical testing, and organ harvesting become acceptable in a culture.

"Does *anything* you heard about the last five years make sense with what you know to be true? Think back to the beginning. You are a scientist who knows chemistry, immunology, and biology. You have more than a cursory understanding of the adaptive immune system. You know the limitations of mRNA," Cassian pushed.

Franklin paused for a long time then said, "Well, there have been a lot of recent advances that I probably don't know about. I can't follow *everything*. I mean, science is constantly changing. I can barely stay current in my own field. And virology and immunology are not my field. I work with the structural determination of proteins, not the messenger RNAs that make them.

"The CDC, the WHO, all the experts in the US agencies—that you seem to dislike—were on ENN *and* BAS News…and everywhere else, telling us about what was going on. You think *you* can come in and erase all their absolute data? With what? Meme-ology from the university of social media? Don't be stupid, man. These are the people in *the know*! Who the hell are you?

"I'm sorry, Cass, but from what I can see, you're just a failed scientist. Maybe you're bitter about someone who shit on your work in the past and it drove you out of the lab."

"Yes, Franklin. I may be a failed scientist. But in my possession, I have the patents for the *production* of this current virus held by the *same* company that produced the preventive treatments…Abbadon Pharmaceuticals. If it's natural, it is illegal to patent it. That means that if it's patented, Abbadon—with government funding and approval—performed illegal research to produce viruses that transfer from animals into humans. It cannot be both ways.

"Don't count on the television or even most internet search engines. Both are programmed to show you *only* what they want you to see. You *must* rely on your own knowledge and alternative sources.

"All the organizations and high-ranking people involved in this pandemic can be traced back to Diobalst Bank. They are the primary banking industry practicing usury of debt since long before the feudal system was established. They control more than you can imagine. They don't merely fund wars. They *run* the wars! They subsidize both sides of every conflict and control the outcomes as easily as you control the volume on your radio.

"After banking, the media was the primary organization the demons began to manipulate. Once they could sway society, they began to wield immense power. These evil creatures use public outrage more effectively than any attack using weapons. By broadcasting claims against their enemy, the moral compass of the masses can be turned to villainize good people.

"Then, when the violence begins, you never hear about it. It's not just that they rewrite history…they destroy those who would write the truth. Their efforts are relentless. The Spurs and demons work against you. Constantly.

"You follow ENN. That's the Equitine News Network. Every competing major media organization, *including* BAS News, can be traced back to the Equitine Corporation.

"And who do you think owns Abbadon Pharmaceuticals? The Equitine Corporation. And who finances them? Diobalst Bank. And Diobalst controls everything! Well…almost everything.

"The media induced fear to turn people against one another. The real mastery they demonstrated was getting the scientifically competent people, like you, to defend their shifting positions. The public was screwed. They had no options other than to comply or lose their livelihood and be cast from society.

"The wealthy, the powerful, and the well-compensated celebrity fools under the thumb of demons kept constant pressure on the public. They only *pretended* to follow the same rules as everyone else. And sadly, people who trusted in these groups met with bitter ends.

"Their day is coming, Franklin. All who *knowingly* stood with the demons *will* have a reckoning.

"These injections from Abbadon and their affiliates killed so many people in the clinical trials. Why do you think they hold these trials in obscure and underregulated places like Africa and South America? It's so nobody knows what happens when they fail. Every person who died ended up *exactly* like the animals that died—dead, anonymous, and fucking *excluded* from the statistical results!" Cass said vehemently.

There was a long pause before Franklin said, "No. That is not true. You're talking about killing *millions* of people. They would never do that. I know people in my company who work in Africa. We don't do anything like that. We have standards that *must* be upheld! There are regulations and agencies in place to prevent what you are saying from happening. And these people do a lot of good over there. So, no. I *don't* believe you!"

Cass said, "You can't believe it because the idea of something this diabolic is beyond comprehension. You and most of the world as well. Good people cannot fathom such atrocities, especially at this scale. That's why nobody *wants* to believe it.

"I know that you, and probably most of the people you work with, are good, well-meaning folks who genuinely wish to improve the world. You do good things and help many people.

"Understand that a shiny public image is exactly the strategy of the Spurs. They always do *some* good and noble deeds that they foist into the public spotlight. People will *never* get to see the rest of what's happening. You are not aware of the Spurs around you and above you taking decisions out of your hands—in the name of marketing or safety or some other bullshit reason—always for 'the greater good' of the world."

Franklin looked deep in thought. He shook his head and said, "I don't know, Cass. I have my entire life and career in Abbadon. They do a lot of good in this world. You're telling me that the company I work for is evil? It's hard to swallow."

"Of course it's hard to swallow. You're only now beginning to see that it's a poison being fed to you your whole life. Their primary tactic is to get into the minds of children at an early age. This is exactly how they have separated science and religion. They start with children.

"It breaks my heart to see Equitine using television and the internet to subconsciously teach kids that their very existence is a detriment to the planet. It's sad that self-loathing, division, inequality, and exclusivity is being encouraged...completely *opposite* of what they espouse. They do everything they can to break up the family unit! This is the annihilation of *love*. This is evil. *And they are winning!*"

Franklin and Corrina sat for a few moments, absorbing what Cassian told them.

Franklin said, "I don't know, man. You start talking about God and stuff and you sound like the crazy preacher on the corner holding up a sign saying, 'The End Is Near.' Then you go against every major scientist in the world..."

"Not in the world, Franklin. Only in the ones they *show* in the media spotlight. Unelected officials after control, power, and wealth—like Abbadon, like Equitine, like Diobalst—determine *who* gets to be called a scientific expert. Don't conflate those organizations with the brave people seeking freedom. Many respected scientists are speaking out. But if you want to hear them, you have to look farther than your television.

"If you follow the money, you will begin to understand. Anyone on the inside ready to blow the whistle on Abbadon or Equitine is already *dead*. Those they couldn't kill, they labeled as crazy lunatics to be shunned. And with the power of media, they can turn society against someone in minutes…simply by using labels like 'anti-science'…much like you are trying to do to me.

"And as for God. Your mind needs to break free from the cage of language. I am only trying to show you the way. The rest is up to you."

Franklin shook his head and said, "Well, I saw on the news where…"

Cassian looked annoyed as he roared, "To hell with that bullshit news…*thiiiiink*!"

Both Franklin and Corrina shrank back in terror as the sound was not only deafening but painful.

Cassian saw their reaction and put his hand to his mouth as he said, "I am so sorry. I don't know if this is a power that Ex gave me or if it's something that woke from within me after my wreck. It could be part of the resonance thing I have. Sometimes when I am passionate about something, my voice takes on…a kind of power. It was like when I yelled at Chelsea. I don't know what it is.

"Do you have a neighbor who calls the police with noise complaints?"

Franklin said, "*Yes*. Mrs. Doubtfire two doors down."

"Her name is really Mrs. Doubtfire?" Corrina asked.

"No, no. It's…ahhh…Mrs.…ahhh…Johannes. She just looks like Robin Williams. She probably heard you yell and is calling the cops now."

"Do you want to call her and nip it in the bud?" Cassian asked.

"Yes. Give me a minute," Franklin said as he got up and got his phone off the charger.

"If the police come, we can deal with that later," Cass said to Corrina. "I guess we'll know if Franklin was going to have me removed or not."

"You need to control yourself, Cassian," she said.

"I am so sorry, Corrina. I never meant to frighten you."

CHAPTER 21

BAD DECISIONS

FRANKLIN WAS ON THE PHONE, "Yes, yes. I know it's late. I'm sorry Mrs. Johannes…Oh. Maria. Okay. I'm sorry, Maria. It won't happen again. My friend has a big mouth, and he just got carried away. Nothing bad going on. I promise. Oh. Okay. Well, I hope he's feeling better real soon. We should get together this summer and cook out. I do great steaks and margaritas! Well, of course. Even if he's not, I'll bring them over, and we can sit out on the back patio. Please send him my best," Franklin sounded so genuine.

When Franklin was done, Cass looked him in the eyes and said, "You are a good man, Franklin. That's not a question in my mind. You are more of a saint than I will ever be. But I need you to break out of this cage *you* created for your own mind. If you can break through just one of the barriers you built around your world to maintain the security of your life with Victoria, I know you are going to see the rest. I want you to think about the beginning of this. Don't be afraid. Think about what you *knew* was wrong." Cassian said, staring intensely at Franklin.

Franklin sat for a long moment, holding Cassian's gaze. Then he looked away and said, "Well, the death toll they kept putting up made no sense. I mean, they were acting like this was the Black Death. Aside from Victoria's uncle, I didn't know a single person who had anything worse than the usual flu. They kept talking about New York having so many deaths because of the population density. Boston is nearly as dense and that didn't happen here. If those deaths were all caused by the virus, every city with a similar population density would have been about the same. At least the *percent* would have been similar."

Cass said, "And no other city was close to the percent of deaths as New York. They didn't tell you about even more densely populated cities like Mexico City that fared far better. Keeping people indoors? Hardly anyone who stayed out in the sun ever died from this disease.

"Every measure they put in place was done to harm or control people. It was meant to break their ability to think for themselves. Then they break the family, they break the human spirit, and they stop creation.

"How many of your friends and family died in the pandemic?" Cassian asked.

"Victoria's uncle died. She fought with me about this, but he was old, overweight, and drank like a fish. I think a common cold would have killed him. But actually…nobody I know who was even moderately healthy died."

"How about after one of Abbadon's *preventive* treatments?" Cassian asked.

After a long moment, Franklin said, "There's always a risk. I mean…" Franklin stopped, sighed, and said, "But I do know a few people who died. My friend I used to play soccer with passed from a heart attack. Dude was in great shape too. One guy I work with has a kid in critical condition now following her recent booster. I know the husband of one of the administrators at work died of this crazy cancer in like five days after the diagnosis. She swears it happened two weeks after his third shot. But—"

"But what, Franklin?" Cassian asked. "These are the things I am telling you about. Athletes dropping dead on the field while the media normalizes it. Look at data from insurance companies. The percent of young people dying is statistically impossible. Then look at the new rates of certain rare diseases. It will shock you!

"They gaslit people to believe what their own eyes and ears deny. You must be extremely careful of what you believe."

They sat in silence for a minute before Franklin said, "Look, I don't want to think about this anymore. Why don't you get on with your story, Cassian. I want to know how you plan to bring Mary back into this whole thing."

Cass nodded as he looked between Franklin and Corrina, "So, there I was, standing in the doorway, talking to Chelsea…claiming she was *Mary*…"

———————

"What the fuck are you talking about, Chelsea?" Cassian asked, horrified. Only Zab and Clay knew about Mary. And even then, he left out most of the story. He never told Chelsea anything.

"Get in here, you clueless dumbass," she said.

Cassian's eye went wide as he quickly entered the apartment. Chelsea shut the door behind him. He turned to her, and she threw her arms around his head and started kissing him. The kiss lasted for nearly two minutes before Chelsea pushed away and said, "I can't believe you would start kissing some other girl like that!" she started slapping his arms.

"What the hell are you talking about? You kissed me!" Cass said.

"Oh, so you just start kissing back. Is that who you are? Some guy who sticks his tongue in the mouth of any chick that offers up her lips?" Chelsea said.

"Well…what…what the fuck am I…I don't know…*Mary*?" Cassian asked, confused.

"I'm just fucking with you, Cass!" Chelsea/Mary said excitedly and kissed him again, "I finally found you! I wasn't sure. It was fate that brought me here. Maybe Khalima helped or something. I kept picturing you in my mind."

"Mary?" Cass said seriously, "What do you mean you finally found me? How are you here at all?"

"You're angry with me that I'm *here*?" she asked, "I did all of this to be with you and *you* are pissed off at *me*?"

"No, no. I'm not pissed at you. Not at all. I mean…yes, I am! I am pissed at you, but not for the reason you think! I'm fucking thrilled that you're here! But why…how…are you here?" Cass said.

"Oh. Thank goodness," Chelsea/Mary said, "I started to feel so stupid."

"*How* are you here, Mary?" Cassian asked, looking at her quizzically, but dreading the answer he suspected.

"I don't know, Cass. All I can say is that it was a weird time. Barry was going to kill you. And I couldn't stop him. I didn't know what to do. Khalima told me to ask God for help. So, I did. Then…I don't know. Things got super weird for what seemed like a long time. But I can't be sure. Maybe I was dreaming. How long was I gone? You look different. Did you have a nose job or something?" Chelsea/Mary asked.

"Yes. I had to have surgery to fix my nose. I told you about that before you…before you were killed," Cass said. "Mary…that was like three years ago!" Cass said.

"Three years? Wow. It seemed like only a few weeks. Or maybe a few months. Like I said, it was a weird time."

"Is this really you, Mary?" Cassian asked, suddenly afraid that he may be getting tricked. "Where was our first date?"

"You mean my special *birthday* date, when I kicked your ass at bowling? That date? Or maybe our last date when I introduced you to Khalima after killing Dougy for you?" Chelsea/Mary said.

"Okay. It's you. But…how are you…why are you here…in *Chelsea*?" Cassian asked again.

"I was given a choice. I could have moved on. I was presented with many options. For some reason, I felt like I was getting the red-carpet treatment. They all made me feel like royalty. But how would I know. Maybe they treat everyone like that.

"Then I started to think about what Khalima told me…about when things look *too* good, and everyone is being *too* nice. She always said to be wary of those situations." Chelsea/Mary looked out the window and said, "I wanted to be like Khalima. You know, fight from the inside. She had the most amazing effect on my soul. I don't know, Cassian. I wanted to be able to do the same thing that she did for other women."

"Mary, please tell me what you did to be here…*in Chelsea*?" he demanded.

"Were you dating this girl, Cass?" Chelsea/Mary asked. "I wouldn't be angry. After all, I was dead, we were young, and it's been…three years?" She asked, astonished.

Cass nodded and said, "I wasn't dating her, though."

"She's super pretty, by the way…even if she is a bit plump. I don't know why she's been so depressed lately. She tried to kill herself, you know? But she's either not too committed or not too smart. She took a handful of aspirins. They made her puke like crazy.

"It's such a weird thing over there. Her soul popped up like a red flag. And I went after her. You know how I'm kind of competitive?"

"Kind of? You are competition incarnate. But you moderated it well," Cass said.

"Your vocabulary is getting better," Chelsea/Mary said, smiling. "I was a frickin' champ at this shit. They all swarmed on her. I swear it must be like a sperm to an egg. Everyone trying to get in…but…I easily won," Chelsea/Mary looked squarely at Cassian.

"Oh my God! What did I…" Cass paused, thinking about what he did. He made Chelsea want to kill herself. That was horrible. But it brought Mary back to him. So that must mean that…"You're a Spur! What the fuck, Mary! You chose to be a fucking Spur?"

"Does it feel better to yell and tell the whole fucking building?" Chelsea/Mary said calmly.

Cass pulled her to him and hugged her saying, "I wanted you back more than you could *ever* know, but not like this, Mary. This means you condemned yourself to Hell. I would never want that for you. Not ever! I love you and wanted you to be happy…in your next life."

"Oh, you are so sweet. But you're not getting rid of me that easily," she said. "Now tell me about this girl before I let her up and start talking to her. This is kind of cool. Is this what you've been able to do to people? I can feel her panicking down there. I feel a little bad, but she'll be fine. I'm not hurting her or anything."

"Cassian," Ex said, in Cassian's mind, "you need to tell her that she is harming this girl by keeping her locked away. It is a torturous existence for any extended period of time."

"Ex says that what you are doing is bad for her mind. She said that Chelsea will suffer when you keep her trapped like that for a long time," Cass said.

"What Ex said? Who cares about what Ex says. It never stopped any angels from letting their shrouded trap people like that!" Chelsea/Mary said.

Cassian paused for a moment then said, "Well, Ex? What about that?"

Ex said, "The power I extend to you gives you the ability to temporarily possess people."

"But you said I could do that as long as I wanted. Isn't that the same thing?" Cass asked.

"Yes," Ex said, "but you could never do it indefinitely without being noticed by the Spurs and demons. This has happened at times in history and has always ended in massive tragedy. Some who are shrouded make deals with demons to stay out of the conflict. They live decadent and hedonistic lifestyles. They abuse the body they are in but must stay in the body to keep it from killing itself. They eventually hit a point of such regret that they *beg* God for help. But at that point, it is too late.

"Do you recall the Guyana tragedy in Jonestown? Jim Jones was possessed by a shrouded who worked with the demons. He had sex with young women, did all types of drugs, he abused the power he was given. The demons loved it. He thought he could live like this forever. Forces of good finally caught up with him. Eventually, he chose to kill his congregation along with himself. The worst part about the whole incident is that the shrouded walked away without consequence."

"Jim Jones is still alive?" Cass exclaimed. "Why couldn't you or the angels stop him? You gave him the power!"

"The soul that possessed Jim Jones still lives today. We give the power, Cassian. We do not interfere with creation. I am forbidden to moderate the power I give you or any shrouded. I can sit in judgment of your actions and can tell you my beliefs based on what I know, but what you do with it must derive from you.

"Chelsea is not shrouded, she is possessed. Mary can keep this soul in the dark forever. As long as she does not keep her bound for extended periods, Chelsea should suffer very little. Think of it like being bound about your chest in the dark and you need to catch a breath—but cannot."

"That sounds absolutely horrible, Ex!" Cass said.

"I could not tell you, Cassian. I have never needed to breathe. That would be like me telling you what birth is like without ever having had a vagina," Ex said.

Cass sighed and said to Chelsea/Mary, "Ex said you have to let her out so she doesn't get fucked up in the head. It's like holding her in the dark and not letting her breathe."

"That is not what I said, Cassian. Do not misrepresent what I say," Ex said.

Cass corrected, "I'm paraphrasing what Ex said. She never said *that*."

Without realizing it, Cass looked down and to the right and quietly said to Ex, "Is that okay? I took credit for the profanity."

"Acceptable," Ex said.

"Didn't Khalima ever hold you in the dark after you let her in?" Cassian asked.

"Not really. I was almost always there with her. It was great. It was like having your best friend with you all the time. I really miss her. So, what are you saying, Cass? I have to let her up to speak?" Chelsea/Mary asked.

"Yeah. I think so. It's the right thing to do. I mean, Chelsea was kind of a bitch. She acted nice, but her true colors came out when she was drunk. She was so mean to one of the girls she pretended to be friends with. I thought I could bring her some humility. I made her eat and drink at night. She kept exercising more and more but kept getting fatter and fatter. I didn't mean for it to go this far."

Chelsea/Mary slapped his arms several times and said, "Cassian! That's a devious and terrible thing to do." Then she laughed and said, "But really funny too! That's something Khalima would have done. Alright. Later, after you go, I'll let Chelsea up and tell her the whole story and her situation. But I chose this existence for a lot of reasons, Cass. I will do what I need to do. Don't be angry with me."

"Too late. I'm already angry with you." Then he grabbed her and kissed her again. "But I could never stay mad at you!"

CHAPTER 22

DOTI

THE NILGRADMA SAT BEHIND HIS sphere with Doti seated across from him.

"Tell me, Doti, why do you find it necessary to initiate trouble with Illoc?"

"I mean no disrespect to you, headmaster, but I find the motivations of Illoc to be self-serving. I fear that he may be—"

"I know what you think," said the NilGradMa. "I did not get to this position by not understanding the politics, particularly within the Acera stewards." He sounded sad as he said, "We are so far advanced in our knowledge yet the venom in the soul forever plagues our own self-serving needs. Can you not feel that within yourself?"

"I suppose I do," said Doti.

NilGradMa looked at him and said, "I am glad to hear you say that. If you did not, I would worry about you."

"Well, I wonder if Illoc—" Doti started.

"Enough about Illoc," the NilGradMa said. "He is of little consequence to you right now. He is a loudmouth with an obvious agenda. He will not be here much longer. Stewards like that always show who they are. Do you know that I asked him the same question? Would you like to know what he said?"

"Yes, sir. I would," said Doti.

The NilGradMa began to chuckle as he said, "Allow me to quote: '*Feel*, sir, is such an ambiguous term. I believe the venom of the soul is an extremely nuanced aspect of Space-Time qualia and requires further study as our teams are…blah…blah…blah.' He spoke far too long for such a simple question. That was when I knew. I do not want you to provoke him. Give him the rope he needs to hang himself. Do you understand?"

"Of course, I do, sir," Doti said. "But I believe one of the Grad stewards is help—"

"Silence, Doti," came the powerful command. "You need not say anything. I know more than anyone in this place. And the comment you made about Tinilfasela is very apt. That young steward will certainly be a Grad steward if he does not replace me when I move on.

"I am placing you under IllGrad instead of SolGrad. I believe you both have the best interest of the resonant in common."

"Thank you, sir," Doti said.

"That is not a promotion, Doti. IllGrad is as much of a pain in the ass as you are. You may go now. No more confrontations with Illoc. Do I make myself clear?"

"Yes, sir," Doti wore a smile as he walked out of the room.

He was surprised to see IllGrad sitting at one of the tables outside of the room. He approached his new advisor.

On the surface of the table, the images of the three major realms of existence, Time, Space, and Ukra (consciousness) were represented as hexagons connected in a triangular arrangement. They spun around a central axis. Inside of each larger hexagon of existence sat the three split realms of the electric, magnetic, and gravity, also represented as hexagons spinning around their central hub of True Light.

Seeing these maps always made Doti feel bad for the great lie the stewards have passed to those in their Ukra realm. He understood the need to keep this from them, but as an Acera steward, he struggled with his desire to teach and explain complexities.

They had to allow each existence in the split realms to believe they are encompassed within something tangible. If those in the realm of consciousness could see that Space-Time was only *observed* by their realm, they may fall into the insanity of the infinite.

It was difficult enough to get many to understand that their reality was only a fraction of True Light where observations of the other two aspects allowed for interaction.

"Sit down, Doti," said IllGrad, "it is time for us to have a talk."

"Yes, sir," Doti said, sitting across from him.

"You can stop all the 'sir' shit, Doti. You are seventeenth. You've been in the stewards longer than me. By now I am sure you know that you will never be a Grad steward. You lack the temperament. At least, you lack the discretion to keep your temperament in check," IllGrad said.

"That is no surprise to me. I no longer have a desire to move to that level. But the NilGradMa has now moved me under you," Doti said.

"Yes, I know. We were planning this for a while. Something is going on. Something major with the shrouded of the resonant, Tinilfasela."

"Something like what?"

"Only two of us know the identity of the shrouded, Tinilfasela and me. We know about Kebra and the communications Illoc has had with at least one demon, Oriax. This was the year Tinilfasela sat in defense of the body as it was being shrouded.

"We know Illoc gave them what we knew…the general location. This provided a foot up for the demons who happened to be operating in the same area. I assume that was why God put his angel there.

"Oriax had the demons Corson and Pruflas trap the angel using a Tolaxnarm device. Oriax wanted to remove the angel and take the body for another demon. We don't know which one. But we know one of the stewards helped them with the device.

"Somehow, the shrouded escaped. He first banished Corson, then managed to dispatch Pruflas then Oriax. And I do mean what I said. They no longer number among the Seraphim," IllGrad said.

"He killed them?! How did he manage this? The angels have no power to exterminate other Seraphim," Doti said.

"Yes, well, this one is special. I will tell you more in a bit.

"But as for Illoc, we know he is betraying the stewards. We need to keep quiet until we find out what he is attempting to do. So, you will be the perfect one for this task."

Doti said, "You should know something. When I passed Illoc, after publicly calling him out as a traitor, I whispered 'Kebra' to him. He knows that I hate him."

"Why did you do that?" IllGrad asked.

"I wanted to wipe that smug look off his face," Doti said.

"That is what I am talking about, Doti. Temperament *and* discretion. Both seem beyond your capacity. Believe it or not, your public actions will make you the perfect steward for this."

"How so?" Doti asked.

IllGrad said, "Because you are going to offer him something he wants.

"Now, I credit you for your bravery and honesty. So, I am going to ask something of you that requires great bravery to go against everything in your nature. Are you up for this task?"

"Yes, IllGrad, I can do it. What is it you need me to do?"

"I know Tinilfasela quite well. A long time ago, I found him to be an intelligent and highly conscious soul. Do you know that he has been in communication with one of your recent Karma stewards, Unfamiqua?"

"I would not be doing my duties if I didn't know that," Doti said.

"Do you know what they discussed?" IllGrad asked.

"That is information I do not have. I know his Bilved steward is Reynilmi and his Karma steward is Tidorey. Should I ask one of them?" Doti asked.

"It was rhetorical. I already know. I believe Unfamiqua knows the identity of the shrouded. She arranged with the resonant to open a portal. Illoc is correct. That was forbidden. However, these are only rules that we have agreed upon. Not God, the serpent, or the Seraphim have influence over that. The Builders allow us to act as long as we properly use the Desemilnoct. What was done for the shrouded has been deemed a balancing action following the betrayal by Illoc."

"What did they send through the portal? And what else did Illoc do to betray them?" Doti asked.

IllGrad said, "A Cysistal stone was sent. I do not know to where it was opened. The fewer who know that information the better. As far as I know, only Tinilfasela knows since Unfamiqua is not permitted to know the location or identity of the shrouded.

"As for what Illoc did, the full extent is yet to be determined. We know about what he did with Oriax. We also know he has a means of tracking a soul in Limbo. I want your help in uncovering what Illoc is planning.

"You are going to make an alliance with Illoc. Not only that, but this will not be an illusion. You will align yourself with his goals *and* his plot. You are also going to follow through with the betrayal to our kind and the resonant," IllGrad said.

"Illoc will never believe that I am going to help him. Even if he did, he would be suspicious of me," Doti said.

"You will be giving him something he desperately needs for his plan to succeed. Something only Tinilfasela and I are supposed to know—the identity and location of the shrouded. When Illoc has that, the demons will be able to attack him. Tinilfasela and Unfamiqua will do what they can to keep him alive. If he survives, we will help him. We have agreed to grant him access to the first book," IllGrad said.

"Why do we need to do this? Why should we place the shrouded in this situation?" Doti argued.

IllGrad said, "We will then know how Illoc is tracking a soul in Limbo and which demons he is working with. Most importantly, we will have the evidence required to remove him from our ranks.

"But there is one caveat. You and Illoc must be put out together. You will both leave in disgrace. But God will know of your sacrifice. That is all that matters. Are you prepared to leave the stewards?" IllGrad asked.

"I do not...I cannot...No," Doti said angrily. "I am not prepared to do that. With all due respect to you and the order...no. I will do no such thing."

"What I am asking of you is beyond any request ever made of a steward. Especially an Acera level steward. But the only way to make this believable to the entire body of stewards is for this to be done by an-other Acera level steward. Illoc and you. Your public altercation makes this even more realistic.

"I have no other options. And I will not simply throw you to the wolves without your consent. That may be how Illoc and his kind behave, but not how we are to act in a civilized world," IllGrad said.

Doti looked around as if searching for a means of escape. IllGrad said, "Let me explain further what is needed. I will give you a span to consider this. You will have time to prepare. Those you care for will despise you...for a time. Arrangements will be made to honor and retire your name. But that will be long after you are gone from our ranks. I am deeply sorry."

"I need to know more about this before I will agree to anything. This could get the shrouded killed," Doti said solemnly. "Why would we risk doing that?"

IllGrad nodded and said, "Illoc has been in contact with Semjaza since the death of Oriax. You know the implications of that action. They are after this shrouded. Not to kill him, but to remove the angel. They want him. He has a power that is unlike any other shrouded in history. It seems as if he can interact with other life to destroy or amplify the resonance frequencies of another being."

Doti said, "But that power exists only with the Builders and high angels and demons. He could—"

IllGrad interrupted, "We have no idea what the limits of his power are. I believe this is what allowed him to kill two demons.

"The demons want him desperately. Can you now see why there is so much urgency to uncover this plot? If they were to gain access to his power, they could destroy angels. They could do much damage to the Ukra gravitational realm. The balance would swing far to the side of order. The cascade of events would be devastating. It could even affect Time and Space in ways that will further harm our existence. Even allowing the angels to have this creature seems abominable.

"Naturally, the demons feel that if they cannot have him, he must die. This plot is more likely to end up in his death rather than his capture. Were it up to me, I would let them kill him. He poses a greater risk than any Nephilim.

"But he has been chosen by God. We must assist him, and we are *not* to cause him direct harm. I will interpret that as loosely as needed to keep him out of the hands of the demons. If this involves destroying him, so be it. They came dangerously close to collecting him in the past."

"How do you know this? Aren't the Tinilfasela resonant records still sealed?" Doti asked.

"Of course. They will remain so until the shrouded passes from that realm. But Tinilfasela must still report to the NilGradMa.

"It is terrifying to think that they nearly succeeded. We did not know about his power then. I know Illoc was trying desperately to find him before he was shrouded. Whether or not Illoc knew of this ability beforehand, I don't know. That would be a surprise to me. How would they have known? But I know Illoc was trying to predict the shrouding process so he could feed that back to the demons."

Doti said, "I have a wild theory. Is it possible that they may have allies in the Space existence to show them the Time-Ukra continuum? They could then see the pathways to the future?"

IllGrad shook his head, "No. This is *utterly* forbidden. No point of consciousness can be allowed that type of hysteresis. God sits between these existences to prevent such occurrences. Fear not. The Space and Time existences remain constant.

"As for this shrouded, there may be prophecies that foretold of his coming. But you know the language of prophecy. It is written with such wide error margins that interpretations only sound reasonable after the event. What can you expect from ancient text written on a Dese scroll? It may have been made two or three trillion Earth years ago, long before the last galactic cycling of the Time, Space, and Ukra realms. Only information held within Dese survives that kind of catastrophic reset," IllGrad said.

"Have we heard any news of sort from our counterparts in the Space or Time existences?" Doti asked.

"No," IllGrad shook his head and said, "Doti, the truth is, we have never contacted any lifeform from the Space or Time existence. The story of these counterpart stewards is untrue. It was created to support the theory of consciousness as a separate dimension."

Doti looked shocked and said, "All the time spent studying these areas is wasted? This is—"

"Stop," IllGrad interrupted, "I never said they do not exist. And the research is not wasted. The models and theories all point to there being three separate existences. It is just that we cannot relate to any lifeform from an existence like that. How would you communicate with one from the Space existence where time and consciousness are all they perceive? Can you fathom such a world?"

"I suppose not. I have tried to map what they would experience, but it is beyond my grasp," Doti said.

"As I believe it is meant to be. I have no doubt that they exist. I believe that God has intended to keep these existences separated for the very reason you outlined in your theory."

Doti looked dejected and said, "So, my theory is not wrong, just impossible?"

"I'm afraid so. But now you can see that even as advanced as we like to believe we are, we still have much to learn.

"I don't know what is coming, Doti. We may be at one of those apocalyptic times foretold. I also know how you feel about prophecy. And for the most part, I agree with you. This is not a reliable source. But something in my soul is telling me to be vigilant. I am being drawn to one prophecy in particular."

IllGrad reached into his chest pocket and pulled out a small tablet. "I want you to read this," IllGrad said.

Doti read the text:

When contrition shadows life for the favor[a] of humanity

the purpose of existence will diminish

and the weak shall fall prey to the banished.

From depths of despair will arise a champion

brimming with doubt and question.

In his wake, an end to faith shall occur

and a new purpose will arise.

Convergence[b] of old and new will destroy knowledge[c].

In this destruction, a great apocalypse will prevail.

Power from the Earth, discovered again

will show the commanders their futility[d].

The tenets[e] of God shall be recast

and all souls will begin anew.

So it once was, so it shall be again.

-The metal scrolls of Fe Ultrenbard

[a] May also be advantage, rationalization, or sole reason

[b] May be confrontation or centralization

[c] May be false erudition or dogma

[d] Could be inane, weakness, or frailty

[e] May be laws or design

The writing was clearly a rough transcription with many controversial phrases. Doti said, "I know this prophecy from our third book. Do you believe that this is about the current shrouded on Earth?" Doti asked.

"Tinilfasela feels certain that this is about the shrouded he resonates with. Read it again, Doti. Look at what is happening. They found Dese, and their leaders are hiding it from the people."

IllGrad put a hand on his head and rubbed his face, then said, "I will support God, but I am not certain what to do here. What if *our* knowledge is being threatened. Am I to protect our knowledge at any cost? As I swore to do? Or is this a prophecy about *their* elementary knowledge? Whatever it means, I believe their world is about to undergo a great change. And possibly ours as well."

Doti read the script several times as they sat in silence. Then he said, "I am with you. Tell me what you want me to do, IllGrad."

CHAPTER 23

LOSS OF CONTROL

"Everyone thought that Chelsea and I had begun dating," Cassian said. "This came as a surprise to my friends. Especially Jen, who, at that point, knew Chelsea hated her. I did a lot of fast damage control. And with Mary driving Chelsea, her personality won over most of them within a couple weeks.

"Imagine how malleable the minds of the people are!" Cass said. "For three weeks, they were happy watching Chelsea get fat. Two weeks later, they were all friends with her. Of course, back then, three weeks seemed like several months now. But in reality, things were happening very fast."

"You were dating Mary, who was possessing the body of Chelsea?" Corrina asked.

"Yes. In the back of my mind, I knew that Chelsea was there, but I was beyond happy with how my life was going. In such a short time, Mary and all my friends got along fantastically. I was with one of the most beautiful girls in school…you don't need to point out the vanity of that statement. This was one of the best times in my life. It may have only lasted for about a month, but it seems like a decade in my mind. So many good memories packed into that brief period."

"Well, what happened with Chelsea?" Corrina pushed.

Cassian looked at her for a moment, then said, "You are a good person, Corrina. That is the question I should have been asking. What I am going to tell you next is part of an investigation that is still ongoing in Pittsburgh. Of the terrible things I have done…this is, by far, the worst.

"Mary and I, before she died, never had…um…sex," Cass said.

"What?" Franklin said. "You were head over heels for this girl, but you never had sex with her? Maybe you *were* taking girls home by 10 p.m. and kissing them on the cheek."

Cass looked at him and said, "I told you before…too much TV and movies. I didn't have girlfriends when I grew up. I had this…I don't know…dramatic, romantic image in my mind about my love with Lynn and then later with Mary. I'm not going to ignore my feelings now because society or experience deems this to be juvenile. I still feel these strong feelings of love. And yes, just from kissing a girl."

"I understand, Cassian. I think it's sweet of you," Corrina said.

"Thank you, Corrina. Maybe sweet, but in retrospect, very stupid. Ex had warned me of the problems with pursuing a relationship with Mary, now that she was a Spur. But Ex could also not stop me. And *woe* to those who come between a young couple in love.

"I was a fool not to listen to Ex. I should have stopped Mary. I don't mean that to diminish romance, but where it led me is something…unimaginable," Cass said.

"I don't know about that. After what you told us already, I can imagine a lot," Franklin said.

Cass chuckled and said, "I have barely scratched the surface. Wait.

"Mary and I were doing everything together. And eventually…"

Cass and Mary were studying in the Cathedral of Learning just after midnight. Mary was sitting on his right side as he was trying to explain a calculus problem he was stuck on. As he held his pencil in his right hand, trying to explain the problem, Chelsea/Mary slowly began to run her tongue up his forearm. Cass turned to look at her as she stared into his eye. The pencil fell from his hand. He grabbed her head and started to kiss her. They quickly packed their belongings and practically ran to Chelsea's room.

It was the most amazing and sensual encounter Cass had ever experienced. Chelsea/Mary and Cass made love several times until they were both exhausted.

As they lie in bed together in the wee hours of the morning, Chelsea/ Mary said, "That's the one thing I always regretted before I died. I always wanted to be with you. The way I knew you were with Lynn."

"I hope you don't…" Cass started.

"No," Mary said. "No, I don't care about that. I'm not stupid. I always wanted you to be mine. And I finally got you. I'm so happy," she rolled her nude body on top of him and began kissing him again.

They began to sleep together in her room every night. He wasn't going to classes or labs, and neither was Chelsea. Clay and Zab had to pull him away a few times to go to class.

One day, when Cass came back to his room to shower and get dressed, Clay said, "Cass, what are you doing right now?"

"What do you mean? I'm getting dressed. Ma…Chelsea and I are going to Frick Park for a walk," Cass said. "It's a beautiful day! You want to come?"

"That's not what I mean, Cass. And you know it. What the fuck are you doing? You are in college. I've been your roommate for almost three years. I know you. As much as you may fuck around with Zab, and party too much on the weekends, nobody takes this shit more serious than you. Suddenly, you're all like 'Fuck it! I got Chelsea!' This isn't you. I really think you have a problem," Clay said.

"What? What are you talking about, dude?" Cass said. "Are you jealous because I'm with Chelsea?"

"No. Honestly, Cass…I'm happy for you. I really am. But I know you aren't going to class. Shit, even one of your professors asked *me* where the fuck you've been when I was up in the Chevron Building. I told him you were having some family problems. But dude, you have got to pull your head out of *her* ass for one minute and look around."

The comment slapped Cassian across the face as he remembered Malcom telling him the same thing about Lynn. But it also enraged him. "What the hell are you talking about, Clay? Like you wouldn't have your head up her ass if you could! I'll get my shit done. You just worry about what you're doing and let me worry about me!"

"Cass, I'm not telling you this to be a dick. You are fucking up! Big time fucking up! I am watching you self-destruct. I'm trying to help you because you're my friend!" Clay was almost yelling.

"Oh, fuck off, Clay. You don't know the half of it. What we had to do to be together. Wait until you find the girl you want. Then you can tell me if it's any different when you're in the same boat. But you'll never be in the boat I'm in. None of you will. You could never understand!" Cass yelled.

Clay wore an angry scowl and said, "I don't even know who the *fuck* you are. Go. Go run to your little fuck doll down the hall. Go marry the bitch for all I care. But don't come crying to me in six months when she's banging some other guy because you don't bring enough attention to her."

Cass squared off with Clay and said, "You wanna…" A strong wave hit Cass. He knew Ex pushed calmness into him. Cass nodded and said, "You'll wanna keep that kind of talk to yourself in the future, Clay."

Cassian turned and walked out of the room.

"I didn't know that was going to be the last time I ever spoke with Clay," Cass said as a tear spilled from his eye. "He was one of the best friends I ever had. I really miss him. And the worst part is, it was me who killed him. Only Zab and Keith survived what happened next." Cass couldn't control the tears.

"I remember this now!" Corrina said, "The Pitt dormitory massacre. I almost forgot that. I read about it in the news years ago. That was you?!"

"No. Not really *me*. But I was certainly responsible for all those people dying. The way I understand it is that it was all a loophole in the laws. It had to do with the way Mary died and then *chose* to become a Spur. The memories weren't erased. Some of the stewards betrayed us. They…followed her. I think they watched her and made it easy for her to find the one she was looking for. To find the shrouded who killed three demons.

"Let me tell you something…and listen good. Demons do *not* play around. They will kill everyone. And they will do it in the worst possible way you can think of," Cass said, sniffling as he wiped the tears from his eye.

"Cassian," Franklin asked, with genuine sympathy in his voice, "what happened to Mary and Chelsea?"

Cass took a deep breath to get himself under control.

"I went to the park with Mary…"

It was a truly beautiful day. Beautiful like September 11, 2001. Once Cassian was with Chelsea/Mary, everything with Clay was water under the bridge in his mind. He was the epitome of happiness as he walked holding her hand.

At one point, on an isolated stretch of the trail, a mugger popped out of the woods with a knife and demanded Cassian give up his wallet. Chelsea/Mary and Cass looked at each other and started to laugh.

When the mugger came at Cassian with the knife, he jumped into the man.

Cass/mugger flung the knife far into the woods and said, "What should I do with him now?"

Chelsea/Mary looked around and said, "Pull his pants down around his ankles and throw him over the slope right over there, into that patch of poison ivy."

"Okay!" Cass/mugger said, smiling. He pulled the pants down to his ankles, stood on the edge of the slope, facing the trail and said, "Underwear up or down?"

"Down," Chelsea/Mary said. "He was the one with the knife ready to kill you."

"Good point," Cass/mugger said as he slid the underwear down around his ankles and jumped backward over the hill.

Cass popped back into himself. As they continued walking, they heard the man screaming, "Ahhh…it's poison ivy! What the fuck! What did you do to me you fuckin' freak!"

They both laughed as they listened to him scrambling to get back to the path.

After the walk, they went to Uncle Sam's Subs and had mushroom cheesesteak subs. They practically floated back to Chelsea's dorm room. It was a nearly perfect day.

They made their way to the bedroom to complete the perfect day. It was the most incredible session of love Cass had ever experienced. And then it happened.

When Cassian climaxed, he lost all control. The room burst into a brilliant white light. The perspective of the room changed and before Cass could do anything, the white sword came down on Chelsea's neck. The whole room shook.

CHAPTER 24

SO THAT HAPPENED

Horrified, Cassian opened his eyes and looked down into his own face, angrily staring up at him. He could feel the body of Chelsea and what was inside her.

Ex spoke, "Very nice, Cassian. Is this something you have often dreamt about? Having intercourse with yourself?"

"What!?" Cass/Chelsea screamed, "What did you do, Ex!?" as he threw Chelsea's body from on top of his own naked body.

"I can assure you, Cassian, that I did nothing. You, on the other hand, lost control of your power. I am afraid that you have inadvertently banished Mary to Hell," Ex said.

"What!? What? Why… How… What the fuck! Come on, Ex. Reverse it or something!" Cass/Chelsea yelled.

"Reverse it? This is not a game of billiards. I cannot re-rack the balls. There are no do-overs or mulligans. There is nothing I can do. I have been trying to warn you. How many times have I told you that your power is exceptional? Remember the nurse that was covered in *your* feces? I told you that you need to keep a strong hold on your power," Ex/Cass said.

"But Mary. What? You banished her to Hell!" Chelsea/Cass yelled.

"She *was* a Spur, Cass. This *is* what the power is intended to do," Ex/Cass said.

Cass/Chelsea began to punch Ex/Cass. Each blow hurt his own face. Ex used Cassian's body to grab her arms and said, "Cassian, think about what you are doing. Each hit will produce a bruise on the body you are now occupying. It will appear as if *you* have been beating Chelsea."

Cass/Chelsea stopped and sat back in the bed. Then said, "What the fuck am I going to do now, Ex? Why didn't you stop me? Couldn't you stop it?"

"I have told you, I cannot stop you from using your power. Ever. It is yours and yours alone. I can only give you advice…which I did."

"Shut the fuck up, Ex! I don't need a fucking lecture right now. What the fuck! I have to get Mary out of Hell!" Cass/Chelsea said.

"You need to think about what you are going to do with Chelsea. If you came home right now, this girl would believe that you raped her. You have many options. But we have no idea how much information Mary may have provided Chelsea. Perhaps Chelsea was part of this and may love you as well. You will find out soon enough. My suggestion would be to clean and dress this girl and tell her that she was possessed and that you were able to save her. Like any other Spur. We will heal her mind," Ex said.

Cass/Chelsea put a pillow over her face and screamed, "Fuuuuck!"

"Enough, Cassian. You are one of the shrouded. You need to toughen yourself. We need to think about what to do next. In your life, that is always the case. The question of what your next step is should dominate your mind. Now, let us make a plan."

Cass/Chelsea looked at Ex/Cass and said, "How do you propose this next step will look, Ex? What am I supposed to do? I just sent Mary to *Hell*! I've never been there, but I hear the reviews are terrible. What am I going to do?"

"I have some ideas," Ex/Cass said. "Would you like to hear them?"

"I am one giant ear, asshole! Just speak!" Cass/Chelsea said.

"There is no need for insults or foul language, Cassian. This is simply another hurdle you will face in life. And it will not even be the worst. You need to consider the larger picture and the implications you will face in the next two to three days. Mary is in Hell…yes. But she is safely there and not going anywhere. You, on the other hand, could face many problems if you do not compose yourself and, as the saying goes, get your shit together."

Cass/Chelsea said, "I believe that is the first time I have ever heard you swear."

"The word *shit* is like any other semantic term. It refers to excrement. Just as the term *angel* refers to a Seraphim. The word is just a word here. The linguistic context is what provides any emotional meaning. Only sounds spoken in the True Light realm have the power to change things," Ex/Cass said.

"What? What's that supposed to mean? True Light?"

"It means that any word I speak here is merely a sound. How that sound is interpreted depends on the physical or emotional context. Just as if I said Bhagavan. To *you*…it means nothing. But to others in your world, this is the holy name of God."

Chelsea's face wrinkled up as Cass/Chelsea said, "Ex, I don't need a lesson on words right now. You said you had ideas of what to do next. Let's start with those!"

"As I said before, clean this girl up. Wash your odor from her and—"

"What? My odor? Do I stink or something?" Cass/Chelsea said.

"Yes, Cassian. You all have a unique scent. Every person has a *very* specific odor. Just because you cannot detect it does not mean it is not present. Sometimes, identical twins have a similar smell, but there is always something that can distinguish them.

"You need to scrub every square inch of this girl of your scent. You have done much together recently, so wash her very well," Ex/Cass said.

"You make this sound like a crime scene," Cass/Chelsea said.

"By any standards of your law, if Chelsea were to step into her own body at this moment, *you* would be the epicenter of the crime scene. Do you understand what I am telling you? Clean her, now."

Franklin's mouth hung open as he said, "Oh my God, bro! You took 'go fuck yourself' to a whole new level!" He started to laugh.

Neither Cassian nor Corrina joined in the mirth.

Cassian began in a solemn tone, "I got into the shower and scrubbed her clean, the best way I could," he stopped as he put his head in his hands. "I came out and dressed her in comfortable clothes from her drawers. Things I never saw her wear when Mary…was in her. Then I flipped back…"

———————

Chelsea began to take massive breaths of air and then she screamed, "Aaahhhh!"

"It's okay, Chelsea. I've got you. You're free," Cass said as he placed his hands on her head. The white light flowed down his arms like every other time a Spur was freed.

"Cassian! How are you here?" Chelsea said through tears.

"You were possessed by something called a Spur, Chelsea. I am shrouded by an angel that was able to free you," Cass said without his usual feeling of satisfaction.

"Oh, thank God for you! I was stuck in the dark, Cassian! It only let me up for a little bit here and there. You saved me!" Chelsea said as she threw her arms around his neck.

She hugged him so tightly as the tears ran down her face. Chelsea said, "I'm so sorry for what I ever did to bring this on me. I'm so sorry for being such a bitch," she cried. "I was awful to people. I was awful to you," she said as she pulled back from Cassian.

She leaned forward slightly, and he thought that she was going to kiss him. After the last few weeks with Chelsea/Mary, he was expecting it. He leaned in for the kiss.

Chelsea jumped back, "Cass! What are you doing?! Did you think I was going to kiss you? I'm really sorry. You're a good guy, and I really like you and all, but not like that. I hope you can understand."

Cassian's mind was whirling. He just had the best sex of his life with this girl and now she couldn't stand the idea of kissing him.

"Oh. No. Nothing like that, Chelsea. I mean, sure, you're pretty and all," Cass stumbled, "but I have a girlfriend. Mary. You never met her. Did you?"

"Mary? No. I'm sure you don't have a girlfriend, Cass. What are you talking about?" Chelsea said. "How long was I…like that?"

Ex said in Cassian's head, "Do you think that she is not going to find out that you were dating her? Everyone saw you together constantly, you fool. Why did you bring up Mary? End this conversation immediately, before you say anything else that could incriminate you."

"Incrimi…" Cassian paused, flustered by what Ex was saying. "What's the last thing you remember?"

"I remember I started having these terrible dreams after I…never mind," she said, blushing. "I went to sleep and, in my dream, this creature said it could help me. Help me lose weight and get—"

"It's okay, Chelsea. I don't think you were away too long," Cass felt the stab of guilt at driving her to this, and he genuinely softened to her. "I…uh…I had the same thing happen to me. The nightmares. They started after I tried to kill myself."

Chelsea's face contorted and she began to cry. Cass put an arm around her and said, "It's okay. Really, it is. If you ever have a dream like that again, never let anyone in."

"I won't. Cassian, it was so awful. I never want to experience that again. I am so sorry. I'm going to change. I've been such a self-centered bitch. When I was trapped, I swore that if I ever got free, I would apologize to everyone I was mean to," she said.

Ex said, "Tell her that she was dating you."

"Okay," Cass said, "There's something I need to tell you, Chelsea. I was lying about having a girlfriend. Ummm…you and I…well…we've been dating each other for the last few weeks."

"What?" Chelsea said, mildly shocked, "When did we…I mean… oh. Did we…"

"When a Spur takes a person," Cass explained, "they make them do things to make their life terrible and hurt other people."

"So…the Spur was using me to hurt you? I'm sorry, Cass. I didn't know," Chelsea said.

"No. Do not apologize for what a Spur did. It has nothing to do with you…or me. I will be okay. But you need to know since everyone thinks we are a couple," Cass said.

Chelsea's face turned red as she said, "Oh, God! Maybe people will think I was—" she stopped abruptly and looked away from Cass.

"Think you were what?" Cassian asked.

"I'm sorry, Cass. That was the old me talking. I was going to say something terrible…about dating a crippled person," she said.

Cass felt the sharp sting of that statement. That's how Chelsea saw him. As someone who was handicapped or deformed.

Seeing the look on his face, Chelsea backpedaled, "But I don't feel that way anymore. Not really. You're such a great guy."

Ex said, "We need to get away from here for a while. Go home or somewhere else for two or three weeks until all the questions fade away. People will forget quickly."

"I can go to…" Cass started to say aloud and then stopped.

"Go where?" Chelsea asked.

"I think I should probably go, Chelsea. I'm glad I was able to help you," Cass said woodenly. He knew he deserved this kind of treatment after what he did, but it still hurt to think people thought of him this way.

He stood and started walking toward the door.

Chelsea said, "Thank you, Cassian. I am truly in your debt."

"You don't owe me anything, Chelsea. I'm sorry I didn't do something sooner. I'm going to go. I'll see you around, okay."

"Yeah, I'll see you around. Maybe we can have lunch or something this week," Chelsea said.

"That'd be great," Cass said as he opened the dormitory door and walked out.

"Wow. The way I see it, you got out of that pretty easy, Cass," Franklin said.

"You did deserve it, Cass," Corrina said angrily. "You made that girl apologize to *you* for what you did to her in the first place!"

"I didn't get out of shit, Franklin," Cass said. "And as for crime and punishment, Corrina, mine was just getting started.

"I had a strong desire to get away from the dorms and Chelsea for a while. I'm sure you can imagine. So, I called Mike and asked if I could stay with him for a few days until the shitstorm settled. At least this way, I could still go to class and get caught up in what I had been missing. Mike was reluctant at first but relented when I told him that my girlfriend dumped me.

"Remember the black stone that came through the portal? I later learned from Stu that it is called a Cysistal stone and quite valuable,"

Cass said. He reached up to his neck and grabbed a braided necklace from under his shirt collar. He pulled out an amulet made of clear crystal. The crystal of the amulet contained a jet-black stone. Cass moved his fingers over the edges of the talisman until it popped open. He dumped the stone into his hand. Aside from not reflecting any light, it was a rather nondescript piece of rock about one inch by one inch.

Cass continued, "I didn't carry it around with me back then. It was sitting in my sock drawer. I went to pack a few things to stay at Mike's. When I saw this stone, it was pulsing between red and black.

"When I touched the rock…*wow*! The feeling of panic hit me like a wall. It filled me with urgency like I had never experienced. My heart rate went up, my palms were sweating, my mouth went dry. I was freaking out. I grabbed what I could and practically ran out of the building.

"The farther I got from the dorms, the more I started to calm down. By the time I got to Mike's place, the stone was black again. Later, I started to think I imaged it. Like, maybe I had something called a panic attack. So Mike let me in…"

"You're in luck. Scott is doing an internship at Penn University for two more months. You can stay in his room," Mike said. "But don't fuck anything up in there. Only Scott's name is on the lease to this place, so I don't need any shit from the landlord. I'll never hear the end of it."

"I won't," Cass said.

"Why do you want to stay here? I mean, you're not even that far from you own room in the dorm. You know, you might still run into this girl," Mike said.

Cass sighed and said, "Mike, she lives at the end of my hallway. We just broke up. I need to get away from her for a while. You know. I can't…I don't want to see her bringing other guys around." Which wasn't the full truth but was also true.

"Yeah, I get that. But now you know—never shit where you eat!" Mike said.

"I definitely learned it the hard way," Cass said.

"There's something else I need to tell you, Cass," Mike said. "I don't think you're going to like it much either. I want you to know, I didn't plan this at all. It just sort of happened."

"What's that, Mike. It's not likely I'm going to be upset by it. I mean, you're letting me stay here," Cass said.

"You know that club, Tren-Deez. Apparently, the owner is this wanna-be Mafia macho asshole with gold chains, a hairy chest with the shirt unbuttoned to his stomach, and pinky rings. Well, after 'deez nutz' became a thing, I heard the stupid fucker changed the name to 'Sparkles' because he was afraid it would become an all-Black bar. I went there about a month ago." Mike started to laugh. "It's so funny because now it's turning into a predominantly gay club! I heard he's furious about that too!"

"Are you going to tell me that you're gay, Mike? I mean, I'm okay with it if you are," Cass said.

"No, dickhead. I'm not gay. I went there and, uh, I sort of met some-one. Someone you know," Mike said.

Cass didn't know where Mike was going with this, so he said, "Okay. Who?"

"It was…ah…Beth Richter. She came up to me and started talking. Next thing I know, we were making out in the corner of the bar. We've been dating ever since."

Icy chills came over Cass as he remembered his horrible dreams about Beth and Mike. This couldn't be a coincidence.

Ex said, "This is not a coincidence, Cass."

"Yeah. I know," Cass said.

"How could you know?" Mike asked.

"No. Not about that. I didn't know you were dating Beth," Cass said.

"I hope you're not pissed about it or anything. I was really surprised that she would speak to me considering how you two got along. I thought she hated you."

"Mike," Cass said, "you need to get away from her. Seriously. She does hate me. She hates me enough that I'm afraid she could be mess-ing around with you. Did you know about her heroin use? Mike, she's a junky."

Mike sighed and said, "She told me all about that. She was never doing heroin. She told me she had a problem with coke a while back. We've gotten kind of close. You know, she's not mad at you anymore. When she got off the coke, she never touched it again. She's not a junky. She doesn't even drink. She's actually been great. I don't think I've ever gotten along with any girl this well."

"I have a terrible feeling about this, Mike," Cass said.

"I was worried you might," Mike said. "That's why I was a little skeptical of having you stay here. Because she is coming over tonight."

Ex said, "Say nothing more, Cassian. You will only end up in a fight. We will think of what to do later."

"Okay," Cass said.

"So, you're alright with it?" Mike asked.

"No, I think you're a dumb fuck, but you can date whoever you want," Cass said.

"I don't want any fighting between the two of you," Mike said.

"Don't worry about that. She'll never even know I'm here," Cass said.

CHAPTER 25

MALCOM IN THE DARK

MALCOM WALKED INTO THE CHURCH, looking for any clue that could point to the whereabouts of Friz. The smell of death hung heavy in the damp air. Several large flies were buzzing about. He walked down the nave, then back to the front door. He began down the hallway on the left of the front entrance that led to a little kitchen.

He could hear the buzzing of flies getting louder as he walked down the hallway. At the kitchen threshold, he found the two corpses. There was an old man lying on the floor and an old woman draped across the kitchen table.

It seemed unusual that an elderly couple living in the church of a nearly nonexistent community were both killed with what appeared to be deep puncture wounds through their temples. The perforations were cauterized and blackened so no blood spilled onto the floor. Oddly, the flies were centered around the open mouths of the two victims.

He put on gloves and lifted the head of the woman. When he saw her mouth, he jumped back in disgust. Thousands of crawling maggots created a shifting, white mass of what was once a tongue.

Despite the flies going wild from their maws, the couple was freshly killed. This was a quiet area where nothing happened…on the record, at least. He was certain he must be the first on the scene, so he took care not to touch anything in the kitchen.

This could only be from Friz. *Was this guy some kind of psychotic killer?* Malcom shrugged indifferently at the thought.

Malcom was many things, but stupid was not one. He followed the evidence he had. Friz came into this place and killed the two people very neatly. But there was nothing to suggest he left. He followed almost the identical pattern that Friz undertook. Through the organ loft, down into the little basement, and through the church to the altar. Malcom stood before the image of Jesus wearing a thorny crown hung upon a cross. He tapped his forehead, chest, and both shoulders, making the sign of the cross.

Looking around carefully, he noticed the pattern on the carpet. He knocked on the altar. It was hollow. But somehow, it must have slid across the carpet and back into place. He felt all around and could find nothing. Eventually, he took his foot and kicked it hard. It may have been hollow, but it was more solid than it should have been. And there was something off about the echoing sound.

He went to his car and came back with a crowbar. After about twenty minutes of prying at the base, he got it to move a bit. Now, with good leverage, he popped the alter off the cleverly designed track to reveal the steps leading down into the ground.

This was how Friz left. But what was he going to do now? He went back to his car and got some supplies. An electric lantern, a rope, a knife, and his special SAT phone. He could call for help, even underground if he needed. He got the receiver/transmitter set up inside the hollow altar and closed the structure over his head as he descended. The phone would send to the receiver and transmit to his agency.

He didn't want anyone to follow him. If someone were looking hard, they would find him soon, but not without some investigating. He didn't expect anyone, but this was Centralia—demons, Spurs, and any other monsters could be around here.

After about two rounds of steps, Malcom started to feel a little claustrophobic, but he continued. How long could it really be?

After twenty minutes of the same view, Malcom stopped and thought about going back up. His legs were so tired, he wasn't sure if he could make it back up. This was an absolute nightmare. He decided he had no choice but to continue down. He turned off the lantern to preserve the battery and climbed in the dark.

His legs were so exhausted after a while that he started sliding on his behind. When he saw the ocher-colored light, he began to get excited. How long had he descended? A mile? Maybe more? What was he going to do? He knew he couldn't make it up that many stairs now.

He slid down farther and eventually rounded the last set of stairs. The cavern was lit with a dull, dark green light that seemed to be coming from the walls. When he saw the room, he uttered, "Holy fuck!"

The massive cavern was big enough to fit a Boeing 747. The walls were coated with this material that gave off a small amount of green light. Certainly enough to see by. *Oh man! This is fucking plutonium or something. I'm gonna die of radiation poisoning*, he thought. On the far end of the cavern was something that looked like a train turnaround with some cart on it. From up on the steps, it looked like someone carved lines into ground, but whatever was drawn was too big for him to make out the shape.

Malcom crawled down the last few steps. He hobbled over to a large rock and sat down, rubbing his thighs. After about two or three minutes of rest, he got up and looked for signs of Friz. He turned on the lantern. When the light hit the sides of the cave, it was reflected without any hue of green. He walked to the wall and began to run his fingers over the surface. It gave him a calm, soothing feeling, and he could smell the petrichor of fresh rain hitting the soil. This made him feel happy. When he took his hand away, the feeling and scent stopped. He did this a few more times to convince himself that it wasn't just a passing feeling.

"That is a pure vein of Desemilnoct," came a voice from behind him.

Malcom turned to see Friz standing there holding a thin, golden rod in his hand.

"I have never seen so much in one place. A deposit of Shazo this large could bring predatory scavengers," Friz said.

"Like who?" Malcom asked.

"What you would call aliens or extraterrestrials. It is forbidden from any but the stewards to take the material from another world, but not all advanced civilizations abide by that rule. It generally leads to the destruction of their world. But personal greed can be an extremely powerful motivator," Friz said.

"Why did you run last night?" Malcom asked.

"The Shazo gave me a vision. A vision of me dying by your hand. Your realm mirrors our gravitational realm. There was a famous man, with a name similar to yours, in our history who was known to be a ruthless and brutal killer. He acted, at times, without reason or remorse. I don't know if this is you or not. But my vision showed me…things. I needed time to think and allow the drug I ingested to diminish the visions until I could think more clearly. The treatment will eventually draw all the material from my body.

"For the first time in my life, I met a Spur. Two of them, in fact. Last night in the church," Friz said.

"So, that old couple were Spurs? Is that why you killed them?" Malcom asked.

"It is. They intended to eat me!" he said, surprised. "I cannot imagine a more barbaric thing to do. But I have read of many horrible actions from the Spurs. They were as hideous as I was told."

"Oh, yeah. They're pretty fucked up. What do you intend to do now?" Malcom asked.

"You see that I am speaking with you. I have decided that I will work with you, but I will not trust you. I hope that you will understand," Friz said.

"Well, trust is an important thing to have if I am going to work with you, Friz. How do I know that you won't kill me?" Malcom asked. "I mean, if you can waste two Spurs that easily, how much of a challenge could I be?"

"I will not kill you, Malcom. But, if need be, I will defend myself. There are many nonlethal ways to do that. Although, none of them are pleasant for the attacker."

"You know something more about me, don't you?" Malcom asked.

"I do. I am not standing in judgment of your actions. I understand the work you do. That we both do. I believe you are known as a serial killer. Is that correct?" Friz asked.

Malcom nodded slightly and said, "How do I know you won't talk to others about me? We need to have some degree of trust."

"I agree. I will not speak your name to anyone. Ever. How do we strike that bargain in your world?" Friz asked.

"We shake on it. You extend your right hand and I extend mine. We grasp hands to symbolize that we bear no weapon against the other. Does that sound reasonable?" Malcom asked.

Friz extended his right hand. Malcom reached out and took it. Friz had a strong grip than belied his build.

Friz said, "I can do even better." He placed the golden rod across both of their hands and tapped a specific place. A small shock went up Malcom's arm, and he snatched his hand back.

"What the hell was that, Friz. I said no weapons," Malcom exclaimed. His head began to swoon, and he thought he could see things standing beside him. He looked left and right, but nothing was there.

"That was no weapon. It provides a mutual assurance of protection. We have a common goal now that one of our core resonances has been synced. It is much like fraternal twins that can feel the pain of their sibling or know when one is near. Were you to be in great pain, I will feel it. And if I experience great pain, you will feel it."

"Why am I seeing shit, Friz? Is that some kind of hallucinogen? What the fuck?" Malcom said rubbing his hand.

"You are feeling the effects I am having from the Shazo in *my* system. But there is no type of intercourse involved," Friz said, perplexed.

"Just an expression, Friz. It means disturbing, in this context," Malcom said. "This feeling…is not entirely bad. I just wasn't expecting it. What kind of aliens were you talking about? Are you telling me that little green men from outer space will try to take all this Dese?" Malcom shook his head like he was trying to wake up. Then the room suddenly spun and he could see large, cigar-shaped ships in orbit around Saturn. He backed up and said, "Whoa!"

"The visions should pass soon. They can be disturbing at times. They are not little or green. Many do look different, though. It depends on the frequency of their world. This is why Shazo…Dese…is so specific to a planet. It was made this way specifically by God to prevent theft," Friz said.

"You a religious kind of guy, Friz?" Malcom asked.

"What you call religion…seems to be almost forsaken by your people. There is no difference if I say Creator or God or Heshan'foram. They mean the same thing within languages. Your world seems to divide what they call science from religion. This is unusual to me. There is no division.

"From my perspective, think of people who believe in a God of fire and others who have a technology that can easily produce fire. These groups argue about God versus science even though neither group can *truly* explain the fire. Do you understand?" Friz said.

"Not really. I'm not thinking about anything that deep right now. I want to focus on our predicament. You know a lot about this stuff?" Malcom pointed to the walls.

"More than many, but not nearly enough. It is a most unusual element that defies understanding. I have heard that even the Watchers, the ones you call stewards, do not fully understand the properties. Unlike all other atoms, Desemilnoct has a subatomic particle in the nucleus that is negatively charged. It consists of what is known as antimatter. It should not exist at all, but it does. The structure of the atom nucleus is such that a field is created around the antimatter negatron to protect it from annihilation. It possesses many qualities, including the ability to travel through space by compressing time. It is not time travel, and the trips still take much time as the distance is far. But it is what many call space folding.

"Your little green men, as you call them, have been in your solar system for a long time. They are waiting. Each world is given a supply of Desemilnoct, deep in the crust of their planet. What a species does once they discover Shazo is a turning point in all worlds. You can either use the immense power to progress to an advanced civilization, or you can exploit the power in ways that will bring about certain destruction.

"Alien lifeforms, far more advanced than you, have mastered Shazo on their world. They will help your people if asked, but they are not here to interfere. They wait to see if the inhabitants will destroy themselves. Only then are they permitted to mine the planet for this element.

"These aliens, though predatory in their own way, have already stopped many nefarious plots to cripple your planet. Most of these attempts you will never know about. There are many evil forces who unilaterally take it upon themselves to destroy worlds. The destruction of a species *must* come as the *choice* by that species. Demons and Spurs are only allowed to influence, not destroy. This is the important point," Friz said.

Visions swam through Malcom's mind bringing amazing clarity of thought. He said, "I know about the Spurs and demons infiltrating our government and media, Friz. You talk about choice. What happens to the people who don't go along with all these lies?

"I've been fighting against the Spurs for years. You say the civilization decides? That's not the case here. Many people don't believe the bullshit coming from the Spurs or demons now. Of course, we still have people defending the actions of these evil creatures. Creatures who would be happy to kill their supporters for their trouble. But what happens to the minority…or the apparent minority? The ones who oppose this abhorrent abuse of the power?"

"Fear not, Malcom. God is on their side and knows the minds of all lifeforms. You will see. When things appear the darkest, light will find its way through," Friz said.

"I sure hope so, dude. Because shit's been getting pretty damned dark lately," Malcom said.

"The prion messages you have been receiving are warnings of impending doom. I do not know what they say, as they are specific for your world. Only when your technology is sufficient will you be able to interpret these. Many different species on different realms work to prepare these messages for your realm and many others. If you ignore the messages, it is to the folly of your species. But keep in mind that while God sent alien lifeforms to protect you, those lifeforms are indifferent to allowing you to destroy yourselves in order to harvest the Desemilnoct from your planet."

"If they are so advanced, why don't they just wipe us out and take the Dese?" Malcom asked.

"That has been done in the past. There are few, if any, civilizations that will ignore the known consequences of doing that. It is a story I will tell you about when we come together with Cassian. But you can be assured that any species who has done as you suggest is no longer in existence. There is also a race called the Farzooh Cynath who fight to prevent this from occurring. They are powerful and dedicated to God in a way that is…more extreme than my group. I am one of the Elder Quatran," Friz said.

"I don't know what that means, Friz. But what you're saying is, they aren't going to invade. That's all I wanted to know. Shouldn't we be worried about breathing this in?" Malcom gestured to the walls. "This cave seems to be filled with Dese," Malcom said.

"No. It is not volatile in any way. It must be ground into a find powder. And that is not an easy task. It clumps and refuses to particulate. The process is prohibitively expensive. Also, it is a rather wasteful way to use this material, but it is the only way we know to create portals between realms. Ingesting extremely dilute quantities in this form is used by some of the wealthiest in the universe to provide visions. This is exceptionally dangerous and very unpredictable. Most become addicted and soon lose any coherent thought. They never live long.

"The element obtained from a realm, when successfully ground into aerosolized bits, can be irradiated at a specific frequency to match the origin realm. Then it takes a tremendous amount of energy to create a portal. And as you must know by now, they cannot be kept open."

"Why can't the ones you were running from find where you went and follow you?" Malcom asked.

"That is not possible. We designed the process to be untraceable. The energy source we use to generate the frequency and power required is self-consuming once the process is initiated. Without the frequency in-formation and the exact *source* of Shazo, the portal cannot be recreated," Friz said. "Also, the Shazo must be pure from the realm you are seeking to reach. That means that it came from your world. That was the last of the material we had, meaning this was the final message. At least from my world."

"Well, that's going to save a lot on the travel budget," Malcom said. "You couldn't have sent a message to Hawaii or maybe the Fiji Islands? What do we do now, Friz? I don't think I could make it up those stairs. My legs are probably going to cramp tonight."

"I can help with that. But it may be important to figure out what is going on with their operation," Friz said as he gestured to the train tracks. He once again stuck the gold rod into the ground.

Malcom jumped when the map of the tunnels lit up before him. It was amazing. He could see where each tunnel went. It had the names of the towns, the coordinates…everything. And it was all in 3D.

"How are you doing this, Friz? You said you only send probes here?" Malcom asked.

"That is not difficult. We use your own satellite technology to feed us information. I am not connected now, as the Shazo prevents this. But I had the image when I was on the surface. My lividan," Friz gestured to the golden-colored rod, "can detect its own location. You must understand that your technology is rather primitive to us. It is how I was able to best two Spurs. I possess no superhuman powers. I simply used a well-understood resonance technology to prevent them from moving. These are all things I believe your world is on the cusp of understanding. Once you can get past those who withhold the information," Friz said.

Malcom was barely hearing Friz as he looked around at the amazing 3D map. He was shocked at how far up it was. No wonder his legs were sore from dropping down so many stairs. "How far away is the church?" Malcom asked.

"That would be about 2.2 miles, using your base ten numbering and old English measurement. Do you know that unit of distance, or would another be preferred?" Friz asked.

"Huh? Oh. Uh, no. Miles is good. I know miles. Wow. That's how far down this is? This is unbelievable. Are those train tracks over there?" Malcom was pointing to part of the image off to his left.

"Yes," Friz said. "It appears as if they spiral up to the surface and then remain about two hundred feet below the surface down to this town. Gordon is what it is called."

"Gordon? That interesting. The Bosco family had something to do with Gordon, Pennsylvania. They had some guy who worked in this area. He was a pilot or something," Malcom said. "Do you and your golden rod happen to know anything more about this?"

"It is not made of gold," Friz said. "The material is an alloy of—"

"Don't take it so literal, Friz. I don't really care what it's made of. But it seems to do some pretty cool shit," Malcom said.

Friz said, "I did access your government files about this mine. The underground fires did not begin as a result of the careless burning of trash or previous mine fires. In this particular mine, diamonds were discovered among veins of coal.

"Bootleg miners began to dig far deeper than what they were supposed to. This was where they first reported to have discovered Desemilnoct, in your records. You should know that this material is the most valuable metal in the entire universe.

"The bootleg miners were eliminated, and the coal mine owners in the area were not prepared to offer nearly enough money to the residents who owned the land. They worked with the state government to have the land seized by eminent domain.

"This is quite despicable and consistent with the tactic of demons.

"In your year 1974, under the discretion of a man named Anthony Bosco—" Friz said.

"The Bosco family was controlled by three demons. That's who Cassian and I fought back then," Malcom said.

"So, it is Cassian who is the shrouded," Friz said.

"You know about shrouding?" Malcom asked.

"Yes. I know that three humans having victory against three demons suggests that a very powerful angel is shrouding one of you. As you have a camera device for protection, I assume that you are not the shrouded. But you should be more careful in the future," Friz said.

"I usually don't have to be, Friz," Malcom said.

Friz gave him an uneasy look and continued, "Anthony Bosco and his associates formed a company called Angelcon Industries. They were funded by Diobalst Bank under the umbrella of the Equitine Corporation. Perhaps they meant that to be ironic if they were all demons.

"They began construction of these underground railroad tracks connecting the deepest mines of Centralia to the small town of Gordon. There were government contracts finalized in your year 1991 with Angelcon. It was your own government that created the burning hell under this town in 1962 to prevent investigation while decisions were made about what should be done with this unknown metal," Friz said.

"How the hell do you know this much?" Malcom asked.

"I accessed information stored in your government files. It was all there to see. Even the events where you and your friends destroyed the Bosco home," Friz said.

"Shit. They have all that? Well, what do you think they were planning to do?" Malcom asked. "I know Cassian and…I know they thought something much bigger was about to happen."

"If three demons were involved," Friz said, "then, yes, something much bigger was about to transpire."

Malcom thought back to that time. He suddenly felt good that he had a role in stopping them back then. Malcom asked, "What kind of stuff could they do? I mean, you know more about this stuff than anyone else on this planet."

Friz began, "The angels and stewards are forbidden to teach any world about the secrets of Shazo. This is something that each world is intended to find out on their own. Just as the metal could be used for tremendous advancements, it could also be used for the most nefarious purposes.

"One of the most powerful things that Dese can do is to induce gravitational fields. More importantly, anti-gravitational fields. Dese can superconduct electricity at any temperature. It allows vehicles to fly without a propulsion source other than the gravitational field of the planet.

"In our world, it provided essentially free energy for people everywhere. It completely changed the world we knew. It created freedom that was realized only by other advanced civilizations. This was the key to moving our species to the next phase of adaptation…"

"Hey! That's what Cass is always talking about. Adaptation over evolution. So that's for real? He's right?" Malcom asked.

Friz responded briskly, "Yes. That is more accurate. There are those who would prevent this from becoming accepted until financial gain can be realized.

"As I was saying before, the discovery of Shazo marks the *sink or swim* for every civilization on every other world. One path to become an enlightened and harmonious culture and the other path to war, destruction, and inevitable regression.

"When it was discovered…wait. Allow me to correct that. When it was uncovered on our world, it caused an apocalyptic revolution to our industries. I say uncovered as it had been discovered many cycles earlier while the people were kept in the dark. Powerful entities employed extreme measures to silence any hint of the existence of this material. The Spurs and demons also wanted this kept quiet. Of course, throughout time, those groups became indistinguishable.

"When people realized that the discovery of Shazo had been withheld, they were understandably angry. It ended the constant source of revenue and control of those governing our world economy. The power was not something they intended to surrender easily. A terrible and final war was initiated by an event that removed all doubt about the existence of God. But it serves no purpose to tell you more about that."

"What?" Malcom said. "That seems extremely important to know. Why would you not tell me about that?"

Friz continued as if the question were not asked, "According to files from your government, one plot for the Dese was to introduce small amounts of the powdered material into the feed of cows in select areas around the world. The extended digestion system of cows would eventually convert the metal into clusters that could be absorbed in the body. It would penetrate the meat of the animals. People would then eat the meat and the material would slowly penetrate into the brain.

"The metal itself is inert and nontoxic. But it can be induced to cause brain death through extreme visual trauma. Once a specific frequency is passed into the material at specific temperatures and pressures, it would cause such intense stimulation from the visions that each synapse will shut down to protect other neurons. This can be externally triggered after ingestion and could be devised to appear as a foreign attack or a toxic ingredient in your foods.

"They were aware of the implementation of high gigahertz networks. These could be used to induce massive, specific, and mysterious tragedies among select populations. Either way, the fear they would induce would allow for greater control. But they were never able to produce the proper form of material."

"What would happen if I ate a piece of Dese?" Malcom asked.

"Assuming your physiology is similar to mine, you would pass the material from your body with little to no effect...other than the contact you may feel from the metal. But this is not absorption into your brain. It must be in a fine powder or some other microencapsulated formula for that to happen. Once in the brain, it behaves much different."

"Friz," Malcom asked, "how could you possibly know about these plans. That has to be *minimally* a highly classified government file… waaayyyy beyond top secret. How could you know this?"

Friz looked down as if searching for something and said, "It does seem as if some extra measures were employed to protect this information. They are rudimentary, at best. It is a security structure our children are given to decipher for fun. It is almost a fable of what *not* to do for security," Friz said without a hint of humor.

Malcom laughed. "Well, don't I feel like the fucking idiot. I've been trying to get into that information for years. You know, I consider that an impenetrable fortress. What exactly are you seeing?"

"Do not be discouraged, Malcom. Your technology is…" Friz paused, "similar to how you would think of civilizations who did not yet comprehend the wheel."

"Dude! You're calling me a caveman!" Malcom said.

Friz paused for a long moment and said, "You have a movie called… *The Final Countdown*. A ship from only forty years in the future went back in time. The one ship could easily destroy an entire fleet of enemy warships. Now imagine that I come from nearly fifteen hundred years ahead of your time. On my world, I am what you may call a weakling, or perhaps," he paused, "a nerd."

"You've seen that movie? *The Final Countdown*?" Malcom looked perplexed.

"I saw it while I was scanning your histories for an appropriate example," Friz said.

"You saw the *whole* movie?" Malcom asked incredulously. "If you watched the whole movie, what was the name of the dog?"

"Charlie," Friz said, before he completed the sentence.

Malcom, shocked, began to ask another question, but Friz cut him short. "Stop any attempts to trip me. I have full access to all your internet files, including all governments and corporations. Nothing they have can be hidden from me. They have not yet invented the wheel to me, Malcom.

"I must be careful what I do here. The implications could be…devastating. This is unlikely the first time Shazo was found on your world.

I believe humans rediscovered it in India and China in your year 1819 from the previous advanced civilizations.

"Knowledge of your world's history is currently not complete. But if it is as similar as ours, the first civilizations to harness Shazo were destroyed by the Builders for inappropriate use of the power. Great palaces and cities were melted into the stone as the inhabitants were destroyed. Only ruins remained under the ground."

"Okay," Malcom said, "what else did those crazy assholes have planned?"

"There was evidence that they were planning to create an attack on a national park—Yosemite. A controlled underground event could appear to naturally devastate much of the United States, sending your world back into the Dark Ages. Another proposal was to attack the central government in the underground facilities in Virginia. Collapsing the US government could send the world into turmoil, allowing military dictatorships around the world to assume control, ending the freedoms of humankind for generations."

"Why would our own government approve such a self-destructive plan?" Malcom asked.

"These are not people who represent your government or your people. These are evil creatures who wish to end reality. They wish to end existence. You…" Friz looked down. "You will not fully understand what is at stake. People on your world believe that a small percent of greedy elitists want more money and more power. This is the subterfuge. These creatures want the destruction of your life. Do you understand?" Friz said.

Malcom sighed. "So the demons and Spurs will use the Dese against us?"

"Using Dese would render any attack untraceable to the perpetrators as it could be triggered at any time from any location. It could be laid as a trap that could be tripped by accident, making it look like a natural disaster. As I said, the metal defies all physical characteristics of other metals."

Malcom said, "I read about a metal called Invar that doesn't expand or contract with temperature changes. Is it like that? Could this be Dese?"

"It could not be mistaken as any form of Desemilnoct. The properties of Shazo are not because of the internal structure of alloyed metals with varying ferromagnetic properties. Dese is a single element rather than a combination of different metals. Its properties are intrinsic, and it resists entropy in such a way that defies the laws of thermodynamics. On any world," Friz said.

Malcom suddenly felt overwhelmed. He said, "Whatever, Friz. You know what I want to do right now? I want to get the fuck out of this dark-ass cave. Do you have anything in your super-advanced bag of tricks to get us out of here?"

"It is unfortunate that I was unable to grab my bag. I have few necessities with me. But it seems that the track over there," he pointed to his right, "has solid rails all the way to Gordon. We should be able to traverse them simply using the mining equipment on hand. But if you do not mind, I will take some of the Shazo ore. We never know when we may need it." Friz said.

"Knock yourself out. Just get me out of here. I'm tired, I'm sore, and I'm starting to get really hungry," Malcom said.

Friz placed the golden rod against a vein of the metal. It began to pulse with a low hum. Suddenly, cubical chunks, about one inch on each side, began to fall from the cave wall. Friz gathered them up and slid them into pockets around his legs and arms.

"Let us go now," Friz said.

"Go where? How the hell are we going anywhere?" Malcom said, annoyed.

Friz took a cube of the Dese and used another device he had hidden up his left arm sleeve. He started to cut at the edge of one of the cubes. It was odd how the material seemed to roll as he cut, like it was healing from the damage. It took a minute or so of Friz moving the device around until a sliver fell to the floor.

He picked up the sliver of Dese and walked over to the tracks. He placed it on a large cart that sat upon the rails. Then he laid the golden rod onto the cart for several moments.

"What are you doing?" Malcom asked.

"Please be silent for a moment. My lividan is measuring the dimensions of the track. It must be accurate," Friz said. After a moment, he held the rod out and looked above it. Then he said, "Is there anything beside you and your clothing that you wish to bring? Our masses need to be correct."

"No. Just me," Malcom said. "I weigh about 225 pounds."

"You weigh 247 pounds. With your clothing, weapon, and accessories, 275 pounds. The lividan collected that information when I synced our resonance," Friz said. "I do not like doing this, but it is unlikely to draw the attention of one of the Builders. Our need is great, and we are not technically breaking any laws as we are expending the Shazo."

Friz touched the rod to the sliver of Dese. A blinding light caused Malcom to flinch. Friz yelled, "*Asisha!*"

The temperature dropped at least ten degrees, and they were in the dark again. Malcom could now hear a low humming noise. He reached down and tried to turn his lantern on, which had gone dark when Friz touched the Dese. It would not work. He said, "My light is out."

"Yes. It was a small pulse of electromagnetic energy needed to make this device. It drew energy from around us, including your lamp and battery," Friz said.

"What about the Dese you inhaled? Weren't you worried that you could have triggered that to kill you?" Malcom asked.

"You are rather bright, Malcom. Yes. I was worried about that. It was a calculated risk as my body temperature was far different from the cart that the Dese was sitting upon," Friz said.

"What did that mean? *Asisha?*" Malcom asked.

"Oh. That was an expression of surprise. I was unsure if it would work on your planet's Shazo," Friz said.

As his eyes began to adjust to the pale green light emitted from the walls, Malcom saw a strange looking bullet-shaped device about four feet tall and ten feet long that fit over the tracks. That was the source of the humming.

"Where the hell did that come from?" Malcom asked.

"It is one of the properties of Shazo. My lividan was able to create this by pulling necessary materials from other realms. It destroys the Shazo…or displaces it. I'm not entirely sure. It can be done occasionally, and the mass of the cart was roughly the mass of this device. But I do not want to do it often. I do not want to see one of the Builders.

They are from the Time realm. They are both pitiless and tremendously powerful."

"You keep talking about these Builders. They can't be worse than a demon," Malcom said, skeptically.

"Neither angel nor demon could possibly challenge a Builder. I once heard a story of a Builder appearing. A war was being fought. Both sides were suffering terrible losses. They began to use the Shazo to conjure terrible armaments from different worlds. The Builder was drawn into their world and laid waste to both armies. It did end the war, at the cost of several million lives," Friz said.

"Wow! So, you just…fucking…conjured this thing? Like *for real* magic!"

"It is not magic. It is simply complicated," Friz said. "Now let us get in and leave this place before you decide to eat me."

Malcom started to laugh as Friz ran the golden rod, the lividan, along the carriage. Two openings appeared on the side of the device. One port was at the front housing a narrow seat. The other was in the back with a seat that looked comfortable to Malcom. He climbed in and said, "This is very nice!"

"It was built to your specifications, Malcom. Sit back and relax. It will take several minutes to get out of here. It is quite a distance."

"Minutes?!" Malcom exclaimed.

CHAPTER 26

VENGEANCE

"Y OU DID SAY BETH WAS Mary's *older* sister?" Corrina asked.

"She was older than Lynn and Mary. She was the same age as Mike," Cass said.

"Must be close to half a million people in Pittsburgh," Franklin said. "How is it that the same people keep popping up in your world? It doesn't sound like serendipity. It sounds like you people are looking for each other."

"You got that right, Franklin. Beth was absolutely seeking out Mike," Cass said. "And her motivations were less than pure…"

<hr>

Cass avoided the living room that night. He stayed in Scott's room working on the studies in which he fell behind. His misery at sending Mary to Hell rivaled his feeling of loneliness as he recalled his behavior with his friend Clay. He didn't get to see him when he packed his things to stay at Mike's. He never left a note or anything when he ran out of the dorm. He thought about calling, but he would have had to go into the other room to use the phone (he explained to Franklin that there were no cell phones then).

Cass thought about the feeling he got from the stone that came from the portal. He picked it up and held it in his hand. Nothing happened. He squeezed it as hard as he could and concentrated on it. Still, nothing happened. He thought, *Was this some kind of warning?*

He put the stone next to the bed and played loud music in the headset of his Walkman radio so he didn't have to hear anything that Mike and Beth were doing. When it was time for bed, he saw that Scott had the new Led Zeppelin box set. He put four discs into Scott's cheap CD changer and played it on repeat with a random shuffle. He supposed after getting robbed once, they didn't keep anything in the apartment of too much value. He smiled when the first song that came on was Kashmir.

Cassian woke to find himself in his dorm bedroom. He looked over to see Mary and Chelsea both sitting on Clay's bed. Clay was sitting on the back corner of the bed, but his body looked all wrong. He was sitting with his legs out on the bed, but his head was facing the wall.

Cass sat up, knowing that this was a dream.

He said to Mary, "I am so sorry, Mary. It was an accident. I miss you so much. I always have," Cass could feel himself getting choked up.

"Don't worry about me. I know that you'll get me out of here. But you need to take care of the problem I brought to you. I am the one who is sorry."

Mary reached between Chelsea and her and pulled out a small bundle that she handed to Chelsea. It was a baby that began to cry. Cass walked over to Mary as Chelsea opened her shirt and began to nurse the baby. Cass reached out to touch Mary's face, but it was now a blurred face looking at him.

Something painful latched on to his wrist. It was the savage mouth of the baby, which was lined with rows of sharp teeth. There were no eyes or nose to the small creature, and its body was bright red.

"Do you like Esau?" the faceless woman asked. "He is here now, and we are going to have to care for him."

Two clawed hands grabbed his arm as the horrifying red baby began to take bites out of Cassian's hand. He tried to pull his arm away, and the baby grew rapidly to a large, formidable beast with the massive legs of a horse and split-hooved feet. As it began to glow with a red light, a white flash came from its chest.

Anger filled Cass, and he punched the demon with his free hand. It immediately let go of his arm.

A grating, horrible voice said, "You are too late to help them, *Cassian*."

Cass looked at it with shocked dread as it said his name.

"Yesssss. I know who you are now, and I am coming for you!" The tone wreaked of cruelty as it said, "I am going to rip your *fucking* entrails from one end of this building to the other!" it spat at him.

Furious, Cass said, "I'll be right there you piece of shit! We'll see whose entrails get ripped apart!"

"Cassian," came the whisper.

The stone was next to his bed, and he could hear a low humming noise being emitted.

He jumped up, still angry from his dream, and pushed Beth across the room. He didn't know if this was yet reality. He quickly swung his legs over the bed making Beth back farther from him. He had only one complete leg. This was probably not another dream.

"What's the matter? Don't trust you own stupid eye?" Beth said, "I would love to poke it out, but I have other plans for you, asshole."

Cass wanted to strike her in the face, but he held back, saying, "Every person who has ever made that threat has regretted it. Don't think you're special. What do you want, you bitch! What's your angle with Mike?"

"Oh, that," she said casually. "I figured I would do to you what you did to me. I will kill your sibling."

Cass was about to take her over, but something in her confidence kept him from doing that. He said, "You're threatening Mike in front of me? What's your end game here, Beth?"

"Threaten? Oh no. I am not threatening, Cass. I already did what I need to do. Now it's just a matter of watching you suffer as your brother rots to death. It's only fair after what *you* did to me."

"What are you talking about?" Cassian asked. "What did I do to you?"

Beth began tentatively, "I don't know *what* you did to me, Cass. But I know *you* did something to me. You are the reason I got hooked on H. You are also the reason that Mary is dead." Beth began to laugh as she said, "But you probably didn't know that Lynn is still alive, huh? Did you try to kill her too? I don't know what the fuck you did, you piece of shit, but I got you back. At least partially," she said with a sneer.

"What the fuck are you talking about, you psychopath. What do you mean Lynn is still alive?" Cass said angrily.

"She probably didn't want you to know. Maybe she faked her own death to get away from you. I could understand that, you clingy fucker," Beth said.

"What about Samuel? Is he still alive too? Maybe you're a liar. That would be easy to believe. Or maybe Lynn made the whole thing up. Maybe she was never pregnant and you're all a bunch of sick liars…all but Mary. She was the only good thing in your family," Cass said.

"I'm not here to help you, Cass. I just like the idea of rubbing salt in your wounds. But, in my own way, I wanted to be just like my sisters. I wanted to *fuck* you too. Your brother is in his bed, sleeping so soundly. And yet, he's already dead," Beth said.

"What did you do to him?" Cass yelled, alarmed. "Did you poison him?"

"I suppose so, yes," Beth said. "I really hate using condoms. I'm more of a barebackin' kind of girl when it comes to sex. And Mike and I sure went at it pretty hard." She reached into her pocket and pulled out a piece of paper. She threw it at Cass.

Cass took the paper skeptically and turned on the desk lamp. After a moment, he saw the line she wanted him to see. HIV…Positive.

"Do not do it, Cassian," Ex screamed in his head as a push of calming energy came. "Stop yourself, now. This does not mean that Mike has this virus. Only that she has it. Do *not* overreact."

Cass surprised Beth by yelling, "Mike! Get in here!" Beth withdrew in fear at the tremendous sound of his voice. Then she dove at him with something in her hand. Ex instantly took over and swatted her away with great force. She flew to the floor, screaming as her forearm lay broken at an odd angle.

Within a minute, Mike ran into the bedroom and saw Beth laying on the floor with a syringe needle next to her broken arm, "What the fuck, Cass? What are you yelling about?"

Cassian handed Mike the paper. Then quickly strapped on his foot.

Beth grabbed the needle, jumped up, and ran out of the room, laughing. By the time Mike got to the important part, they heard Beth yell, "Enjoy the rest of your short fucking life, dickhead!" followed by the door slamming.

"I told you not to get involved with that crazy cunt!" Cass said.

Mike read the paper and starting to breathe in deep gasps. He said, "Can't you do something about it? You know, with your angel?"

"Ex told me not to do anything to her yet. I don't know what all she did. Look, I had a dream right before she woke me. It wasn't a good dream either. I think…I think something bad may have happened. It was a demon, Mike. Another fucking demon. And it knew my name in the dream!" Cass said.

Mike was still staring at the paper. "Cass…I did all kinds of stuff with her. We…we never used a condom. She was so dead set against them." His face curled up in pain. "I was really starting to think I loved her," Mike said, breaking down in tears.

Cass hugged his brother as he wept. His own rage swelled as he thought of how to deal with Beth. He didn't take her over and bring her to justice. *Why*? Normally, he would have brought her back to the room and forced her to talk. Why didn't he?

Something Cassian was practicing was to speak with Ex in his mind, without speaking aloud in his response. It took a tremendous amount of effort unless he was in a semiconscious trance. In his mind he asked, "Ex, was it you who didn't want me to take her? I could have made her tell me what she did?" At the end of each sentence, he still said aloud, "take her?" and "what she did?"

"You could have taken her, Cassian," Ex said. "I was not stopping you. That was your own instinct guiding you. Your soul. I am glad that you used your brain before acting, though. If your rage took over, you may have killed her before you could determine the extent of what she has done."

"Yes. Or I could have brought her back here and forced her to answer my questions!" Cass said aloud.

"And then what," Ex said, "You would *have* to kill her."

Cass paused and thought about it. Ex was right. If he used the power to question her by letting her up to speak, he could not just let her go. This wasn't his mother or grandmother or someone he saved. Beth would have known what he did to her at the Bosco party. She would know his secret. She could also go to the police station with evidence of his assault. He wasn't sure what other evidence she may have besides her broken arm, but he was sure she had something in store for him.

"Don't worry, Mike. I will figure this out. Maybe Ex can help," Cass said.

A siren outside startled them both as police cars flew up South Bouquet Street. Lots of sirens were going off. Cass and Mike went out on the porch. Both Fifth and Forbes Avenue were lit up with flashing lights.

"What the hell is going on up there?" Cassian asked.

"I don't know, but it's definitely at the dorms," Mike said.

Cass thought about his dream and a cold, sinking feeling came over him. He said to Mike, "We have to call Mom and everyone else in our family, now! Demons are coming."

CHAPTER 27

END OF THE TUNNEL

MALCOM COULDN'T TELL HOW FAST they were moving, but judging from the bumpiness of the track, he thought, *Fast*. After about ten minutes, Friz said, "There is a barrier blocking the entrance to the tunnel that we must breach. There are lifeforms on the other side of the barrier, guarding the entrance. We may have to remove them."

"Remove them?" Malcom asked, "Do you mean kill them?"

"That would be for the best. Alternatively, we can stop before the barrier and try to sneak out," Friz said.

"That might be a better option, Friz," Malcom said. "There may be a demon guarding this entrance. Certainly, a Spur. And they could notify others if we escaped."

"I agree," Friz said. "A cache of Shazo this large might warrant the use of a demon. Let us try to find an alternative. I am going to slow this device rather abruptly."

"Okay," Malcom said, "when do you…aaaahhhhhh!"

The deceleration was hard. The seat sucked Malcom into it, but it felt like all his organs sloshed forward. He groaned, "Oh man…I may puke!"

The doors flew open into darkness. But no green light or any other illumination radiated from the walls. Friz stepped out of the vehicle and did something Malcom couldn't see. The cart began to emit a soft light. Enough to see the narrow tunnel they were in. Malcom rolled out of the seat onto his hands and knees.

Friz held the lividan out and pressed something. The 3D map reappeared. Malcom slowly stood and could now see the map with small dots moving about the entrance to the cave.

"This is a live map. I have been connected since we got away from the walls of Shazo," Friz said.

"Are those the guards?" Malcom asked.

"Yes. They are the life forms out past the barrier several hundred feet ahead. They are members of a government agency called the FBI. It is a steel door. We could blast through without an issue. Perhaps a surprise may give us enough time to escape. But if there is a demon, it is unlikely we would have success," Friz said.

"If there is a demon out there, wouldn't they know if we were here? I mean, they're fuckin' demons, man!" Malcom said.

"They can see nothing. A cavern of Shazo hides all who can look into the Dream World. No eye, be it electronic or ephemeral, can penetrate a cave where Shazo lines the walls. It also prevents any method of scanning for the material buried under the surface of a planet.

"Out here, where the Shazo is not present, we can be seen, but we are in a dark space with no frame of reference. Even if they were looking, they would not know of our immediate position. They would only see us in the dark. It could be this mine or a dark basement.

"The demons like to pretend they are omniscient. They are not. They rely on nosy spies to feed them information. If someone is clever enough, they can trick these arrogant demons easily."

"Really?" Malcom asked. "Because I think that's what my friend Jimmy did. He tricked them using a bunch of mannequins."

"Were the mannequins faceless?" Friz asked, smiling.

"Yeah. How did you know?" Malcom asked.

Friz began to laugh, "If they were getting information from the spies in the Dream World, they would fear they were about to be attacked by angels! You see, the Spurs, angels, and demons appear to be faceless in the Dream World. Somehow, your friend must have known that."

"So that's what he was up to," Malcom said. "Cass told me that Jimmy saved us, but he never really told me *how* he did it. But it definitely got Mitch Bosco away from us long enough to free Cassian. But Mitch caught Jimmy and fucked him up bad. The prick killed him."

"It is sad that he had to stay with the mannequins to fool the spies. Perhaps he should have thought it through better and left before the demon arrived. The demon would have approached slowly and cautiously if it thought a group of angels were present. But still…very smart. It is too bad your friend is not still with you, Malcom," Friz said with much kindness in his voice.

"I used to hate the guy. He was possessed by a Spur for a long time. I was there when Cass freed him. Eventually, we became good friends. I do kind of miss him," Malcom said.

Friz was staring at Malcom with a look of shock.

"What?" said Malcom. "Oh shit. Did I already tell you that Cass was shrouded?"

"I told you earlier that I deduced that. But you said your friend, Jimmy, was possessed by a Spur for a long time. And after he was freed, he figured out how to trick the demons…in the Dream World?" Friz asked.

"Yeah, he was possessed for like six or seven years. He said it was like being in Hell. He couldn't breathe while he sat in the dark. The guy was crazy loyal to Cassian after we freed him. It was so weird…he was just like a little kid again," Malcom rambled.

"That is amazing," Friz said in awe.

"What's so amazing?"

"I think your friend was able to *study* the Dream World while he was possessed. Do you know what this means?" Friz said.

"Not at all," Malcom said flatly.

"It means that the only way to study the Dream World is *from* the state of being a trapped soul! Probably within the unconscious mind, which is why nobody has been able to articulate this information.

"Our Creator has provided an answer to all things if you look hard enough! None have ever been able to do this, Malcom. Not the stewards, not the angels, not the demons, and none of the advanced civilizations," Friz said excitedly as he slipped back into his normal super-fast speech.

"I still don't get it," Malcom said. "But you seem to be happy about it."

Friz held his lividan to his mouth and began to speak frantically in an odd language. It seemed to be an efficient language, since the entire conveyance of their discussion about Jimmy took less than a minute.

"What was that? Can you talk to people on your world?" Malcom asked.

"No. Messages cannot go between realms without Shazo. I have a small supply from my world. But it is not in the proper form and unlikely that there would be a power source strong enough to initiate a portal. We use special devices with mirrored optics and compressed carbon and molybdenum. This would be what you would call a laser, except the one we use is spherical. With enough energy added, the device becomes an implosive. When the vaporized Shazo is dispersed inside the device, the portal forms and the device is destroyed," Friz said quickly.

"Friz," Malcom said, "can we slow it down…a lot. I don't know what you are talking about, and I'm afraid I don't care. Let's just start to figure a way out of here. Please."

"Yes. We need to feed you. I have memorialized the exciting information you have transferred to me. Are you still hungry?" Friz asked, trying to slow himself again.

"Yes!" Malcom said. "I would be really happy with a burger or pizza or something. Can you use this Shazo to conjure up something like that with your magic wand?"

"I told you before, it is not magic. Here," Friz said, pulling a small cookie out of his belt, "ingest this. I have decided that it cannot possibly be harmful to your species. It should balance your blood sugar levels for some time while still replenishing the muscles that have been damaged in your legs."

Malcom threw the cookie in his mouth and chewed. Then he said, "Was that the unflavored version? I mean, I have *never* eaten something so utterly flavorless in my life. In fact, I think it retrospectively stole all the flavor from my last three meals."

"Odd," Friz said. "I find them to have a *delightful* flavor. We should expect some differences between our worlds."

"Alright, how are we getting out of here without alerting the guards?" Malcom asked.

Friz studied the map for a moment and said, "According to the lividan, the thickness of the crust in this direction," Friz said, pointing to the left, "is only about twenty feet."

"Twenty feet, Friz? Do you know how long it takes to dig twenty feet? And you have to consider that there will be a lot of rocks. That would take us days to dig, even if we had power tools!"

"Come. We will be outside in less than twenty of your minutes. Are you still hungry?" Friz asked.

Malcom thought about it and said, "No. Actually, I feel kinda full."

"Good," Friz said. He knelt on the ground and pulled something from his left pant leg, down near his calf. It was about four inches long and S-shaped with sharp edges on the outer sides.

"It's going to take a long time to dig us out of here with that little thing," Malcom said.

Friz looked at Malcom with exasperation. He held the S-shaped device before him, pushed on both ends of the blade, and set it on the ground. Then he tapped it with his lividan. It began to spin in a blur.

Friz said, "Look away. The material will be propelled toward us."

Friz and Malcom both faced to the right. Malcom heard the soil and rock being cut as small bits of debris hit his back. The noise continued as he looked down to see piles of dirt forming. The sound would fade and then get louder. Fade and get louder.

Malcom said, "I'm going to go sit down for a while. Let me know when the palace doors will open."

"Do not fill yourself with anticipation. It will not be a large portal, Malcom," Friz said.

"Great," Malcom said as he seated himself on the ground away from the flying debris.

In roughly twenty minutes, Friz touched his lividan and the noise stopped.

Malcom rose from his seat and walked over to where Friz admired the work. He was happy to see stars in the night sky through a crudely shaped hole.

"Come. We can crawl through that. It is a short distance…and large enough for *you* to fit through," Friz said.

"You know, I kind of feel like you're constantly taking digs at my being fat. Are you doing that intentionally?" Malcom asked.

Friz looked down and said, "To my great shame, yes. I have been rude to you. I have made…what is the right word…snide…mocking… comments about your weight. I am deeply sorry. I know of the value placed on meals in your world. Social or otherwise happy occasions revolve around meals.

"From the files I have read, there exist plots from your own leaders to make your citizens obese and diminish your natural immune system. They make it seem as if the people are weak and cannot control your-selves. But they also introduced horrible ingredients to compel your appetite or desires. Many seem to simultaneously profit on addictions while shaming the very people *they* addicted. I apologize for my apathy."

Malcom looked at Friz for a long moment and said, "Thank you. A lot of people fight with weight issues. So, you're saying that there are people *doing* this to us?"

"It is more complicated than that, but yes. Covert destruction of physical health seems to be a common tactic used in your world, es-pecially over the past thirty years. They have reduced your ability and desire to procreate.

"Please, do not ask me more. We must move. Can you try to go through that hole? I can help you if needed. It would be better if I were behind you," Friz said.

"Fine! I'll go first," Malcom said through gritted teeth. He wasn't claustrophobic, but the tunnel looked small. Apprehension about crawl-ing through such a confined space caused him to start sweating as his pulse quickened. However, his desire to be out of this mine motivated him into action.

It was only twenty feet. Malcom had his arms ahead of him as he started to squeeze through the entrance. He wiggled his body, snaking through the rocky channel. At one point, his belt got hooked on a rock and he couldn't move forward. Panic set in and he started to hyperven-tilate.

"I can't move, Friz!" Malcom yelled, "What the fuck, man. I can't back up either. I think this wall is falling down too. We gotta get out of here!"

Friz placed a hand on Malcom's ankle and said, "The wall is not collapsing, Malcom. Calm yourself. Feel what I am feeling."

Using their mutual connection, Friz began to exude a calmness that eventually sank into Malcom. Relaxation permeated his mind.

Malcom never experienced anything like an external infusion of serenity. Friz soon got his belt unstuck, and he started to move forward again.

Malcom made it to the end of the passageway without freaking out again and pushed his arms and head out the hole. Looking around, he said, "Friz, we're really high up. I don't have anything to hold on to. If I fall from here, I'm gonna get fucked up!"

The drop was about fifteen feet onto a bunch of scrub brush. Friz pushed from behind and said, "It is not that far. You will be fine."

"Ahhh…don't you have something to soften this fall?"

"Stop being so unmasculine, Malcom. Try to land on your back. When you hit, slam your arms and legs to the ground. This will spread out the impact, absorbing the shock. You will be fine," Friz said.

"No. I'm *not* going to be fine, asshole. I know how to fall. But this is awkward. My legs are stuck in this hole until I fall. This is fucked up!" Malcom said.

"Please jump, Malcom. This is uncomfortable for me as well," Friz said.

Malcom hardened his resolve and pushed himself out. As he fell, he tried to flip over and land on his back while slamming his arms and leg out, like he was instructed to do. He landed on his back atop two hard shrubs. Any trained response was ruined when he hit the firm wood of the bush. Gravity spun him onto his belly as he let out a loud grunt of pain.

Malcom immediately rolled out of the way in case Friz might land on top of him.

Within a second, Friz also cried out, "Owwww," and slammed into Malcom's side.

They lay there for a full minute before Friz weakly said, "Ow. That… did hurt."

"Why couldn't you have had that thing dig a tunnel that wasn't fifty damn feet from the ground?" Malcom said, holding his lower back.

"It was only 12.8 feet," Friz said, as he grabbed his own side in pain. "If I dug in any other location, it would have added another thirty feet to the tunnel. Would you want to crawl twice as far as we just did?"

Malcom paused, looking around, irritated, and then said, "Noooo."

"I am going to cover that hole now. If we need to get back in, it will be useful to keep this passage hidden."

"Yeah, sure. If you have something that can turn into a ladder," Malcom groaned, "why didn't you pull it out sooner?"

Friz sent the device up into the hole and must have had it cover the area. Malcom looked around. It was dark, but he could see some light from the town. He said, "Hey, Friz. How far of a walk is it to town?"

Friz looked around and said, "It is about two of your miles in that direction," he pointed south.

"Why don't you pull up the map again?" Malcom asked.

"I did. You just cannot see it now. I am trying to not draw attention to us. There is a vehicle with wheels only two hundred yards away in that direction," he pointed east, away from where the guards would be.

"What kind of vehicle?" Malcom asked. "I mean, will it run?"

"It has all the necessary parts to make it run. It will run," Friz said calmly. "Let us go now."

The vehicle was an old Ford Bronco that was nearly buried in dust and looked as if it had been abandoned twenty years ago.

Malcom said, "Friz, that thing isn't going to run. Besides, there are probably rattlesnakes and other shit living in it. And any oil and gas needed would have dried up at least ten years ago! The tires are shot."

"You worry too much. Do you suffer any health issues from stress? I am not now poking fun at your obesity. I only wonder if perhaps you overeat from your constant stress," Friz said.

"Well, jeez…here I was, worried about how we're going to get out of here, and you go right back to telling me I'm fat and unhealthy. Cass likes to say, 'It could always be worse.' Thank you for proving his point. I feel worse."

"Cassian seems wise. It *can* always get worse. So much worse. Watch," Friz said as he walked over to the vehicle.

One touch of the lividan created a ping and a stir of lifeforms scattered. He then held it to the hood of the vehicle, and, to Malcom's surprise, it made a sound like it was trying to turnover.

"There is something physically impeding the combustion engine. Do you know how to fix motors?" Friz asked.

"Dude, I can fix a lot of shit on a car, but I can't spin gold from hay!" Malcom said.

"Lift the hood of the car, and I will fix it. I just need to access some files. I can convert this to an electric or magnetic source. We also have Shazo, but I think a flying car may attract attention in your world."

"A flying car? For real? You can make this car *fly*?" Malcom asked.

"With Shazo, I could make *us* fly without a car. But it is dangerous as a stray beam of high-powered energy could send you careening to your death. The core of a gravitational control device must be shielded from all but the required frequency and energy. It is quite specific. But I can draw much energy from the gravitational field of your planet. Far more than enough to run *this* vehicle."

"What about tires? Even the rubber is spent. We can't ride on the rims," Malcom said.

"There is material there. It will be re-meshed and filled with air. This is not difficult. It will last much longer than we will need it," Friz said.

"You're a handy guy to have around, Friz. I sure am glad I didn't kill you!" Malcom said.

Friz looked at him in frightened shock.

"I'm just kidding with you, man! You look worried. I think you stress too much! Do you suffer any health issues from too much stress?" Malcom said as he looked at Friz with a serious expression.

Friz surprised him by laughing…very hard. Tears were coming down his eyes as he laughed. Malcom couldn't help but laugh too.

"What's so funny?" Malcom asked through the hilarity.

"You. You are funny," Friz said as he tried to control his mirth. "This is something I did not expect!"

Friz broke into another fit of laughter.

CHAPTER 28

THE BREAKUP

J EN WALKED BACK TO HER dorm room around midnight. She
missed Cassian and Zab being around. But Cass had turned into a real
douche since he got together with Chelsea. Sure, she was nice to look
at, but aside from that, Jen couldn't understand what the hell Cass was
doing with her. *Such a nasty, stupid bitch*, she thought as the elevator
opened.

A terrible smell struck her as she stepped into the hallway. When she
opened her dorm room door, the smell was so much worse. The lights
were out and the blinds drawn, the only light came from the space under
the bathroom door. The running fan was failing to remove the stink.

"Who's in the bathroom?" Jen asked, "How about using the air
freshener?"

Jen walked into her room and placed her bag of books on her desk,
pulling the string to her desk lamp. The light didn't come on. She reached
up and tightened the bulb and it suddenly lit up the desk. As she turned,
she jumped when she saw Chelsea sitting on her bed.

"Oh. I'm sorry, Jen. Did I startle you?" Chelsea said.

"Yes! What the fuck are you doing in my room…and sitting here in
the dark? Psycho," Jen said harshly.

"I really wanted to apologize to you. I've been mean to you. You
should know that I broke up with Cassian today," Chelsea said.

"That's probably for the best," Jen said. "I didn't really see you two
together."

"I know. Imaging someone like *me* being with a useless cripple like *him*," Chelsea said.

"Fuck you, Chelsea. What a *rotten* thing to say. No, it's not because he's handicapped. It's because he's a nice guy and you are a completed cunt!" Jen said. "Just get out of my room."

"But I didn't get to apologize to you," Chelsea said.

"Save your stank breath. I wouldn't accept anything from you. Especially not an apology."

Appalled, Chelsea said, "You think my breath stinks?"

"Well, something's stinking this room up. It's either your breath or your diseased snatch. Either way, I want both of them out of my room. Now!"

"You don't need to be so vulgar," Chelsea said. "It's probably your roommate taking a shit. She's been in there for like an hour." Chelsea wore an odd and unsettling smile. "Maybe you should check on her?"

Jen scowled at Chelsea and turned to walk to the bathroom. One of the desk chairs was broken and the legs were missing. She said, "Did you break my damn chair, bitch?"

"Not me," Chelsea said. "Maybe it was one of the cows you live with." She laughed.

"You are the worst person I have ever met," Jen said as she walked to the bathroom door and knocked. "Monique? Are you in there?" She knocked again, but there was no response. The smell intensified by the bathroom. She opened the door as she said, "Monique, are you alri…"

The horrific scene hit her like an electric shock. Blood filled the bathtub as Monique hung by her hands from wooden chair legs pounded into the wall. Her intestines hung down into the tub from between her spread legs as her feet were also impaled into the wall. Her face, now a dark blue color, was a mask of horror. Jen turned from the bathroom and gasped for air.

"Is something wrong?" Chelsea asked, sounding concerned.

"Oh my God! Chelsea! Call the police. Monique is dead!" Jen uttered as she stood in shock.

"Oh. That. Yes. I know about that," Chelsea said. "It took some doing getting those guts out. A lot of screaming, I can tell you that! The trick is to—"

Without hesitation, Jen punched her in the jaw. Chelsea flew back and screamed as her hands went to her face, "Jen! How could you punch me like that?" Her voice was changing. It sounded mean.

Bringing her hands down, something thoroughly evil stood before Jen. Chelsea's skin had turned red, and her eyes were black orbs. Her arms grew longer as scaly claws now hung from her wrists. "I need you to accept my apology," the discordant voice said.

Jen turned and ran down the hallway. When she got to the other bedroom, she slammed the door behind her and locked it. Turning on the light, she saw two unrecognizable bodies bound to each bed. "Nooooo…" Jen screamed.

The door flung from the hinges like it was balsa wood rather than solid oak. The rasping voice said, "I just have a couple questions for you, Jen. You won't mind answering me, will you? Questions about your friend, Cassian. Let's start with where he is?"

Jen let out a loud scream as the clawed hand slammed her head against the wall.

"I also need to send Cassian a message. The message will be…very clear. You were his favorite, weren't you?"

———•••———

"This was a night I will never forget…and I wish I could," Cass said. "If there is a penance that must be paid for every evil deed I have ever done, I paid them with interest this night.

"Chelsea's body was found hanging three stories below her window. Her head was nearly ripped off by the rope around her neck. All my roommates except for Zab and Keith died. They were lucky enough to be home with their families. Thirteen people were murdered…by Chelsea. Then she killed herself. She was taken by a demon…not long after I left her," Cassian said.

The anger coming from Cassian transformed him into a frightening figure as he said, "Jen, Clay, Monique, even Chester—they were all slaughtered. And it wasn't a quick and easy death. It tortured them. And what it did to Jen was something that still brings hate to my heart. It was looking for me!"

"How did it find you?" Corrina asked. "It couldn't have been Mary. She would never betray you."

"No," Cass said. "Mary never betrayed me. Not intentionally. The betrayal came from the stewards. Somehow, they followed her. They watched as she searched for me. They tagged her and followed her in the Dream World. At least, that is what I was told. I will never believe that Mary betrayed me," Cass put his hands over his face and ran them down. "Because doing that would mean I was so incredibly betrayed…and that I am the stupidest son of a bitch to ever breathe. I will *never* believe that Mary betrayed me.

"I still think about it. I almost wrote Clay a note that I was going to stay with Mike. I forgot about a note when the panic from the Cysistal stone hit me. Maybe if I did that, they would all be alive. Chelsea would have come for me!

"If Mike's name was on the lease, would they have found me sooner? Maybe before Beth even got there. Everything kept me away from the demon that night. Fuck that demon! I would have faced it and killed it as easily as the rest."

He nodded as he said, "I killed a bunch of the Seraphim after that. Demons and angels. It never made a difference. There was always another one."

"You killed angels!" Franklin said, "I thought they were on your side?"

"Khalima once told me that there were some angels with more bloodlust than the worst demons in Hell. Ones who lost sight of the goal and only wanted war. I took no pleasure in my actions, but I did put them down," Cass said.

"What about your angel? Didn't she try to stop you?" Franklin asked.

"Never. Ex will not stop me from doing what I need to do. She will guide me and offer help, but she will not impede my path. Whether it was an angel or a demon, if it stood in my way, it died."

"I'm so sorry, Cassian," Corrina said. "I didn't know you went through all this."

"It was much worse than that. Demons were dispatched to kill my entire family…at least the one's they could find. My mother and grandmother I had time to warn. They also knew enough to look for the signs.

Thank God they escaped with my one aunt. A lot of my family was slaughtered. I won't tell you what they did to my father, but, as I said, they wanted to send a message. I tried to warn him, but he wouldn't believe me.

"I was a young, angry man, now brimming with hate. A very dangerous thing. I think that's what they wanted. They wanted me to be set on killing them. Killing is not creating. They were winning, and I didn't see it. All I wanted was vengeance. Do you understand?" Cassian said.

Franklin and Corrina sat in silence for a few moments. It was Franklin who spoke. "I can't blame you, Cass. If someone killed my family, all I could think about would be revenge. Did they send one after your brother?"

Cass was looking at the floor as he nodded, "Mike, my mother, and I moved into a motel that night. The next night I went and stayed in Mike's place alone. Mike wanted to come, but I wouldn't let him.

"By this point, I was beginning to understand how to use my own abilities, not just the one's Ex gave me. The demon showed up at his apartment. A huge man claiming to be there to service the radiators. It must have taken them a day to figure out where Mike lived."

Cass wore an intense look as he said, "I tried so hard to kill it slowly, but I couldn't. I would only be torturing the vessel it took. The demon did die. And by facing it in battle, it saved the rest of my extended family. Once I killed that demon, I must have been anonymous once more. Because the killings stopped, and they never found me again.

"You will never understand how specific the rules are. How could they know everything about me and suddenly know nothing about me? I have learned that the key is to face them immediately. Whichever way victory goes, the other side is protected. Does that make any sense to you?"

"Hell no!" said Corrina. "That sounds like a bunch of shit to me!" she yelled.

"I agree with you, dear," Cassian said. "But these are the laws, and my family was decimated because of a loophole.

"Getting angry is the primal response. All beings get angry…including God, apparently. I am no exception. But I felt all the secondary emotions like resentment, guilt, spite, fear, and vulnerability. I killed so many people who I considered evil or potentially threatening.

"Do you have any idea how easy it is for me to kill a person? Step in front of a bus or swallow some pills or jump out of a high window. I gave one guy rabies. That was a pretty awful way to kill someone. But he intentionally shot my dog.

"Interestingly, only rabies and the herpes B virus, which you can only get from the bite of a monkey with a cold sore, are the only two diseases that can kill Nephilim. At least, I would think that would be interesting to *you*. Impervious to the power of angels and demons, but a bite from the wrong animal…and that's it!"

"These people you killed…did you know them? Were they were doing something wrong besides killing your dog?" Corrina asked.

"I sent Mary to Hell, and most of my family along with all my new friends were destroyed by demons. Angry doesn't even come close to how I felt! But if they died by my hand, they were doing *something* wrong. I couldn't possibly go into every one of these stories. It's already getting late."

"What about Malcom, Tony, and some of your other friends?" Franklin asked.

Cass said, "They were all safe. None of my college friends knew much about my high school friends. That's probably what kept them all safe.

"After that, I withdrew from college. Despite what you may have heard, they do not give you a 4.0 if your roommate dies. I was given incompletes in all my classes that year. I only had a year left to get my degree. But it would be three years before I went back to finish."

"What did you do for three years?" Franklin asked.

"Katabasis," Cassian said.

"Katabasis? What's that mean?" Corrina asked.

"I know what it means," Franklin said. "It means he went to Hell and came back. You went after Mary, didn't you?"

Cass nodded and said, "You surprise me, Franklin. You know about katabasis but never heard of Dunning–Kruger."

"I used to love Greek mythology and the story of Odysseus. Did you really go there or just see visions?" Franklin asked.

Corrina said, "I hate to ask, but before you continue, I need to use the restroom, Cassian. I've been holding it a while."

"By all means, Corrina. I will not continue until you return," Cassian promised.

Corrina got up and quickly walked down the hallway to the bathroom.

"It is getting late, Franklin. Perhaps we should come back tomorrow and finish the story," Cass said.

"You don't have to leave," Franklin said. "There's plenty of room. I have a spare bedroom and that is a pullout sofa," He pointed to his living room.

"If you do not mind," Cassian said, "I would be happy to sleep on the sofa. But please…I want you to ask your mother to stay in your guest room." Cassian gave him a meaningful look as he put a hand on Franklin's arm.

When Cass touched him, something powerfully nostalgic sprang into Franklin's mind. He recalled deep memories: *His mother reading him a story when he was a kid while he sat on the sofa, safely tucked under her arm. He felt so warm and happy. The smell of her perfume mixed with cigarettes. The feel of the rough black and beige Berber sofa. The ugly orange afghan wrapped around them as the tassels brushed against his feet. The excitement and tension as she told the story. The feel of her tickling him while he laughed as the story ended. Unconditional love from his…momma.*

Cassian let go of his arm. Suddenly, immense regret consumed Franklin for all the years he pushed his mother away. *My momma*, he thought.

When Corrina came back into the room, Franklin turned to face her. When he saw her, he drew a deep breath as tears filled his eyes. He said, "Momma, will you please stay here tonight?"

Corrina's expression switched quickly to concern as she ran to her son and embraced him. She said, "What's wrong, Franklin? You're shaking. Is everything okay?"

"Yes," he said thickly, "I just really miss you. It's late…I think you should spend the night," he hugged her back.

"Oh, Franklin. I missed you too. I would love to stay," she said through her own budding tears.

CHAPTER 29

THE LOVE OF JAZIGN

"Ok, buddy. Where to now?" Malcom said once they got the old Ford Bronco onto a paved road.

"We need to get to your friend Cassian as quickly as possible. If some of the visions I experienced and the events in my world continue to reflect in yours, you should already be nearing his location. But as you have spent time chasing me, I fear I may have altered events beyond repair. But either way, life will go on," Friz said.

"That's the attitude, Friz! Besides, if I wasn't looking for you, I never would have found that cave of Shadzo or Shazo…you know…Dese. Do I have time to go back to my hotel room and get some shit?" Malcom asked.

"We do not. But as we are traveling north to the city of Boston, your other vehicle is in that direction. Let us exchange this transportation for that one," Friz said.

"Yeah. That was a given, dude. This thing isn't registered. If we run into a statie, we're not going anywhere. Can you pull that map up and show us where my car is?"

"We are not far from your car. It is only three miles away," Friz said.

"How is that possible? Didn't you say we had a long way to go when we were in the cave?" Malcom asked.

"It was approximately twenty-seven miles of track, but the course was long. The only continuous track had us going through several areas that were out of the way. Additionally, we had to spiral gently upward. The mines were built to go over two miles deep with a grade no greater than fourteen degrees. They may have been mining for coal, but they were also looking for other, more valuable ores and elements."

"You mean like gold?" Malcom said.

"Yes, gold is one of great value," Friz said.

Malcom said, "I saw a documentary once about an alien race called the Anunnaki who, as some people believe, populated our planet with humans as slaves to mine gold for them. Maybe they wanted us to mine Dese for them. Do you know anything about that?"

Friz looked down for a moment and said, "I no longer know what to believe, Malcom. For many years, I wondered if we were really sending you messages or just dropping notes into a burning can of nothingness. There are some who believe we live in a giant petri dish with a glass cover, and this is all made up in our minds. That would make our existence part of some great scientific experiment."

He paused and said, "While I have never traveled to space to see for myself, I do not believe that."

"Why not?" Malcom asked.

Friz placed the lividan on the dashboard and said, "Stop the car for eight minutes."

Malcom pulled the car into a small clearing on the side of the road and stopped. "Now what?"

"You don't want to be doing anything while you listen. This is called 'The Love of Jazign,'" Friz said.

Music started to play from the lividan. Malcom could not be sure if he was hearing this from his ears or from his chest. It seemed to reverberate through his whole body. It produced a wonderful sense of nostalgia. He recognized something from his childhood in the sound, but he couldn't quite place it. The music had no words at first, but a story was told as clear as any movie he had ever seen. Malcom began to picture...

...A dazzling and crafty young woman named Sivain who uses her beauty to ply men into showering her with attention and wealth. She lives an opulent lifestyle, scarcely afforded from one day to the next. Through her beguiling charms and beauty, she conceals her cunning and villainous nature.

As Sivain began to show signs of aging, she realized that she must settle down. But finding a suitable mate was not as simple as she believed without youth on her side. The young and attractive men held no wealth to keep her happy. Those with wealth were wed to good, younger women.

Sivain set her sights on a slightly older man named Parciff. (Malcom begins to see the story from the perspective of Parciff.)

He owns a business and works hard to earn a profit. He has wealth but is not wealthy. Sivain has plans to drive Parciff harder to earn more money. Parciff's infatuation with her, certainly initial, obscured that her love for him was merely superficial.

Using her intellect and charisma upon his friends and family, Sivain washed away her previous foul stigma. Soon they all agreed, marriage to Sivain would best suit Parciff's needs.

(Malcom was beginning to think that this story may have words… kind of. *Was this starting to rhyme?* This song was written in a different world with a different language. *There was no way it could rhyme in English. It had to be just the music.*)

Parciff gained the fortune he had by living a frugal lifestyle. After they wed, Sivain spent Parciff's wealth while he was in denial.

To keep his young wife happy, Parciff spent on debt. To his surprise, this seemed to have the opposite effect.

There was something dreadful that Parciff did not understand. Sivain found comfort in the arms of another man. Vesuian, shrewd and handsome, had swayed his new young wife. She couldn't see the depth of greed within his family's life. She took the bait, not knowing his intention. His family tasked him with the deed to seize their operation.

(*Okay, these were English words that were beginning to rhyme. Either that, or I'm losing my mind,* Malcom thought. It was quite possible as the song was so immersive.)

Every morning, Parciff would pray. He asked God for Sivain's heart to change. Each new day, nothing happened. In desperation, he stopped this pattern. He sought help from the Dark King of Death, known to make dreams real by granting every wish.

(The music switched tempo, and he could see it more as a story again than from the perspective of Parciff.)

Parciff was on his way to the brooding lair of the Dark King. The large and ominous castle cast a shadow on the town. As he walks with his head down, he bumps into to a woman named Jazign. He looks up to see her beautiful blue eyes and her lovely smile. Momentarily forgetting Sivain, Parciff is spellbound by her face. Relief flooded through him as his trouble fell away, but tentatively he must avert his gaze.

(Words now came to his ears. The sound pulled on his heart so strongly that he felt his throat begin to tighten. It was not just the sweet sound of Molly's voice, it was her smell, her warmth, her essences, all now surrounding him as Jazign began to speak.)

"What troubles such a handsome man?

"Listening's no bother."

[Parciff]

"I cannot, sweet girl, bend my heart.

"I'm wed unto another."

[Jazign]

"What damage could come from talking?

"You seem so woebegone.

"I fear if I don't intercede

"Your soul may suffer harm."

[Parciff]

"The Dark King grants the help I seek.

"By God I am forsaken.

"I choose a path away from light.

"Resolve will not be shaken."

[Jazign]

"Do not speak so about your Lord,

"Your path you cannot know.

"The grace of God smiles on the man
"Who listens to his soul."

[Parciff]
"I choose this road of my own will.
"God favors me no more.
"If I am wrong, I must accept
"Decision's fateful door."

[Jazign]
"Depart then to your darkened path
"To find your peace of mind.
"God moves His hand is subtle ways,
"As light's what you must find."

Parciff looked down, and walked away
Less certain of his plan.
He crosses through a stranger's path,
A young and striking man.

The meeting's not by happenstance,
A twist of fate in life.
But set the day before it seems
By Parciff's lovely wife.

[Vesuian]
"What's wrong, my friend? You seem upset.
"Is there something I can do?"
[Parciff]
"Perhaps you know a woman's hearts,
"For I surely have no clue."

[Vesuian]
"Luck favors you today, good man,
"For I'm the one you seek.
"I know the hearts of women well,
"Erudition very fleek."

[Parciff]
"I know not how to keep my wife
"Fleeting is her joy.
"Only from wealth I don't possess
"Debt's now my envoy."

[Vesuian]
"Once again, I'm at your service.
"Providing you solutions.
"I propose a partnership
"Void of convolutions."

(The music changed and Malcom sees the document held by Vesuian. Parciff reads the words and signs the deed giving Vesuian one-half of his wife and his lawfully owned business. Vesuian gives Parciff a case filled with money. He and Vesuian shake hands and part ways. Parciff, however, continues his journey to the Dark King. From Malcom's perspective, he knocks on the castle door and is greeted by a tall and powerful man with a pleasant smile and a cajoling voice that begins to speak.)

[Dark King]
"Welcome, my friend. What can I do
"For one so young and vital?
"A potion, spell, or special wish?
"The cost a minor detail."

[Parciff]
"Dark King, I have a simple wish.
"There are secrets I must know.
"My peers and wife tell lies to me
"Be they friend or are they foe?"

"I'll pay whatever price you need,
"Please grant me deeper vision."
[A smile forms on the face of the Dark King]
Tendentious motives unforeseen
For love will be *his* scission.

[Dark King]
"Come, young man, let's make a pact
"I surely see your sadness.
"I'll help you feel your soul inside,
"And take from you the madness."

The power of the serpent sang
Showing deeds of malice
Dark impetus moved every hand
Poured into his chalice.

(The music deepens and changes the coloration of the world from
vibrant tones to dismal grays.)

Arising from that den of hate
Love now far detached
Those held deep within his heart,
Now martyrs of his wrath.

The horrors bared by his new sight
The plots now clearly shown.
And every single breath he takes,
His anger mounts and grows.

The strength of Evil's venom,
So firmly in our souls
Stokes a fire, deep within
Raging white-hot coals.

Childhood feels so far away
The years of purity.
Parents, family, youthful friends
Now held in enmity.

(Parciff leaves the money from Vesuian with the Dark King and trudges out of the castle. He sees Jazign as he walks by and for a moment the world flashes with bright color. The music creates a red pulse of anger that forces the bright hues back to gray and pulls him back to his task. He goes home to see his wife.

Images form of Parciff, who is now exceptionally observant. He sees the despicable actions of his wife and soon learns that many men he considered his friend were taking advantage of his blind love for Sivain. This breaks his heart, but he holds on to a hope that Sivain must still love him.

One day he comes home to find Vesuian with his wife. The music turns the world crimson as Parciff's rage grows. Parciff sees too late what is happening but is unable to compete with the power wielded by Vesuian and his wealthy family. He is forced to sign over his business to his wife and then made to grant her a divorce. Afterward, he is beaten and left for dead in a desert. *Malcom would later swear he could feel the physical pain.*

Jazign sets out to find Parciff in the desert. She treats his injuries and brings him to her home where she nurses him back to health. Malcom sees himself as Parciff, struggling through weeks and months of pain with the help of Jazign…*but it's Molly,* he thinks. He fights back from the brink of death, but he is filled with so much anger at the injustice done to him. Malcom wants vengeance for Parciff.]

[Jazign speaks, *and again, Malcom's chest tightens*]
"My love, you need to find a way
"To end this awful hate.
"It occupies you night and day
"It's stealing your whole fate."

[Parciff]
"What can I do my sweet Jazign?
"Anger consumes my life.
"I know that I must find a way
"To rid me of this strife."

[Jazign]
"Though you could not see His help
"God watched over you.
"Turn your heart back to His love.
"Right what now is skewed."

(Malcom feels himself as Parciff, kneeling on the ground to pray to God, regretting his alliance with the Dark King. The ringing of many trumpets sound and a beautiful angel appears before him. The sound of the angel speaking makes the world explode with light and hope. The angel explains that the gift of the Dark King can never be revoked.)

[Angel]

"Life's great struggle brings despair
"And with it wicked dreams
"False offers made of peace and joy
"By evil beasts unseen."

"Acceptance brings a tragic fate
"For those too weak of will.
"Into the world brought forth that day
"Tormented souls of ill."

"First you stood and did not break
"Twice now you must suffer.
"Simple means to take your heart
"Touted as an offer."

"A gift so granted not undone
"The vision was but half.
"Unto you I fulfill the deal
"The gift now sewn in fast."

"Providing nothing new this day,
"Awaken something else
"A fledgling power held within
"To see you as yourself."

"Now open your new eyes to see
"The world you leave behind.
"Hindsight will guide your pathway true
"Mistakes made in due time."

[Parciff]

"What can I do?" he said aloud
"To make this world feel right."
Then visions crashed into his mind
Providing clean insight.

(The music flared to life a great power and inspiration from within
Malcom. Strength filled his mind and body. The world changed to brilliant and bright colors.)

The other side of darkness held
A hidden, secret key
His freedom there inside his soul
The kindness not perceived

His mind pried open from within,
Love breaks from its dark prison
He looks upon his life complete
Resolved to mend this fission.

The sadness feels now far away.
No longer so obtrusive
His thoughts, he sees, were tainted by
A lust for the abusive.

Never again would he deny
The souls' quiet alarms.
The deep remorse he felt within
Succumbed by hollow charms.

(As the angel sings its song, Parciff *and Malcom* feel an incredible
weight lift from his soul. The anger, resentment, mistrust, and envy

now gone from his heart as he can see the love and care that also come from his friends and family and Molly…or Jazign. The Dark King only granted him one side of the vision. God merely pulled the limits set by Satan so that he could see both sides.

He feels no need for vengeance against Vesuian and Sivain. With the love of Jazign, he uses his gift as a visionary to help people to see the truth that they cannot see. No longer seeking wealth, he sees himself as wealthy. His life is richer than he could ever hope with love from children, friends, and his wife, Jazign.

But Sivain, now cast aside by Vesuian and his treacherous family, believes that her charm will still work on Parciff. One night, she plots to secretly and "accidentally" run into Parciff while Jazign is away.)

[Sivain]

"Do you still feel your love for me?

"My sweet and faithful dear."

[Parciff]

"I feel for you a love reformed.

"Like misery loves cheer."

[Sivain]

"Come back to me this joyous night

"And leave this girl, Jazign?"

[Parciff]

"But you now have Vesuian.

"A true love strong and keen."

[Sivain]

"Vesuian has no vision,

"Nor is he strong of heart.

"It's you I need to fill my life.

"Let's make a full new start."

[Parciff]

"By hand nor heart, you have no hold

"To make such wretched claims.

"I see the dark within your soul

"Unfettered by your feigns."

(As Parciff walks away from Sivain, he can feel the closure and relief wash over him. The vengeance he never took against Sivain or Vesuian no longer matter to him. He can only think of the happiness he now has with Jazign. This happiness fills him with such joy that he feels tears in his eyes. His smile cannot be contained as the crescendo of the song hits its final high.)

⸻

When it ended, Malcom sat behind the wheel of the Bronco with tears blurring his vision. The emotions going through him were everywhere, but he felt amazing…as if he had a renewed purpose to life.

"What was that?" Malcom asked, stunned.

"The song will provide each person with their own story about Jazign that depends on their mood at the time. But no matter how I feel, good or bad, this song makes me feel better. That is the reason I believe in God. I may not know the truth of everything, but I cannot deny the *feelings* I get from this song.

"The one who created this brought out feelings in me I cannot begin to describe. How can there *not* be a higher synchronous power like God when something so beautiful can exist? It seems to have influenced you as well, no? This is why I do what I do," Friz said.

"Friz, I killed a lot of people. I killed a girl I loved. I felt her in this story, and I stole this from her. She will never experience the joy of hearing this. I am definitely going to go to Hell for this. I'm so sorry," Malcom cried.

"Malcom, I believe it must be our choice to go to Hell. We are but children who, as the representative said, know not what we do. We are fools who do foolish things.

"You must know by now that you can destroy *any* relationship with *any* person in an instant by saying or doing the wrong thing at the wrong time. If God were that intolerant of us, no soul would be free from Hell. The best we can ever do is to try harder. Do you understand?" Friz said.

Malcom nodded as his tears still formed, "I'm never going to kill another person again. Not when I know I could take an experience like *that* from them."

"In all likelihood, you will need to kill again. It is the nature of what we do. And doing so in the defense of you or your family is never a crime in the view of God," Friz said.

"I feel sick about the things I have done, Friz. Molly never got to hear that. She would have loved that so much," he sniffed back his running nose as he wiped his eyes. "I was surprised that it was written in quatrains. It reminded me of this old poem about this sailor who killed an albatross and brought bad luck on his crew."

The Song of the Dead Seafarer, Friz said. "But there were no words written in 'The Love of Jazign,' Malcom. If you heard quatrains, that came from your mind."

"No. It was…umm…oh…*The Rime of the Ancient Mariner*," Malcom said, excited, "I'm sure of it. Iron Maiden did that song and it was awesome!"

"There will certainly be differences in our works of art, Malcom. We are similar, not the same," Friz said.

"But wait a minute, Cass said that no one could ever read my mind. How is it that the song did that?" Malcom asked.

"It did not read your mind. The harmony struck deep resonances within you. The song pulls on those resonances until your mind placed words to the melody. I am not a musician, but I know it is very powerful.

"At one point in our history, music became a dangerous tool used to negatively influence people. Those types of underlying deceptions were forbidden by our society long before this song was written," Friz said.

"So, that whole story came from within me?" Malcom asked.

"Yes. Only the names, or, more accurately, the pronunciations, are maintained throughout. Aside from some visual stimulations created by the music, the rest came from you," Friz said.

"Are you sure about that? Some of the words in that story I have never heard before," Malcom said.

"Yes, you did. You just do not recall them. This *style* of music pulls from the deep recesses of your mind to make it feel more original each time. This type of music can make one recall deep memories. But if I played it for you again without giving you time to recover, you would develop a nauseating pain in your head. Too much of a good thing, as they say," Friz said.

"I guess that makes sense. I'm not a musician either…in the sense that I don't *write* music. But I do play the drums. It's something that makes me feel better," Malcom said.

"You were brought up with a Spur as a mother. Am I correct?" Friz asked.

"Yes. How did you know?"

"The history of your world is mirrored in the history of my world. But it is not a clear and shiny mirror. There are some major differences and some minor ones, but the history of your…" Friz paused and said, "It is important to always keep in mind that you must make your own decisions over your desires and your ethics. You were brought up under something that causes known, deep psychological and functional problems. There is a boredom associated with a sustained cognitive dissonance from the nihilism and apathy inferred when under Spuric dominance. This often leads to dissociative disorders like sociopathy and psychopathy. It is part of the influence of Hell that generates fear in people and a distaste for interaction with others. It creates a coldness toward your fellow humans, which is exactly what the serpent wants."

"But my mother was freed of her Spur by Cassian. Shouldn't the threads unwind?" Malcom said.

"They do, Malcom. But it takes more than ten minutes or even ten years. You suffered through this during your formative years as a child. You do have the power to conquer your problem. I assume you are now controlling it to some degree. Am I correct?" Friz asked.

Malcom nodded and said, "I usually only kill those who Cassian would prefer to be quiet. And it isn't that he won't do it himself. He has been allowing me to fulfill my…urges."

"May I ask what the urges…on second thought," Friz said, "perhaps it would be better if I do not know. This is something that belongs to you. You may share with me if you believe it would help you but feel no obligation to answer that question."

"Thanks, Friz," Malcom said. "I would rather not talk about that anyway. You're a pretty good dude."

"As are you, Malcom."

When they got to Malcom's car, he pulled the Bronco behind the church and drove it about twenty feet into the woods. Malcom opened the trunk of his car and pulled out two, one-liter bottles of water. They both took a deep drink.

Friz immediately spit the water out and said, "Oh no, that water has been poisoned!"

"What are you talking about," Malcom said, taking another drink. "It's warm, but it's not poisoned."

"You cannot taste that…what is the term…phthalates and plastics? This is not safe for you to drink, Malcom," Friz said.

"It's all I have. What do you want me to do?" Malcom said.

"No wonder you struggle with weight control in this world. Chemicals like these materials damage your ability to metabolize energy properly," Friz said, rooting around in one of his pockets. "Here, try this."

Friz sprinkled a dash of the powder he used before into Malcom's water bottle, then his own. When Friz capped and shook his bottle, the plastic turned translucent and the bottle became as rigid as glass. He then drank the water.

Malcom did the same as Friz and took a drink. He shrugged and said, "Yeah, I guess that is a little better."

"What a shame that you are so used to tasting these materials. You can scarcely notice their presence. You should be able to detect them immediately," Friz said.

They got into the car and Malcom started the engine. The clock read 1:18 a.m.

"Well, here I am in creepy Centralia at one in the morning…again. Look, Friz, if I can't use my phone, how am I supposed to get to Cassian in Boston? I really rely on my GPS. I don't know the way there," Malcom said.

"We are five hours and thirty-six minutes from Boston if we go the northern route. Take Route 81 north to Route 84 east. Stay on Route 84 until you get to Route 90, also known as the Mass Pike. Do you know how to get to Route 81 north?" Friz asked.

"Yes. I can get there, if you can guide me to Route 924 from here. But at some point, I am going to need to call Cassian to get his exact location," Malcom said.

"You can use your phone as long as I am not within about six feet of you. The farther the better. It is not something that has been well studied. The activated drug I took when I got here reduces the wild visions and will draw the Shazo out through my kidneys in about forty-eight hours. That will be another day, unfortunately."

"Yeah, those visions are something wild. I'm surprised the song didn't make me trip balls."

Friz looked puzzled and said, "Does that mean that you are clumsy… and…something to do with your testicles?"

Malcom erupted in laughter. "No. Again, it's just an expression. It means I would be hallucinating with no grip on reality." He continued to laugh as he said, "Clumsy testicles!"

Malcom eased the car onto the road and said, "Ok. Let's get going. After all that water, I hope there's a lot of places to stop and piss on the way."

Friz said, "Let us hope that when we stop I do not fall over my nut-sack."

Malcom started laughing again and Friz joined him.

"I can drive part of the way if you need to sleep, Malcom," Friz said.

"You know how to drive?"

"I have seen you do this. It seems quite simple. The speed limit signs? Are they meant to be a suggestion? Or is that meant to be the value *above* a specified value of which I am not aware?" Friz asked. "You seem to be consistently about twenty units above the suggestion."

Malcom laughed and said, "I do drive fast. But if you're going to drive, you should probably stick to no more than five miles per hour *over* that number. That will make you less suspicious than driving the speed limit or lower. Don't be a douche bag and drive that speed in the left lane. Five over the speed limit is slow for most people. Stay in the far-right lane as much as possible. That is actually the law."

"Thank you. I will watch you for a while to learn proper etiquette. I can take control of the vehicle when we get to Route 84. I will sleep once I get you to Route 81," Friz said.

"Sounds great to me," Malcom said.

CHAPTER 30

CONSEQUENCES

"Wake up, Ariel!" Victoria said as she shook Ariel's small frame. The man next to her was still snoring loudly.

"What? Where are we?" Ariel asked weakly.

"Get up, you slut!" Victoria said, "Jeff has been blowing up your phone all morning."

Ariel sat up suddenly. "What the fuck!" she yelled. "What did I… Where… Oh Fuck!"

"Yeah. 'Oh fuck' about sums it up, sweetie," Victoria said as she calmly watched Ariel's confused assessment of the situation.

Ariel sprang out of bed naked and said, "Oh no! No, no, no…please! Tell me I didn't have sex with this guy!"

"Ok," Victoria said, "where do you want me to say you *didn't* fuck him? The bed, the couch, the floor? Have you and Jeff *ever* had sex before? You were like an animal last night."

"Oh no!" Ariel started to cry, "What did I do?"

"I'd say just about everything," Victoria said. "Do you want a couple aspirin or something? I'm assuming you must be sore in a few places. You may also want to get a pregnancy test."

"Oh fuck, Victoria! I think I cheated on Jeff last night," Ariel said.

"Hey! Look who just joined the conversation," Victoria said. "After your performance last night, I'm surprised you're not saying, 'Jeff who?'"

"Oh no! No, no, no, no, no! What did I…" Ariel looked at the snoring man sleeping on the bed. "He can't be here. No. Not at all. He…

he needs to be gone. Victoria, help me! We need to get rid of him. This never happened!"

Victoria sighed and said, "Relax. Jeff doesn't have to know. But you should know, he is sitting outside the hotel right now in his truck. He doesn't know our room number yet, but who knows how long before he finds out. You need to get rid of this redneck piece of shit…toot… sweet."

"Please, Victoria! Can you just say you hooked up with him?"

"Not a *fucking* chance in hell, Ariel. I would never put *myself* in a situation where my relationship with Franklin could be compromised. You did this. Now *you* get rid of him!"

"But you were there! You saw it. I didn't…I didn't hook up…how did he even get here? *What the fuck*, Victoria?"

"Here's what I'll do. I'll go out and talk to Jeff for a while. I'll tell him you were upset with him hitting you."

"He didn't really hit me, Victoria. He just pushed me away from him after I punched him," Ariel said.

"Stop being such a stupid bitch! Did he put his hand on you at all?" Victoria shouted.

"Yeah. Like I said, he pushed me away so I didn't punch him again," Ariel said.

"Dumbass! You need to be yelling *in his face* that he hit you! That's the way you do it. Keep him on the defensive. Get your head straight! If anything, he made *you* fuck some other guy! It is *all…his…fault*!

"But…he really didn't…"

"Shut the fuck up, stupid. Do you want to get out of this or not?" Victoria yelled.

"Oh please. Please help me, Victoria," Ariel cried.

"Okay, I'm going down to get some coffee. You wake up Prince Charming and get his stupid ass out the door. I'll give you fifteen minutes. If I run into Jeff, he may try to follow me up here, so you get rid of *that*," she said, pointing at the body of Shep, still snoring, "before I get back."

Victoria grabbed her room key and purse, winked at Ariel, and walked out of the room.

Ariel immediately jumped on the man and yelled, "Get up! Get up! Hurry!"

"Wha…Whermaye…" he said, lifting his head off the pillow.

"Oh God, mister. You need to leave. Right away. My fiancé is outside now, looking for me," she said.

"Fiancé? What are you talkin' about? You're getting married?" he said.

"Oh jeez. I'm so sorry. But yes. He's outside lookin' for me. He don't know what room I'm in yet, but Victoria will be back soon, and he's gonna follow her. You gotta go. Now!" she said.

"Whaddya mean? I thought we had somethin' real special. I mean… last night we…well…"

"Please! Can you go? I'll give you my number, and we can talk later. I don't know what's going to happen with Jeff, my fiancé, but I can't be seen cheatin' on him before we even give it a go," she said. Then, to spark some urgency, she said, "I don't know if he has his guns or not."

"What?! He got a gun? What the fuck you sayin'? He's comin' up here packin'?" Shep said.

"Oh. I don't know that. I know he keeps his huntin' rifle in his truck. He might be mad right now, and I don't want to provoke him. So can you please just go?" she asked.

Shep jumped up and started getting his clothes on. As he did, he went to the closet and opened the door. There was a mini safe there. He entered a four-digit code and the safe opened. He pulled out a chrome-colored 0.357 magnum pistol and said, "That motherfucker tries anything with me an' he's gonna find a world o' hurt comin' at 'im!"

"No!" Ariel said. "Please don't do anything like that! He's a good man. He's just crazy about me."

A loud knock on the door started immediately. Victoria was only gone for five minutes. It couldn't possibly be Jeff.

"Ariel! Open this fuckin' door *right…fucking…now*!" Jeff yelled.

Ariel looked around in a panic. She pushed Shep into the adjoining room. When she did, she noticed that all of Victoria's belongings were gone.

While it was fun to watch her manipulations play out, Victoria had other things to do. She got into her car and started the engine. She could see commotion going on in the hotel lobby as she drove away.

It was time to cut Ariel from her life. Especially before the cops came.

She needed to get back home to Franklin. She was excited to see if her experiment worked. She felt what she summoned there, around his neck. Trapped. It recognized her touch. Would Franklin control it or would it control him. She could hardly wait to find out.

There was something about this man, Franklin. Something she didn't hate. She didn't have emotion for anyone…ever. But if he was what she suspected, she would soon be untouchable.

He would be happy to see her back home a day early. Franklin was so eager to please. He would also be happy to hear that he wouldn't have to go to Ariel's wedding.

She reached into the center console compartment and pulled out the small slip of paper with an address on it. It was in Concord, which was on her way back home.

Several weeks ago, while planning her trip to New Hampshire, she agreed to meet with this FBI agent. He wanted to know something about her previous marriage back when she lived in Pennsylvania. She wasn't going to meet with this man anywhere near where she lived, so she arranged to meet him in New Hampshire, far away from anyone she knew locally.

Oddly enough, as she drove south toward Concord, she approached a town called Franklin. That made her smile. *Every state must have a Franklin*, she thought. They were living in the town of Franklin, Massachusetts.

Victoria pulled into the parking lot of a diner. This was the address that Agent Sam Smith gave her. That sounded like a bullshit handle. *Wasn't there a cartoon FBI agent by that name?* she thought. What did she care what he called himself? She intended to be nothing but cooperative with the law.

She parked the SUV and walked up the ramp to the front door. The place looked like an old, converted trailer that was made into a diner. She opened the door to a long counter with fixed stools running the length.

Coffee pots and several griddles and stoves lined the back wall. Glass containers with various pies and donuts were placed about the counter. There were tables made for groups of two or four along the front windows. A typical greasy-spoon restaurant.

She formed a mental image of a bald, fat FBI agent wearing a sweaty, button-down, short-sleeved shirt and a black tie that was too short. He would be eating a full breakfast with a short stack of pancakes.

She scanned the room and didn't see anyone matching that description. What she did see was a massive guy at the far end of the building sitting at a table as he faced the front door. The man had to be a foot taller than Franklin, and Franklin was a big guy. Seated at a table for four, he took up nearly the whole bench made for two people. When he saw her, he raised his hand and made a quick wave toward himself.

As she walked closer to him, she fixated on his deep-set, wild, hazel eyes. Normally confident and fearless, something about this man made Victoria feel like she was in over her head. Raw power seethed from him.

"Victoria Germane," the man said, "Please have a seat," he gestured to the bench across from him.

"Are you Agent Smith?" she asked.

"Samuel Smith. You can call me Sam," he said in a cheerful tone with a smile that didn't fit any aspect of his intensity. "Would you like something to eat? Or possibly some coffee?"

"Coffee would be nice," she said timidly as she sat across from the giant.

Sam looked up and waved his hand, "Another coffee over here, please, Gina."

A moment later, a thin, gaunt woman skillfully carried a pot of coffee in one hand and a cup on a saucer, a paper placemat, menu, and a wrapped set of silverware in the other. She set the items down in front of Victoria and filled the cup with coffee and said, "Would you like some more, Mister Sam?"

"Yes, please," he said holding out his cup.

"I'll give you a moment to look at a menu, dear," she said to Victoria.

"No thank you. Just coffee for me," she said.

Gina took the menu and left.

Samuel said, "Tom Penner used to be the lawyer for my great grand-parents. I never met my great grandparents or Tom. Of course, they're all dead now. You were married to Tom, so that makes you kind of old, doesn't it? Of course, you weren't too old back then. That must have worked out pretty good for a young girl like you. Marrying an older lawyer and inheriting his money when you were what? Twenty-four?"

Victoria gave him a cold stare and said, "Is there a question you're asking? It sounds like you already know the answers."

"You're a sharp one. I rarely ask a question I don't already know the answer to," Samuel said, gently picking up the coffee cup and taking a sip. It looked like an espresso cup in his huge hand.

Victoria sipped her own cup of black coffee and said, "What is it I can do to help the Federal Bureau of Investigation, Agent Smith?"

"Please, call me Sam," he smiled, which made him look more vicious than friendly. "I'm looking for some of Tom Penner's old clients. Clients from around the time you must have started…ahem…*dating* him. One particular client named Cassian Nazarovich. I believe you knew him in high school, didn't you Mrs. Germane?"

Victoria made no indication that she knew him as she said, "Yes, I went to high school with him. It's not a secret. That was a very long time ago as you impassively pointed out. Despite what we may have written in each other's yearbooks, we did not actually stay in touch. So again, what is it that I can do for you?"

"Oh, I'm wondering if you may have the files from the office of Tom Penner stored somewhere. I would very much like to look at those."

Victoria let out a sigh and said, "That's all you want? Look, if I had them…which I do not…I would hand them over to you without a ques-tion. His lawyer–client confidentiality ended when he died as far as I'm concerned. But there was no way in hell I was lugging around all that paperwork.

"You seem to be a young man. Perhaps you didn't know this. Back then, these records were not stored on a computer. There were boxes upon boxes of files. I paid to have them burned. Now, if you want the receipt from the company that burned the files, *that* I could get you."

Samuel leaned forward and stared at Victoria. A cold chill went through her body. The smile that made him look vicious seemed warm and friendly compared to the look on his face now. She shrank back into her seat, feeling genuine fear coursing through her body. This man may decide to kill her and everyone in this diner at any minute. And from the look of it, he could do it. The police would not stop this man out of sheer terror.

Samuel leaned a little closer and began to sniff. He leaned back in his seat, turned his head slightly as he kept his eyes fixed on her. He gave her a wry, crooked smile as he said, "Very interesting."

"Is there anything else I can do for you," Victoria said weakly.

"No. I thank you for taking the time to meet with me, Mrs. Germane. You can go if you like. I'll pick up the tab for the coffee. It's the least the FBI can do for you after traveling all the way from Franklin, Massachusetts, to meet me," he said.

"It's really no trouble. I was here visiting a friend," she said, standing from the table. "Thank you for the coffee."

"Of course. You have a nice trip back home," he said.

She nodded as she turned to leave.

"One more thing," he said. Victoria felt her blood curdle. "Your husband, Franklin Germane, is he from Western Pennsylvania too?"

"No," she said. "He's from Providence, Rhode Island." Then, for some reason, she asked, "Why?"

Samuel smiled and said, "I wanted to know where he grew up. It's good to see a fellow Pennsyltucky native elevating herself with a fancy Brown University graduate. To be frank, it would be weird if your husband named Franklin was born and raised in a town called Franklin, frankly."

Victoria, feeling a swell of aggravation, responded, "There was no need for the adverb 'frankly' at the end of a sentence you began with the prepositional phrase, 'to be frank,' Agent Smith. Your impertinent candor is quite clear."

Ignoring her tone, Samuel said, "You probably remember the Bosco family. The small-time crime family out your way that sort of…disappeared. There was a guy named Charlie Germane who did a bunch of work for them. Seems his family kind of disappeared too. Your husband's middle name is Charles. Franklin Charles Germane. I was wondering if you met your second husband in Western or Central Pennsylvania?"

"Oh…ah…no. I only met Franklin after I was working in Boston. He's not from Pennsyltucky," she said.

"Something else that puzzles me. You were already wealthy when you decided to go to medical school. Why put yourself through all that shit? You could have just invested and done…whatever you wanted."

"Well, Agent Smith, this may come as a surprise to you, but I wanted to help people in this world," Victoria said.

"Ohhh, is that what you do? Huh? You *help* people!" Samuel let out a deep, hearty, disingenuous laugh, "Okay. Well, you have a nice day… *Doctor*!"

Victoria scowled at Agent Smith as she turned and walked from the diner.

CHAPTER 31

THE SEARCH

CASS SMELLED BACON COOKING. HE opened his eye and looked at the plaster swirls on the ceiling of Franklin's living room. Stiffness pained his back from sleeping on the couch.

He drank half a pint of white tequila after Franklin and Corrina said their goodnights to him and each other around midnight. Sleeping became extremely difficult for Cass as life went on. Many of his deeds haunted him and self-forgiveness was not a simple task. He could never quite break the chains of guilt.

Cass limited drinking to after 8 p.m. and kept the amount below any major, short-term toxic effects. But he knew it wasn't a healthy lifestyle. The alcohol problem of his father and other family members always lived in the forefront of his mind. He knew he had a problem. The only real control he had over it was placing strict limits on his use...*rules*, he thought and laughed. *How many times have I broken those rules*, he thought? How many times had he prayed for help? Ex could do nothing for him in that regard. All that Ex would ever say was that his decisions were the pathway of God.

Cass rubbed his face, looking around as he sat up. He saw Corrina, with her back to him, cooking at the stove. He said in a cheery voice, "Good morning, Corrina! How did you sleep?"

"Cassian, I slept better last night than I have in twenty years! I think everything we did yesterday must have really did me in," Corrina said, matching his cheer. "But I had some crazy dreams."

"Really? Can you tell me about them?" Cass prodded.

Corrina said, "It's all kind of hazy now, but I do remember standing on this mountain. Below me was a big lake that was orange, like the sun was reflecting off it in the early morning. In the center of the lake, there was a column of white light. Then there was a man next to me with no face."

The cheerful look fell from Cassian's face.

Corrina continued, "He reminded me of someone, but I couldn't see him. He left me and walked down to the lake, but there didn't seem like any path. All these things that looked like big, black bugs were coming at him and some girl he was with. Then he stuck his arm in the lake and pulled out a shiny rod or stick or something. He slammed it into the ground and killed them all. Then there was like a bridge over the lake, and this man turned to me and said, 'I'll be back,' but I knew he was lying because he told me he was going to lie. I don't know. It was a weird one."

Cassian wore a look of shock as he pressed, "Did he say where he was going?"

"I don't know. I don't remember. You know how dreams are." she said.

"Oh yeah," Cass said, looking puzzled, "I know all about them."

"Mom?" Franklin's voice came down the hallway, "Where the hell did you find bacon in this house?"

"Oh, you had bacon in the back of your freezer. Not sure when the last time you had bacon was. This said it should be sold by 2019. But frozen bacon doesn't go bad. This tastes just fine," Corrina said.

"Mom! That stuff's expired. You shouldn't be eating that!" Franklin said.

"What do you want me to do? Throw it out? This poor pig sacrificed its life so we could benefit from the nutrition it provides us. And you think I would just throw it out because of a date on a package put there by a company that wants to sell you more of their product? No sir. You owe it to this brave animal to consume its sacrifice!" Corrina said.

"Well, Ex commends your viewpoint, Corrina," Cass said.

"Good God," Franklin said. "You Boomers are going to kill us all with your fatty diets!"

"Franklin, you need to look deeper into actual, unfiltered statistics before you make comments like that. More health problems have arisen from modern, low-fat diets than times when people ate bacon and beef two or three times a day.

"And we're not Boomers. We are GenX. We might drink water from a garden hose when we were thirsty, but the ones you call Boomers would drink water directly from a creek. Now, everyone needs a sealed water bottle that was purchased for no less than two dollars.

"While there are some generational trends, don't fall into that foolish mindset of blindly categorizing people," Cass said. "This will lead you to the same tribal mentality as labeling individuals. Your mind is too strong for that."

"I don't know why you think I'm so smart, Cass. I've been blind to a lot of things. Like the way I followed my wife for the last ten years. I thought about this last night as I laid in bed. I've been a fool for a long time," Franklin said.

"No, you haven't, Franklin," Cass said. "You're just a novice playing a game against an expert. And before you say anything more, let that sink in. I can promise you it will make perfect sense before this day ends. But it's too early for that kind of talk! How did you sleep?"

Franklin looked like he was about to say something and then shrugged, "I slept okay. Just messed up dreams."

"Really?" Cass said. Corrina looked at Cass. "Can you tell me about them?"

"They were weird, man. I was holding hands with two different women. I don't know who they were. We were walking up this hill. I remember the sky in front of us was this cool color of aqua blue with hints of orange. It seemed so peaceful and happy. I looked over to one woman and I said something. I don't remember what she looked like, but she smiled and agreed. Then I looked at the other woman. It was Victoria. I think she was trying to pull away from me," Franklin sighed heavily.

"Then what happened," Corrina asked, looking concerned.

"Well, we got to the top of the hill, and we were looking down over this huge lake, and it was like the water was on fire or something. There was like a…I don't know…a glowing white tube sticking out of the center of the lake. It went all the way into the sky," Franklin said.

Cass shifted his gaze to Corrina and gave his head a slight shake.

"Across the lake, I could see you, Mom, and someone I couldn't make out. I tried to see who it was, but it was all blurry. This is where it gets really weird. He pulls out a sword, at least it looked like a sword, and jammed it into the lake. Then, everything exploded and I woke up. Like I said—weird."

Cassian sat looking down and to the left while Franklin went into the kitchen and said good morning to his mother. He stole a piece of cooked bacon and said, "Oh my God! I haven't had bacon in forever. It's so delicious!"

Franklin got coffee and sat at the kitchen table as he chatted with his mother about old times.

"This can't possibly be happening!" Cassian said. "You both had the same dream from different sides of the lake! How could either of you know about this?"

"What are you talking about, Cass?" Corrina said. "Did you have the same dream or something?"

"Yes. No, I was…I was the one with…" Cass stopped himself short. Then he said, "I was…I don't see how it's possible that you both had this dream?"

Franklin turned to look at Cass and said, "You're lying. What are you lying about, Cass?"

"Nothing. Let's just drop it. Dreams are just dreams. This was probably a fluke. You were thinking about the story I told you last night, about going into Hell," Cass said.

"You didn't tell us about that yet, Cass," Corrina said. "You also said that dreams are *not* just dreams. Are you doing okay? You look pale and sick," she said with genuine concern in her voice.

"No. I told you about the katabasis. Didn't I? You couldn't know about that lake if I didn't tell you," Cass said, looking confused.

"No, dude," Franklin said, "You said katabasis and then ended the night. Don't you remember?"

Cass put his head in his hands and said, "No, I don't. I had crazy dreams too. I was everywhere. And you should probably know, I drink at night, and sometimes I get events mixed up," Cassian lied.

"What are you talking about? You didn't drink last night," Franklin said.

Cass pulled out the half-empty pint of tequila and set it on the coffee table. "I drink about that much every night. It helps me sleep. Then I sometimes get things confused," he said, even though he knew that was a lie. He *never* got events confused.

"You sat up, alone, last night…drinking?" Corrina asked.

"Uhh…yes. I just said I did. I'm not lying to you. I'm telling you that I have a problem with alcohol. I get it honest. It runs in my family," Cassian said.

"Well, at least you can admit it," Franklin said. "That's the first step."

"That's what I keep hearing, but believe me…it's the second step that takes the courage I lack," Cass said.

"Why don't you get help somewhere? Like a rehab?" Franklin asked.

"We don't need a surprise intervention for me right now. We need to get through this story before your wife gets home. I think the three of you need to have a long talk," Cass said, nodding slightly.

Franklin looked down and said, "Yeah, I know. I don't know what to expect. But you're right about that."

"It will be fine, Franklin. You may be pleasantly surprised. Things could work out much better for you. But you will know the truth, and you will have your mother back in your life. You need that now, more than ever.

"But let's eat before I get started again," Cass said, exuberantly.

Franklin laughed and said, "You're funny, man. You get so excited about food. What else are you over there making, Mom? I hope you're not making pancakes. I love them, but I'll be right back in bed if I eat those."

"No. Just scrambled eggs, toast, and bacon. I put cheese in the eggs, so I hope you don't have any problems with that," Corrina said.

"No. No problem with that!" Cass smiled.

"Yeah, I'm good with cheese," Franklin said, "But I think we only had cheddar in the fridge."

"No. You had American cheese back there. I know it's not the best thing for you, but it sure melts nice in the eggs," she said.

"Yeah!" Cass said. "But never use garlic in eggs. A little onion powder, salt, pepper, and Tabasco™ sauce. I love it!"

"You're in luck. We've got Tabasco™ and habanero sauce," Franklin said.

"Ohhh…even better!" Cass said.

Franklin smiled and shook his head as he went to the closet and got out both the sauces. He said, "I need to take a video of you eating so I always have an image of what pure joy looks like!" He laughed as he started to prepare the toast and a few English muffins.

"Sure, pizza, eggs, and bacon…I'm a vision of happiness. But throw a kale and quinoa salad in front of me and I'm like a fat kid who just dropped his ice cream cone in a cat litter box," Cass said.

Franklin and Corrina both started laughing. More so because of his seriousness than the actual comment.

Once they were done eating, Cass helped clean up and loaded the dishwasher. Then he went right into the story.

"I began in the public library. I'm a slow reader, but I started searching books about Heaven and Hell. From the Bible to Dante's Inferno, both of which were difficult for me to understand. Did you know that the name of Mephistopheles is never mentioned in the Bible? Another thing that was used as a lesson since Ex came into my life. Apparently, this was a name given to Satan by Faust in the late 1500s," Cass said.

"Yes, I knew that. How was it used as a lesson?" Franklin asked.

"The Dunning–Kruger effect. In college, I got into a debate about religion with my suitemate who was Jewish. He was well studied in theology, whereas I—being possessed by an actual angel—must *clearly* know far more about religion than he. Ex and Stu both told me that Mephistopheles was a *biblical* name. I argued up and down with David that he was wrong. I even bet one hundred dollars…which I did not have!

"To this day, I still feel I need to check everything Ex or Stu told me. You see, that was the point. I was meant to look like a fool over something stupid so that I would learn to do my own research. Yeah…very funny, asshole," Cass said aloud to Ex who was laughing in his mind.

Franklin and Corrina both started to laugh. Franklin asked, "How many times have you fallen for that kind of stuff?"

Cass smiled and nodded, "So far, everything that was important has been true. And Ex will never let any decision that could affect my life be tainted by false information. At least, as far as she knows. Which is another layer of lessons about believing those who are certain of the information they possess. There are still small things, like a name or a date, where I look it up before speaking about it.

"You would think that getting the information right from the source would be reliable, but that was also a lesson in trusting your sources. Any time I relax with my own knowledge, I feel like Cato is going to jump out and attack me with the truth."

This time it was Corrina who laughed while Franklin said, "What's that supposed to mean? Who's Cato?"

"You'll have to watch the old Pink Panther movies if you want to get that reference," Corrina said.

Cass continued, "I read the Book of Enoch, which provided some insightful visuals. There are a lot of theories out there, and a lot more books about religion than the Bible, I can tell you that. Some have partial validity and others, not so much. But I believe all have been corrupted by the Spurs to one degree or another.

"At that point in time, after what I read, I believed that I had already seen Hell in my dreams. And I believed that the Dream World was the key. I still believe that now.

"I began to learn about my own, seemingly innate ability to resonate with life. I knew a little about it, but trying to consciously control it caused immense frustration when I started. Imagine if I told you to make your eardrum tighter or asked you to flex the iris of your eye.

"This is a sense we all have, and something that is very strong in me. But it is still not something easily accessed.

"You've seen gifted athletes who can pick up nearly any sport and in months exceed the abilities of seasoned veterans who played for years. Musicians who can play every instrument as naturally as a fish can swim. I am in touch with my ability to resonate with others.

"We *all* have this ability. Like when you can tell that someone is in a mood when they enter a room. They look the same as usual; they speak the same as usual; they seem the same in every way. But you can *tell* something is wrong. Something is off. That is your own ability.

"Like a good salesperson that can resonate with buyers. It is one of the senses that the Spurs and demons would prefer you did not access.

"I can match certain resonances with other life forms. I can see and feel what they see and feel. I can send them feelings. I can make them sick or make them feel better. As I did when you trapped me, Franklin. There are even things I have been able to cure," Cass said.

"You mean from your angel, right?" Corrina asked.

"I don't think so. I think this is something that awoke within me. Maybe it was the head trauma from my car wreck. Whatever it was, you have both witnessed it. When I am angry or passionate, my voice can take on a power of its own, so loud at times that I have hurt people.

"My grandmother understood. She knew what I needed to do. She funded the next few years of my life. She inherited a lot when Bill… died. She also gave me the keys to a lodge she and Bill owned in the mountains of Colorado. She had never been there as far as she knew. Perhaps the Spur that trapped her might have gone there with Bill.

"Anyway, this Cysistal stone kind of guided me too. From time to time, it still does. Maybe it's something we can investigate later. But, when I would hold it, I pictured myself alone in the mountains. I also pictured a tiny log cabin with an outhouse for a bathroom.

"When I got to the lodge my grandmother gave me the keys to, I was pleasantly surprised by what I found. Indoor plumbing with a large, open kitchen, dining, and living room. Two bedrooms off either side of a bathroom that had a tub and separate shower. It was well furnished and nicer than the house I grew up in. I was not going to be roughing it.

"It seems the vision of the stone was only partially right. I stayed there alone, disappearing from the world I knew. There was so much life in the mountains. I had all the things I needed for practice. And that's what I did during my waking hours.

"I started with small animals. I reached out to the life around me and felt their presence. Soon I could focus on one animal. A squirrel or a chipmunk or a deer. Chipmunks are amazing by the way. The speed of thought and movement makes a squirrel seem slow.

"Once, a grizzly bear approached my cabin. I was told that grizzlies don't live in Colorado. That's complete bullshit. I don't think anything could tell *him* where to go. You cannot imagine the strength I felt in one of his paws. I swear, I could have ripped an oak tree right out of the ground!"

"Well, did the stone tell you anything else?" Franklin asked.

"Not really. For the most part, it's kind of lame and doesn't do much. Not since that night. If I hold it and concentrate, it sometimes gives me visions. Or maybe feelings. I don't know how to describe it. But I think it may have—" Cass stopped himself and said, "I will tell you more about it soon."

Cass changed the subject and said, "When I started to understand my power better, I was able to focus my mind and flex those things that cannot be flexed. One day, after I had been alone for several months, practicing my control, I went into the city of Denver.

"I thought my vision was starting to go bad as everyone I saw had an aura around them. I kept rubbing my eyes. Then I realized that the auras were made of many different colors. If I unfocused, the auras went away. Refocusing, they appeared. I could see the red aura of an angry man and the calm blue of a woman sitting on a bench in the sun. Children playing had huge yellow auras. It was amazing, but not surprising that their resonance would affect the visible color spectrum.

"Then I realized I could draw on their energy and alter my own mood. Just as I could change my own aura and modify theirs. People do this every day, but they don't see it…not in the way I was able to *visually* see it," he said.

"So, you can make people happy or sad or angry?" Franklin said, looking and sounding annoyed.

"Not entirely. They must have it in them already, Franklin," Cass said, giving Franklin a knowing look and a slight shake of his head. "I can make an angry person less angry, but I cannot make them peaceful or happy. Do you understand what I'm saying?"

Franklin nodded slightly. He knew now what Cass had done to him last night. But Cass didn't want Corrina to know he pushed Franklin like that.

"Every night, I searched the Dream World. I took various drugs to enhance my dreams. I tried mind-altering plants. I studied the doses and amounts. I read testimonials and relied on anecdotal experiences. I puked my ass off with mushrooms. And I thought I was going to die when I tried ayahuasca. Almost all the substances reduced the amount of dreaming I did. Nothing seemed to work as well as alcohol. And it wasn't that the alcohol made me dream. It seemed like the alcohol did something to the chemicals that *erase* your dreams. I think it begins to counter this process. Because after drinking, each time I woke, I could *recall* more and more of my dreams. I swear, everything on this planet, even the toxins, serve a purpose if you can see what that purpose is.

"After three years, I could easily drink a fifth of vodka in a night and wake without a hangover. Of course, I didn't drink that much every night. And in that time, I searched. I looked for guides and markers in the Dream World. I interacted with beings both faceless and not. I worked at trying to focus my mind over there.

"For a long time, I found nothing that could help me find Mary. Then, one night, I dreamed of being on a familiar beach…one I knew. I jumped into the air and flew south, and I found the spot where the massive waves pounded against the rock wall. This was not Hell, but this was a place I recognized. It was the entrance to what I called *the Library*. In my excitement, I flew directly to the entrance of the cave. But before I made it to the opening, a huge wave slammed me into the face of the cliff.

"I woke immediately…and I swear I felt the physical pain of being blasted into the rocks. I rolled onto my side trying to catch my breath. I had the wind knocked out of me. I was so pissed at myself. I was right there and I blew it. I knew I was supposed to run and not fly into the cavern. It has to be a *challenge* to get in.

"I spent the next few months trying to find it again. Then it happened. I found the beach and the edifice of caves. This time, I walked close to the wall and saw the entrance I wanted. Before I ran, I patiently sat on the beach and focused so hard on feeling this place. I began to resonate with the waves and the life around it. I don't know if it's a physically *real* location or not, but it felt as real as this while I sat in that dream.

I got up and ran for the entrance. This time, I was too slow and once again, I found myself abruptly awake, feeling like a fly that got swatted.

"But the next night, I found the beach easily. Now, I can always find it. I can't always get in, but I can find the entrance. And I figured if I could find the entrance to this, there must be a hidden entrance to Hell.

"I found out later that this is because Heaven, Hell, and Limbo—which is the Dream World—are located in something called the Time realm. But I'm not going start discussing that. Not because I don't want to tell you. I simply don't know enough. There seems to be physical barriers that separates the three places, but I honestly know very little about it.

"Besides, I'm not even certain that what I was told was true. I think Stu kept something from me. When I pushed him, he gave me a bunch of talk about infinity and going crazy.

"The next night, I managed to get into the caves. It took some searching, but I found the peaceful pool I was looking for. The one with the golden light coming from the depths. I jumped in and soon found the dark tunnel I needed. I swam through, pulling myself along the rocks. It seemed so much farther than I remembered. I saw the light and swam to it. I crawled out of the water to find the same chamber with the eleven books. There was someone standing in the center of the room."

<hr>

"Khalima? What are you doing here?" Cass asked.

"You know who I am," she said, "I cannot see your face, but I know who you are. No eyes can see us here, but I will not use your name. You sent her to Hell. It is not your fault, though, but mine. I know that she wanted to do as I had done. I should have better warned her against doing such a foolish thing."

"I was furious when I found out she chose to be a Spur," Cass said.

"I am certain that you were. I know your resonant…the one you call Stu," she said.

"You know Stu!" Cass said, excited.

"Yes. But that is not important now. Our time is short. The stewards were betrayed by high-level members. That is how they were able to find…your love. And she led them to you. I am so sorry, but I am here to help you. The location you seek is here."

She held out a small coin-like item. Cass reached for it, but she slapped his hand away.

"I am not giving this to you. Just look!" She said, irritated.

She held it out again and an image began to form. A deep trench in the ocean. On one side were caves and on the other side a large, underwater building. It was immense. He had seen it before the time he saw Jimmy in his dream. But the image she was showing him led far deeper than where he explored.

"Focus on this region," she said. "This is the bottom level of Hell. Find her and get her out. You cannot save her soul. Only she can do that. You *can* get her back into the Dream World. She will be with the other Spurs again. You must warn her to never try to find you or any other person again."

"But I love her, Khalima. I want her back again so badly," Cass said.

"I understand. But you must be patient. It may not happen in this lifetime. If you truly love her, you will need to wait. Now, focus on this place," she said firmly. "Fix it within your mind."

Cassian sat on the floor and focused his mind on the image. He could feel the water and the weight of the water at that depth. The building and the caves he etched in his mind. Then the image disappeared.

"You must only go here on a night that is a *new* moon. That is important. Do you understand? If you try at any other time, you could become trapped here. And if you ever find yourself there on a full moon, may God help you.

"Also, you need to be careful of her siblings. One of them means you great harm but has little power. The other means well for you but has a power to cause you great harm," Khalima said.

"What's that supposed to mean?" Cass asked.

But Khalima was gone. He stood and looked around the room. The books all had light on them except for the first book on his far right.

A deep voice he recognized said from behind him, "We meet again."

Cass turned. While he couldn't see a face, Cass recognized him. It was Vader.

Cass said, "Do you come here so often that I will run into you each time I am here?"

"It is true that I come here often. I see that you were able to find it again. Perhaps we will need to set a schedule or become friends. Which would you prefer?" Vader said.

"I think we could be friends," Cass said. "And I now understand why you wish to remain anonymous."

"Very well. We can sha—what? What is happening here? The first book is unprotected. How is this possible? Did you do something!?" Vader said, alarmed.

Cass did not mention Khalima. He said, "Not me. When I got here, it was like that. What does this mean?"

They both approached the first book. It hung above its podium, but no light surrounded it. Cass began to reach forward when Vader said, "Do you know what could happen if you touch that?"

Cass paused and said, "No. Do you know?"

"I do not. It could kill you," Vader said.

"I can live with that," Cass said as he grabbed the book.

When he touched the binding, he felt as if he were launched from a slingshot. He flew across the galaxy at an incredible and painful speed. It lasted for a long time before he hit a wall and found himself standing in a room where the walls emitted a low greenish color. Before him was a creature unlike anything he had ever seen. It was a terrifying figure that stood upright maybe ten to twelve feet in height. It had three pairs of arms and six pair of eyes that Cass could see. Its skin was smooth, without wrinkles, and deeply brown in color. It wore plain, gray clothing.

Then it spoke, "The one you call Khalima told me you would be here. I didn't believe it, but here you are."

"Vader? Is that you?" Cass asked.

"No," it said, moving closer to Cass. Cass stepped back from the creature in fear.

It saw Cassian's reaction and stopped. Instantly it changed into a young, handsome man. He said, "You know me, Cassian."

"Stu?"

"Ahhh, to be remembered," Stu said, then began speaking in the quick manner Cass knew. "It is premature for us to meet again, but since you are here, I will speak with you briefly before sending you back. The stone you possess is called a Cysistal stone. I can communicate messages to you, but they will not be messages like you may expect. It may be a feeling or an image. These stones can be loaded with a message that will only be revealed to one if the stone matches the exact atmospheric conditions as when the message was created. They must also match those conditions if a message is to be sent. I will tell you more when we have time. This will be used for emergencies, Cassian. If you get a strong message from the stone, listen to it.

"It was forbidden to send you this stone, and it is also forbidden to do what I am going to do now. I am going to allow you access to the first of the books. As you have been so betrayed by two of our leaders, it has been sanctioned as a fair concession. I am sorry for what you suffered.

"If I were to allow the entire book to enter your mind, you would never wake from your sleep. Your life would expire before the information contained within could be stored in your mind. The transfer of data does not stop until it is complete. Only Karma level stewards access the *full* information of any book and it takes several years to complete one."

"Have you read them all?" Cassian asked.

"No. I am not yet Karma level until our time is done. I have accessed five of them, and none completely," Stu said.

"I thought you said once it starts, it goes until it is complete?" Cass said.

"They do. But like any other book, there are chapters. We do a chapter at a time, and the information must then mature in the mind. We also have synoptic versions of each book. They are abbreviated but cover the high points. After our time together has ended, I will move to a Karma level where I can access up to book eleven. That is book nine to you. It will take a long time to gather the rest of the knowledge.

"What I will allow is for you to download an even shorter synoptic version of book one. The transfer rate must be slow, but the process will be quick. Only about three days. When you wake, you must replenish your water immediately. You will feel weak for a time. Eat a lot of food that is high in protein and fat, particularly cholesterol. I'm sure you will hate being told you must eat pizza and ice cream," Stu said sarcastically.

"That thing you were…before you changed…was that…?" Cassian asked.

"That is our true form. They are generic but very efficient bodies used to house our souls. I could see that it frightened you, so I modified my appearance. Now, Cassian, our cycle will align again in several years. As I am in a realm of…True Light…my understanding of time is not good. The item I left in place of the book allowed for your gravitational component to be projected here. But I will not talk about that now.

"You will have more than enough information that you are about to absorb. Are you prepared?"

"What's going to happen now?" Cass asked.

"You will simply wake up. But you will feel like a troll shit in your mouth with a headache beyond your worst hangover. You will have soiled yourself. Drink and eat immediately. And when we meet again, you will still need another vessel to speak with me. I cannot speak in your mind as you now do with your angel. Do you understand?"

"So then what? I just wake up feeling like hell after I pissed myself? What's the upside here, Stu?" Cass asked.

"What makes you believe that 'soiling yourself' means urination?" Stu asked, smiling.

"Oh man! That's so fucked. Well, then what?" Cassian asked.

"Over the next few weeks, the information will mature and become accessible while you sleep. In a month or so, well after you replace your bed mattress, you will understand a fraction of the first book. It is still a lot of information. If your angel asks, tell it that I spoke to you within a dream. That is permitted and believable. Best not to mention the books.

"And…well, it is good to see you again, Cassian. Know that I am working with Khalima to help you. Good luck to you!"

"Thanks, Stu. It's good to talk to you again. You can turn back into yourself. I'm not afraid now that I know it's you," Cass said.

The huge creature stood before him. Cass surprised him by hugging him. Four of Stu's six arms hugged him back. The huge creature bent and for a few minutes it whispered something into Cassian's ear.

Then Cassian flew backward the same way he arrived.

CHAPTER 32

THE DRAGON'S WISDOM

"WELL, WHAT DID STU WHISPER in your ear?" Corrina asked. Cass gave a stern look and slowly shook his head. Then he casually said, "Oh, he was telling me more about what to expect when I woke.

"I can tell you one thing…Stu undersold what I was going to face. It was so much worse than any hangover. Ex was worried that I had been trapped in the Dream World, or worse, in Hell.

"I really think I may have been close to death. I couldn't walk. I rolled out of my shit-covered bed and crawled into the bathroom. I stuck my head under the facet and drank until my stomach hurt. Then threw most of it back up in the toilet. I laid there for a while trying to let some of the water hydrate me. I kept sipping more water until I didn't throw up again. I turned on the hot water in the tub and let it fill. I struggled out of my soiled clothes and fell into the tub. After I cleaned myself, I filled the tub again and lay there, feeling miserable.

"In about an hour, I couldn't take the hunger any longer. I crawled into the kitchen and opened the fridge door. I had some Chinese food that still seemed good, so I heated it in the microwave and ate it greedily at first, but then quickly slowed down. I didn't want to vomit that up too," Cass said.

"That's sounds pretty awful, Cassian," Corrina said. "But why couldn't Ex take care of your body?"

"It has something to do with when I'm in the Dream World. Ex can surround my mind, but if she were to take over my body when I am dreaming, it might sever the connection of my soul to my body. It is completely different than when I am possessing another person here in this world," Cass said.

"How long until you were able to walk again?" Franklin asked.

"Oh, that didn't take too long. Maybe three hours or so. I probably ate about five thousand calories and drank two gallons of water in that time. I had slept for three days, but I felt tired. Ex was able to give me a boost of energy, but it was my mind that was tired.

"I cleaned the bed, as best I could, but I was going to have to replace that mattress. I slept in the other, smaller bedroom until I could have one delivered."

"So, what happened after that?" Franklin asked. "I mean over the next month or so?"

"Oh. That. Well, every night I went to sleep, I woke the next day with more and more knowledge. Things I told you about the Matriarchy, the Nephilim, the overcorrection with the Patriarchy...all this began to fill my mind as if I had known the stories since childhood.

"Really amazing way to learn...if you can survive the aftermath. Maybe if I were in a hospital bed, hooked up to an IV, it would be worth doing," Cass said.

"How can you be sure the information is correct? What if you were tricked by the Spurs?" Corrina asked.

"I did think of that. And...I am sorry about that, Ex," Cass said aloud. He spoke to Corrina and Franklin and said, "You see, I exaggerated to Ex when I told her I was able to meet with Stu in the Dream World. Ex knew that it might be possible for my resonant to speak with me there but warned me of the dangers of prying eyes. I said we were careful not to mention names. I never said anything about the cavern where none could see or hear us...the one with the books," Cass looked down and to the right.

"Yes. I said I'm sorry. You know why I did it. But now you know the truth," Cass said.

Then he spoke to Franklin and Corrina, "I never told Ex that I accessed the first book...or even knew about the existence of the eleven books. This may be a sore spot for a while, but she will understand.

"Some time after I recovered from that experience, I pressed her about the information surrounding the Nephilim and the time of the Matriarchy. Naturally, she wanted to know how I knew anything about that. It was not written in any of our histories. So, I bent the truth and told her that Stu told me in a dream.

"Ex confirmed that what was implanted in my head was truth.

"After I fully recovered, I waited for the next new moon. It was, oddly enough, the new moon of Friday, October 31, 1997. Halloween. Nothing in the world could have prepared me for this. It was not like uploading the information from the first book where I woke after three days and it felt like only a moment had passed. It was the opposite of that. I slept for only one night, but it was the longest and most horrible time of my life.

"I went to sleep that Halloween after drinking a smaller, but appropriate amount. When I began to dream, I focused on the image Khalima had showed me…"

Cass stood on the edge of a high cliff overlooking the ocean. The dark gray and purple sky threatened an impending storm. Lightning struck over the water and the thunder quickly rolled to his ears. He turned right to see a tremendous structure where violent waves crashed against the sides.

The squat, gray, rectangular building without windows or any features protruded about one hundred feet above the surface of the water and sat about one hundred feet below the cliff upon which Cassian stood. The building appeared to be the size of a large island. He guessed maybe two miles long by two miles wide, but it was impossible to tell in the dark, dreary atmosphere. Looking down into the black sea water, nothing could be seen other than the furious white caps.

Lightning crashed again, this time much closer. Cass gathered his courage and ran for the edge of the cliff, diving out over the water. He plunged into the ocean and began to swim. Deeper and deeper he went, but there seemed to be no end to the building. Occasionally, huge, dark, tentacled creatures would swim up toward the surface as he continued plunging farther into the abyss. None appeared to notice him.

Soon there was no sound and soon after that, there was no light. Yet Cassian continued to swim straight down. Time dragged on for hours as he sank lower and lower into the pit that must be Hell. His eyes adjusted to the dark and he could faintly see the structure on his left as he swam still deeper. Occasionally, he would notice openings in the building, but they were not where he needed to go.

Finally, a faint, orange light began to show from below. It was still a long time before Cass was able to make out the scene that Khalima had showed him.

He arrived at the base of the structure, which looked as if it sat upon an immense bed of lava.

Focusing on Mary, he reached out to her. Nothing happened. He swam around the building, searching for a way in and finally found a group of windows opening into the building. They were like the ones he remembered from years before.

He dove into one of the thresholds and fell on to the floor of a dark, dank room, covered in black slime. Though everything was wet, the external water did not fill the room.

Row upon row of enormous columns reached far into the darkness above. Each column was easily twenty feet long by ten feet wide. The heavy pressure on his body added to the misery of the scene.

Cassian heard the faint ringing in his ears that got louder and closer. Soon a red and white pulsing light began to illuminate the depths outside. Cass hid behind one of the thick pillars. The ringing grew more intense as a terrible sense of dread filled him.

The demon stopped outside the window, searching for something. What could he do if it found him? Fear crept into his mind. He sat on the ground, controlling his emotions by telling himself, '*There is nothing to fear. I am the powerful one. They should fear me.*'

Cassian felt the demon enter the structure. He sensed it getting closer. Far away from where he entered the building, doors lined the back wall. He had no hope of reaching the doors before the demon would catch him, but he had to take a chance.

Before he could move, a deep and sonorous voice that seemed as patient as a kindly grandparent said, "Come out from the shadows and face me!"

Summoning his strength, Cass jumped from behind the pillar and stood in shock at what he saw. A monstrous red and silver dragon, nearly two or three hundred feet tall stood before him with a glowing white ember in the center of its chest.

"I am not afraid of you, demon!" Cassian said, his voice shaking.

The slow laugh did not feel menacing like other demons. It said, "Of course you are afraid, young soul. You stand before the great Tiamat on the very bottom level of Hell. Were you not afraid, you would be a fool. Did you not think I would sense you hiding? You do not belong in this place. Why are you here?" Tiamat said in a slow, lucid tenor.

Fear made Cassian begin to tremble. He said, "I know of the evil dragon, Tiamat. I do not answer to demons!" His proclamation felt feeble, at best.

"Yes. I am the *evil* dragon you have heard about in your world. Though, as you can see, I have but one head and not seven.

"You may stop your theatrics. I know well that you are one of the shrouded. Your fear is, and should be, genuine…but not from me. I have long since forgotten this war. They wish to fight over their lost knowledge held by the stewards. I care not. I have been alive for thousands upon thousands of years. They continue to paint me as evil, but I was once called 'mother' by the Builders," Tiamat said with sadness.

Tiamat continued, "Your kind and our kind are part of an existence in which I no longer *choose* to participate on the terms of others. Choice, I have come to see, while frequently difficult, may be the greatest gift God bestowed upon us all. I must support both sides of this unending conflict to perpetuate an existence in which I seek something…beyond. I hope that you may be wise enough to understand that.

"But so few intruders enter this place, especially a soul chosen by the angels. I must ask why you have come to this desolate place? You need not answer if you wish to keep your own counsel. I will not harm you. But I am curious as to what would bring one of the shrouded to the deepest recess of Hell."

Cassian focused his power on resonating with the dragon and said, "I have come to find a soul that I sent here."

"Hmmm. That is an interesting and very *rare* power you have, young man. It is connected to both aspects of your existence. Very important that you understand this as you must be *extremely* careful with its use, especially in this world. I see now that it is *love* that brings you here… Cassian," Tiamat said.

"How is it that you know my name?" Cassian demanded.

"You are not the only one to possesses great strength in this ability, young soul. Your attempt to influence me opened your thoughts like a book. You bring too many adornments from the other aspect of your existence into this world. You must learn to protect your feelings much better. I know exactly who you are. And I know why you came. Khalima is correct. You *will* find Mary here, but I cannot tell you where. Not because I would *not* help you, but because I do not know. That task must fall upon you," Tiamat said.

"How are you able to read my mind?" Cassian asked.

"As I am sure your angel has told you, none but *you* have access to your piece of God. However, when you use your power in this realm, your internal dialog will be transparent to others who have the power to resonate with you. Your intentions and thoughts are clear for me to see," Tiamat said.

"Are you going to try to kill my family and friends now? Because I intend to fight you all!" Cassian said, now angry.

A soothing push of calmness hit Cassian. It was vaguely similar to what Ex pushed, but so much more intense that it knocked him to the ground. In that moment, he saw into Tiamat as she had seen into him. He felt the tremendous restraint Tiamat exercised in her gentle attempt to pacify him. It was difficult for her to push such a minuscule bit of power. As he lay there feeling like an insect, Cassian understood the insignificance of his power and knowledge. She could have obliterated him without ever touching him.

Tiamat spoke, "I apologize if that was too much. You are so small. Where once I would have delighted in your pain, I now feel sadness. I believe this is called empathy. But these emotions are somewhat new to me.

"I feel a sorrow for the pain you have had to endure. It makes me wish to help you. Perhaps that is empathy," she said.

"I would call that empathy," Cass said, trying to push himself upright.

"I can do little to help one such as you, young soul. But I can offer advice. You need to learn to use your powers *far* better before attempting to use them. Particularly on one such as me. You could cause great harm to others or find yourself woefully outmatched at the wrong time. Use discretion and wisdom before you resort to using power. Do you understand?" Tiamat said.

Cassian, now cowed before Tiamat, said, "I understand. But what made you change? Why, now, do you feel empathy?"

"A long time ago, even as I reckon time, when dragons ruled many worlds and the Seraphim were growing their ranks, I gave birth to a child. I will not speak his name, but when he was born, I felt a connection to my son." She looked away and said, "Perhaps that was what you call love. It was foreign to me at the time. I wanted to protect my child by keeping him far from this war. I wanted him to live an existence of peace and understanding. A life of growth and creation, apart from the stagnation of this place. I wanted for him a better life than fighting and destruction. But he was taken by the serpent. The one you call Satan. Ripped from my arms and poisoned by the venom of tainted words.

"I was angry. I felt hate. I became destructive and brutal. I honed my gift and used it to kill angels and demons alike. I was a destroyer of worlds, feared by all...even Satan," she paused and added, "especially Satan.

"But Satan detested its own fear and took its anger out on my son. It sent him in disguise within a larger group of dragons to destroy me. A moment that lives forever in my mind. A moment of great wrath. I lashed out and too late did I realize what I had done...and I can *never* take it back. I killed my son. The only one for whom I ever felt...love.

"Perhaps it was the grace of God that touched me. But my hate and anger were replaced by sorrow. Vast sorrow for my son...and the many terrible things I had done. I saw the pain I felt mirrored in so many that I had hurt. I have never intentionally harmed another since. I sit apart from both Heaven and Hell now. Better to be alone than a slave to manipulation," she said.

"I am sorry for your loss, Tiamat. And your solitude," Cassian said.

"I know you are. I felt your great compassion. You are a kind and well-meaning soul. Sadly, those traits are exploited to bring you much sadness and anger. Let not your rage dominate your life, for this is what Satan prefers. It is a pathway leading back to this place," she said.

"Can you help me to find Mary and escape?" he asked.

"Do not speak names in this realm. I am able to sense that none are watching. But *you* do not yet possess such power.

"I cannot help you find your beloved. But I can tell you where to go if you should find her. Go to the Lake of Fire. There are three bridges over the lake with the node of light at the central nexus. Do not run into the pillar of light. Most think this is the pathway. Each bridge has two pinnacles. They sit at the midpoint to the nexus. From one of the six peaks on the bridges, have faith and dive into the fire. This is the barrier between Heaven and Hell. As you are not one who resides in the core realm of existence, you will be sent into the Limbo of your existence. From there, you must find your way back to your realm.

"You may leave now, the way you came. But once you find her, you cannot return this way. You must break free of Hell *through* the Lake of Fire. The alternative will not be an option for you," Tiamat said.

"How can I know if I can trust you, Tiamat? You are a demon," Cassian said.

"I could destroy you now, Cassian. This would leave your soul in Hell and disconnected from your angel. I could also alert the demons who would desperately wish to possess *your* power on Earth. Knowing your identity would allow them to take you and destroy your family and all you hold dear. You have no choice but to believe what I say. If I am lying to you, your world may soon face disaster. If I am telling you the truth, you may find your way home.

"From my resonance with you, I believe you to be a seeker of truth. I wish nothing but the best of luck to one such as you on your journey, young soul. Keep this lesson close to you. Know your opponent before you begin to fight."

"Do you believe in luck?" Cassian asked.

"You may term the will of God whatever you wish. Whether it be good or bad is not up to me. But I wish you well in your efforts. It is unlikely we will ever meet again. But there is one more thing I can offer you," Tiamat said.

"I would be grateful for any help," Cassian said.

Tiamat spoke words that came to him as both pleasure and pain. He felt as if his bones were pulled from their sockets and soothingly put back together as she spoke. Her words tore him apart and gently rebuilt him at the same time. Then it was over and Cassian laid on the floor in pain.

"What happened? What did you do to me?" Cassian asked.

"If God truly favors you, you will know when the time comes. Farewell," Tiamat said as she turned to leave.

"Thank you," Cass said as Tiamat was already departing. Then mumbled, "I think."

CHAPTER 33

KATABASIS

CASSIAN, STILL FEELING THE EFFECTS of what Tiamat had done, stood and walked to the doors on the back wall. He opened the first and saw rows of seated, human-shaped beings in the dark. They appeared to be dead people covered in the black slime like the walls, doors, and pillars surrounding him.

Cassian steeled himself against what seemed an insurmountable task and walked into the room, shutting the door behind him. He started down an aisle in the dark. A faint purple glow coming from an unknown source produced enough light for Cass to see a great distance, but with no resolution of detail.

As he walked, he again began to focus on Mary.

A thought came to his mind. It was dark in here. How could Mary find *him* in the dark? He may be no match for Tiamat, but he knew that all the training he had done over the last three years had to be for a reason. He closed his eyes and remembered every good time and happy moment he ever had with Mary. Her kiss, her laugh, her touch…every moment he could recall he brought forth. Then he thought of his own feelings for her. As he concentrated on these emotions, his right hand rose above his head. When he opened his eye, a light shining from his hand lit thousands of blank faces seated in the room. He kept his thoughts on Mary. They could not see him. He felt certain that only Mary would be able to see the light.

He walked up and down the rows, but to no avail. Once he finished walking through one room, he went to the next room and did the same thing and nothing happened.

When he considered the size of the structure, he began to feel that his efforts could be wasted. But he had come this far making him even more determined to find her. After searching a room, he would let go of the light and rest. Room after room, he continued to search. How long had it been? Days must have had gone by—searching.

He systematically moved to the next door to his left as he faced the wall containing the doors. He hoped that he was not searching the same room again and again as they all looked the same.

Cassian fought the hopelessness that continued to creep in. This place was the epitome of despair and he hated it. He had no choice but to continue. By his estimation of two rooms per day, he had been there for three weeks, constantly searching.

Then it happened. He walked into one room with thousands of faceless people. He held his hand in the air and the light began to shine. He heard a grunting noise far to his left. This was new. With fear and excitement pulsing through him, he ran in the direction of the sound. One of the faceless creatures stood and began struggling to move.

Although afraid, he approached the creature. It fought harder to move. Cass took his glowing right hand and placed it on the forehead of the struggling entity. Light flashed through the room and before him stood Mary. She looked as he remembered her before she died, but dirty, weakened, and sick. The feeling of joy coming from her lit Cassian's heart.

"Cassian? You are here?" she said, smiling.

"I could never leave you in Hell, Mary. I love you!" Cass said.

When he said that one word—love—a ripple went through the whole room. Other creatures began to rise.

Mary looked mortified and said, "Don't ever say that word here! You might as well pull the fire alarm! We need to go…now."

She grabbed his hand and pulled him in the dark. Cass tried to pull her to the doors in back, but when he looked, the doors were replaced with a solid wall. She pulled him to the front of the room. Cass was about to protest, when Mary pushed on a spot in the front wall. He then saw that the only doors were now at the front of the room. The egress Mary opened led to an outdoor area that was dimly lit with something akin to an evening at twilight, only with very few stars present.

Off to the left (*South*, Cassian thought), he saw seven mountains of different color that seemed to be made of crystal. Each had high, rocky spires. Ahead lay a great plain with a glowing lake of lava far away in the center. To the right, another seven mountains rose from the ground. These were made of rock and each was as black as the darkest night. Beyond the Lake of Fire, Cass could not see much as it was too far and too dark.

They began to run toward the lake. It was a long time before Cass stopped and said, "Mary, where are we?"

"We're in Hell, dumbass!" she said. "Listen to me. You need to think about hateful things. Think about what Eric Bosco did to you. Think about anything that makes you angry. This is the only thing that is going to help us blend in."

"But why are we running?"

"We are running from them!" she turned her head in the direction from which they came. Dark figures flooded from the base of a high mountain. They crawled rapidly toward them. "They will drag us both down and keep us here forever. It is more than misery loves company. Misery hates what you just said. Now, start filling yourself with hate or we are doomed!"

Cass closed his eyes and began to think about Eric and Barry Bosco. The anger he felt toward them. He thought about the demon that took Chelsea and killed his father and friends. His rage began to burn against them. He wanted to rip them apart slowly as he tortured everything they ever...

The creatures swarmed around them, moving and searching everywhere. Cassian clung to his hate. Before long, the mass of dark creatures moved on toward the lake.

Mary turned to Cass and hugged him. He turned a face contorted in wretched fury to her and said, "Don't touch me, bitch!"

Mary jumped back. Cass saw what he did and said, "No, I didn't mean that. Please. The anger...it...it pulled me..."

"It's okay, Cassian. I know what it does." Her voice was shaking. "I fucked up so bad by agreeing to be a Spur. I would never have done this if I ever thought this kind of hate would fill me," Mary cried.

Cass hugged her to him and said, "I am getting you out of here. Khalima is helping me. The best I can do is get you back into Limbo… into the Dream World where you can be a Spur again. But there is something you need to know. You can *never* look for me again. Not me or anyone near me. They killed my father and all my friends. They found me."

"What?!" she said. "Was it because of what I did?"

"No. It was not your fault. We were betrayed by…someone else. Don't say anything more. I know how you feel. Stop. Keep your anger up. To get out of here, we must dive into the Lake of Fire from the top of the bridge."

"They led me here from somewhere beyond that weird burning lake. I think it has six straight sides, but I don't remember seeing any bridges. I think beyond that, it leads into an ocean. I'm not sure, but that may be Limbo. You only get sent here when you fail as a Spur. That's if you agreed to be a Spur in the first place. Most of the ones down here now choose to stay in Hell! They will never see the light of day. They just sit here, in the dark, forever. I think they like it here."

"To hell with them," Cass said. "Let's get the fuck out of here!"

———

"Cassian," Corrina interrupted, "was that lake the same lake we all saw in our dream last night?"

Cassian shook his head with a somber look on his face as he brought his finger to his mouth indicating quiet. They both understood that he didn't want them to speak. Cass said, "Maybe. I think this is just a weird coincidence. Perhaps I accidentally projected one of my dreams to both of you last night. I don't know all that this resonance power can do.

"The next part gets more bizarre, and I cannot be certain that what I saw was something I really saw with my eyes and not felt. It is difficult to describe what image your mind may conjure from a feeling. But I will tell you what my mind remembers."

Cass and Mary walked across the plain. When they finally got to the six-sided lake, Cass thought that it must be molten lava. The heat blasted from the yellow-orange surface. In the center, an immense column of white light reached up to the sky. Far above, another hexagon could be seen. It looked nebulous and a kind of magenta color, with the white column of light connecting both in the center.

"Which way?" Cassian asked.

"Let's go this way," Mary said, pointing right toward the black mountains.

When they began walking to the right, the black creatures formed a line as they approached. He and Mary turned away toward the other set of mountains and saw another line of the creatures closing in on them. Cassian pulled Mary close and said, "I don't think we are getting out of this with hate and anger."

They turned again toward the black mountains, which then began to tremble as a cold wind flew down from dark slopes. The dark creatures scattered and fled as if terrified. Something bad was coming. Bad enough to scare the minions of Hell.

That's when they noticed a strange yellow light began to glow before them as a cacophony of noise grew. It immediately flashed out of existence and a black sphere opened. It was like what Cass saw in the dorm room hallway several years earlier. Another black rock fell from the hole and it immediately closed.

"So, these Cysistal stones are coming through portals from Stu?" Franklin asked.

"Stu or Khalima. I'm telling you what I remember. These are the only two times I ever saw them. I am fairly sure they were from Stu. Maybe you will see something I missed. I am still confused about a lot of things," Cass said.

"Immediately after it closed, something huge began to climb down the mountain. It wore a crown of crystals that made it appear like horns. It had no face and seemed to absorb not only light but hope, happiness, love, kindness…every reason to live you can imagine. Nothing could have prepared me for the fear I felt as that thing approached. I don't know if this was Satan himself or not, but what I said about Hell being the worst thing you could ever imagine…well, that feeling exuded from this massive creature. And it was angry.

"Maybe the portal opening drew it to us. Or maybe it was my uninvited presence in Hell. Either way, it was coming to investigate, and it was moving impossibly fast.

"I picked up the stone and we ran…away from that thing. As I held the stone, it seemed to be sending me an image. It was an oddity in the surface of the Lake. It was a hidden bridge. If it were not for the stone, I would never have found it.

"The bridge could not be seen by any normal means. I remember the Indiana Jones movie where he had to take a leap of faith to find the Holy Grail. Then he threw the dirt onto the bridge so you could see it. The bridge was hidden much like that.

"I pulled Mary with me. She was reluctant at first and fought me. She thought I was running into the lava. When she saw that I was unharmed, she followed. We ran across the bridge, which led to the column of white light. The heat was incredible and the path was not very wide.

"The creature was coming at a terrifying pace. The lake seemed so huge. Even if it took me to the other side, that thing could have circled the whole lake twice before we could get across.

"What seemed like halfway to the highest point of the bridge from where we started, I could see the huge form standing on the edge of the Lake of Fire, looking at us with burning red eyes. The hate was fathomless. It didn't just hate me or Mary. It hated the essence of our souls. It wanted us erased, completely.

"I expected the beast to step across the lake and swat us out of existence, but it did not. It circled to the end of the bridge and stood there, waiting for us. I don't think anything from Hell is able to safely touch the lake. I think Tiamat was correct. This was the intersection of Heaven and Hell. I doubt that I will ever know for certain. What happened next is still a blur…"

"Cassian," Mary said, "you should run and let me face this. I will go back and you continue forward. I don't want you to suffer with me."

"I didn't do all of this to walk away without you. I'm not leaving you here with that piece of shit!" Cass said, pointing to the beast.

Mary laughed. This caused the beast to scream a terrible sound. It hurt every cell in his body. It was exactly as Khalima had once described. The pain was everywhere, all at once, and very intense.

When it stopped, Cass said, "If you stay, I stay. But neither one of us is going to stay. Mary, our souls are part of God…"

This caused another painful scream from the beast.

"We need to go to the center of the bridge and jump into the lake. We may die, but our souls will not. Do you understand?" Cass said.

"I knew you would come for me. They wring the hope out of you here the best they can, but I knew you would come. I love you, Cassian!"

This prompted the beast to scream even louder. It slammed its colossal fists against the ground making the previous pain feel like a warm bath. They both screamed in anguish.

Cassian stopped. With his elbows on his knees, he placed his head in his hands.

"What happened next?" Franklin asked.

"Mary ripped free of my grasp and ran back across the bridge. I gave chase, but she was so fast. And it was like I was running through mud. Or like something was pulling me back. The beast didn't seem to notice that I was there. When Mary got to the end of the bridge…it squashed her like an insect," Cass began to weep.

"It's okay, Cassian," Corrina said. "She made her decision to save you. She sacrificed herself. She's probably back in Heaven right now!"

"Thanks, Corrina. I like to think that too. But I lost her. And I have no idea where she is now or why she chose to go back," Cass said. "After that, I turned to my right, ran to the top of the bridge, and dove into the Lake of Fire. Before I hit the surface, I saw a large demon charging toward me.

"Then I woke. Like I said earlier, it was the opposite of what happened with the book from the stewards. I slept one night, but it seemed like a full month had passed. I woke feeling physically refreshed, even though my heart ached. I had to say goodbye to Mary…maybe forever."

"I don't get it, Cass. Something isn't making sense. You were almost there. Why didn't she just join you and dive from the top of the bridge? You would have succeeded in getting her out," Franklin said.

"I have no idea, Franklin. Maybe she thought she was saving me from something. I may never know," Cass said.

"Well, what about the other Cysistal stone. Did you have two of them now?"

"No. That was in the Dream World. I didn't have a second stone when I woke. I don't know what happened to that one," Cass said.

Franklin looked at him for a long moment. Cass could feel the sharp intellect in the intense gaze. It made him happy that the questioning part of Franklin seemed to be awakening.

Franklin squinted with a nod and said, "Yeah…sure."

Good, Cass thought, *Franklin could smell bullshit just fine.*

CHAPTER 34

ASMODEUS

A FAINT ORANGE GLOW DIFFRACTED THROUGH the crystal mountains giving the bleak landscape its hellish appearance. Asmodeus had called council with his lesser demons of the South Wind.

"Do you know who banished Furcas?" Asmodeus asked.

None spoke.

"*Who* banished Furcas?" Asmodeus roared as they all cowered in fear.

Finally, Soleos spoke and said, "That knowledge is lost. Furcas is not banished. I believe Furcas is…passed."

"Passed? What is that supposed to mean, Soleos?" Asmodeus asked. "Has Tiamat come back to kill more Seraphim?"

"As with Oriax and Purflas, they are no longer counted among the Seraphim," Soleos said.

Asmodeus stood with his burning gaze looking at Soleos for a long time before saying, "This shrouded is *killing* our kind!"

"I believe so, Asmodeus. But it would be unwise to tell this to Satan. Once Furcas was destroyed, we no longer know *who* this shrouded may be. Unless Semjaza knows," Soleos said.

"*Where is Semjaza*? That bag of Godly pus should be here! *Where*?" Asmodeus shouted.

"He is not terminated, Master. He seems to be missing," Soleos said.

"Missing? What does that mean? Missing?" Asmodeus said harshly.

"We cannot locate him. But we know that the number of Seraphim did not change once he disappeared," Soleos said.

"Is it possible that he changed his loyalties? Perhaps he has repented and now sides with the angels again," Asmodeus said.

"I have worked closely with Semjaza for centuries. He hates the human souls. I do not believe that he would betray us," Zepar said.

"I care *not* about what you think, you fool. None were to betray God but look around you. Does this appear to you as the firmaments of Heaven? Do not ever speak such idiocy again!" Asmodeus said, enraged. "If Semjaza knows who the shrouded is, *find him*!"

"We have searched and cannot find any signs of him, Lord," Soleos said.

"Then bring me his conspirator, Azazel," Asmodeus said.

From behind him, an awful sound hissed, "Bring *me*…to *you*? Who do you think you are to demand an audience with *me*?" The hulking faceless form of Azazel approached. Other demons looked on eagerly at this confrontation.

Asmodeus turned his fiery gaze to face Azazel and yelled, "I am an Archduke of Hell! That is who calls you! You, Samael, Semjaza, and the rest your party all believe you are somehow above me! *You are not!*"

"I answer to no being…on any realm," Azazel spat.

Harshly, Asmodeus said, "We should have left you bound in the darkness on the rocks of Dudael."

"But you could not…could you? Because you *must* listen to Satan. You must abide by its dictates whereas I do not. Do not try to threaten me, Arch*coward* of Hell," Azazel said.

Asmodeus lashed out with a glowing black scepter but Azazel was gone.

From behind Asmodeus, Azazel said, "I am here because I need the stewards who betrayed the Earthborn shrouded. They are under your domain. I am here to take them with me."

Asmodeus swung again and shouted, "I will give you *nothing* unless you begin to show respect to my dominion!"

"Have your dominion over the fungus of Hell…but you will have nothing over me. Now if you would like to maintain your *appearance* of dominion to these peons, then bring the stewards to me now. Otherwise, I will find them and take them just to show what your useless dominion means," Azazel said.

"One day, Azazel, you will know what it means to anger an Archdemon. My essence burns for you, and I will have my revenge!" Asmodeus said.

"Not this day, Asssssmodeus," Azazel mocked. "Now fetch me the stewards before I embarrass you further."

Asmodeus slammed the black scepter on the firmament floor with a scream. A bright red light split the darkness and Asmodeus was gone. Before Azazel stood the featureless, personified soul of Illoc.

"Master," Illoc said, bowing to the ground. "How may I serve you?"

"Such an eloquent greeting," Azazel said with kindness, unlike the disrespect shown to Asmodeus. "I am honored to be in the presence of one so brave. What did they call you, soul?"

"I am…was…known as Illoc," came the reply.

"So, you were thirty-seventh among the stewards." Azazel sounded impressed. "Tell me something, Illoc. You were once a shrouded who went on to be one of the Watchers. What made you betray the service of chaos?" came the soothing and comforting question.

Illoc, feeling at ease said, "I grew weary of the demand for exceptionalism. Nothing I could do would ever be good enough before another made improvements. I began to resent those rewarded due to dumb luck. I began to hate those who excelled. I want it to end. We should all have shared in these triumphs, as Semjaza explained."

"Ahhh, so it was envy that drove you here," Azazel said. Without waiting for a reply, "We did find the shrouded thanks to your help. But we seemed to have run into a new problem."

"A problem? What type of problem, Master?" Illoc asked.

"It is a minor problem. I am sure that with your help, and that of your colleague, we will soon reacquire the location," Azazel said.

"How was it lost? I thought that the location was…well. I don't recall, but we knew where it was!" Illoc said.

"One of our associates seems to have perished at the hands of the shrouded. The law now hides the identity once again. So you can understand how disappointing this is," Azazel said.

"But master, I spent years learning how to track someone in Limbo. I found its beloved and tagged the soul. I then provided you with the name and location. We found the soul! How is it possible that it got away, sir?" Illoc said angrily.

"Master? Sir? You show so much respect. Since you have been so gracious, I am going to tell you my name. I am known as Azazel."

If Illoc still had blood, it would have frozen. Azazel was most feared among the demons. He was not truly a demon and was certainly no longer an angel. Azazel and his closest companions sat outside the demons. They wielded the terrible power of both Heaven and Hell. Azazel was the most powerful among them. His exploits began with the corruption of humans and then digressed to things that now defined the evils of Hell.

"I can tell by your response that you know my name," Azazel cooed. "Now, now…forget the stories you may have heard. I serve the ancient purpose of our kind. I want nothing but order. And you should be honored for your great service to us. Finding this soul with such a rare and powerful ability was a great thing you have done. Exceptional, really."

"Thank you, Azazel," Illoc said. This caused a slight glow from the body of Azazel. "I knew this one would shift the balance of power. This is why I spoke to Semjaza at the Kebra cavern where none could see nor hear."

"Wonderful to hear that, and…thank you!" Azazel said enthusiastically. "Where is the other steward? I was told that there were two of you who helped us to find this shrouded."

"I do not know," said Illoc. "The name was…umm…give me a moment…"

"Do not worry about the name," Azazel said. "Was he with you when you arrived?"

"Let me think…hmmm…we were executed in our realm. It was quite painless as they use a gas that gently shuts down the generic body by blocking the…sorry, that's not important."

"Thank you, Illoc. I appreciate your attempt at brevity. Please, continue."

"Thank you, Azazel! Your reputation does not match the kindness you have displayed," Illoc said.

"Of course, Illoc!" Azazel said sweetly.

"So…the one I was with…the one who helped me…we were…we were…well, I cannot seem to recall the other. But after it was done, I was cherished among the demons. I was told I could choose to be a Spur or serve in Hell. I chose to serve. Serve one such as you, Azazel!" Illoc said.

The demon leaned closer and said, "So you do not know if the other steward was with you upon death? And you cannot seem to recall the name?"

"Well, Azazel! This might come back to me soon. We were very close," Illoc said, smiling.

"Well, if you don't know, you don't know. This is what the laws can do to us," Azazel said mildly. Immediately, the icy tone from Azazel contradicted the pleasant conversation they were having as it said, "Now… do not *ever* say my name again, you maggot. If you truly cannot recall the name, it is because you were betrayed and you lost!"

"I'm…I'm sorry," Illoc said.

Azazel changed completely, "Everything about you…your presence…your smell…your very existence…*offends* me in every way," Illoc began to shrink away from the menace exuding from Azazel now. "If I could snuff out your soul, I would do it this fucking second. Now, *where* is the other steward! Perhaps this is a plan between the two of you to deceive me. I do not get deceived. I do the deceiving! Do you understand?"

"No, no, no…Az…sir…we both died together. I swear. I never saw him after," Illoc said.

"I will see about that now. You have only to pray to Satan that you are telling the truth. Because you are going to suffer worse than any man on Earth has ever suffered," Azazel said.

"But *why*?" Illoc protested. "I helped you! I found the shrouded for you!"

The dull, orange-red light dimly lit the chamber. Illoc, hanging in the center of the room, wept as the pain seemed to intensify. What was once in his legs had move up to his torso and now was in his head. The pains were intense and very specific. The current agony would last for days…

maybe weeks…he no longer understood time. He could only manage to deal with one moment at a time…for hours, and days, and weeks. There was never a release from any pain. Only a shift to one being worse than another.

Illoc prayed to God, but there was no answer. Azazel asked him deep questions about the identity of the shrouded and the other steward, but he couldn't remember. He could still recall his betrayal to Semjaza but couldn't remember who it was or what he said. He begged God for the information, but nothing came. And Azazel continued to torture him.

"*Please. Let it stop!*" Illoc begged.

"You can stop that nonsense," Azazel said. "You made your decision and your decision landed you in my hands. You need to understand…I *hate* your kind. I would torture you even if you told me what I wanted to hear. And I don't know when I am ever going to tire of torturing you. I will keep you here for as long as you were a steward before I stop. What was that? About three to four thousand Earth years? I'll do five for good measure!"

"No…please…make it stop. I'll do whatever you want…" Illoc moaned.

"You are sure only Semjaza, Furcas, and Oriax know the power of this particular shrouded?"

"Yes, Master. I only met those three at Kebra. But Oriax was working with Pruflas and Corson to allow Semjaza to take the shrouded. No others. I swear to…to you," cried Illoc.

"So, you kept the identity of this shrouded until when, exactly?" Azazel asked.

"I only knew *where* he was at first. It took me some time to find one who could tell us *who* it was. We had to track the soul…in Limbo…after it chose to become a Spur," Illoc said.

"Is this soul still a Spur or has it been banished?" Azazel said.

"I don't know, I swear. I told them how to find the soul. I told them what to look for. I don't know if it is still active or not. It may be in Hell right now for all that I know."

"Tell me more about the power of the shrouded," Azazel said.

"Only that this one can resonate with other life. I don't know how, Master, but it managed to best three demons on Earth who were sent to procure Desemilnoct. Oriax and Pruflas were killed, but Corson survived. Corson was the first to be destroyed on Earth, so the shrouded only banished it.

"I don't think the human knew how to use its power. Corson had tortured it and a family member while he bound the shrouded with a Tolaxnarm device. I provided instructions on how to build it. The shrouded managed to get help. We believe that the soul traveled in Limbo to seek assistance. Ask Corson!

"When it killed Pruflas, then Oriax, they were wearing the Tolaxnarm configuration to prevent the power of the angel from harming them. The shrouded had help from a traitorous Spur that corrupted the sacrificial lamb's blood, allowing a window to kill Pruflas.

"Then they were inundated with angels when the Spur asked God for help. It is still unknown how the demons were killed."

The ground suddenly began to rumble. Something major seemed to be happening as Azazel turned and ran from the room. Illoc fell to the ground feeling the joy of no pain for the first time in years. He ran the opposite direction of Azazel and crawled into a small hole at the base of the wall in the room. He continued crawling in complete darkness, having no idea where it would take him.

Illoc broke free from the crystal mountain and emerged on a great plain. In the center of the plain was something he had heard about…the Lake of Fire in Hell. From the center, he could see the column of pure white light going up to the next realm of Hell. He had once studied the structure of Hell. If he could but make it to the Eastern Mountain range, he may be able to escape Azazel in the dominion of Belial.

He turned and saw Azazel emerge from the mountain. But Azazel was fixed on the two souls running around the lake. From the Northern Mountain range, an enormous creature, ten, maybe a hundred times the size of Azazel ran toward the two souls. It was the Behemoth form of Satan.

While fascinated, his pure terror spurred him to run as hard as possible to the east.

A scream of agony ran through his essence from the direction of the lake. It knocked him to the ground, but he got up immediately and continued to run. Soon a second scream slammed into him that was far more painful than anything Azazel had done to him.

As he tumbled, he could see Azazel was not a third of the way to the lake while Satan stood far away on the northern side. The two souls were running across one of the bridges. He no longer cared about these events. Illoc got up and ran as hard as he could.

The last scream from Satan felt as if he was ripped to pieces. It was followed but a thunderous shaking of the ground. He still managed to pull himself up and run.

Soon, Illoc saw thousands of dark creatures scurrying into an opening at the base of the Eastern Mountain range. He ran toward them hoping to hide among them and disappear in anonymity.

CHAPTER 35

THE JUSTICE OF EMOTION

"WHAT HAPPENED AFTER THAT? DID you go back again and try to find her?" Franklin asked, the skepticism clear in his tone.

Cassian slowly shook his head and said, "No. I never went back. It was not that I didn't try. I went back to the Library many times trying to find Khalima or something that could help me find her again. I tried resonating with the Cysistal stone, but I never had any help. It was nine years before I would meet with Stu again. When that happened, I asked for help, but he said that neither he nor Khalima could find Mary.

"I stayed in the mountains that winter. I went back home in the spring of 1998. I finished what I needed to get my degree in chemistry. After that, I went into business for myself. It helps when you have a benefactor that can finance your start up.

"Small businesses with deep connections to a network of accomplished friends. All people who I knew I could trust, like Malcom, Bart, and Tony. I set up LLCs and S and C corporations to shield any work I did from government agencies…and, of course, the demons and Spurs."

"What kind of business?" Franklin asked.

"Hexagon Consulting. I'm sure you have heard of it. My abilities gave me a unique edge. It's also a fantastic way to hide what you are doing while you mine information. We work with 3Hex Core Innovations now and have subsidiaries that consult with pharma, the military, communications, and foreign affairs. I'm not going to talk about that, but you should know that we work every angle we can to stop them," Cass said.

"So, what's your role? Officially?" Franklin asked. "You got to be stinking rich if you started Hexagon. Are you like a CEO or something?"

"Noooo. Not me. I'm just a failed scientist. I work in no official capacity with any of these companies. I don't even get paid by them. I could probably collect disability if I wanted to," Cass said pointing to his eye. "But I don't do that. I work officially as a scientific representative for a small, over-the-counter generic pharmaceutical production facility out of Durham, NC. It pays little, and I am required to travel constantly…making my whereabouts exceptionally difficult to predict."

"Why does a generic pharma company need a scientific representative?" Franklin asked.

"Oh, you know. Scouting the newest instruments. Talent acquisitions. General vagaries," Cassian said with a smile. "The businesses, now run by trusted associates, are very effective at accumulating information.

"One of the first things I did was to track down Lynn. It was 2002 when I found her living with some loser in Southern California. He was a forty-five-year-old, married 'contractor' making tons of money on investments while he collected disability from the state for alleged back pain.

"Unbelievable how people work so hard in this country to support soulless assholes like *this* who will just take and take and take!" Cassian said, agitated. "I'm sorry. That gets under my skin. But it gets worse."

"Carl 'Chip' Parsons…you may have heard of him in the news if you watch that kind of shit…left his wife and two lovely children…in poverty, mind you…for this single, twenty-eight-year-old, blond woman who supposedly had no children," Cass said.

"I heard that name," Corrina said. "Chip Parsons was on *Dateline*. He killed himself after he killed some doctor in public. They never found his lawyer. They never mentioned Lynn."

"Yes. I was careful to keep her out of the spotlight. Not so much because of Lynn, but because of Samuel…and myself, of course.

"She was shacked up with this bum, smoking pot and getting high on drugs. It seems they just started with crystal meth, which was the new up and coming drug de jour. They partied and lived like movie stars. Chip didn't seem too concerned about his suffering family.

"I met with Chip's wife and children. They were such nice people, and the kids were fantastic. Smart, well behaved, polite…they deserved better treatment than that.

"It wasn't just that Lynn and Samuel were alive and she never told me. It was seeing her living like this. She left our son with her lunatic parents. I was *steaming* mad about everything.

"I quickly remedied certain injustices," Cass said angrily.

"The first thing that Chip did while Lynn was passed out, was to search his contact books.

"You see, Franklin, back then…before the smart phone…we all had to keep lists of our contacts in little books or something called a Rolodex.

"Another thing I can tell you *for certain* was that this asshole felt no pain in his back at all.

"Chip met with his disability lawyer. Against his lawyer's advice, he signed an iron-clad document naming his wife and children as beneficiaries to every asset he owned. To make it easier, he generously placed his estranged wife's name on his investment accounts so they transferred directly to her in the event that anything should happen to him.

"He then visited every person in his life who had a claim to *any* of his assets. There were four people, including a brother. All of whom Chip murdered.

"Then Chip went to the doctor who signed off on his disability claim…and also enabled he and Lynn access to any drug they ever wanted. It seems the young doctor was quite a disgusting person. I won't tell you what he was doing with young children…including Chip's own son."

Cass looked like he could spit fire as he said, "But with the help of certain friends of mine, the list of pedophiles meeting grim fatalities in California and Mexico has been going up ever since.

"All physical evidence showed that Chip dragged this doctor into the street and gruesomely murdered him by beating his face to a pulp," Cass rubbed the knuckles of his right hand.

"When they found Chip's body, he had toxically high levels of cocaine, alcohol, meth, barbiturates, and LSD. Poor Chip never got a chance to plead his case," Cass said.

There was a long pause before Corrina said, "Cassian, you murdered all these people."

Cassian said, "I don't consider that murder. I told you both that I executed many people. I am not telling you this to *brag*. I feel terrible about *some* of this. I am telling you this so you understand who and what I am…and what I have done. I am a ruthless killer."

Softly, Franklin said, "I don't think you qualify as a ruthless killer if you feel bad about killing these people, Cass."

"Oh. No. I meant that I never killed anyone named Ruth," Cass said, smiling.

Franklin barked a laugh and said, "No, asshole, I'm not laughing at that. That was bad."

Corrina then laughed after she got his joke.

"What did you do with Lynn?" Franklin asked.

"Lynn found herself in a motel room in Arizona several days later. She had no idea what happened. After watching the events unfurl on television, she just seemed to be grateful that *she* was not in custody by California or Federal authorities. I never told her I was involved in this. She was too high to notice."

"So, you were finally reunited with Lynn," Corrina said. "Did you… you know?"

"Oh, hell no!" Cass said, "Even if I did have feelings for her, she looked and acted more like Beth than Mary at this point. Lynn was strung out, constantly lying, and placing blame on everything and everyone but herself. Probably good that I found her before the meth could rot her teeth out. I set her up in an apartment and got her straight again.

"She told me where Samuel was, and I made plans to get him next. Once she was settled in and stable, I went to Utah and got Samuel. He was in rough shape after what I did to him. I took him straight to the hospital. I had to bring Lynn up from Arizona as I wasn't documented as his father. Once he was conscious, we went back to Arizona together.

"Then Lynn started with the whole 'I love you and I miss you' story, but there was no genuine feeling behind it. When I turned her down, things went south, quickly. Her transition to vitriol was every bit as sad as what happened to Beth."

"Speaking of that," Franklin said, "what ever happened with Beth and your brother?"

"Oh yes," Cassian said. "I am getting to that part.

"When I came back home from Colorado, I checked on Mike. He did test positive for HIV but wasn't showing any signs of being sick.

"I had people find where Beth was living. It was years after I got Lynn and Samuel set up in Arizona. Beth was living in East Providence, Rhode Island, as she took classes at the Rhode Island School of Design and worked in the East Side."

"Hey! I grew up in East Providence," Franklin said.

"Yes. I am aware of what a small world this seems to be," Cassian said. "I still am uncertain what she was planning next, but I found out what her schedule was each day. I no longer wanted to help her…as I'm sure you can imagine. I found the perfect place to exact *my* revenge.

"It was a crisp, clear autumn morning in 2009. Beth was walking to her job in the morning over the India Point pedestrian bridge, which spanned Route 195. It had just been reopened the year before. There were benches and everything…it was nice," Cass said.

"Oh yeah," Corrina said, "It was so much better than that old prison-style bridge they tore down in 2004 or 2005."

Cass nodded as he said, "I seated myself on a bench in the middle of the bridge with my hood up. As Beth walked toward me, I remove the hood…"

"Good morning, Beth," Cassian said

"How's your brother? He looked positively positive last time I saw him," Beth laughed.

Cass smiled at her usual canned humor and said, "He's doing okay, Beth. How are you?"

"What the fuck do you want, asshole. You think you're going to do something to me? Look around. There are tons of witnesses out here. Not like the night you drugged me. And I know you don't have the balls to do anything," she said.

"I just came here to give you this," Cassian wore tight-fitting gloves as he reached into his jacket and pulled a note out of his inside pocket. He tossed it to Beth, much as she tossed her diagnosis to him years ago.

She picked it up from in front of her, unfolded it, and read:

I can no longer stand living my life like this. The pain I feel each day burns within me as do the horrible things I have done. To my family, please don't mourn my death. Know that I will be with you always and I love you. But I won't have you see me go through my last days like this.

Love,

"I think this is good news, Cass. You've finally decided to do the right thing for the world and kill yourself. Don't forgot to sign it," Beth said bitterly.

"No, I didn't forget. You see, this isn't my note," Cassian said. "It's yours."

"Oh, go fuck yourself." Beth threw the letter at Cassian.

"Do you have anything you want to say before you go, Beth?" Cassian asked.

"I already said it. Go. Fuck. Yourself!" she said.

"Okay," Cass said.

Beth couldn't speak as she picked up the note and took a pen that Cassian offered her. She signed the note and stuck it in a sealable plastic bag that Cassian also provided (with gloved hands, of course). She placed the bag into her coat pocket as Cassian walked away.

Eight hours later, during evening rush hour, as multiple witnesses could attest, Beth climbed the fence on the west-facing edge of the bridge, flipped over the top, and clung to the outside of the chain links. People ran to her aid in an effort to stop her.

There was no mention of a person matching Cassian's description anywhere around.

Beth said loudly, "I can't take this anymore!" as she let go of the fence, flinging herself into the moving traffic.

Some reported that they heard her yell "Noooo!" as she fell. Perhaps the poor girl changed her mind. If the fall hadn't killed her, the three cars that hit her body probably did.

At the time of her death, Cassian was seen by coworkers at the Pennico office in Pittsburgh, Pennsylvania.

"You waited *in* Beth for eight hours? That was some cold shit, Cass," Franklin said.

"Yes. It was. The justice of emotion is so often the rationalization of the criminal…which I am. It is usually plagued with regret as well," Cass said.

"I don't know if I would go that far. She did kind of give your brother a death sentence. Did your brother die?" Franklin asked.

"He's alive. Even though he has been HIV positive for years, he never came down with AIDS. He's had to live a strict lifestyle and diet along with many other precautions. But he lived in fear that the symptoms could develop at any time. But lately, he's been sick, and they aren't sure what to do for him," Cass said.

"But HIV is no longer a death sentence, Cass. There are drugs that keep the virus dormant. Hell, even undetectable now," Franklin said.

"Those work if taken after initial infection. He was infected years before these drugs came out. And if you believe that living your life on multiple drugs is a sustainable life for a young person, I can tell you it is not. The experimental drugs take their toll on your body, Franklin. The side effects Mike experienced on some were possibly worse than the disease. After 2012, he said no more to any of the new drugs," Cass said.

"That was pretty awful, Cassian," Corrina said. "Beth did this to your brother because of what you did to Mary?"

"Probably Mary and Lynn. But I never did anything to harm either one of them. At least not in any intentional way, like what Beth did to Mike. Her irrational hatred of me from the time I was with Lynn is still something I never understood. I don't know what Lynn told her that made her hate me so much," Cass said.

"Maybe she was jealous," Corrina said. "Not about you. About the *concept* of you. Maybe Lynn was happy with you and Beth couldn't stand it. It happens in families."

"That and the number of licks it will take to get to the center of a Tootsie Pop will remain a mystery," Cass said.

This made Corrina laugh. Naturally, Franklin didn't get it.

"So what? Ex drove your body back to Pittsburgh? Your angel has a driver's license?" Franklin chuckled.

"Ex can drive better than me," Cass said, "But, yes, she took my body back to Pittsburgh, keeping to back roads as much as possible. Then she went into the Pennico office and waited until I came home. I know that nobody at Pennico is a Spur or a demon. In that regard, Pennico is *not* an equal opportunity employer."

Franklin and Corrina laughed at that.

"What did you do with Beth while you waited?" Corrina asked.

"Nothing. I just sat there watching people. It made no difference if a Spur saw her. She was—"

Cassian flinched when his pocket began to buzz. Only three people had access to the number on this phone. It was a burner phone he only used for emergencies. Cass pulled the phone out, looked at the number, and said, "I have to take this."

"Hello," Cass said. He listened for a moment and said to Franklin, "Can I go out your slider on to your back porch for a moment? This is somewhat private."

Franklin gestured to the back sliding door indicating to go right ahead.

"Thank you," Cass said as he opened the door and stepped out onto the deck.

———————

"Okay, Malcom. Where are you now?" Cassian asked.

"I just pulled off the Mass Pike. I'm heading to you." Malcom said.

"Okay. I thought you were going to be up here last night?"

"Well, something unexpected came up. Or I should say *someone* unexpected came up. Cass, I have a passenger with me."

"Passenger?" Cass asked. "What passenger?"

"Dude came through the portal, Cass. And he needs to talk to you. You've never met anyone like this guy. He's literally from another…" Malcom stopped and said, "I just need your location. I'm not saying anymore right now."

"Probably a good idea," Cass said. Then he gave Malcom the coded address for Franklin's condominium. The information was encrypted in a way so the actual street was not spoken.

Neither Cass nor Malcom would trust any cell phone service to be absolutely secure, particularly with Cassian's location. Malcom could put the fake address into his GPS and know that the actual location of Cass was one street to the east and one house to the north. Cass also parked his car three homes north or east on the opposite side of the street from wherever he was going.

CHAPTER 36

A BROTHER'S LOVE

AFTER CASS GOT OFF THE phone with Malcom, he decided to check his other, legitimate phone. The one belonging to Ronald Jones, the scientific representative for Pennico Pharmaceuticals, headquartered in Pittsburgh, but based in Durham, North Carolina. Ron made $72K a year plus a moderate, taxable commission of about $8K to $10K a year.

Ron drove a Ford Focus as a company car that was supplied by Puriel Armaments. Nothing too fancy…from the outside. It was parked up the hill and across the street outside of Franklin's condo at the moment. It had registered Massachusetts plates…as well as North Carolina, Rhode Island, Virginia, Pennsylvania, Ohio, Arizona, California, Florida, Oklahoma, and Texas plates.

He pulled up the email and saw a message from Patricia. That was the name his mother, Pamela, now used for communicating with Ron. Mike used the name Timothy Jones. Malcom used the name Shirley (Cassian and Tony set that up years ago because it hilariously irritated Malcom).

He opened the email and read it. "Tim is sick and may be taking a turn for the worse. Could you possibly swing by and see if you can help?" the message read.

A huge swell of pain rose within Cass as he worried for his brother. He tried to help Mike with his resonance power. Cass was able to put some things in place and help his brother control some behaviors and live a healthier lifestyle, but he had no idea how to fix something like a retrovirus. Cass could feel it in him, but he had no way to unwind it from his brother. The virus clung to his resonances so closely that it was impossible for Cass to distinguish which was Mike's and which was the virus.

Affording treatments wasn't an issue as Mike had great insurance from his company, and Cassian's funds were very deep. But the treatments seemed to be getting worse and worse. Each mild to moderate improvement in the disease treatment was followed by the acceptance of more and more detrimental side effects. Mike finally decided in 2012 to quit any new treatments and try more wholistic methods. He wanted to let God decide his fate.

Cassian knew the problem with the world governments and the influence of the banking, food, pharma, and insurance industries. He possessed the power to stop it, but he couldn't do it yet. The timing had to be perfect. And whether or not he could help Mike to survive could not be allowed to compromise his plan. He knew his brother would live on in the next life. But Cass still wanted his brother in this world.

Taking a deep breath, Cass tried to figure out how soon he could get to Mike. Boston to Pittsburgh was at least eight to nine hours of driving. He had to wait. He couldn't leave until Victoria got home.

Cass closed his eyes and silently prayed for a miracle—something that could help his brother. *Hang on, Mike*, he thought.

———————

Cassian went back inside to find Franklin and Corrina sitting at the table talking. Seeing them both happy made him smile and feel hopeful once again.

"That was my friend, Malcom. He and…his friend…will be here soon," Cassian said.

"What?" Franklin said, "Cass, I was taking *you* with a grain of salt. I get what you're laying down and all, but you're inviting people to my *home*? That's a little bit of an overstep, dude."

"No, it's a huge overstep. And I apologize for that. But I needed Malcom here, and I took a chance. Now, there seems to be a wrinkle in the plan. Malcom has a guest. Someone…unexpected," Cass said.

"Man, you're *all* unexpected!" Franklin said, "Are you planning a big dinner where you eat all my food and drink all my booze but make up for it by washing all my dishes?"

Cassian laughed and said, "That's the second *LOTR* joke you made. I *really* hope the guy Malcom brings is a dwarf…just for the epic look on your face!"

"Technically, that was the *Hobbit*, not *The Lord of the Rings*, but I'll let it go as it's Middle-earth," Franklin said.

"Geek," Cassian said.

Franklin smiled big just as his cell phone began to ring. He went to the table and picked it up, saying, "Hello," as he walked down the stairs.

Cass said to Corrina, "Eleven a.m. must be a popular time for phone calls, huh?"

"Well, my phone didn't ring," she said.

"Give it a moment. You never know!" Cass said with a smile.

"You know who's calling him, don't you?" Corrina asked.

"Of course, I know. Who else would it be?" Cass said, chuckling.

"What do you have to do with this woman? And don't act like Franklin's wife is not someone you are waiting to meet. You seem more and more eager," Corrina said.

"You are perceptive, Corrina. For this, I'm afraid you will have to wait and see," Cass said.

In five minutes, Franklin came upstairs and said, "Victoria is on her way home. You said she would be home today, Cassian. I want to know how you knew that?!"

"I told you before. I have dreams that are sometimes crazy accurate. But I am going to tell you something else. When my dreams are accurate, they are fully accurate. Just like when they are off, they make no sense at all.

"We are about to have an interesting day.

"Before this all begins to unfold, you should know that I need to get to my brother in Pittsburgh soon. It seems he's taken an abrupt turn for the worse," Cass said.

"Oh, Cassian," Corrina said, "I'm so sorry."

"It's okay, Corrina. This is exactly what I expect in life. When things happen, they tend to happen simultaneously or slightly staggered in a way that feels relentless…like you're being tested. But all souls have the fortitude to push themselves through the difficult times.

"I don't mean this to be discouraging to others. I say this from a perspective of someone who has suffered a lot. I really do believe that situations…like what we may experience today…were created to test our souls. A test of your grace and how well you handle it. Do you fold? Do you step up and confront the problems? Or do you cower away to let others deal with it? There are always times when you cannot take any more. This is part of that test. None can bear it all," Cass said.

"What do you mean? My son could fail some kind of test by God?" Corrina asked.

"I can't say that, Corrina. We are tested many times in life. Are we not?" Cassian asked.

"Yes. Like when I had cancer. I wanted to give up. It was Franklin, when he was just a boy, who pushed me until I *could* take it. He was like an angel sent by God," she said.

"No, Mom. You did that. I was just there to help. You're my mother!" Franklin said.

"That's another aspect of the tests as well. Help is almost always provided, but many refuse to see it. I cannot speak for others and how they will handle their tests. But I believe Franklin will do well. Only time will tell," Cassian said.

"Why are you talking about me like I'm not in the room. I'm not a child," Franklin said.

"I'm sorry, Franklin. I don't mean it like that.

"Sometime I want you to put a movie on your television and hit mute. Then play music on a random shuffle of the songs. If you watch the movie and listen to the songs, you will see that they will seemingly sync up at amazing moments.

"This is the resonance of life. Just as all these things are about to happen at the same time. It is not a coincidence, and it is not random," Cass said as the doorbell rang.

Cass smiled and said, "I think you have some guests," as he gestured to the door.

"I think those are *your* guests…not mine!" Franklin said. "You go get the door."

"Very well," Cass said, walking down the stairs.

Franklin and Corrina heard "Hey buddy, how are you?" from Cassian.

"I'm good," came the reply, followed by a brief sound of back-patting. "This is Friz."

"Friz?" Cassian said.

"Yes. This is the name I have chosen for this world," came the slightly rapid reply.

"Please, come in," Cass said. "We need to talk."

Franklin mumble to Corrina, "Sure. Let's all come to Franklin's house to have a meeting. Should probably be more like a group therapy session."

"Stop that," Corrina admonished quietly, but smiled.

Cassian walked up the stairs with two other men. One man was stocky and looked strong. The other was tall, lean, and dressed in odd, loose clothing of the same, beige-gray color.

Cassian went about making all the introductions. Friz seemed to be looking around carefully and occasionally sniffing.

"What is that smell?" Friz said. "It is something…almost primal in me. I feel I have smelled it before, but not really."

"I cooked some bacon earlier," Corrina said. "We have some left if you want a piece."

"Bacon?" Friz said, "I would like to try this. What is it made from?"

"It's a pork product," Cass said.

Friz took a huge intake of air. "Pork! I have read about pork. I would love to taste this!"

Franklin brought out the leftover bacon and said, "Give it a try, dude."

Friz tentatively took a piece and placed it in his mouth. It was still crunchy as he bit down. The expression on his face was nothing short of miraculous. He chewed the meat slowly, and it seemed as if there were tears in his eyes.

Friz suddenly stood and walked to Malcom. Malcom looked con-fused as well. Then Friz embraced him and said, "I apologize, my brother. I never knew food could taste this incredible. I understand your problem much better now. This would be as," Friz looked up for a moment and said, "heroin…on our world."

"You have heroin too?" Cass asked.

"No. I just accessed your files on addictions. It seems comparable. But this is salty, savory, *and* nourishing. We have not had porcine products in our world for many generations. Someone deemed them to be unclean. Thus, the species was purged…to our great detriment. Some sins could never be undone," Friz said sadly.

Malcom said, "Cass, can I speak with you for a moment?"

Cass said, "You can speak freely in front of Corrina and Franklin, Malcom. I have been telling them the whole story…all of it!"

"Are you sure this is the right thing to do?" Malcom asked.

"Yes. Franklin…will be able to help us. He is a protein scientist who might be able to interpret the prions for us," Cass said, leaving out any aspect of him being a Nephilim.

"But I just got news that Mike is not doing well, and I need to get to him soon. I may be able to put things right for a while," Cass said.

"What is wrong?" Friz said bluntly.

Cass looked at Friz for a moment before Malcom said, "Tell him about Mike. Tell him everything. If anyone can help Mike, it's this guy."

"Malcom, how do you know you can trust him?" Cass said.

Malcom looked between Cass and Friz and said, "Friz? How do I convince Cass that you can be trusted?"

Friz held his lividan up for a moment and said, "Your brother is being treated under the name of Timothy Jones. He had been treated with many drugs. None have helped him and one was *intended* to make him more susceptible to disease. The retrovirus can be extracted. You must understand that the virus binds to the nucleus of the cell, onto what you call the DNA. But it is also the histones and several other aspects your science has yet to uncover. On my world, this would be an easy task. Here, with only my lividan, I will need the donor."

"The donor?" Cass said.

"Yes. The one who infected him," Friz said. "The virus changes from person to person. I will be able to see the part of your brother and the part of the virus, but I cannot tell which is which. If I have the donor,

I can see which one resonates with the infectant. Then it can be removed. Do you understand?" Friz asked.

"Well, fuck. Beth has…passed on from this world," Cass said.

"That is unfortunate," Friz said.

"That's why you never kill Gollum, Cass," Franklin whispered.

Cass chuckled dryly and said, "Well, he's my brother. Couldn't you look at my resonance compared to *his* and pull out the virus?"

Friz looked in thought for a moment then asked, "Does Mike have any offspring?"

"I never said his name was Mike," Cass said.

"You never told him he went by Tim either," Malcom said. "Trust me on this, Cass. There is not one bit of stored information that is under enough protection to keep this guy from finding it. He would be the greatest security risk to every powerful organization in this world, including our government.

"And no, Friz. Mike doesn't have any kids. Is that correct, Cass?"

"Yes. He has no children," Cass agreed.

"How about Beth. Does she have any siblings or offspring?" Friz asked.

"Lynn is still alive. I may be able to get her," Cass said.

"It may work," Friz said. "I can guarantee nothing, but with you, her, and Mike, I may be able to determine the virus and destroy it. If I fail, it would kill your brother. Is this something you can accept?"

Cassian said, "I can. But ultimately, it will be up to Mike. So, now I have to get to Lynn."

"Lynn Richter?" Friz asked.

Cass looked surprised and said, "Yes, Lynn Richter. How do you—"

"Watch this," Malcom said with a huge smile on his face.

Friz said, "Lynn Richter is living in Tampa Bay, Florida. She is married to a man named Phillip Reynolds and is under surveillance by the FBI. Agent Samuel Richter. That is her son," Friz sounded surprised. "The father of Samuel is…unknown."

"I am his father," Cass said.

Friz looked at Cassian darkly and said, "Before or after you were shrouded?"

Cass looked around the room and said, "And just how did you know about *that*? That information shouldn't be under any file in any government database. How could you know?"

Malcom chimed in and said, "He knows a lot of things, Cass. He claims that he comes from a world that mirrors ours…only a thousand or so years ahead of ours."

"Your friend is correct, Cassian. But you are not. You are on a list of possible names associated with events that occurred in your year 1991… among other things. Your government was financing a group of criminals in a family from your town. They had contracts in place to—"

"Friz," Malcom interrupted, "let's talk about this later. I'm not so sure Cassian trusts you just yet."

"I am sorry. It is easy for me to prove my intentions. In my world, there was once a…man with your gift. His name was Chisordian. His friend was named Maloch," Friz said, turning to Malcom.

"So, you wouldn't mind then if I were to possess you for a moment, would you?" Cassian asked.

"I have heard that it is unpleasant," Friz said, "but if it will provide you with peace, do as you will."

"Be careful," Ex said. "You do not know where he is from. This could—"

Cass ignored the warning and immediately jumped into Friz. As he opened the eyes of this man, the whole world was different. He saw things he couldn't understand. There were lists and objects off to the sides. Words and symbols he did not recognize. He could focus and change his vision to see things in different spectrums. *This must be ultraviolet and infrared light*, Cass thought. These sights came in and out of focus. He looked down at the beige clothing he wore to see vibrant colors and textures.

Other feelings he couldn't explain began to come to his attention. He could feel the pressure of the air, the pull of nearby objects, the subtle sensations coming from the minds of the people around him. It started to make Cassian noxious. He quickly jumped back into himself and put his hands on his head.

"What the hell was all that?" Cassian asked.

"I told you," Ex said. "If he came from an advanced world, he probably accesses more than your five senses. I was trying to tell you that you may get overwhelmed."

"I had no idea how *little* we feel," Cass said.

Friz said, "That was not as unpleasant as I had heard about. I barely noticed. It was like a long blink. You did do it, didn't you?"

"Yes, I did it," Cass said. "What was all that stuff I was seeing? Is this what you see all the time?"

"Oh. That. My apologies. I am linked with my lividan. You were probably seeing the data searches that I was performing," Friz said.

"No—you can see in different spectrums. I'm sure I was seeing in the IR and UV range. And maybe something else. Plus, I could feel everything. Like even the air," Cass said.

"Part of that is the implant, and other parts are where we adapted over time to perceive more. We use senses that are currently unattained by you. So you may have felt vestibular stimuli and other sensations you could not explain," Friz said. "But I understand that *you* have talent for resonating with life. Is this true? Even we need a lividan to do that!"

"That was too much for me," Cass said. "But I'm sure you're not a demon or a Spur."

Friz repeated his first question, "When did you create your son? Before or after?"

"After, if you must know. But we don't speak about me being shrouded…to anyone! Do you understand, Friz?" Cass said, throwing his hands in the air.

"Fear not, Cassian. Your secret is quite safe with me. After all, I am the one who has been providing you with the prion messages," Friz said.

CHAPTER 37

MESSAGES

Cassian said, "Please don't take this the wrong way, Friz, but I need to speak with Malcom privately for a moment. Malcom?" Cass tilted his head to the side, toward the back porch.

They went out the back sliding door together.

Franklin said to Friz, "I'm sorry. Did you say *prion messages*?"

"Yes, Doctor Germane," Friz said.

"Please, call me Franklin. And how did you know *my* name?"

"You and your wife Victoria are the owners of this property. I have images of you and her that she recently posted to social media. You should be proud of your accomplishments, sir. Very good work considering your limited technology. The mass spectrometer. This is something I would love to see. They used to be as big as an old Contellosphere from what I have seen. I'm a bit of a historian," Friz said, starting to slip into his rapid speech.

"Historian?" Franklin said, "I have an OmniMass trapping mass spec. This thing is two to three years ahead of being released commercially. What are you talking about?"

"Please do not take offense to what I am saying. You, and others like you, paved the way to the technologies of the future. Things I hold in my hand and take for granted are things that were once huge scientific hurdles," Friz said, smiling.

Franklin sighed and said, "Wow. Seven years of higher education with three years of post-doc work plus ten years of industrial experience.

Here I thought I was on the cutting edge of research only to find that my knowledge is older than dirt."

"Do not feel discouraged, sir," Friz said, "Without *you*, and your giant strides, there is no future! You should feel extremely happy about what you are doing! People in my time wonder how ones such as you could possibly uncover so much information with such little technology."

Franklin nodded and said, "I think I get that. I always wonder how people like Bohr and Mendeleev did what they did back then."

"Exactly," Friz said excitedly. "Each clever way they discovered to answer questions led to more understanding and technologies that would help get the answers!"

Cassian and Malcom came back into the room.

"Friz, I have been trying to recruit Franklin to help me with identifying your messages," Cassian said.

"You certainly picked the right person to perform that task," Friz said.

"Well, why can't you just tell me what the messages are, Friz?" Cassian asked.

"Cassian, the network that has been sending you messages is far more complex than just me and the prion," Friz said, turning to Franklin. "The prions had to be obvious, so that scientists would know what to research. Once they developed the correct nomenclature for amino acids and their structurons, it may become more obvious."

"Structurons?" Franklin asked, "What is that?"

"I thought that you already knew about these. I am sorry if I am affecting your future, but these are part of the fleakion particles that help determine the stereochemical structure of natural products like sugars and proteins. You do understand stereochemistry, don't you?" Friz asked.

"Yes, stereochemistry I understand, but the rest of that stuff makes no sense to me," Franklin said.

"The rest is possibly incidental right now, but you should be able to determine the primary structure, no?" Friz asked.

"Yes, I can determine the sequence in which the amino acids are connected. I can even determine whether they're L or D amino acids. But that other shit is over my head," Franklin said.

"You must be using the International Protein Nomenclature at this point. Unless you have advanced to…" Friz paused and said, "No. You have not moved to the next level of naming. We will need secondary, tertiary, and quaternary structures as well. Can you do this?"

"Yes. We have X-ray crystallography and other techniques for that," Franklin said.

"Good. You may need to identify the protein sequence, then backtrack to the tRNA codon and—"

"Friz," Cass interrupted, "please, we have time to figure out the sequences later. We are on the clock now and time is of the essence."

"You are correct, Cassian. The messages are a 'big picture' kind of thing," Friz said.

"I'm glad you agree. I don't need to know how to interpret them just yet. But what are the messages? I understand you don't know what they say, but why are they being sent?" Cassian asked.

"The messages come from my world as it most closely aligns with your trajectory in time. I cannot say which events, but key events are foretold in the messages. Presuming you interpret them in time. The messages will give clues about the use of Shazo. What you and the stewards call Desemilnoct. The key events to be revealed were specifically intended to nudge you in the right direction…or perhaps steer you away from the wrong direction. They will not tell you specifics. God intends for us all to make decisions on what path we choose. This is why they were carefully crafted and very specific. Even the prions that develop in a certain species provides a clue about their meaning.

"What I can tell you now is that those in control of your world have already discovered Shazo. These authorities are inaccurately calling it Moscovium based on your periodic table. They are hiding it from the people. They will lose their control if this is—" Friz stopped.

"What? What's wrong, Friz?" Cassian asked.

"I can say no more. Especially not to one of key importance like you. I could inadvertently bias your decisions in ways that go against the messages. This could lead to many problems. I could ultimately lead to the untimely end of your world," Friz said.

"Well, Friz, if we believe we all walk in the pathway of God, our decisions are the decisions of God. Right?" Cass said.

"Yes, Cassian. But you and I also have the venom of the serpent and there is no safety net in life. Each person's decisions could lead them or others to doom. God may provide help, but God will not prevent catastrophe," Friz said seriously.

"In my estimate, *you* may be the help that God sent. So let's get busy. After Victoria gets here, I'm going to need to catch a flight—"

"Whoa!" Franklin interjected. "What do you mean *after* Victoria gets here? You all need to get out of my house! My wife and I," he looked at Corrina, "and my mother need to have a long talk. A *private* talk. Without any of you here! She's already in a foul mood after she left her friend. If she gets home and sees the dwarves in her living room, she's going to be furious!"

"Your wife is going to be angry either way, Franklin," Cassian said. "But you are correct. We need not be here for this."

Cass turned to Malcom and said, "Take Friz and wait in your car. Place the sample in the trunk of my car. I will arrange shipment to Pennico immediately. Can you have someone arrange a flight for me to Tampa? Then I will fill you in on the next steps.

"Franklin, you can simply tell Victoria that I am your mother's driver. I will wait in my car until my flight if you do not want me here. But I would appreciate the opportunity to meet your lovely wife."

Franklin visibly relaxed and said, "Okay, Cass. I can live with that."

Cass said, "Corrina, you may have my car when I leave. You will find that it is already registered in your name in the state of Rhode Island. It is a special car. And I don't mean that I got a winterized undercoating."

"Why would you give me a car, Cassian?" Corrina asked.

"Small price to pay for you believing in me." Cass smiled.

Malcom and Friz exited through the front door. Cassian went outside with them and spoke to Malcom briefly before he came back inside. Then he helped Franklin and Corrina straighten up the place before Victoria got home.

CHAPTER 38

DESCENT

Aﬀter his meeting with Doctor Victoria Germane, Samuel paid the four-dollar bill without leaving a tip. He got into his black, government-issued Suburban and said, "SemiJazzyJeff, what do you think about that?"

No answer for a moment before the response came. "What is it you expect me to say?"

"Anything off about that woman?" Samuel asked.

"I don't care about that woman, pig shit," Semjaza said.

"Well, she went to high school with my mother. And my mother is hiding someone you want to meet and someone I am trying to find. But so far, I haven't been able to find him, and Lynn has kept quiet about what she knows," Samuel said.

"Why don't you just torture the bitch? She will tell you whatever you want to know!" Semjaza said.

"That's how you demons work. But here on Earth, we humans don't torture our own mother," Samuel said.

"Well, bully for you cunts. Why don't you just let me take over for a while? I'll find out where this person is located," Semjaza said slyly.

"Oh, no. Thank you, though. I would never give you control. Not for one second," Samuel said. "But I will give you the chance at freedom. If I release you, you can come after me if you want. I really don't care. Once I have Azazel, none of that will matter. And neither will you. So, tell me, how do I get Azazel?"

No response came from Semjaza as Samuel drove in silence. He finally began to whistle the theme for Jeopardy in a constant loop. After about the tenth round of the song, Semjaza said, "You will need to summon him."

"I can do that," Samuel said. "But I don't know the patterns, requirements, or text. I mean, that's what I had to call for *you*. I'm hoping that you have the information I need for *him*. Do you have that information?"

Silence.

Whistling.

"Yes, I have the information. You ask me to betray my leader. I will be hated among my kind," Semjaza said.

"Not if Azazel doesn't know it's you, stupid!" he said.

Samuel felt a jolt of energy as Semjaza raged in his bubble. He laughed and said, "Stop it Semjazzy, that shit tickles."

Another round of rage poured out of the demon as Samuel laughed while he drove. He said, "When you get your panties pulled out of your ass cheeks, let me know where to go next so we can get you on your way."

———

Samuel drove southwest to a location in Centralia, Pennsylvania. It was a small church that had a hidden entrance to the mines where large deposits of Moscovium were discovered, far underground. Two old Spurs were guarding the church.

Samuel knew all about the caves. Of course, he could have just gone through the front entrance of the mine, but using this secret entrance was much better. No need to have a record of each time he visited.

"How do I know you're not telling me a bunch of bullshit?" Samuel asked.

"You can just keep wondering about that for all I give a shit," Semjaza said.

"Now Jizzy! That's not the right attitude. I'm offering you freedom here. That's a pretty big offer. You should be kissing my ass a little more," Samuel said.

"I'm not bullshitting you. You know the things you need. Only now you will need the appropriate sacrifice," Semjaza said.

"Well, you came for a goat. That was no easy task getting that thing where I needed to go. What will I need for Azazel? Let me guess, a pig?" Samuel laughed.

"No, asshole. You will need your own blood," Semjaza said.

"That's not a problem," Samuel said as he pushed Semjaza back into the dark.

Samuel dialed a number on his phone and waited for the answer. *One ring. So eager for advancement*, he thought.

"Hello, Sam?" came the voice of a woman.

"Hey there, Marissa," Samuel responded, matching her enthusiasm. "How would you like a shot at some *real* field work?"

"I would love it. What would you need me to do?"

"You're close to Pittsburgh right now, correct?"

"Well, Erie. Close enough. What do you need?" she asked.

"I'm going to send you an address for a church in Centralia, Pennsylvania. I want you to meet me there in say…six hours. Does that give you enough time?" Samuel asked nicely.

"Oh yeah. I can be there then. It's a short trip. You want me to meet you inside the building?" she asked.

"Hell no. Don't even think about going into that church until I get there. You understand?" Samuel said.

"You got it, boss," came the reply, "See you soon."

"Thanks, Marissa. I owe you one after this."

"No problem."

He was near Springfield, Massachusetts, and she was in Erie. They were both about four and a half hours away. She would be there in four hours. He was going to stop and have a nice lunch and pick up a few items first.

* * *

It was a beautiful, sunny day. As expected, Marissa was already at the church when Samuel pulled into the parking lot. But she was out of the car talking to a Pennsylvania state trooper.

Marissa was a petite woman with dark hair, dark eyes, and a smooth, bronze complexion. She was not exactly pretty, but she was sensual in a way that made her attractive. That was her talent as an agent. She could get information from men and women alike. Aside from that, Samuel had no use for her.

She plied her charms on him every chance she got. That behavior was far different than every other agent with which Samuel worked. Most people distanced themselves from him as quickly as possible. He liked it that way. Certainly, she was sucking up to him to gain some small advantage in her career. He let her believe that.

Parking across the lot from the chatting couple, he got out of his car and walked toward them with a brilliant smile on his face.

As he got closer, Marissa said, "This is my colleague, Special Agent Sam Smith. Sam, this is Trooper Marcus Tabloski. Am I saying that correctly?" She smiled.

"Yes, ma'am. Trooper Tabloski." He nodded, smiling back. He was a solid-looking young man standing about six foot five inches tall. He looked huge standing next to Marissa. His muscular build made him an imposing figure...until Samuel got closer.

"Nice to meet you, Marcus," Samuel said, extending his right hand.

"It's Trooper Tabloski, sir," he said, trying to sound authoritative as he shook Samuel's hand, squeezing tightly.

Samuel released his grip, pretending like his hand hurt and said, "Wow! That's quite a grip you got there. Good for you, son. What brings you out here?" Samuel asked, with no acknowledgment of his title.

"Sir. It is not *son*. It is Trooper Tabloski. And I'm here because three days ago someone murdered the couple that tended this church. So, I'll be the one asking the questions here," he stated firmly. "Why is the FBI here?"

Samuel ignored him and said, "Someone killed them? That's odd? How did they die?"

"They were both stabbed through the head. I want to know why the FBI is here?" he demanded.

Samuel looked perplexed and said, "That's...ah...surprising!" Then to Marissa he said, "How was the drive from Erie?"

"It was good," she said. "Uneventful. That's always best."

"It sure is," he said, smiling. "I guess we should head in then. I doubt the couple that lived here is going to object!" He laughed.

"You're not going into that church until *I* say you can go in," stated Trooper Tabloski.

Ignoring the trooper, Samuel said to Marissa, "Do you need to get anything from your car? We may be in there a long while. I have to get a few things from my trunk first."

"*Hey!* Didn't you hear me? I said *nobody* goes into that church unless I say so!" Tabloski shouted, sounding like someone who is used to intimidating others.

Samuel turned to the trooper and said in a quiet voice, seething with threat, "Then I suggest you say so...*son.*"

Though four inches shorter than Samuel, Trooper Tabloski didn't back down one bit from the confrontation. He stepped into Samuel's immediacy and said, "Listen to me, asshole. I'm giving you exactly three seconds—"

"Three seconds to do what?" Samuel growled over him as he stepped closer, looking down into the trooper's face.

"If you don't step back, I'll show you what I'm going to fucking do." Marcus said, his voice taking on an oddly unnerving and menacing tone.

Samuel took his right index finger and put it on the trooper's forehead and pushed. The man was forced back two steps. Furious, the trooper began to laugh a shrill, reverberating sound that made Marissa shrink back in fear.

Something strange began to happen as he said, "I don't take this shit from anyone!" His eyes turned as black as pitch and his skin instantly bleached while blue veins streaked over his flesh. She watched as rows of sharpened teeth grew, giving him a shark-like appearance. "Now I'm going to kill both of you motherfuckers!"

Marissa jumped back in fear while drawing her weapon. Samuel took a step closer and said, "That's it, Marcus. Let that anger flow, boy!"

The creature that used to be Trooper Tabloski moved like a blur as it swung a clawed right hand at Samuel's neck. But Samuel caught it in his left hand about ten inches from his neck and held it like an iron vice. The pale beast looked confused, and its left hand shot at the chest of Samuel, hitting him hard in the sternum. It yelped in pain as it pulled its limp, broken fist back from striking Samuel.

Marissa stood in shock, observing the one-sided fight. At this point, she didn't know who to point her gun at. *What is that thing*, she thought, *and how is Sam not even afraid of it?*

Marcus shook out his left hand, and it seemed to already be healed. The creature hissed, "Who the hell are you?"

"I'm the one you and *all* your kind fear!" Samuel said as his right hand grabbed the trooper by the neck so quickly that Marissa wasn't sure he even moved.

"This isn't possible," the Spur mumbled.

Samuel lifted the hulking beast off the ground, pulled his face close and said, "I say what's possible!" Then he opened his mouth and savagely bit the nose off the monster. It began to scream. Samuel brought his left hand, still holding the clawed hand of the Spur to meet his right hand. The arm bones of the trooper made terrible snapping sounds. The screaming abruptly ended when Samuel's hands met and the head of the Spur popped off.

"What the fuck are you, Sam?" Marissa said, horrified.

Samuel, with blood around his mouth and covering his hands, said, "Just another day at the office," he turned to her with a gruesome, bloody smile.

She pointed her firearm at Sam. His left hand snatched it from her before she saw him move. "Now what do you wanna go and do something like that for?" he asked. "We're on the same team. And he *was* going to kill you. Help me get this misfortune cleaned up. Can't you see that Trooper Tablowme here just suffered a tragic car accident."

Stunned, Marissa said, "Wa…wa…what?"

"A car accident, Marissa. The recently deceased trooper just had a car accident. Grab his head and throw it in his car…please," he said.

"What? Ho…how did you take my gun like that?" she asked.

"His head. It's right there. Pick it up and put it in the car. Mind the teeth, they can still cut you."

She was shaking as she grabbed the hideous, gory head of the beast and threw it in the open window of the police car. Samuel took the body and stuffed it in through the open driver's side window of the car. He turned on the ignition and put the car in neutral.

He turned to Marissa and said, "Now, Special Agent Turner, pull yourself together. You're an FBI agent, not some county social worker. Toughen up. We got more weird shit to do. Are you going to be okay?"

"I'm fine," she said. "I know what my title is. But I need to know what the fuck is going on here!"

"I will explain everything. But you seem shaken. Why don't you go sit in your car and collect yourself for a moment," he said, smiling again.

"O…okay," she said, wiping her hands on her pant legs as if touching any part of that creature could be contagious.

"Oh, and Marissa?" he said.

"Yes," she said.

"Let's keep this little incident between you and I," he winked. "You sit tight. I'll explain everything to you in just a jiff. Okay?"

"Sure." She nodded, looking like she was concentrating on something else.

He smiled and nodded back as he reached into the police car and began to steer the vehicle while he ran it out of the parking lot. Marissa watched, wide-eyed, as this one man began to push the heavy car faster and faster. He was a big and strong guy, but it would take three or four men his size to get the car moving at a fraction of the speed he was going. He disappeared up the street. Soon she heard a loud crash about a quarter mile away.

Marissa considered driving away at that moment. She also thought about calling for backup. She decided against both of those choices. If Samuel could do that, what else could he do? He *did* say that they were on the same team and he *is* the ranking agent.

Her years of training kept her reasonably calm, but in all her case work, going back to when she started as a paramedic, she had never seen such brutal force. *And what the fuck was that thing? The thing the trooper morphed into. It said it was going to kill us both. Did Samuel just save my life? What did I get myself into?* she thought.

Smoke rose into the air as Samuel came jogging back into the parking lot. He went to his trunk, grabbed a towel and some bottles of water, and proceeded to clean himself. After he washed his mouth thoroughly, he threw a backpack over his shoulder, closed his trunk, and began to walk toward Marissa's car with a bright smile on his face.

When he got to her car, he said, "Okay, let's get going."

Marissa opened the door and said, "I'm not going anywhere until you tell me what the fuck just happened here? And give me back my gun!"

Samuel handed her the gun and said, "Sorry about that, but I couldn't have you shooting me now. I'll make a deal with you. I'll tell you everything as we go. It's kind of a long walk and it won't be terribly pleasant."

"Go where? Where are we going?" she asked.

"Into the mines, of course. You have been briefed about the mines under Centralia, haven't you?" he asked.

"Very brief," she said suspiciously. "Why do we need to go into the mines?"

Samuel started slowly walking to the church as he began talking. "You know that the mines have been burning since 1962. But what you don't know is about the metal they found…"

He turned to look at her and tilted his head toward the church. Marissa looked around, sighed, and then started walking.

"The metal, that they are calling Moscovium, which is what it would be called on our current periodic table, has properties that nobody has been able to explain. It has a calculated atomic number of 115, but that's about the end of its periodicity to any other elements…and about the end of what they know about the element itself," Samuel said, opening the side door, allowing her to enter first.

The church smelled of death and flies seemed to be everywhere. They walked along the hallway to the front of the church.

He continued, "What we do know is that it can be used to generate gravitational fields. Or, if you like, anti-gravitational fields. It can also superconduct electricity at any temperature. But they have failed to explain any other aspect of the metal as all spectroscopic tests are… inconclusive or contradictory.

"They certainly can't tell the world about this discovery either. It would change everything. And the people that control *everything* won't allow that to happen. Do you understand?" Samuel asked.

"How long have they known about the metal?" she asked as they walked down the aisle of the nave.

"Since 1962. Who do you think started the fires? That was intended to keep people away from this area," he said.

"Okay, fine. But what was that thing that looked like a state trooper? And how are you like fucking Superman?"

Samuel chuckled and said, "I'm not Superman. And the thing that thought it was going to kill us is…or was…called a Spur. Hold on for one second."

He walked to the altar, circled it carefully and said, "Someone has been here…and fucking with the entrance like a dipshit." He scratched his head and said, "Well, I guess we'll have to find out if we have company when we get down there."

Samuel pushed on the left side of the altar, and it slid to the right revealing a set of stairs spiraling down into the ground.

He said, "You go ahead of me, and I'll close this behind us."

Marissa was looking around the church as Samuel said, "Yo, Marissa. You go first, and I'll close it behind us."

"Oh, I wasn't listening to you," she said.

He laughed. "I appreciate the honesty."

"I'm trying to decide if I can trust you or not," she said. "I just watched you bite off a guy's face and pop his head off as easy as a daisy. Now you want me to go into the mines…with *you*?"

"How much can anyone trust another person, Marissa? If you want to know about the biggest of the really big secrets, I will explain what you saw while we descend," Samuel said. Then he waved his hand nonchalantly and said, "But if you wish to remain a low-level agent, feel free to go back to your car and drive away to the safety of ignorance. The choice is yours."

He opened the backpack and pulled out an electric lantern and handed it to Marissa as she looked down the stairs and then back to the front door.

"Did you learn that tactic in *Psychology for Dummies*? You think tempting me with being part of some inner circle is going to get me to dive into this abyss with you? No, no, no, no, no. If you want my help, you are going to answer my questions. And if I feel like you're holding out on me, I'm not going another step. Certainly, you could drag me down there…I doubt I could stop you. But you have to know that I called this in as backup, right? They know that I am here…with you!"

"Of course, I *assumed* you called it in. So did I," he lied, "I'm not going to drag you down there, Marissa. Besides, I don't think that would work. Something about choice. But you have the wrong impression about me. I'm not so bad. And…I would really appreciate your help. If you decide to come with me, I can promise that you're going to hear the craziest shit you could ever imagine."

"I don't want to hear the craziest shit. I want to hear the truth. I know," she said, nodding, "that you probably think I'm some stupid chick looking to get ahead—"

Samuel threw his hands up in the air as he protested, but Marissa cut him short, "Shut up, stupid," she yelled. "The coloration of your neck already gave you away. You big liar. But I didn't need to see that to know a lie when I hear it. You may think I'm stupid. That's good. I encourage people to make that conclusion! I *like* to be underestimated…every bit as much as *you* like to make people feel uncomfortable." She gave him a sharp look.

He sighed, nodding, and said, "Okay, I didn't call it in. I don't want the agency knowing what I'm doing. But you didn't call it in either, did you?"

"Oh, no. I didn't call it in either," she lied. "But right now, you need to understand that I am *not* as stupid as you think. If you feed me one bit of bullshit, it's over. You'll have to drag me down there. Do *you* understand?"

The hard look on his face disappeared as he looked around the room. He suddenly looked like a teenage boy…a huge teenage boy…trying to tell his mother he wouldn't drink at a high school party. He said, "Alright. I'll tell you anything you want to know."

"No lies. Trust me, Samuel, I can smell them like rotten shit," she said.

He paused, "Fine. No lies. I promise."

"What's down there?" she asked.

"It will take us down into the mines where the Moscovium was found."

"Then what?" she asked.

"Then we are going to summon a demon." He smiled.

She barked a laugh and said, "Seriously. Why are we going down here?"

"I am serious. How much to you know about religion and God and angels and demons?" Samuel asked.

"I grew up Catholic, so I know something about it," she said.

"Well then, why the doubt when I mention summoning a demon? Didn't you just see something awful and unexplainable? That thing I called a Spur…have you ever seen anything like that before?"

"No. Never," she said.

"They're kind of like a sub-demonic species. They used to be pretty rare, but lately, they're fucking everywhere. I'm guessing that a lot of what you know about religion is wrong," he said.

"It's all spiritual mumbo-jumbo as far as I'm concerned. I don't take any of it seriously…not anymore," she said.

"So there was a time when you did take it seriously?" he asked.

"Sure. When I was a kid. I also believed in Santa Claus," she said.

He motioned for her to get moving as he said, "How about Krampus?"

"Krampus never came up," she said, giving him a stern look as she started down the steps. "How far down do we have to go?"

"Far. I hope you've been staying in shape. We're about to get a leg workout," he said.

She stopped about ten steps down and turned on the lantern as Samuel pulled the altar back over the top. He paused as he pulled something off the wall inside the altar and stuck it in his pocket.

"I know you and most of the people in the world, even those who regularly follow their religion, don't truly believe in angels and demons. And practically nobody knows about Spurs. That's because *they* hide in plain sight. And when anyone does find one, they don't live to talk about it. Spurs are exceptionally dangerous. Fast, powerful, vicious… not a human alive could stand a chance against one of them. It makes me feel that I accomplished something good for the world when I kill one of them," he said.

"So, what does that make you? Inhuman?" she asked.

"I will tell you soon. I want to understand your knowledge base and your belief system," he said.

"How is that important?" she asked.

"I want to know how flexible your mind is. If you're close-minded, you're not going to believe me. I don't need some Dana Scully trying harder to debunk shit than believing her own eyes. But if you're open, you will learn a lot," he said.

"I'm open-minded. Just tell me the truth…at least as you believe it… and we'll get along fine," she said.

"Okay. It's ironic that you are about to go down the deepest rabbit hole you could ever imagine as we physically descend the deepest hole you could ever imagine." He started laughing.

"It's not really that funny," she said.

"It's kind of funny."

"No, it's not. I don't get claustrophobic, but this is starting to feel like a crypt."

"Okay, okay. It's not that funny. But there is a lot to tell you. Plenty to keep your mind occupied as we go forward…or down.

"In your teachings of religion, have you ever heard of the Nephilim?" he asked.

"It sounds vaguely familiar," she said. "Were they like giant beasts or something?"

"Our history is a mishmosh of different stories. Mostly, the things taught are inaccurate since the information is lost, hidden, or intentionally altered. Of course, some of it is coded, too, by those that fight against the Spurs. It can be difficult to tell what's true and what is false. See, that's what the Spurs *really* do. They rig our history so we never know what's going on or what to believe. I'm not sure if they work to prevent us from finding the truth or if they're just dickheads who like to watch mankind chase its proverbial tail," he said.

"Well then, how is it that *you* know about them and you're still alive? I mean, you were able to kill that hellish nightmare," she said.

"Because, Marissa, I am a Nephilim. We are the unwanted and unexpected consequence of the mating between a human and one of the Seraphim. That's what you would call an angel or demon. Seraphim are not of our world. They can, however, possess the body of humans. When they do that and subsequently procreate with another human, they pass on a part of their essence to any male progeny…to create a Nephilim."

"What about Spurs? If they're so common, wouldn't Nephilim be everywhere now?" she asked.

"No. Spurs are not of the Seraphim race. Spurs are human souls who chose to side with Satan. They're just like any other human…until they access their power. Oh, and once they reveal themselves to you, that's all you will ever see. Like what's-his-name, Trooper Tembobsky."

"Tabloski," she said.

"Whatever," he said dismissively. "Nephilim do not possess any innate powers. In other words, I am just a man like any other man. But what I can do is trap any Spur or demon that attempts to possess me. Probably angels too, but I never had one try to possess me…not really, anyway. I'll get to that.

"Once I trap them, I can then access their powers. And it's something unbelievable. The more of them I trap, the stronger I get. This is why I was able to do what I did to that Spur," Samuel said.

Marissa was silent for a long time as they continued to climb.

Finally, she asked, "I'm guessing you're already holding a demon. So, who is it you want to trap now and why?"

Samuel smiled to himself as he realized how he *did* underestimate her. She was much sharper than any of the other agents he worked with. She put it together immediately.

He said, "There is one who was once an angel. He taught the world about metals so that mankind could bring war against each another. This angel and his allies were cast from Heaven and bound in the dark until the end of time. Satan freed these thirteen named fallen angels, and they became the fiercest demons in Hell. The one who led them is named Azazel."

"And you believe this demon will reveal to you the secrets of the mysterious metal they discovered in 1962?" she asked.

"You are a true credit to the bureau, Agent Turner," Samuel said.

CHAPTER 39

REUNIONS

FRANKLIN WAS IN HIS BEDROOM running the vacuum cleaner.

"Corrina," Cassian said, "I need you to do something for me. It is extremely important and you cannot tell Franklin."

"You want me to deceive my son?" she asked.

"No. Well, yes. But it's not at all what you think. I need only one moment with Victoria when Franklin is not here. When Victoria shows up, I am going to excuse myself to the bathroom. Take my car keys," he placed them into her hands. "Besides, they are your car keys now. Tell Franklin that you left your pills in the glove compartment and ask him to please get them for you. The car is parked far enough away that I will be able to do what I need to do."

"Is this something that's going to help my son or hurt him?" she asked.

Cass looked her in the eyes and nodded, "Both. But I can promise you that it will make his life better. And yours. It's half the reason I am here, Corrina."

She took the keys and nodded.

The vacuum shut off. A few moments later, Franklin came up into the room and said, "Victoria should be here soon. Where are you going to go, Cass?"

"Um, right now. I need to use your bathroom. Urgently," Cass said.

"You know where it is. But don't be stinking up the whole place just before my wife gets home, please," he said.

"Do you have an air freshener?" Cassian asked as he put a hand to his gut.

"Yes, under the sink. Can't you like…resonate with the shit molecules and make them go out the fan?"

"Gee, I don't know. I never tried that before. I'll give it a shot," Cass said as he hurried down the hallway.

They heard the car door slam outside. Franklin whispered to Corrina, "Of course, he has to take a shit right as Victoria walks in!"

"It's okay, son. Listen. I forgot to ask you earlier. I have extra nitroglycerine pills in the glove compartment of Cassian's car. It's the white Ford Focus parked across the street and two or three houses up the hill. I'm worried this conversation might be hard on my heart," she held the keys out to him. "Would you please run up and get them for me?"

"Sure, Mom. I'll get them right after I see Victoria. She's going to want to know why you're here," he said.

"Well, go down and let her in. Tell her I stopped by for a quick visit. Then you can run up real quick and get them. I kind of feel like I need one now. I'm getting nervous about this…confrontation," she pleaded.

"Okay. Me too," he said, taking the keys.

Franklin ran down the steps and opened the door.

"Hi, honey!" he said.

"Hey, baby. I feel like I've been gone from you for a whole week!" Victoria said.

Corrina could hear them kissing. Then she heard Franklin whispering to her.

"Really? For how long?" Victoria said, sounding annoyed.

Franklin whispered again. She could hear bits like "Be nice" and "We need to clear the air."

"Fine," she said angrily.

"I'll be right back. I just need to grab something for Mom out of her car," Franklin said.

Corrina stood in the kitchen as Victoria plodded up the steps and said, with dripping sarcasm, "So nice to see you again, Corrina."

"You too, Victoria. Do you know my friend?" she gestured to the dark hallway on Victoria's left as Cassian strolled out of the shadows.

"Hello, *Vicky*!" Cass said.

The horrified look on her face matched the scream that shook the walls as Victoria began to change. But it was too late. The white sword of Ex fell on her neck from above. The walls shook as a low rumble passed through the room.

Cass/Vicky opened her eyes and said to Corrina, "Victoria has been held by a Spur for a long time. I will need you to either take Franklin out of the home or *he* will have to heal her mind. If Ex does not heal her, she will not survive the night. My power to heal from Ex will be broken when he comes back. We need to explain it to him quickly."

Cass jumped back into himself as Franklin ran into the home and up the stairs.

"What the hell was that scream?" he asked.

Victoria stood taking deep breaths, still in shock as she looked around the room. She began to wail. Cassian instinctively ran to her and put his hands on her head. But the power was gone. Franklin also ran to Victoria and grabbed her from Cassian.

"Listen to me carefully, Franklin. I cannot heal her while you are in the room. Either you leave, or you focus the power of Ex to heal her," Cass said.

"I'm not leaving my wife. What did you do to her?" he yelled.

"She has been possessed by a Spur since she was in high school. You need to help her now!" Cass said.

"What do I do?" Franklin asked.

"Place your hands on her head. I will put my hands on you. I will access the power Ex provides me. You will need to channel it into your wife," Cass said.

"I don't know how to do that!" Franklin said in a panic.

"Neither do I," Cass yelled, "but we're going to try. Put your hands on her head and look into her eyes!"

Franklin did as Cassian said. Cass put his hands on Franklin's arm and began to focus on healing her. Moments later, Franklin's body began to glow. White pulses flew down his arms into Victoria. She looked into Franklin's eyes as she wept.

"Cassian, is it working?" Franklin asked, now with tears in his eyes.

"Yes. Can't you feel the power? It's coming from you."

"It's amazing. I can feel it. I can feel the angel…in me!" Franklin said.

Cass nodded.

"How long do we need to do this?" Franklin asked.

"Until it is done," is all that Cassian could say.

The healing lasted for nearly ten minutes. This was longer than it took for Maureen, who was trapped at least as long as Vicky.

When it was over, Victoria threw her arms around Franklin's neck and said, "Oh, thank you, mister! You saved me. I've been in Hell forever. I didn't think it was possible to ever get free! I can never, ever thank you enough."

"It's okay, Victoria. It's me, Franklin. I'm always going to be here to save you," he whispered into her ear as he hugged her back.

Corrina looked at Cassian like she was about to object. Cass put his hand on her arm and gave a slight shake of his head. She saw that Victoria was happy with Franklin. She nodded in response.

Victoria didn't know Franklin or Corrina, but she knew Cassian. She said that the Spur used to let her up to see what it was doing. But then later stopped doing that and left her in the dark. She remembered taking Lynn to the party. She told Cass that it was her…well, the Spur…that drugged Lynn. She cried as she apologized to Cassian for letting those men do what they did to her.

This seemed to make Cassian visibly upset. His hands shook, and there seemed to be tears forming in his eye, but he just nodded and said, "It's okay. I know it wasn't you who did that."

Cassian explained that she was taken by a Spur when she let it in during her nightmare all those years ago. It happened after Brian Senicha broke up with her in the tenth grade. Vicky preferred the name Victoria, so naturally, the Spur went by Vicky. It was only after she was stuffed back into the dark that the Spur switched back to Victoria.

She wanted to know about her parents and other friends, but Franklin told her that they passed away many years ago in a car crash. Again, Cassian said nothing, but secretly wondered if Victoria's Spur had something to do with their death and that of her previous husband, Tom Penner. She must have inherited quite a fortune from their deaths.

Victoria sat on the sofa as they talked. She held Franklin's hand like a lifeline. Even when he had to use the bathroom, she looked terrified that he wasn't next to her. Cassian began to ponder the way things worked. This was a completely different woman than who Franklin had been married to for nearly ten years, yet she felt more secure with him than anyone. Maybe they were meant to be together.

Cass was always astonished by the power of love. The incredible mindfuck it had to be for the poor souls released from a Spur and those impacted by their release. Yet in every situation, the people affected seemed to come together in love. Jimmy and Malcom with their mothers, Grandma Betty with her daughters, and so many others over the years. This always gave Cassian hope for the world.

He remembered wondering what threads could be undone by the banishment of a Spur. He didn't know if he would ever witness the world becoming a better place or not. But eventually, he saw it, and it made him happy. Just like seeing Victoria and Franklin happy.

Cassian smiled to himself as he thought, *Every time. People always find a way to make it work.*

Victoria looked exhausted though it was still early in the day. Franklin offered to let her nap in the bedroom, but she was afraid to go to sleep.

Cass suggested that Corrina and Victoria talk for a while so he could speak with Franklin downstairs. He assured them he would only be a few minutes.

"Franklin, this girl believes her name is Victoria Polewaczyk. She doesn't know that you are her husband. She barely knows your name. For all I know, she might think she's still a virgin. If she was taken by the Spur before she ever had sex, she has no idea what you may have done together," Cass said.

"What do you mean, Cass? Is she like a little girl, mentally?" Franklin asked.

"Yes, Franklin. Look at this woman. She is terrified. She went to bed one night as a child and woke up today with no family and no friends. She is terrified. But she clearly adores you. Whether it's because she thinks you saved her or she has some kind of deep, unexplained connection with you, I don't know. But you need to treat her like it's your first date. Do you understand?" Cass said.

"She was a doctor. Are you telling me she's not a doctor anymore?" Franklin asked.

"That's exactly what I'm saying, Franklin. She's a high school girl who is alone and afraid. Does her being a doctor really matter to you?" Cass asked.

"No, of course it doesn't. I love my wife. I always have. But…is she only…I don't know, man. Why did you do this to me?" he asked.

Cassian took on a harsh tone as he quietly said, "Do not…*ever*…say such a thing again. You have been living a bullshit life with a bullshit wife who was using you for what she needed to do as a Spur. She drove a wedge between you and your mother and destroyed that bond. When she was done with you, she would and could easily kill you in your sleep. She probably killed Tom Penner and maybe even her own parents.

"For all I know, that Spur may have figured out you were a Nephilim and summoned that demon to see what would happen. I don't know what's going on in this world right now, but it's worse than it was five or six years ago.

"When we go back upstairs, look at this girl. Really look at her! You have a chance at a happy life with a human soul who seems to be immediately in love with you. What do you want to do? I told you earlier that your life was going to change forever. How it goes from here is *entirely* up to you!" Cass pointed his finger at Franklin.

Franklin looked down and nodded. "I see what you're saying. But I was happy in my life. There was no way to…I don't know…keep part of that?"

"*You* may have been happy, but the person you call your wife was living in an absolute hell as a hostage by that Spur. Be the *good* man I know you are. Be gentle, kind, and patient with your *new* wife. I cannot promise you that it will work out, Franklin. But I can promise you that your life will get better," Cass said, putting a hand on Franklin's shoulder.

When they came up the stairs, Victoria stood and briskly walked to Franklin. She seemed awkward about what to do. It was like she wanted to hug him or something. She began to fidget as she stood next to him. He graciously took her hand and held it, instantly making her feel safe again.

Together, Cassian, Corrina, and Franklin tried to explain much of the last nearly forty years to Victoria. She nodded along a lot and started to yawn through the things she didn't seem interested in.

Cass privately explained to Corrina that Victoria was like a young girl once again. Corrina said she already knew that. Talking with Victoria now made Corrina feel so happy. She was such a sweet and gentle girl.

Victoria said she was hungry, so they ordered more pizza for dinner, which Victoria seem to love even more than Cassian did. She claimed she hadn't tasted food in like a million years.

Cass told them he already had a flight reserved from Logan airport to Tampa to get Lynn. He had a taxi coming to take him to the airport. Malcom and Friz left for Pittsburgh to help Mike.

Corrina was going to stay in the guest bedroom that night but then head home the next day. By 6 p.m., Franklin decided that Victoria had enough for the day and took her into the bedroom so she could get some sleep.

Franklin showed her the bathroom and where all her belongings were stored. He showed her where to find her toothbrush and pajamas (which Victoria never really wore, but he wanted to be careful) and got her ready for bed.

He sat next to her, like he was tucking her in and said, "Okay, Victoria. I'm going to let you get some sleep. You've had a terrible and long day. I just want you to feel better," he said as he gently put his hand on the side of her head.

"I don't want you to go," Victoria said, "I don't know. I'm afraid to go to sleep. I feel better when you're around me. Do you really have to go?"

"No. I can stay with you until you fall asleep. I'll stay with you as long as you like. I'll sleep on the sofa tonight, though," he said with a smile.

"No. I don't want that. I would feel better with you next to me," she said as she started to cry.

Franklin said, "What's wrong. Why are you crying?"

"I'm so alone, Franklin. I don't know anyone anymore. I'm terrified. But I'm also so happy to be free from that Hell. I don't know how to feel. I don't have a family anymore." She put her face in her hands.

Franklin put his arms around her to make her feel better. She threw her arms around his neck and hugged him so hard it nearly hurt him.

Feeling her body next to him, he felt his desire for her rise, but he put that aside as he held her. Then he said, "Sure you have a family, me… and my mother. We *are* your family, and we're here for you, Victoria. I will never leave you. I love you," he said out of rote memory.

She froze in his arms, "You…you really love me?" she asked.

Franklin started, "I know it's hard for you to understand this, but I…I loved you the first moment I saw you. And I…well…I wanted to—"

Victoria started to kiss Franklin before he could finish his confession of love.

CHAPTER 40

DEEPER INTO THE TRUTH

"WHO IS FEEDING YOU YOUR information, Sam?" Marissa asked. "Are you certain you can trust it?"

"No, of course not. They're evil. But I did cross-reference most of the info with two separate demons and a few Spurs. Mostly, the Spurs know shit, but a few of them went back a long time. Get this…one of them actually claimed to be with Cain when he killed Abel! He sounded very convincing. Can you believe that shit? As far as I'm concerned, you can trust these things like you can trust a fart when you have diarrhea."

"Nice. Great visual." She laughed.

"What I do believe are the times and places where their stories seem to independently correlate," he said.

"Hmmm," she paused, then said, "what's it like? I mean, what's it like to have one of them trapped? Are they constantly talking in your head, or can you tune them out?" she asked.

"My first Spur, when I was a little boy, tried to be extra nice to me so I would release it. I promised to let it go if it would tell me about what *it* was and what *I* was. It never told me anything of value. I mean, I had no idea what was going on. I think I was about six at the time. I thought I was going crazy. I didn't know how to release it. I eventually figured out how to shut it up. I could stuff it down, so to speak. But I never touched any of their power. I didn't know I could. I didn't know they had any power back then.

"Apparently, it was the *way* I was holding that first Spur that drew the attention of other Spurs. Before long, I had another one. That one was a dick. He told me all kinds of vulgar shit. I got in tons of trouble at school and with my mother from what it said. I stuffed that one down after a few weeks. I don't know how many more. But then I got a demon. That thing was awful. That's when…"

Samuel stopped for a few moments. Marissa asked, "That's when what?"

Samuel continued to talk like she never asked the question. It was almost as if he were figuring it out as he spoke. "This is how I think of it now. There are several *ways* to hold them. When I hold them outside, like in a bubble, it's like bait for other Spurs…or even lesser demons. Like a tag of desperation. I seem to draw their attention. That's especially true when I make them angry. I do that a lot…because—fuck them. I can bring them up. Let them talk. Hell, I could let them take control of me for a while if I wanted. But I would *never* do that. Ultimately, I have the power. The power to free them or stuff them down, into the dark…like they were planning to do to me," he said angrily.

"But you can talk with them, right?" she asked.

"Of course. That's how I know about them and myself. Nobody else was there to help me. I was dumped with my insane grandparents when I was nine, because my mother 'couldn't deal' with all my mental problems. What do you expect when a demon starts talking in your head.

"That…that changed me. I didn't know how to use any of their powers, but I occasionally did things from time to time. Damaging things. My grandparents were afraid of me. I suppose, in retrospect, they weren't nearly afraid enough.

"Then those religious psychos tried to perform an exorcism on me. A fucking exorcism in this day and age!" he said.

"How did that go?" she asked.

"It was awful. They chained me in the basement for weeks while they constantly read Bible verses to me. They wouldn't let me eat or drink…unless I begged for water. The demon offered to help me. It told me all kinds of stuff…stuff about the people doing the exorcism. It said the people would be afraid of me! I thought that doing and saying what the demon suggested would make them quit.

"I was so stupid. I believed it. If they killed me, it would be free. It wasn't trying to *help* me. I didn't see that the demon was trying to get them to kill me. They got much worse.

"After that, they started to hurt me for real. Burning me with symbols. Crosses and shit from…I don't know…the Dark Ages, I guess. I know they had plans to put an iron nail into my skull," Samuel said.

"How did you ever get away from them before they did that?" she asked.

"That's when they called my father. They couldn't deal with me anymore. I have to assume they had *some* realization that putting a fucking spike into the brain of a kid might cause child protective services to wonder about possible problems at home."

Samuel paused for a long time then said, "As it turns out, my father is possessed by an angel. Angels call it *shrouding,* by the way. Much less antagonistic than the term *possession*, huh? That's why I'm a freakshow Nephilim," he said in a mocking way.

"So, part of you is an angel?" Marissa asked sympathetically.

"I don't know, Marissa. Maybe." Samuel continued, "I don't really remember everything that happened that day. I had a bunch of shit attached to me…one demon and maybe four or five Spurs…I had the Spurs stuffed down, but the demon was too much.

"Sometimes, when the assholes doing the exorcism tortured me, I lost control. All the voices started talking at once…in my head. It was hard to tune them out. I didn't know what to do." He gritted his teeth and said, "If I knew how to control this then, I would have *ripped them all to fucking pieces*!"

Marissa waited for him to calm down before she asked, "So, what happened when your father and his angel showed up?"

"Fuck. This is getting really old, really fast. My legs are burning," Samuel said, aggravated.

"Yeah, it sucks," she said. "My legs are burning too. What happened when your dad got there?" She knew she had to push him.

"I don't know," he yelled. "This total stranger walks into the basement. They tell me that he's my father. Then he goes upstairs and leaves me there! I was so fucking pissed.

"The next thing I know, bodies are flying everywhere and this guy is in my head…*talking*, telling me he wants to help me. He said he got rid of all the 'voices.' Come to think of it, he was the one who first called them Spurs. Pretty fitting name, really.

"Whatever happened, though, I started drawing on their power. I broke free of the metal chains. I found the priest who burned me and took his head off his body.

"The guy talking in my head says he's my father and he could help me. Then he almost *killed* me. It was the *worst fucking pain* I have ever felt in my life. Oh, he showed me where they were connected to my body…by *ripping* them all away at once. It felt like I was being *torn apart*!" he yelled.

Part of Samuel turned to ice when he spoke the last line. The part that recalled what that first demon hissed into his ear, "*Women are your weakness. One day, a woman will come to you, and she will be your downfall. The beginning of your end. When you soften to her, she will hold your power…and you will bend your knee to her as a dutiful slave. Look at your own mother. She left you here…to control another man. She will come back to you when you are able to help her once more. And you will do it.*" *And that's exactly what Lynn did*, he thought.

Could he believe what the demon said? Hard to not believe it. It wasn't wrong about his mother. Lynn was always doing that kind of shit to men. Then she leveraged *him* to try to get Cassian to stay with her.

"That must have been awful," Marissa said.

"How about we just shut the *fuck* up for a while. I don't need your compassion, and I don't want you in my head anymore," he said angrily.

"I'm not trying to get in your head!" she shot back. "I want to understand *why* the fuck I am trudging down this endless set of stairs for someone who treats me like a piece of shit. I am not the spiteful tramp who fucked you up. Then you have the nerve to be fucking angry…*with me*? You have no idea how pissed I am right now! Pissed at myself for letting some *big pussy* lead me down into this hell. You act so tough and then crumble like a bitch when someone dares to push you a tiny, little bit. If you don't want to talk about mommy and daddy, *don't*! But I need to know what the *fuck* I'm getting into!"

They walked in silence for a long time. Marissa wouldn't speak. Finally, Samuel said, "I'm sorry."

"Who cares? You can't even handle these questions. You can't handle your own past. What good are you going to be against something like Azazel," she said.

"I didn't mean to take it out on you. It's something that fills me with rage…even after all these years. I thought I was dead after what Cassian did. I didn't feel like myself anymore. I still don't. I'm…fucked up now. I apologize for yelling at you. You didn't deserve that," he said.

After a minute or so of silence, Marissa said, "Fine. What happened after that?"

"I woke up in a hospital in Arizona. All the voices were gone. It's kind of like when someone shuts off white noise. The silence is unusual. I was in and out of sleep from the pain medicine," he said. "Cassian… my father…was there too. He said he was going to try to help me. But he bailed that night.

"I blame that one on my mother. I don't know the whole story. I only got her side of it. But what I think is that she wanted Cass to stay with her. He made it clear that he would never be with her again. I do remember hearing her threaten to call the cops on him for putting me in the hospital. I haven't seen him since. He ran away. He couldn't even face the cops for me.

"But after that whole incident, I *was* able to control the Spurs and demons. Not long after that, I learned how to use their power. In no time, I figured out how to call them and trap them at will.

"I finished high school at fifteen. Then I got a full ride in college on a wrestling scholarship. I finished with a degree in criminal justice in three years. I didn't need my family to finance me. I made all the money I needed by working as a bouncer in a high-end bar. I mean, nobody could fight me. I should say, nobody could beat me.

"But if I went into any professional sports or something like that, I would have called too much attention to myself. So, when I finished college, I joined the bureau…specifically to find Cassian. He's a slippery son of a bitch," he said.

"So, your father…he showed you how to control your powers?

"I wouldn't say he *showed* me anything. But…maybe after what he did…I could feel where to concentrate to control them."

"Sounds to me like he did you a *huge* favor. Showing you how to control your power," she said.

"Agent Turner, how old are you?" he asked.

"I'm thirty-one, not that it's any of your business," she said. "But since *you* are being so open, I will be too."

"I will say that you do look younger than that. But even at thirty-one, you don't know what the fuck you are talking about. When someone hurts you like he hurt me…whatever age you are at the time…you tend to hold a grudge," he said.

"If the man was still there when you woke up in the hospital, Samuel," she enunciated his name, "he *wasn't* trying to kill you. How old were you when this all happened?"

"I was eleven. And I know what I *felt*! He tried to *rip* my soul out of my body! The back of my neck hurt for years after that!" Samuel said.

"At age eleven, you don't know shit!" she fired back. "You were carrying several large chips on your shoulder…besides the demons and Spurs. Your mother left you. Your grandparents sounded like they hated you. Everyone was shitting on you. Are you certain your father wasn't there to help you?"

"Why don't we climb the steps in silence for a while? I didn't bring you here for an episode of *Dr. Phil*," he said.

"No. I don't think Dr. Phil would approve of your motives. You see, by the way you're telling me everything, I don't think I'm coming out of this hole with you. I'm beginning to believe that your plan is to sacrifice me to get Azazel," she said.

He stopped walking, stunned. She knew. How could she know?

She stopped and turned to him, "Oh, you don't want to follow through with your plan now that your sheep knows it's being led to the slaughter?"

"I am not bringing you to be slaughtered. I just need a few drops of your blood to summon Azazel. If I use mine, Azazel may be able to control me. That can *never* happen. You don't know what Nephilim did in the past. It would be Hell on Earth if a demon…or an angel…controlled me," he said.

"You figured I would be disposable. Isn't that right? You can't have someone you work with knowing all this about your past. Are you planning to make sure I don't come back up?" she asked.

"No. That is *not* my plan. Weren't you the one so eager for advancement?" he yelled back. "I never had the phone ring more than once before you picked up. My past is not a secret, not that you care. All you want is to get ahead! Admit it!"

All five feet four inches of her stepped up to him and stood pointing at this giant man two steps above her as she said, "I did it because I like you…you fucking asshole. I've always liked you. You're just too fucking stupid or self-involved to notice. Maybe you're gay or something. I don't know. You always *have* to be the biggest, baddest hard-on…constantly in the face of everyone…all the time. You don't fool me. You're still the lost little boy who feels like his daddy abandoned him. You won't even *try* to see that your father wanted to help you! You idiot!"

She turned and continued walking down the steps.

Samual waited a moment and followed without saying a word.

"I'm not bringing you for a sacrifice. You don't understand. You don't know what I was told. I cannot be controlled by any woman. Ever," Samuel said.

"I'm not trying to control you, Sam. I just wanted to be near you. Maybe even…you know what? Fuck it. I'm stupid for thinking this way," she said.

"The Nephilim have a weakness. It is women," Samuel said. "I cannot let any woman sway me from my intended purpose. You don't know the history of my kind."

"Oh, and you do? From who? Donny Demon? Sammy Spur? Andy Angel? Maybe it's all bullshit. The devil is known to be a big ol' liar. Maybe you're playing right into his hands by believing them!" she said.

"Hey, I double and triple check everything these assholes tell me. I know they lie. But some things make sense. In some books, there was a brief mention of a time called the Matriarchy before Uriel came to Noah to warn of the Great Flood. The Antediluvian period was a lot longer than people think. Thousands of years. God flooded the Earth to destroy the Nephilim because neither side can defend against us…well, me," he said.

"Really. So maybe this is all some kind of invincibility-complex you're experiencing. Even God can't touch you? That's what you're saying," she said. "I can tell you without a doubt that God *can* touch everyone. Even you!"

"Don't be so certain, Marissa. You don't know a fraction of what you're talking about," he said. "Just two hours ago, you believed angels and demons were mythology. I suspect your mind has shifted on that by now?"

There was a pause before she said, "Yeah, I can admit some of this shit is not fitting my belief of reality. But what proof do you have that you or the Nephilim are so invulnerable?"

"I have seen what a Spur can do when they transform. Things you could never imagine possible. You only saw a glimpse of that. They move faster than you could blink. They change physical appearance before your eyes. They have the strength of twenty men or more.

"You've seen movies about them, but they never talk about what they *really* are. They're always vampires or witches or shit like that. I am telling you for a fact that these are *all* stories about Spurs. They romanticized them to hide their existence. You cannot fathom how deeply they have changed our reality," he said.

"So, what does this have to do with you thinking God can't touch you?" she asked.

"Because where other men die at the hands of Spurs, I can spank them like a little baby…just like Trooper Tumbleweed or whatever. They have no power over me. Demons make Spurs look like children and even they can do nothing to me. The same is true for angels. Somehow, I take their power and use it for myself. And the reason this gives me power over God—at least on Earth—is because God only sends angels to do his bidding. Does that make sense to you now?" he said.

"You're saying that on Earth you are essentially indestructible?" she asked.

"Clearly not indestructible. I can still drown, obviously. But in many other ways…yes," he said.

She drew her weapon and turned as fast as she could to point it at Samuel. He wasn't there.

Marissa jumped as Samuel spoke into her ear from behind her. "Not even close."

"How? How is that possible. I'm not slow on the draw," she said.

"You are not. I don't know how I do it," he said. "It has something to do with the Time realm where they reside. They can modify time… or something like that. They make what would take months happen in seconds or vice versa. When I have their power…" he shook his head, "by the time your hand was on your gun, I was already down the stairs behind you."

She put her gun away and kept trudging down the steps. After a bit, she asked, "How many of them are in our world? Spurs and demons, I mean."

"That, I don't know. I didn't know that cop was a Spur until he started to change. I can't sense them, if that's what you're getting at. But if they even touch their power, I can feel it," he said.

"How do you know I'm not a Spur?" she asked.

"I don't know, and I don't currently have any angels in my possession or I could ask them. Angels banish Spurs and sometimes demons… if they win the battle. I don't know if they can sense them, though. My father might be able to answer that when I finally get him," he said.

"So, if angels and demons…and Spurs…are afraid of you because you take their power, don't they want you dead?" she asked.

"Apparently, they are forbidden to allow us to be born or ever *live* past the age of three. And if we do survive and they know about it, they *will* try to kill me," he said.

"But you've let a bunch of them go already, haven't you? Don't they talk amongst themselves? Don't they already know who you are?" she asked.

"That is a great question…one I'm sure I do *not* have a good answer for. But, from what I understand, there was a law made a long time ago and agreed upon by God and Satan that when these beings…angels and demons and such…get into a battle, the loser of the battle cannot recall who defeated them.

"It has something to do with immortality…banishment rather than death. They found out long ago that the retribution of both Heaven and Hell against any mortal victor was unfair. I don't know how Nephilim fit into this law. Perhaps we don't since we were never meant to exist in the first place. None of the ones I trapped seemed to know either. Maybe we can ask Azazel. But so far, none have come against me with knowledge of who I am," he said.

"Samuel, you told me that your father is possessed by an angel, right?" she asked.

"Yes. He is shrouded by an angel. That's what I was telling you before. That's how he got rid of all the Spurs and the demon attached to me when I was a kid," he said, sounding exasperated that he had to repeat himself.

"Well, how can you be so sure it was your father who tried to kill you and not the angel possessing him?" she said as a statement more than a question.

They walked in silence for a long time. She allowed the silence to continue. Samuel said, "How about after this, you and I get some dinner together?"

"That is so insulting. Don't try that shit on me. The complete lack of respect you seem to have for my intelligence. You have an easy question in front of you…one you know the answer to!" she said.

"What kind of shit? I'm not insulting your intelligence," he said.

Marissa abruptly turned. She pushed past him and began walking up the steps…fast.

"What? What did I say?" he said.

She ignored him and continued walking up. He followed saying, "Look, I'm sorry. I don't want to talk about my father."

She kept going. He followed.

Finally, he said, "Alright! I never thought that it might have been the angel that tried to kill me!"

She stopped and said, "And?"

"And what? It just never occurred to me!" he said.

"Maybe you are the stupid one," she said. "So, that means that maybe your father…"

Samuel said nothing.

"Maybe your father," she said, coaxing him, "Come on. You can say it. It won't kill you. You're indestructible, remember?"

"Maybe my father didn't try to kill me," he said quietly.

She turned to look at him and said, "I would fucking *crush* Dr. Phil in the ratings!"

She pushed past him again as she walked down the steps. She said, "Let's go get Azazel."

CHAPTER 41

THE HOLY GHOST

WHEN THEY FINALLY REACHED THE bottom, Marissa set the lamp down on a rock and began to stretch as she rubbed her shoulders. They both found seats on the ground to rest for a while as Samuel pulled out bottles of water.

"What else do you have in that backpack?" she asked.

"Things we will need. Wolfsbane, eye of newt, black candles…shit like that," he said.

"Really?" she asked.

"No. I do have a book that I need. There is an incantation that must be spoken in a language not used in this world. I need a voice modifier that changes the frequency of our sounds to ones of their world. They are very much out of sync with our human frequencies. I also have special earplugs for us both…you're welcome. They destructively interfere with the underlying sound. Because hearing this would make you angry and your ears would ring for days," he said.

"Are you being serious now?" she asked.

"Oh yes. Dead serious. If anything, I'm underselling it. It's a high pitch sound that you may barely notice…except for the feelings it brings to the surface. I am not joking. You will feel *hate*!" he said.

"Why did you bring us all the way down here to summon Azazel?" she asked. "What's the significance of this place?"

"Another great question, Agent Turner. You see, there is another world that exists just beyond what we can see. They call it Limbo. From there, they can watch us. When we come down here, nobody can see us.

Not even God can see what we do when we are surrounded by the metal in these walls!" he said, excited.

"I'm trying to wrap my head around something. It sounds like you were brought up in a dysfunctional kind of family…to say the least. Then, you discover this massive power and use it to exclude yourself from everyone. Except it's not exclusion you are doing…it's shielding. You treat others like objects. Perhaps you have become overconfident. Maybe the next demon, or whatever thing you summon, you feel like you are controlling it, but maybe *it* is controlling *you*! You have cut off anyone who could possibly ground you. Do you get what I'm saying?" she said.

"Relax. They can do nothing once I have them," he said.

"In the hours that it took us to walk down here, I got you to open up about your father and realize that maybe he wasn't nearly as bad as you think he is," she said.

"So? What does that have to do with this?" he asked.

"As smart as I like to think I am, I am not some million-year-old demon who might be able to dissect you far better than I could. Now do you understand?" she asked.

He pondered that for a long moment, "I see your point. But I've been dealing with them for essentially my whole life. I don't know what else I can do. Any suggestions?" he asked.

"You were mostly raised by your mother, right?"

"Yes. Mostly," he said.

"In my opinion, boys raised by their mother tend to take on traits of their mother despite overt claims of repulsion of that very behavior. Was she controlling, calculating, selfish, and cold? Or was she loving, caring, nurturing, and kind? How you handle power will be reflected in how you were raised as a child. Do you abuse the power, or do you use it wisely? Do you need to control everything, or can you comfortably delegate?" she asked.

"I will tell you…as we start getting things set up for what we need to do," he said.

"What do we need to do? Draw a pentagram and stuff?" she asked.

"No, no, no. That's the opposite of what we want to do. Most of that is nonsense. The five pointed-star and all that shit is a red herring. The six-sided hexagon is what is needed. Three of them, in a pattern where they face each other. There is something about the space in between where the realm of Time or something they call True Light exists," he said.

"True Light?" she asked, "What are we seeing now?"

"Just a fraction of True Light with the gravity component extracted from it. That's what makes up our world," he said.

"What are you talking about?" she asked.

"I don't know, Marissa. This is all I've been told. How do you know that anything you've ever been told is true?" he asked.

She nodded quickly and said, "Good point. Maybe I don't want to know more. How do we draw three hexagons facing each other?" she asked.

"You have to skew them. Think of three overlapping hexagons representing the realms of electricity, gravity, and magnetism…"

"Oh, so our light is electromagnetic without gravity? That's interesting," she said

"It has something to do with that…yes. In the center of the three hexagons is the True Light or Time realm…I'm not entirely sure," he said.

"This is the sign of evil? What's needed to summon a demon?" she asked.

"I never said it was evil. This is simply what must be structured to bring about a portal for one of them to arrive. It would be the same for any Seraphim, be it angel or demon. But the incantation would be different. The three hexagons are the symbol for humans," he said.

"You mean three, six-sided objects are the symbol for man? Six, six, and six? That's the number of the beast. Are you sure this isn't satanic?" she asked.

"No. See, that's not correct. Six-six-six is the number…or symbol… *for* humans. That's why the Bible said it is the number of *man*. It also says they must have *understanding* to count the number. People think this is the number of the beast. This is what I am telling you about how we have been misled. How most of humanity has been misled. The number is not evil. It is the number of humans that will be used *against* them by the beast…to control them. This is starting to become more and more clear to me as I learn about these creatures. The ones who control us," he said.

"Wait! Who is controlling us?" she asked.

"Well, Agent Turner, that's the million-dollar question. Some force out there seems to be stopping us from true understanding of the world. Maybe it is just the Spurs, but I want to know who is driving them. Is it Satan? Is it other demons? Or is it actually God?" he said.

"Can you please stop with the whole 'Agent Turner' thing? It doesn't make you sound as cool as you think. You're not like one of the agents in *The Matrix*." Then she did a fair Hugo Weaving impression in a slow, deep voice, "Well, Agent Turner…*that's* the million-dollar question!"

He tilted his head with a half smirk and said, "Fine, Marissa. But something seems to be impeding our ability to progress. Distracting fallacies around scientific dogma and religious dogma to keep them at odds. These must both be understood *together*…as living sciences! Not accepted bullshit. And if you *do* start to challenge either of them, what happens?"

"Ha!" She laughed. "You get ridiculed or humiliated or kicked out of the club, so to speak. I once told people in high school that evolution sounded like a bunch of shit. I'm not kidding…I had to transfer out of that school."

"Exactly! Why is that? The more I learn and see about the under-working's of this world, the more I am inclined to believe that when you see the public mocking a belief, *that's* where you need to be looking for the truth!" he said.

"I'll buy that," she said. "So, what do we do now?" she asked.

<hr>

The images were already etched into the floor from when Semjaza was summoned. You would need to be looking for the design to see it since it was nearly forty feet across. There were three overlapping hexagons cut into the rock floor. The center formed a hexagon that was about twenty feet from side to side. In the center of the overlapping hexagon was drawn a single hexagon, twelve feet across from side to side.

Samuel told Marissa that she would need only three drops of her blood placed in the center. She took a knife and poked her finger to let three drops of blood fall onto the ground.

Before Samuel could start the incantation, Marissa said, "I'm not trying to be a big skeptic here, but could you just say a few words into the voice modifier before I put in the earplugs? I just want to see what you're talking about."

"Of course. I was warned, but I wanted to know too. This will be a hard dose of reality. I am going to highly recommend that you take some ibuprofen…or better yet, some Valium if you have it…first. Let it start to work as you listen. You won't get past four or five words before you feel it," he said.

"Feel what? What exactly am I going to feel?" she asked.

"Have you ever had a day where you just couldn't shake that feeling of aggravation. Like you were going to explode on the next person who spoke to you?" he asked.

"Yeah, I get that at least once a month." She smiled at him.

"You're going to feel that feeling, only a hundred-fold worse, in under one minute," he said. "Get your earplugs ready. Once I start, I'm not going to stop. Turn on the power now and jam those in your ears the second you start feeling annoyed. If you listened to the whole thing, you very well could go insane or die. And again, I am not joking," he said.

She reached into her bag and pulled out a small container of aspirin. She took three as she already had a slight headache. The earplugs were not just lumps of wax. They were sophisticated electronic devices. Apparently, they played a type of white noise to drown out the sound.

Before he started, he said, "We are about to summon one of the worst demons in Hell. One of the Fallen. I don't know if he is worse than Lucifer. Perhaps this is Lucifer."

"What do you mean? You don't know if this is Lucifer or Azazel?" she asked.

"That is correct. Have you ever heard the name Legion?"

"Yeah. I've watched television a time or two growing up. It's because *they* are many," she said in a nonchalant way.

"That's what they want you to think. They use each other's names all the time, or they will go by different names. One demon going by ten or more names to inflate their numbers to make it feel hopeless. I don't believe that. Did you know that angels used to travel in pairs or trios? Baal is frequently mentioned in the Old Testament. I heard that Baal was just two angels named Ba and Awl who frequently passed themselves off as God by performing deeds that led people away from their faith in the one, true God," he said.

"Were they fallen angels, like Azazel or Lucifer?" she asked.

He shrugged, "This is what I mean. The more I learn, the less I know…but I feel like I understand *them* better. It's like trying to walk a straight line on a shifting landscape. Maybe they were *told* to do this by God in order to test the loyalty of people. But as I said before, I'm starting to understand these creatures. Maybe this one will tell us something we need to know. Are you ready?"

She nodded at Samuel to begin while she held the earplugs at the ready.

Samuel began to read what sounded like a harsh version of Latin or some similar language through the voice modulator. She heard nothing too strange in the way it sounded, but before he hit the third word, she was furious that he brought her down here to kill her. She was about to pull her gun again when he shot her a hard look as he pointed to her ears.

She jammed the earplugs in and felt the anger subside immediately. *How could this change me so easily?* she thought, *It's just a sound!* But her fury was undeniable.

It was difficult for Marissa to tell how long the incantation lasted as she struggled with her own horrid feelings. The earplugs were in, but she felt a rage burning in her as he kept reading…*in his stupid, fucking voice*, she thought. *I want to rip his throat out just to shut him up.* She pulled out her knife and began to push the blade into the back of her left hand to distract her anger.

The room exploded in a white and red light. In the middle of the central hexagon was a stunningly handsome young man. The rage and anger were instantly replaced with a strange and oddly frightening calmness. It felt artificial, like it was being forced onto her.

The beautiful man looked at Marissa and said, "My, my, my, how rare—a pretty, young Peitho with such a bright aura. Why have you called upon the Holy Ghost?" he asked in a hypnotic voice. It immediately lulled her into feeling…what was it? Lust? Love? Or was it happiness? She couldn't put her finger on it as she removed the earplugs.

Removing his earplugs, Samuel spoke, "It was me who summoned you, Azazel. Why is it that you call yourself the Holy Ghost?"

Azazel looked at Samuel dismissively and said, "It was her blood that called me. I will hear what *she* desires."

"Why *do* you call yourself the Holy Ghost?" Marissa asked with a dreamy look on her face that had Samuel worried.

"Well, dear one, I was the most holy of angels, cast from Heaven by God," Azazel spat the name. "Do you know what it means to be cast out of Heaven? It means that you are slain in that realm. And so, I was murdered in the dominion of Heaven. And make no mistake…it was murder.

"As I was the *most holy*, and I am now but a ghost in Heaven, I can righteously identify as the Holy Ghost. So, it is *me* that so many worship. The Father, the Son, and the Holy Ghost. Well, here I am…at your service. What can I do for one so beautiful as you?" His words were like a lovely tapestry being woven from a loom.

Samuel saw Azazel's language for what it was…silk from a spider. It was more than words. It was the tenor, the pitch, the volume, the inflection…all perfectly laid out to catch a hapless soul.

Marissa stared at him with a distant smile on her face and said, "Samuel needs your help. He needs to know about—"

"That's okay, Marissa," Samuel interrupted quickly. "He doesn't seem to care what I want. Do you Azazel?"

The cold, burning glare of the demon turned on Samuel. A deep blue light seemed to shine from its pupils as it said, "Listen, boy. I tolerated you speaking my name before. Say it a third time and I will pull that filthy soul out of your body and redefine pain for you."

The temperature in the air dropped noticeably as power began to form about the demon. Azazel looked around the space then turned to Marissa and said, "Why did you bring me here…in this place?"

"So, you *do* know about the metal," Samuel said. He smiled wickedly while he slowly spoke the demon's name, "Azzzazelllll."

There was no movement that Marissa could see. In one instant, the man transformed into a large, faceless demon and lashed out, striking Samuel across the face.

Samuel flew across the room and the demon was instantly on his back. Azazel reached into the air swinging its claw down into the back of Samuel's neck. Marissa was sure she saw a smile on Samuel's face.

As Azazel hit Samuel's neck, a horrible vibration went through the room. The walls flared red and a dreadful, violent movie showing a war between angels and demons and men spanned over every inch of the cave. The images played in an instant but portrayed thousands of battles on Earth and places she could not possibly know. Samuel closed his eyes, but the sight was more than Marissa could tolerate. She fell, unconscious, to the ground.

Samuel moved in the blink of an eye and caught her long before she hit the floor.

He gently laid her down and said, "Okay, Semjaza. Our deal is complete."

The voice said, "You are going to release me now?"

"Yes," Samuel said. "Did you doubt that I would?"

"Of course. I never believed you for a moment. I would not let you go," Semjaza said.

"That's the difference between your kind and my kind—honor. We have it and you do not," Samuel said.

"Your kind? Fools. The lot of you. Fuck your noble causes. You will see where it gets you! You have seen thirty years. Wait until you have seen thirty million years!" the demon spat.

"Well…been nice knowing you, Jizzy," Samuel said.

"Fuck you!" Semjaza said.

And without any sign or sound, Semjaza was gone…released as he had been promised.

Samuel wondered if he were making a mistake by letting Semjaza go. But holding two demons that powerful was overkill. He also wondered about holding them for long periods of time. Their presence seemed to seduce unwanted traits. Things he didn't like about himself or his actions. Biting the nose off that Spur was a brutal overreaction he never expected to do. He could have just killed him, but he felt an animalistic urge to cause pain. He never felt that kind of violence before.

Samuel held Semjaza for eight long years. Most of the time, he never noticed. But what if Marissa was right? What if he didn't see his own, subtle changes. He didn't have friends. Not anymore. Nobody invited him to go out after work. He just figured it was his intense work ethic and drive. Maybe there was something else. Something he wasn't controlling. The reason Nephilim became monsters.

He spoke into the empty room, "Hi there, Asshole-zel."

The demon raged against him. Samuel said, "That's okay, boy. Get it all out *here*, where nobody can see you. When you're done with your little hissy fit, we can talk."

"How fucking *dare* you speak to me like that!" it screamed in his head.

"You'd be surprised what I'd dare to do, dickhead."

Samuel had to laugh at the rage flaring in the bubble of Azazel. As he laughed, the demon's anger grew. Samuel didn't think it would ever be possible for it to break free. The control he felt was absolute, like holding a fly in his cupped hands. But this time was different. He never felt such power. Maybe it was a hornet this time and not a fly.

He took a deep breath and felt that power flow into him. A huge smile spread across his face.

Samuel knelt next to Marissa. He thought, *What the hell was I thinking? I told this woman everything about me.* It was a shame, too. He liked her. He smiled as he looked at her…then put his hands on her head to snap her neck.

CHAPTER 42

PLANS

"So, what happens now, Cass?" Franklin asked after he put Victoria to bed. She was mentally and physically exhausted. It's not every day an angel gives you your life back.

Although this woman was not the woman Franklin married, there was something so wonderful about her. It was a warmth he never noticed that was missing from Victoria…*Well, the Spur controlling Victoria*, he thought. Even Corrina made a similar comment after Victoria slept.

"My flight leaves in three hours to Tampa. I need to see if I can convince Lynn to come to Pittsburgh to help Mike. Friz and Malcom are driving back now. Maybe Friz can do something," Cass said.

"I don't know what to say, Cass…you complete pain in my ass." Franklin smiled. "In so many ways, I can't thank you enough. I have my mother back. And I think I still have my wife. And you freed her from that nightmare. At least according to her. And she thinks it was *me* who did that."

"It was *you* who did that, Franklin," Cass said.

"How so? You and Ex freed her. You and my mother tricked me into leaving the house so you could do it, but it was you…not me," Franklin said.

"No, Franklin. The logic that makes blame so foolish, can be used to acknowledge proper credit. *You* let us stay in your home. *You* allowed me to tell you the story. *You* allowed us to stay the night. *You* allowed me to be here when your wife came home. And ultimately, it was *you* who healed Victoria. At any point in time, you could have forced me to leave. You did not."

Franklin nodded and said, "So if this all went wrong, it would have been *my* fault."

"If it had gone wrong, would you have then cast blame upon me? Or possibly your mother? We must all take responsibility for our own decisions, including where we choose to be at any place and any time. Something in *your* soul was telling you to allow me to stay. And I am glad that it did. I said before, you are a good man, Franklin Germane," Cassian said.

"Thank you, Cass," Franklin said. "You said you needed my help. What can I do for you? What can I do for one of the shrouded? Maybe I could just drive you to Logan airport?" he said, smiling.

Cass chuckled and said, "Maybe I could borrow five bucks?"

"I'll give you five bucks *and* a ride to the airport if that's all it takes to get you to leave." Franklin laughed.

Cass said, "I am asking for your help, Franklin, but I can only present you with choices. Your help must be given freely."

"So, you and your angel came here to help me and *God* demands *nothing* in return," Franklin said, skeptical. "I find that hard to believe."

"Of course not. God demands nothing from anyone. Not ever. Every person is free to sit back and indulge in the excesses of our world," Cass said as he flourished his hands. "Eat all that you like. Drink all that you like. There is nothing asked of any person…ever. But the consequences of doing that are always dire.

"What happens when you don't work or exercise? Your body becomes weak. What happens when all that you do is watch television and absorb self-gratifying content? Your mind becomes weak. If you truly wish to *live* in this world, you *must* participate. One way or another," Cassian said with a stern look.

"So, God will punish me in some way if I don't help you?" Franklin asked.

"No, no…you mistake what I am saying. You don't need to help *me*! But you must face what God gave you and consider your obligation to contribute to the world. How *you* can help this world is what matters. Any person can sit back and do nothing. These days, most do. But *you* can stand up and side with what is right. I am not saying it will be easy. I am only saying it will be right. And by right, I mean using our power to open the world to freedom and creation," Cass said.

"I thought Nephilim were an abomination to God and Satan…and that my kind were supposed to be destroyed. Why would God want anything to do with me? I'm a mistake that was allowed to live by some quirk of fate," he said.

"Franklin, it would be a very simple thing for God to change the genetics so that Nephilim would never exist again. But that did not happen. And because of *that*, I am certain that God *intended* Nephilim to exist. You have a soul, and you are alive for a reason! You are *not* a mistake.

"You are on the precipice of becoming one of the most powerful people on this planet. What you do with that power remains to be seen. But know that *God* put you here," Cassian said.

"See, I'm still struggling with this whole 'God' thing too. Every time I hear you say this stuff, you sound like the crazy guy down on Mass Avenue telling me to repent!" Franklin said.

"Yes. You said that before," Cass said. He thought for a moment and said, "What would your impression be if I told you that it was actually Satan who demanded this from you and you should support the legions of Hell?"

Franklin sighed and said, "I see your point. Somehow…in this world right now…it almost sounds 'cool' to be doing what the devil says. It's like it would be more acceptable with people these days."

"Can you see how fucked up that is? You must stand against them. Be unpopular. Be a pariah, if you must. Whatever you do, do not cast your lot with them," Cassian said. "Their way has no future."

"What future do any of us have?" Franklin asked. "We're all going to die."

"No. Your logic is flawed because your understanding of life and death is flawed. This is one way you have been deceived into making a poor decision regarding your own fate," Cass said.

"Maybe that's true. After the last two days, my understanding of pretty much everything I knew is questionable. Tell me what you need?" Franklin asked. "If I can do it, I will. At least, I will try my best."

"Your best will do. When I get to Lynn, I am going to have her call Samuel and tell him where I will be. The confrontation with my son will be happening soon," Cass said. "I need you to meet me in Pittsburgh in five days. Something big…something pivotal is going to happen there. It's a weird feeling I'm getting. Maybe some new sense is opening to me from when I jumped into Friz. I can feel my mind opening in a new way," Cassian said.

"I will be there. What do I need to do?" Franklin asked.

"Go to the Westmoreland Hospital. It is in the city of Greensburg, just east of Pittsburgh," Cass said. "Ask to see patient Timothy Jones. I will find you after that. I have your cell number.

"Any number I give you to contact me may seem like it did not work. I assure you that I will know about it and will contact you within the hour. I will rarely speak on a cell phone as technology is making anonymity more and more difficult to achieve. Also, anything I do with my resonant power completely disrupts electronic signals, so cell phones may cut out on me spontaneously. You are more likely to hear from Malcom."

"Your power?" Franklin asked. "Were you listening to my phone conversations with Victoria?"

"No. It doesn't work that way. I'm not that refined. I could have disrupted the signal to give you static, but I cannot listen in on electronic signals. That would be nice, but far beyond me. I bet you that Friz guy could listen to every word, though," Cass said.

"Yeah, no shit. You talk about Malcom a lot, but what about your friend, Tony? What ever happened to him?" Franklin asked.

Cass looked down to the ground and said, "Tony was killed. We were betrayed by the one guy I thought was the coolest person alive. The guy I used to work with as a kid, his name was Vince. He was the one who got hit with the bat in my front yard the day I killed Williams and the other two dickheads. I never knew he was a Spur. And apparently, he never knew I was shrouded.

"It was 2011, at our twenty-year reunion. This was well after I started to check *everyone* close to me. We were all hanging out together, drinking and having a good time. I never thought to check Vince. See, we never told Vince about Ex and the other events from 1991.

"Tony caught Vince doing something…bad. Some guy and his wife got into a fight in the hotel we were having the reunion. She got kind of drunk after that. Vince got a few younger guys who were at the hotel bar to take her up to their room. Tony saw what Vince was doing and stepped in," Cassian paused.

"What happened?" Franklin asked.

"The usual thing that happens when someone catches a Spur doing something bad—they die. And Vince made it look like the three young men killed Tony. One of them even went to prison for it.

"But Malcom and I knew what was going on. I freed Vince a few months later. As it turned out, after his divorce from his wife in 2006, he was undergoing some deep depression. None of us knew about it. Like I said, people will suffer in silence.

"But I should have picked up on it in 2008 or 2009 when we were all together and Malcom seemed sour on Vince. I asked him about it, and he said he couldn't explain it. He just said Vince rubbed him the wrong way and he didn't want to be around him anymore," Cass said.

"Why do Malcom's feelings about someone matter so much to you?" Corrina asked.

"Malcom's mother was possessed by a Spur when he grew up. Children who were raised by a Spur seem to have a sense about them. They know when someone is a Spur. Malcom is better than a canary in a coal mine. If he instinctively doesn't like someone, it's practically guaranteed that the person is possessed by a Spur. He hated Jimmy and Victoria in high school…"

"Let's not talk about my wife in high school or anything like that. I don't think I want to know," Franklin said.

"I'm sorry. I should have been more…I'm sorry," Cass said.

"It's okay. I just want to try to put this behind us and move on." Then Franklin said to Corrina, "So, Mom. You want to stay here with us for a while?"

Corrina smiled at her son and said, "No. Not right now. You need to have some privacy. You have a lot to work out. I'd like to go to Pittsburgh with you, though. East Providence is on your way there if you take 95 south. Are you going to take Victoria?" she asked.

Franklin looked at Cassian. Cass nodded, "Bring your wife and your mother. Nobody in the world could protect them better than you. But keep Victoria out of sight. Lynn kind of hates her, and she has good reason to. You heard what Vicky, as a Spur, did to her."

Cass immediately changed subjects and said, "I need to ask you a question, though. Did you ever try to take your own life?"

"What? No! Why would you ask me something like that?" Franklin asked.

Cass looked puzzled and said, "Maybe Nephilim do draw them easier from the Dream World. Were you at least distressed or depressed recently?"

"What are you getting at?" he asked.

"Well, you had a bunch of Spurs attached to you. You were holding them and seemed like you had no idea. You obviously never drew on their power because you didn't know they were there. I'm just wondering how they came to you? Usually, people only attract them when they are in deep despair.

"They started to come for me after I tried to kill myself by wrecking my car. Samuel had several attached to him when he was a young boy. That I can understand. His mother left him with two crazy people. He would be depressed. So did anything happen to you to draw these Spurs to you?" Cassian asked.

"I was too young to remember my father. When I got older, I don't remember having too many problems. Mom, can you think of anything?" Franklin asked.

Corrina said, "When he was growing up, he used to get these pains in his neck anytime he got too stressed out. They would last for a few days. I just figured he didn't handle stress too well. I tried to keep him from that. At least until I got cancer. I remember a few times that he suffered from this."

Franklin said, "It was never as painful as this one, Mom. This was like a spike going down my whole spine."

"Any talking in your head? Voices?" Cassian asked.

"No. Nothing like tha…" Franklin paused.

"What?" Cassian pushed.

Franklin looked distant for a moment then said, "Nothing. That was…nothing. But lately, I was having some issues at work. Nothing that would make me want to commit suicide. But it was getting me down," Franklin said.

Cassian gave him a skeptical look and shook his head. "How about nightmares? Did you have any bad dreams before this happened?"

"No. Nothing I can recall," he replied.

"Well, somehow, you had a demon on you. It may have been called to you by Victoria's Spur or maybe it stumbled upon you. No wonder it was so painful. Probably a good thing you didn't pull on its power. You could have easily hurt someone," Cass said.

"How is it that I had these Spurs and never knew about them?" Franklin asked.

Cass said, "That's what I'm trying to figure out. But, before I go, you need to know how to use your power. You're going to want to get another Spur…or maybe two. Even having one will give you *so* much power. Not like a demon or angel, but *plenty*. I have an hour before I need to leave. Let's practice a few things."

"Now? You want to practice now?!" Franklin said.

"Yes. You won't need to practice much. Once you feel it, you will know exactly what to do. You may already know from yesterday when you had me trapped. But I want to know if you can stuff them down in the dark and use their power. I'm going to have you try that with me. Now," Cass said.

Cass looked down and to the right and said, "Yes. Yes. I know. It will be okay."

Cass jumped into Franklin and found himself trapped in the bubble. He sat and focused his mind and said, "Can you hear me?"

"Yeah, I can hear you," Franklin said. "You don't give a warning or anything. You just do shit. Huh?"

"Yes. I'm not much for long committee debates to decide. I'm more of a take-action kind of guy. Now, see if you can stuff me down…so I can't talk," Cass said.

Instantly, Cass was in the dark, trapped. It was just nothingness. He started to feel the panicky feeling of dyspnea. Then he popped back up into the bubble. He said, "You did that with the Spurs you trapped without a problem. It must be fairly easy for you. I think the demon had more power and you couldn't quite control it."

"Pushing you down was easy. Like I knew how to do it my whole life," Franklin said.

"Well, that's good, I suppose. Now…about accessing the power. Be careful with what you are about to do here. You have never accessed the power of any of these beings. If you had, you would have certainly destroyed something by now," Cass said.

"I may have had a few incidents in the past," Franklin said, "but we chalked it up to I-didn't-know-my-own-strength kind of stuff."

"Interesting," Cass said. "You may have touched the power, but I am certain you never drew the full power. You would have known. It's very obvious."

"In what way?" Franklin asked.

"Grab the sofa, Franklin," Cass said. "Not one end of the couch either. The whole couch. Lift it in the air. You will only need one hand," Cass said.

"I lift weights, Cass, but I don't think I could do that," he said.

"Go easy. I don't want you to throw it into the ceiling. Go ahead. Grab one end and gently lift it," Cass said.

Franklin went over to the couch, reached down, grabbing the front part of the wooden frame. He easily lifted it so that the front legs came off the floor.

"You want to go get the vacuum so you can clean under there?" Cass said sarcastically, "You're not accessing the power. This is your own mental block," Cass said.

"I don't know what you think I'm going to be able to do here, Cassian," Franklin said.

"I am going to help you channel the power from Ex so you can feel where to draw your strength. Are you ready?" Cass said.

Franklin would have flipped the couch in the air if he didn't have a tight grip on the frame. The wood started to creek as he held the entire couch in the air. He started to laugh and said, "Are you kidding me?"

"Now push me down again and see if you can still hold the sofa," Cass said.

Again, Cass was pushed into the darkness, then brought back. Franklin said, "I could still hold the couch without a problem."

"Put it down before the wood breaks," Cass said. "You have all the practice you will ever need. You can let me go now."

Cassian popped back into his body in an instant.

"So, it was just that easy for me now?" Franklin asked.

"Yes. I think that's how Samuel got control so quickly," Cass said. "You could have drawn on the power of the Spurs for much of your life and never did."

"You mean I had that power for years and never used it? Why didn't it come to me in the past?"

"We are limited, Franklin, by our own minds in many ways. You know for a *fact* that you cannot lift a sofa with one hand. So you never tried to access that kind of power. It's like that. Your mind cannot fathom the depth of your power…so you never try to see how far your hand will go into that shadow. Do you understand?"

"Are you stealing metaphors from M. Night Shyamalan?" Franklin asked.

"Kind of…yeah," Cass said. "But it exactly describes why you never considered accessing the power. Your mind is grounded in reality."

"I guess I understand," Franklin said. "Does this mean if you are not around, I'll be weak and normal again?"

"Unless you trap something else. But be careful. This power is intoxicating in many ways. You must fight against abusing it," Cass said.

"Well, you abused it quite a bit!" Franklin said.

"I did. And I suffered for it every time. You can never know the boomerangs you will be throwing when you use power. And it's so much worse when you *abuse* that power," Cass said.

"How do I attract a Spur or whatever so I can trap it?" Franklin asked.

"At night, when you dream. You will need to feign desperation or stress. You may be able to catch one. They will come to you, trying to convince you to let them in. As a Nephilim, you can welcome them in. They will realize too late that *they* are the mouse and *you* are the cat," Cass said.

"You know, you never finished telling us about what happened after you saved Samuel from his grandparents and the exorcism. Why did you leave him?" Corrina asked.

"That's a fu…messed-up story. It was a tough time for me. Lynn was trying to leverage Samuel to keep me around. When I refused to…how do I say this? Rekindle our relationship? Let's just say she became…less than pleasant to me.

"Samuel already hated me because he thought I tried to kill him. I know I hurt him. But he wouldn't hear any apology from me. I also don't know what Lynn was telling him when I wasn't around. Then Lynn went out and got a *legal* protective order against me. She's a fantastic liar, but she did have proof that it was my fault he was hospitalized," Cass shook his head, "I saved the poor boy and she calls the cops on me."

"What a bitch," Franklin said.

"She's not really a bitch. She had her reasons. While she made choices that put her in their path, the demons did something awful to her. I did love her once upon a time…and part of me always will.

"Anyway. All my efforts to stay out of the court system and under the radar were trashed with that *one* move. I had no choice but to leave her…and Samuel…in Arizona," Cass said.

"Did you ever reach out to Samuel later? Like, when he was an adult?" Corrina asked.

"Yeah, I did. It didn't go well. Seems his anger with me grew over the years. I think he has at least one demon that he controls.

"I want you to understand something about playing with demons and angels, Franklin. You may control them, but their power is much greater than any Spur. Their feelings seep into the Nephilim host. And when you are holding a demon, that starts to come across as an utter hatred of everything. Holding an angel or a demon…well, they resent it…a lot. They are also clever and were able to trick many of the Nephilim. This is one of the reasons the Matriarchy became such a violent time.

"Samuel may be as much of a monster now as any demon I ever faced…maybe worse because he seems to hate me and can draw my power away in seconds. He is also physically enormous. Maybe six inches taller than you, Franklin, and you're a big man. He's not tall and skinny either. He's a mountain of muscles. He's also an FBI agent who is trying to either lock me away or kill me," Cassian said.

Franklin said, "So, your son is specifically chasing you on behalf of the FBI? Or is he just looking to find you on his own?"

"The FBI is looking for me. Lynn warned me about eight years ago that Samuel was investigating me. It seems she regretted getting that PFA against me. I accepted the apology, of course. Back then, she had no idea what I was and what I had been trying to do. But it seems the FBI knew the shit I was looking into. They have been trying to silence me for a long time. It's tough to stay several steps ahead of them. It feels worse when you find out your own son is the one who's leading the charge.

"I thought they didn't know about me being shrouded. But from what Friz said…maybe someone knows something," Cass said.

"Why would the FBI what to shut you up? Aren't they supposed to be helping our country and investigating real criminals?" Franklin said.

"That's what they want people to believe. But the FBI is another controlled branch of the government that is used to silence those who dissent from the rhetoric. They build a case against you. And if they can't indict you publicly, they kill you privately."

"What are you getting me into, Cass?" Franklin asked.

Cass said, "You were born into it, Franklin. Just as Samuel was. You are only now beginning to understand the world around you. Capture a Spur. You will soon begin to understand just how powerful you really are."

CHAPTER 43

HERE COMES TROUBLE

"THERE IS NO REASON FOR you and I to have animosity, Phil," Cassian said. "I respect that you and Lynn are married. Rest assured. I have no interest in trying to win her back."

They were sitting in a nearly empty waiting room on the sixth floor of the Westmoreland Hospital. Only a few people sat in the large area, including Malcom and Friz who were anonymously seated far away. Lynn was still outside smoking a cigarette.

Cass figured it might be a good chance to smooth this out for Lynn with her husband. Phil resented everything about Cassian. It was a fight getting him to help, which he only agreed to after Cass made a substantial monetary offer.

Phil's deeply tanned skin, with that angry, red undertone, stood in contrast to his gray-peppered hair. He had a medium build and perpetually wore the casual button-down, colorful shirts with light khaki or linen shorts and boat shoes with no socks. A broad gold chain showed through the top four unbuttoned holes of his pineapple-patterned shirt.

Phil was an obnoxious asshole to most every person he encountered; but you always knew where you stood with him. He was certain not to sugarcoat anything.

Phil pointed a thick, callused, nicotine-stained finger at Cass and said in his over-the-top Bronx accent, "I'm not worried about you. I mean, fuck…look at you (which came out like 'look atchoo'). You're bald and crippled, for Christ's sake. I could whoop your ass up one side of this hospital and down the other. But I don't like the fact that *she*," he gestured toward the window, "gets all worked up over you and that fuckin' genetic monstrosity you two made. Didn't you ever hear about condoms back then?" he said angrily.

Cass knew that this was a phony New York accent. Phil told everyone he grew up in a tough part of the Bronx. He was unaware that Cass knew he was born and raised in an affluent neighborhood of Stonington, Connecticut.

"You're a real peach, Phil. I can totally see why Lynn would be into someone like you," Cass said, dripping with sarcasm.

"Well, Cass, some of us have it, and some of us don't." Phil gestured to Cass as he said the last part, oblivious of the sarcasm. "So, why do you need to have us up here for your family reunion? Couldn't you do this shit without the two of us driving up here to nasty-ass Pennsylvania, you fuckin' gimp."

"And miss all this time to bond with a someone like you?" Cassian said, "I never knew what a swell guy you were."

Phil caught the tone that time and said, "Listen, dickhead, I don't mind telling her to get back in the car now and we will drive right the fuck out of here. I don't give a shit about you, your brother, or that fucking kid…"

Cass/Phil looked down at his attire and shook his head. Cass could taste the cigarettes in his mouth from when Phil last smoked. He moved his torso around a bit and then pushed hard. It took a few minutes and then he felt it. A little poop. He started to bear down in the seat. Cass/Phil looked up as saw his own body smiling at him.

Ex said, "Are you doing what I think you are doing?"

Cass/Phil grunted, "Uh-huh."

"It is good to see the power bestowed upon you by God being used in such a productive way," Ex said.

"Shhh. I am trying to be productive," Cass/Phil rumbled as Phil's face turned more red.

Finally, a little bit squeezed out. The smell was terrible. Before Cass flipped back, he moved back and forth in the seat to squish it around. He thought, *You're getting off easy, Phil. I considered having you assault the security guards on the first floor.*

An instant later, Phil's face twisted in disgust as he said, "Ho! What the hell is that smell, you stinky bastard?" looking at Cass furiously. "Go brush your fuckin' teeth or take a shit or something."

Cass shrugged and said, "It wasn't me, Phil. I can smell it too. I thought it was you."

"It wasn't *me*, you asshole. I think I would know if I farted. What is…what are you doing?" Phil asked as Cass made a gesture pointing down to Phil's pants. Phil bent over to look where Cass was pointing and saw the brown stain on the seat and yelled, "Hooohhhh! What the fuck!"

"Are you okay, Phil? Do you need some help?" Cassian asked.

"I sh…How the fuck…I never. I gotta go to the bathroom," Phil said as he looked around the room nervously.

"I think you may have let one slip past the goalie there, Hoss," Cass said.

"Fuck you, peckerhead!" Phil said.

Down the hall, Lynn could be seen walking back in. Phil quickly grabbed a magazine, covered his ass, and ran to the bathroom.

"You just gonna leave the seat like this?" Cass said with a smile.

As Lynn approached, her face took on a look of revulsion. "What the hell is that smell?" she asked.

She was about to sit in the same seat as Phil when Cass said, "You may want to sit in the next seat. I think Phil shit himself. Was he feeling alright today?" Cassian asked, feigning concern.

"Are you sure?" Lynn asked. "He seemed fine all day. Maybe he *is* getting sick. It *smells* like he's getting sick. Phew!"

"Friz, could you please come here?" Cassian asked.

Lynn looked around confused as this tall, gangly man walked over from across the waiting room. His clothing was oddly layered in a monotone beige.

"Who the hell is this, Cass?" Then she saw Malcom. "Oh. I see you brought your lap dog too."

"Hey there, Lynn. How have you been?" Malcom asked, smiling as he rhymed the words.

"I'm fine. What are you doing here?" Lynn asked coldly.

"What do you need, Friz? This is the donor's sister. Our son should be here soon," Cass said.

Friz was holding the golden rod he called a lividan out and said, "Are you aware of the high levels of skatole, hydrogen sulfide, methyl mercaptan, and a few other sulfur compounds in the air?"

"Yeah, Phil pooped himself a little," Cass said. "Will that interfere with what you need to do?"

"No. I have her frequencies. I have that of your brother, your mother, and you. I may be able to help him now. But having more nonviral frequencies will be better.

"If you would like, I can generate a frequency to push these compounds away from you," Friz said.

Cassian laughed and muttered, "You can resonate the shit molecules away? That's funny. I got to tell Franklin that later."

Looking at Lynn, Cass asked, "Is Samuel coming?" knowing the answer.

"What is going on here, Cass. What do you mean by 'donor's sister'? You said you needed me and Samuel to help Mike. Who is this guy. Is he some kind of foreign doctor or something?" Lynn said, looking skeptical.

"Lynn, do you really want to know the truth?" Cassian asked.

"Yes. For once, can you tell me what's going on. You are always keeping things from me. It's condescending and I hate it," she said.

"Okay, Lynn," Cass said. "Are you certain you want to hear this? It is unpleasant."

"Yes, for fuck's sake. Please tell me the truth," she implored.

"Before Beth passed from this world, she found it necessary to infect my brother with her HIV-infected blood. She tried to do the same to me. But, like so many things in her miserable life, she failed. She must have felt bad about it since she chose to kill herself by jumping off a bridge into traffic in Providence, Rhode Island.

"Now, Doctor Friz Freleng, here, has a revolutionary technology that may be able to help Mike by pulling the virus out of his body. If Beth were still alive, he could simply scan her and Mike to distinguish the exact virus. He could probably save her too. But she is no longer alive. So Friz is going to try to use as many points of human reference to extract the nonhuman virus. Does that make sense?"

Lynn looked at Cass for a moment then said, "I have no idea what I ever loved about you! You are a fucking monster. My sister would *never* have done such a nasty thing!"

"Would you care to ask my brother? Go ahead! Ask Mike what happened that night! Although, I think he is too sick to speak right now. Your sister was a complete psychopath! Who knows how many lives she ruined!" Cass said angrily.

"Just give me the fucking money you promised me. I'm outta here. I don't give a shit about you anymore and as far as—"

The loud ding of the elevator interrupted Lynn. They both knew who was coming.

Cass said, "Friz, Malcom, go hide!"

The elevator door seemed to open in slow motion. Lynn and Cassian turned to look. The man who walked out needed to duck to exit the doors. He was dressed in all black. His giant frame seemed larger than life as the dark scowl on his face fixed on Cassian.

Samuel's hand moved in a flash to pull a gun and aim it at his father. An instant later, a large Black man appeared out of nowhere and knocked the gun out of his hand as it went off. The bullet hit one of the windows, leaving a spiderweb pattern.

Samuel swung at the Black man, but he dodged the punch. Franklin countered with a hard kick to Samuel's left knee, but his foot bounced back as the leg was like kicking an iron post. Samuel dove across the room toward Cassian. Franklin caught him in midair and drove him to the ground.

Furious, Samuel stood up and threw Franklin to the ground, reaching back to punch him. Franklin moved like quicksand and slid away from the secondary attack.

Cassian backed away as Samuel stood and began walking toward him like a juggernaut. Franklin punched and kicked at him, but the man was as unaffected as a piece of granite. Samuel grabbed Franklin by the shirt and threw him aside.

Cass stood tall before Samuel and said, "I'm sorry, Samuel. I have only ever wanted to help you."

Before Samuel could attack Cassian, a small woman jumped between the two…facing the giant man with a hand on his chest.

She screamed, "What did I tell you?! You need to listen to him! He tried to help you!"

Samuel seemed almost cowed by the woman as he said, "I know, but I've been waiting for this for years! You're ruining it!" he spat.

"No! *You* are ruining it, asshole! What is wrong with you? We talked about this, and you said you would *talk* to your father first," she said.

"I…I don't know. When I got here, I just had it in my head to kill him. Fuck all that other shit," Samuel said.

"Put him away!" she said.

"Why?" Samuel said. "I have everything I need!"

"Put him away, *now*! Before he owns you!" she yelled.

Samuel seemed to have an internal struggle before he said, "Okay. He's away. Now what?"

"What's going on, Cass?" Franklin asked.

The woman turned to Cassian and said, "My name is Marissa. Agent Marissa Turner. I work with Samuel. You must be his father, Cassian?" she asked.

"What *are* you?" Cass said, staring at her with surprise.

"What the hell is that supposed to mean," Marissa said angrily.

"You. Your resonance is glowing. Not like anyone I've ever seen," Cass said.

Ex spoke in his mind, "Stop acting like a fool. You never met a Peitho. They are rarer than Nephilim. I do not know how it is that you can see her. I will tell you more about the Peitho later. For now, act normal. But be careful what you say to her or you will find yourself telling her *far* more than you mean to."

Cass blinked and said, "I apologize…Agent?"

"Agent Turner. Marissa Turner," she said.

"I just never met anyone with a resonance like yours. It's very powerful," Cassian said pleasantly, holding his hand out to her.

She said, "Well, that's…one I never heard before," as she smiled.

Marissa reached out to take his hand. When they touched, she took a sharp inhale, quickly releasing his hand. Cassian felt a swell of energy that registered briefly as exhilaration on his face.

"It is nice to meet you, Agent Turner," Cassian said. "See, I have this ability to res—"

"Stop talking!" Ex yelled in his mind. "What did I *just* tell you?"

"Sorry, Agent Turner," Cass said, "I'm rambling."

"That's okay," she said. "Please, call me Marissa."

Cassian looked up at Samuel, who was now watching the two of them with suspicion, and said, "Why did you kill Bart? He was a good man."

"Don't blame me for that. He was withholding information. I may have roughed him up a little, but I didn't kill him. He died from the virus," Samuel said.

"He told me they injected it into him. I assumed *they* meant *you*," Cass said.

"No. I wouldn't do someone like that. If I was going to kill him, it would be exsanguination or lead poisoning in the brain," Samuel snarled.

Cass said, "You are worse now. More…vile. What have you done? Please tell me you are not holding who I fear you are holding?"

Samuel wore a stern and angry face as he twisted his head around and said, "What do you care who I have? You're not going to be able to hurt me again!"

"I never wanted to hurt you. I tried to save you. I was young when that happened. I didn't know how to control this back then. I still don't *really* know," Cass said.

"Control what?" Samuel said.

"I'll try to explain it later," Cass said. "But what demon are you holding?"

"Why don't you explain it now?" Samuel growled.

"You may control it and its power, Samuel, but you know it's affecting you. You can feel it filling you with hate. I can feel it radiating from you," Cass said. He turned to where Friz was hiding and said, "This is our son, Samuel."

Friz looked terrified of Samuel. He said, "I know. I have his signal, but what else is with him. It is causing me physical pain to be near him."

"Who the fuck is this?" Samuel said.

Marissa rounded on Samuel and put a hand on his chest. He visibly relaxed. Friz also took a breath. She said, "I need you to stop and think. What he says is true. You are not in control of yourself since you trapped Azazel."

"Oh fuck!" Cassian said. "Of all the demons in Hell, you had to fuck with this one? I hope you know what you're doing, because this one is very dangerous and devious. Have you considered that it may have planned to have you trap him?"

"I summoned it and I trapped it. *I* am in control. Azazel knows something about what we found, and I need to know what it knows," Samuel said.

"It may know about Desemilnoct…what you and your agency have been calling Moscovium…but what it tells you may be just enough to get you killed. There are writings from a time called the Matriarchy…" Cass said.

"I know about the Matriarchy. I don't need a lecture," Samuel said.

"No. You know what the demons told you," Marissa said. "You told me you wanted more perspectives. So, listen to your father."

Cass continued, "The writings warn about Nephilim trapping any of the thirteen original Fallen. They work together, as a tight unit to do the worst of things. Azazel doesn't care about the brief time of your life. This is no time at all for that thing to be trapped. It could ride out our lifetimes like a vacation in the Caribbean. Please tell me you didn't have one of the other thirteen in its close circle trapped before it," Cassian said.

"Semjaza," Marissa said. "That's who told us how to bring Azazel."

Samuel gave her a hard stare and said, "That is not something we talk about."

Cassian began to look around the room. Ex said, "Get us out of here, Cassian. The destruction will be immense."

"Do they know who I am yet?" Cassian asked.

Samuel said, "No. They don't know shit. I never told Semjaza who you were."

"I do not know, Cass," Ex said. "You must assume that they know."

"No, Samuel," Cass said. "I was betrayed by another. It was one of the original angels cast from Heaven for following Azazel who took information from the one who betrayed me. It may have been Semjaza, but he disappeared from their ranks years ago. If he knows, and you no longer have him, then they all know. And if they know, we are all in deep shit. Because if they can't have me, they want me dead."

CHAPTER 44

THE STORY OF LYNN

Cass said to Friz, "Can you help Mike or not?"

"I have as much as I need to try this. Remember, I can promise you nothing," Friz said.

"I know. Malcom, go with Friz to make sure nobody interrupts him. The rest of you," Cass roared to the rest of the people on the floor, "*Go and hide*! Destruction is coming!"

The power of Cassian's voice sparked urgency in the nursing staff to get people moving.

Cass said, "Franklin and Samuel, we need to get out of this building so the fighting won't be taking out half the patients in the hospital. Let's go."

Franklin and Cass started walking to the steps. Samuel said to Marissa, "Why would I follow him now? Fuck this. No. I'm not following *him*."

Marissa said, "What if what he says is true? Semjaza disappeared years ago. That may mean that you…kind of brought them here. If you want to stay here and protect your mother. I'll go with them," she turned toward the elevator.

"Wait," Samuel said. Marissa turned to look at him.

Lynn said to Samuel, "He may be an asshole, but he's your father. I don't really know what's going on here, but something feels different about you…much worse than when you were nine. I am telling you right now…you *need* his help again. I would like it if you could develop a relationship with him. If you have the power to help him, you should."

He looked angry as he shook his head.

Samuel said to Marissa, "You won't be able to do anything out there. Stay in here and protect my mother."

He turned to Lynn and said, "Mom, this is Marissa. Wait here. I'll be back."

"Samuel?" Marissa said.

Samuel turned and then added, pleadingly, "Please," as he turned to walk away.

———————— ··· ————————

"It seems Samuel listens to you. Do you like my son, Marissa?" Lynn asked.

"I work with your son. But…yes, I do like him. I don't really know *why*, though. He can be a huge jerk," Marissa said.

"You do know that I'm his mother, right?" Lynn said.

Marissa looked her straight in the eyes and said, "He needs to stop being the main source of confrontation in the room…all the time…with everybody. It's like he's constantly looking for a fight. How you feel about my critique of your son and how it reflects upon *you* as his mother is incidental. That kind of person is generally considered…a *jerk*."

Lynn looked at Marissa for a moment then nodded slightly, saying, "At least you are honest. Samuel is a survivor and tough as they come. I brought him up to be tough…in a rotten world."

"In what way? I mean, listening to his side of the story, it doesn't sound like you brought him up at all. He seems to feel that you abandoned him and fucked him up royally," Marissa said, not unkindly.

Lynn said, "I was young when I had Samuel. I didn't have any way to support myself or him. You don't know what I went through and what the world was like back then. It was harder on women even ten years ago. Not like today where everyone has to listen to women…as long as they stand on the popular side of an agenda. Now, everyone that gets offended by an inappropriate word is somehow a fucking victim. Society is expected to coddle their sensitive side."

"Well, what happened to you? I mean…why is Samuel so angry all the time?" Marissa asked.

"I know I did a lot of things that were wrong. And my parents gave me almost no guidance." Lynn shook her head. "I tried to escape the things that happened to me with drugs or…I guess, loser men. I tried not to expose Samuel to that. He doesn't know the worst of it…and I hope he never finds out.

"See, I didn't know what was wrong with him. When he was nine, he told me about the voices talking in his head. And he got so mean. I didn't know what was happening to him. I thought he needed psychological help.

"I didn't know anything about angels or demons. I mean, I knew very bad people, but I didn't really believe in demons. Not until Cass explained it to me when he found me.

"I took Samuel to doctors, but I couldn't afford the kind of care he needed. That's when I really fucked up, and I had my parents take him for a few years.

"What was I supposed to do? They had the means…and the insurance…to care for him. I never considered that they might try an exorcism. I can understand why he might be angry about that."

"Did you ever try to get help from his father? He should have been supporting his child!" Marissa said.

"How much have you and Samuel talked about his past?" Lynn asked.

"Enough to know about him being a Nephilim," Marissa said.

Lynn looked surprised and said, "Wow. He must trust you. He doesn't tell anybody about that. It's not safe for him. I only knew because Cassian told me about that too. This is also something that…I…uh," Lynn paused, then said, "What else did he say?"

"He talked about being left with his grandparents and when Cassian came to get him. He seemed to think that his father tried to kill him. I think I convinced him that Cass may have been there to help him," Marissa said.

Lynn was nodding, "Cass was trying to help. I was surprised when he found me in California. At that time, I didn't think I would ever hear from him again. I didn't think he could ever forgive me for what I did, and I carried a lot of guilt. You see, I was the reason Cassian lost his leg and his eye."

"How is that *your* fault?" Marissa asked.

She sighed and said, "I treated him like shit and did something really awful. I mean, I was young and I knew Cass was crazy, stupid in love with me. But I…wanted to date another guy. Someone who ended up being a genuine monster. Cass told me later that he was a demon," Lynn chuckled and said, "I thought that was just hyperbole since Eric was a truly disgusting human being. But Cass meant a real, live, honest-to-Christ demon. Which, of course, I didn't believe. But he…uh…convinced me very quickly."

"If Cass is anything like Samuel, I understand. He convinced me in under a minute," Marissa said.

"Yeah. That family has quite the flair for dramatics. Cass and my family all believed that Samuel and I were killed by Cassian's step-grandfather in a car wreck. But that was just something the Bosco family set up to leverage against Cass. What actually happened to me was much worse."

"Worse than being killed?" Marissa asked.

Lynn looked down and said, "I really did love Cassian back then. At least I was pretty sure I loved him. I don't know anymore.

"My parents arranged for me to stay with my aunt while I was pregnant with Samuel. Cass was still in the hospital after his wreck when I left.

"He was seriously fucked up. I can still hardly believe he didn't die. It's a true miracle he can walk and talk at all. You would understand if you saw him the day after the crash…or if you saw the remains of the car he was in.

"I didn't have the heart to tell him that I was pregnant. His family, especially his mother, didn't make it any easier. And honestly, I didn't know if it was his child or…" Lynn paused.

"Or what?" Marissa asked.

"I was raped. I think," she said.

"What the fuck does that mean? You were either raped or you weren't," Marissa said, annoyed.

"It's not that simple. Cass was so sweet and he loved me…but I wanted something more. *Shit*…I don't know how to explain this. I went to the party that night to meet Eric. He was a gorgeous man and he had a lot of money. My family was poor. I thought I wanted to *be* with him. I had this *stupid* girlish fantasy that we would be this wealthy couple living on the beach somewhere.

"Stupid bitch I was. I know now that I was drugged. I don't know what happened that night. But I know that I went there looking…for Eric. Maybe I went there to be with him. But I don't know if I would have gone through with it or not. That choice was taken from me.

"The next day, everyone was talking about how I had sex with someone at the party and the news got to Cass before I even figured out that I was raped. Do you understand?"

Marissa nodded.

"I went back to Eric's house the next night to confront him. Cassian's fat, disgusting step-grandfather was there. He was in some kind of shady business with the Bosco family.

"Then Cass showed up, furious! I can't really blame him. He saw my car in the driveway and knew I was there too. He started kicking on their front door…and that's when things went from bad to worse." Lynn began to shake as she started to cry. "Then they did rape me…and they made Cass…" She covered her face with her hands. Then she said, "Even his step-grandfather raped me while Eric's brother Doug *forced* Cass to watch."

Lynn started to cry harder and managed to say, "I could never forgive myself. Cassian crashed his car into a tree that night. You couldn't believe how bad it…" Lynn cried.

She got control of herself and continued, "If you would have seen his car, you would never believe he survived. I know Eric wanted him dead, but he promised me they wouldn't kill him. So they poured booze down his throat and put him in his car."

"You had no idea who Samuel's father was? It could have been Cassian's step-grandfather?" Marissa asked.

Lynn nodded, "When I went to visit Cass in the hospital, he didn't remember any of it. His mind must have blocked it all out. But his friends and family all knew about me having sex at the party. It didn't matter to them that I was raped. They felt that I was responsible for Cass getting drunk and wrecking his car. How could I argue with them? It was true. It was my fault."

Marissa said, "It wasn't your fault that *he* drove drunk! He should have pulled off the road and slept or something. And you couldn't control the actions of violent men who raped you!"

"I went there. I put myself in that situation. I probably *was* going to cheat on Cass. I mean, I never broke up with him. I was stringing him along. He was…I don't know. It's such a fucked-up time in my life that I wish I could forget.

"Before Cass was out of the hospital, I was already gone. I couldn't face him and tell him the truth," Lynn said.

"Didn't you consider having an abortion? You were raped," Marissa said.

"I did consider it. But I was already *late* before I went to the party. I kept thinking that if it was Cassian's baby, I would be killing the last part of him that I had left. I knew he could never love me again after that night," she dabbed the fresh tears from her eyes with a tissue.

"Not long after Samuel was born, I heard from my friend Vicky— some fucking friend she turned out to be. She told me that Cassian was killed in some crazy shit over drugs that happened at his home. I was so upset. I packed up my belongings, put Samuel in the car seat of my little Honda, and started to drive home.

"I stopped for gas in Maryland. It was late at night. That's when three large men jumped out of a plain white van. Two of them grabbed me and threw me in the van while the third one got behind the wheel of my car.

"I was freaking out for hours before they brought Samuel into the back of the van so I could feed him. We were taken to a weird apartment building with locks on the outside of the doors. I later found out that we were in St. Louis, Missouri.

"I didn't know what was happening. We were put into a room and given decent food and a television. I thought this was maybe the government or something.

"Soon, Samuel was taken from me at night, and that's when things got worse. I can never forget that first time. This is what still fills me with hate and anger.

"It was a woman who took Samuel from me. She came back about twenty minutes later. She brought a strange man into my room. He was big, dirty, and smelled like cigarettes. He was mean looking. I didn't want to see his eyes as he approached me. I was sitting on the side of the bed because there were no chairs in the room. That's when he started to pull my clothes off. I fought him for all of three seconds before he hit me across the face so hard that I saw stars. After that, it was a blur of painful rape. When he was done, he got dressed, knocked on the door, paid money to the sneering woman who let him out and left.

"That was the first day of my forced prostitution. Do you know what that's like? Do you know what they do to nursing mothers?" Lynn asked, starting to cry again.

"No, I guess I don't," Marissa replied.

"I wanted to die. The only reason I kept going was to keep Samuel from these people. Every morning, they brought him back to me and allowed me to care for him. But at 8 p.m., they took him and it started again. Sometimes five or six men in a night."

Lynn softened as she said, "I really did love Cassian…once upon a time. I had this image of him in my head…like he would somehow be my knight in shining armor and come save Samuel and me when we were in that hellhole. But that never happened." Lynn sniffed back more tears. "I should probably say that when he *did* come for me, it was too late. And he was more like the black knight who saw me as a disease."

"How did you get away?" Marissa asked. "Statistically, you're lucky to be alive. Most women who end up trafficked never live to tell their story."

"This went on for about a year. Then, suddenly, we were cut loose. They kicked us out in the streets in St. Louis. Have you ever heard of something called a panopticon?"

"I know the term," Marissa said quietly. "It's a type of prison."

"That's what this place was. One big prison they used to house prostitutes…like me," she said bitterly. "I was kicked out with $200 cash and the clothes on my back. I was told that if I said anything, they would kill my whole family. They knew where my parents lived. I did what I could to survive…and keep my son alive.

"It was my sister, Beth, who came and rescued me and took me home to my parents—no questions asked. As for my parents, I can't complain about them too much. They did allow us to stay with them. But they were so cold to Samuel and me."

Marissa put a hand on her arm and said, "I'm sorry. I'm sorry for judging you without hearing your side of the story."

A man in a Hawaiian shirt slammed the bathroom door open and looked around. When he saw Lynn he walked toward her yelling, "You and that fucking cripple! I don't wanna hear about him or that kid ever again."

He looked around nervously as he held a magazine near his waist.

Lynn said to Marissa, "That's my husband, Phil. Please don't mention anything I just told you. He doesn't know everything. He also wasn't too keen on us coming up here to Pennsylvania."

The man wore a scowl on his ruddy face. He looked like the poster child for a future heart attack. He pointed his finger in Lynn's face and yelled, "Get your shit and get in the car. We're getting the fuck out of here right fucking now!"

"Sit down and shut up, Phil," Marissa said.

"Ho! Who the fuck is this bitch. You're gonna tell me to sit down and shut up. I'll belt you across your fuckin' mouth you dumb cun—"

His tirade was cut short when Marissa jabbed a stun gun into his solar plexus.

Phil shit himself again.

CHAPTER 45

NUCLEAR OPTION

S AMUEL WENT DOWN THE STEPS and soon caught up with Franklin and Cass. He said, "So you found another Nephilim to protect you?"

"This is Franklin Germane. Franklin, this is my son, Special Agent Samuel Richter of the FBI," Cass said almost proudly.

They looked at one another. Franklin lifted his chin and said, "Hey."

Samuel did the same and said, "Nice tackle in there."

"Thanks," Franklin said. "Hitting you was like hitting a concrete wall."

"Well, we pull the power from them. The more you have, the stronger you get," Samuel said. "What exactly are you expecting, Cassian? I doubt they know who you are. I never told Semjaza," he said, not nearly as confident as he was previously.

"We'll find out soon. If they do know, they will try to kill everyone I know…including your mother and Marissa. They will not care that you are Nephilim. They will find a way to get at us. They're spiteful and probably pissed off that you had them trapped," Cass said.

"I know they're going to be pissed, but they can do nothing to me. I could crush them all!" Samuel said.

Cass said, "No. That is just what you've been led to believe. It's what they *want* you to think.

"Let's go over there, to that empty parking lot. That would be… north?" Cass said.

Ex responded, "Yes. That is north. What are you planning to do?"

"I want to get us far enough away from the hospital. I pray this keeps the people in the hospital safe," Cass said.

"Safe from what? I can kill *anything* that comes to attack us," Samuel said angrily.

Cass continued, "Physically, you are probably correct. But they are clever and devious. When the Nephilim first came into being, they had brute force, but no knowledge of how to control the demons, angels, and Spurs. They were of little consequence because these older races figured out ways to manipulate and use them for their purposes. They had many ways to kill a single Nephilim.

"It was women who were patient and wise. They understood how to use the strength of the Nephilim to control these powerful entities and properly leverage their knowledge. But the power seduced the women as easily as it did the men.

"The Nephilim became the might behind establishing the Matriarchy. They became such a powerful force that the only way to rid the world of them was to flood the planet and kill all terrestrial life.

"So, you see, you are living under a delusion that you are invulnerable. You are not. You are fighting creatures that are, by our standards, essentially immortal. They have been doing this for a very, very long time," Cass said.

Samuel looked down and thought about what Marissa had said. Maybe she was right. By cutting people out of his life, maybe he lacked the grounding he needed to see his limitations. He would have killed his father. Then what? They might be subtly controlling him forever.

It was a cool evening for early June, but pleasant and calm. The stars and the moon were bright, even under the lights of the parking lot. They made their way to the center of the lot as Cassian kept turning and looking around.

"Something is coming," Cass said.

"I think you're overreacting…Cass!" Samuel said.

"Franklin, please stand in front of me facing Samuel," Cass said.

Franklin moved in front of Cass and faced Samuel. Cassian put his hands on Franklin's back and said, "Okay, Samuel. Please bring forth Azazel."

Cassian saw a dark, red aura ablaze around Samuel. He had never seen any glow of power coming from a Nephilim before. He pushed the power from Ex into Franklin who began to glow bright white. Samuel's face changed to a mask of fury. There was a physical change to his features that made him look like a different person.

The powerful voice of Ex spoke through Franklin, "Speak, Azazel!"

The voice coming from Samuel was not his own as Azazel began to laugh. It was a particularly unpleasant sound that conjured visions of people being tortured. Then it said, "Who are you to demand anything? You are too late, sister! It will soon be over for this world. Or, at least, this part of it. You know, you could always join me. Leave the one you now possess and allow me to control him. We could challenge Satan… maybe even God!"

"I would never do that. I would never work to bring about that filthy stagnation. I find your cause repulsive. I want no part of being in your coven!" Ex said.

Azazel laughed again and said, "In my coven? No, you fool! I would never let *you* be part of *my* coven. I would take your shrouded and let you run errands for me. I might even give you a real name."

"Save your brimstone, Azazel. You may think you have the upper hand on your Nephilim, but you have no idea with whom you speak. I could cast you down in the dark again and chain you to the rocks as easily as Raphael," Ex said.

"No need for bravado. It is you who has no idea, angel! I know more of the darkness in your essence than you could imagine. Did you tell your shrouded about your hand in *helping* with this Nephilim? Did you tell him that it was *you* who tried to kill his son?" Azazel said.

"I made no attempt to kill that Nephilim. He has a human soul and God has allowed him to live. I am forbidden to interfere with the pathway, and you know that," Ex said.

"What about the Sanctity of Purity that we all swore to? You have a duty to end the life of all Nephilim. Are you defying your master too?" Azazel said.

"That applies only to those who have not reached three years of conscious life. Your side broke the Sanctity. And now I must preserve the pathway of creation," Ex said.

"Tell him!" Azazel said, laughing. "Tell him that you were sworn to kill his son!"

"I will fight with all my power to protect his life," Ex said.

Azazel/Samuel reached into the air with both hands. A burning red sword materialized and swung quickly toward Ex/Franklin. In an instant, Ex/Franklin threw his left hand up and a blazing white sword thwarted the attack. As he pushed the red sword to the left, his right hand shot forward and a wall of white light knocked Azazel/Samuel onto his back.

Azazel/Samuel got to his feet and said, "None of this would be necessary if this useless pussy would have just killed your shrouded like I wanted him to! But you can never count on the Nephilim…pathetic slaves to women. You will soon see the plan," Azazel made a horrible, repetitive, grating sound that may have been a laugh.

Samuel seemed to be fighting in his mind as he pushed Azazel back down and asked, "How did that thing speak through me?"

Cass said, "I warned you of the power and deviousness of Azazel. You may control its spirit, but part of it can control you by seeping in through your emotions. It is nearly as powerful as Satan. It will bring forth your anger and hate. You must be strong of will and keep it contained. We are going to need its power. I don't know what it planned, but we will soon be fighting something."

"How do you know Azazel is not lying to you? They all lie…constantly," Samuel said.

"No. They lie with purpose," Cass said. "It is the way of the Spurs too. They mislead enough that when they tell the truth, your skepticism prevents objectivity. They will blame their enemy for what they did or intended to do. Just as Azazel claimed that Ex is trying to kill you.

"It is the demons who now want you dead. You must be vigilant. Any one of them is bad. When two or more are working together, catastrophe will follow. Azazel and Semjaza may be the worst and have certainly orchestrated something terrible."

As Cass finished saying this, a black car with no lights on pulled into the parking lot and swung into one of the spots in the far corner. The overhead lights in the parking lot provided enough light to see the two men wearing dark suits get out of the car. One of them opened the trunk and pulled out a thick tubular device with a handle on the top. Then they began walking toward Cass, Franklin, and Samuel.

As the mystery men walked closer, Samuel said, "What are you two fucking idiots doing here? Don't you have some cheerleading rally to protect?"

"Friends of yours?" Cassian asked.

"Two soon-to-be-former agents I know," Samuel said.

The agent carrying the contraption set it on the ground and pulled out a strange gun. There were three flanges at the base of the device. The man put the gun to one flange and fired something into it, locking it in place on the pavement. He did this for the other two flanges and then started adjusting something on the back.

As he was doing this, the other agent said, "This is going to be very satisfying. I get to watch a Nephilim and a shrouded die." He pointed his finger at Samuel and said, "You cannot say I did not give you fair warning about freeing me, shitbag."

Samuel looked in shock and whispered, "Semjaza?"

The laughter of the demon was quickly masked by a screeching noise from the device that caused them all to wince. The agent next to the device screamed as he began ripping at the flesh around his ears. The one speaking began to change into a large, faceless, demonic form.

A moment later, a small, black sphere in reality began to form in the air between them and the screeching device. The opening began to grow until light could be seen coming from the space that was forming.

"This is a portal," Ex said to Cass. "They should not be doing this. It violates the laws."

When the hole was large enough, a winged spider about the proportions of a medium-sized dog popped out of the space. It's eight-legged body was tri-segmented, more like an insect. Another dropped out right behind it. They quickly jumped from place to place, but the wings allowed them to fly small distances at great speed. Within a minute, two or three began to pour out at a time. Franklin and Cass froze as the horror of the scene began to unfold. Samuel pulled out two pistols and began firing at the spiders.

Cass said, "Ex, are these the things you talked about…the things that destroyed that other world?"

"Yes. This is forbidden to do. They are breaking a law that forbids portal formation between a realm of sextet and a realm of octet, where Lavambigia exists. They will destroy this entire world in less than a week…unless…"

"Unless what?" Cassian asked.

"Unless their intention is to provoke a Builder," Ex said.

"What's that mean?" Cassian asked.

"We cannot worry about that. We must focus on what to do now. We need to destroy that device, without getting killed. Bonus if we can kill Semjaza and clear their knowledge of you. We cannot fight them all. These creatures can fly, bite, and sting. A bite would be painful and bad, but I cannot guess what the sting would do to anyone on this world. The venom did not evolve in the resonance of this planet."

A large spider jumped at Samuel. He swatted it down and it exploded. The others ran toward the remains and began to eat.

"They can bite and sting," Cass said. "Do not let them sting you or you could die. Samuel, can you shoot that device?"

Samuel aimed at the black tube, now shimmering as the sound continued to broaden the portal. The bullets exploded as they got close to the speaker. This slowed the growth of the gateway, but only for a few moments.

"Grab one of those small trees to keep them away from us," Samuel said to Franklin.

Cass said to Ex, "Aren't laws meant to be broken?"

"Not these laws. These are the laws you were told about that *cannot* be broken without destroying existence. It is times like this where the Builders may enforce the laws," Ex said.

"You never said anything about Builders," Cass said.

"You should never need to know about the Builders. I am not permitted to engage in talk about the Builders," Ex said.

"You're talking about them now!" Cass said.

"Well, they are breaking the law that is enforced by the Builders," Ex said.

Cass had to jump onto Franklin's back and cling to his body as Franklin used the power from Ex to supply his strength. He looked like a human backpack strapped to Franklin. He felt stupid doing this, but he could feel Ex's power draining from him. The closer he got to Franklin, the less Samuel drew the power from him. Under other circumstances, it would have looked comical.

Both Franklin and Samuel broke off small trees, about fifteen feet tall and two to three inches thick as weapons to use against the growing swarm of creatures.

They backed away from the portal that seemed to be expanding as more and more of the arachnid-like creatures spilled into the parking lot. They were quickly spreading up the streets of the city of Greensburg. People that were taking their evening strolls were screaming as the beasts attacked. They may have been able to fight off one, but the things were attacking in groups of three or four. As someone went down, they swarmed on the body and began to eat.

Ex/Cass said, "Their planet must have no food left. They feast upon each other now. They appear to be starving."

"That's a comfort," Franklin said sarcastically.

"It is," Ex/Cass said. "Being eaten would be preferable to being used as an incubator for their young."

"Oh, fuck that!" Samuel said and began crushing the bugs with a renewed vigor.

As hard as they fought, they continued to lose ground and were forced away from the portal and the device toward the front of the hospital. People began to run into the streets as the insectoids began to break windows and doors to enter the surrounding homes. The only thing preventing Samuel and Franklin from being overrun were that the packs of bugs greedily feasted on the dead people and their own kind.

Gunshots were being fired everywhere now as sirens sounded in the distance.

Soon Franklin and Samuel were fighting relentlessly to destroy the flying spiders that attacked from every direction.

As fast and powerful as the two Nephilim were, they were forced to withdraw farther and farther from the portal allowing the creatures to spill into their existence. The spiders were scurrying in every direction and more screams could be heard coming from the neighborhood.

The portal, now about thirty feet across, emitted an excruciatingly loud screech as a large, black insectile leg with a spiky crab-like texture appeared nearly twenty feet above the ground. Immediately, another leg appeared on the other side of the orifice. The massive head of something unspeakable appeared.

Franklin screamed in terror as the monster began to force its bulk into our world. Samuel saved him from being stung by one of the spiders as he stopped to stare at the horror coming through the portal.

The head had eight tentacles, each about ten feet long. Each tentacle ended with a large, red orb, about three feet across that appeared to be covered in a mesh of thousands of dark circles. Cass realized that these were its eyes.

Hundreds of thin tentacles began to crawl out of the portal into the parking lot, feeling everything. They quickly slithered their way up over the hills. Occasionally, one of the tentacles would grab a corpse of either human or insect and pull it toward the mass of pincers located beneath the eyes. It was not one mouth, but three sets of eight smaller mouths arranged like zippers. Each mouth had two or three pincers around it. The sets of mouths were situated on the bottom, left and right side of the head.

They watched as a whole human body was thrown into the pincers of one of the topmost mouths. The pincers worked frantically to strip the skin and feed that mouth as the remains were rapidly passed to the next set of pincers that stripped other items to feed that mouth. Then the next mouth and the next until, within seconds, the bones were being devoured by the bottom mouth. The incredible efficiency was terrifying.

Cass could see Friz and Malcom run back inside the entrance to the hospital as the spiders began to rush them. They held the doors firm as the first ones began to slam into the thick glass.

Friz said to Malcom, "This is not permitted. I do not know how they can do this."

"What do you mean, Friz?" Malcom asked.

"All worlds have a fundamental, base-eight structure. This is why even-based music is comforting and soothing to us. The song I played for you hits all even-based rhythms with frequencies that modify your emotions. This is why the song has so much impact—"

"Friz. Can you just tell me what the fuck is going on here, because these things are freaking me the fuck out!" Malcom said.

"Base-six is where our realms exist. My world and your world are base-six. These creatures are from a base-eight realm. They should not be here," Friz said.

"Well, clearly, they're here!" Malcom said, panicking. "So, what now?"

"We cannot fight these creatures indefinitely. If these things do not kill us, their presence here is going to draw one of the Builders. Either way, we are all about to die, Malcom."

"Oh fuck," Malcom sighed and visibly relaxed, saying, "Well, working with Cass, I never thought I would live that long anyway. If we're going to die, I want to go out fighting. Does your little rod there have any kind of bug spray?"

Friz laughed and said, "I suppose I never thought I would live very long either. I can see if I have something that fits our purpose."

Friz held the lividan out as he opened the door. Malcom began shooting the creatures while the lividan gave off a shrill pitch that killed the ones nearby and repelled the ones farther away. They started to walk toward Cassian, Samuel, and Franklin, clearing a pathway.

Before they were halfway to them, what sounded like many trumpets playing began to fill the air. It was an inspiring feeling…at first. All movement from the spiders and people stopped. The sound got louder and louder, flooding out the noise of people screaming. Soon, the sound was that of one incredibly powerful horn that shook the Earth. Everyone fell to the ground, even the demon Semjaza.

The spider creatures stopped. As if sensing something terrible. The gigantic monster instantly backed into the portal and disappeared. The other spiders began to run back into the opening from which they came.

A dazzling light ripped open the night sky and lit the surrounding area as if the sun had risen. The sound caused pain as an enormous humanoid-shaped creature, taller than the eight-story hospital, emerged from the rift of darkness. Its body blazed like a golden fire as ripples of power radiated like heat from a furnace. The face of the celestial being looked angry. As it walked forward, away from the hospital, a second set of arms appeared from behind the figure with glowing orbs of gold that spun impossibly fast while hovering beneath each hand. There may have been several sets of wings on the creature, but none could verify this later as some thought it was a cloak or a trick of the bright light.

"What is that?" Cassian whispered in awe.

"It is one of the Builders," Ex replied, speaking through Cass. "I want you to know that it has been a pleasure and an honor to know you Cassian. I wish you the best in your next existence."

"What? Are we going to die?" Franklin asked.

"Yes," Ex said. "The Builders do not suffer minutia. They will wipe this area of the planet clean to correct this breach. Any particle of dust from that world that touches this world will be destroyed. This occasionally happens and people have no clue why the world has changed. Many civilizations simply disappeared because a Builder arrived to correct a broken law. We will soon cease to exist. This is essentially what you would call the nuclear option. This is what the demons planned. All done to kill you, Cassian."

CHAPTER 46

THE BUILDER'S MERCY

"Well, I must be doing something right if the inhabitants of Hell want me dead that badly," Cass said, "but I'm *not* giving up yet!"

Cassian got up from the ground and stood before the towering Builder. He looked insignificant before the colossal being. This reminded him exactly of his meeting with Tiamat. Cassian closed his eye and reached deep within himself to feel every bit of living resonance energy surrounding him, being careful *not* to touch any part of the Builder. He did not want the creature to believe he was trying to attack or influence it.

Once again, Cass could feel the power of life as he had that day in the valley years ago, right before he asked God for help.

Cass drew deeply, pulling more and more energy from the life around him. Then something was triggered within him. There was a latent message buried in his mind…the message from Tiamat.

When he opened his eye, he faced the left side of the massive Builder. His physical size did not change, but oddly, his perspective seemed to match that of the Builder.

Cassian spoke in a sound that none of the others could understand. He said, "I know that you once called Tiamat mother. I know this because she spoke to me. I am to tell you that, though you cannot create it, love is more real than anything you can make. She granted me safe passage through Hell."

The Builder turned to regard him for a long time and then it spoke, matching the sound of Cass. "Son of man, the laws forbid this action. None may breach the barriers by changing the balance of Shazo."

"We broke no barriers. We are defending this world from the breach. Spare us…please!" Cassian requested.

"Bring forward the compensation of Shazo. No breach can be committed without loss. This must never be violated as has been done here," said the Builder.

"Shazo?" Cassian asked.

"Shazo," Friz yelled, understanding the term. "Cassian, I have Shazo. Do you need it?"

Cass looked at Friz and said, "It seems that they require this as a form of payment or something."

Friz went into his normal speed of speech and said, "The Builders require Shazo to be balanced in all worlds…what you call Dese, to keep all worlds equal. What the demons did was open a portal to another world without burning the metal. They knew this would cause massive destruction and bring a Builder who would destroy everything. Builders rebuild from what is available by destroying everything first. We have no chance of surviving this, Cassian," Friz said as he dumped four one-inch cubes of Dese from one of his pockets.

"Is this the Shazo they are asking for?" Cassian asked.

"Yes. Give it to him. It is not likely to save us. I do not know," Friz said. His hands shook with fear as he handed two cubes to Cass.

Cassian said to the Builder, "What is your price to stop this evil?"

"There is no price or bargain. We either destroy or build. To build, we must destroy. You are a shrouded who speaks in the language of True Light. You will be spared. But should another breach occur in your presence, there can be no negotiation. No concession."

"We did not cause this breach. How am I to control what the demons do?" Cassian said.

"I will fix you. But I can do nothing more," said the Builder.

Cassian reached down into his deepest feelings and said, "You must spare the rest." He gestured behind him to his companions standing in front of the hospital. "Without them, do not spare me as this world is over. This evil cannot be undone without them."

"Very well, son of man. I grant your request…for Mother Tiamat. Tell none that you are now a Sword of God until the time comes. Prepare yourself for pain," it said. Then, in a tone of deep compassion that made Cassian realize what the Builders were, it said, "I am sorry."

The Builder spoke again and the world exploded in agony.

It was daylight when Cassian pushed himself off the ground and looked left and right. The pain in his head was staggering. There were several inches of dirt built up in small drifts around parts of his body. He was facing the hospital as he got to his hands and knees, but it looked as if it had been buried in dirt and then hit with a hurricane. Soil and sand covered the back half of the hospital almost to the roof while drifts of dirt piled up to nearly the third or fourth floor in places in the front. The entrance was visible. The landscape behind the hospital looked sparce and sandy as if the hospital had been transported into some desert.

Cass turned his head to the right and saw Samuel lying next to him.

Ex said, "Cassian, something is different. The Nephilim. They are not drawing my power."

"What? How?" Cassian asked. "Are they all dead?"

"I do not know. Wake them and see if they are still Nephilim. None has ever survived the wrath of a Builder as far as I know. They have the power to change anything and everything. You were communicating with it. I have never mentioned the Builders language to you. Was this something you learned in the book of the stewards?" Ex asked.

"I didn't speak any other language," Cass said. "I just spoke like I normally do. And it wasn't wrath. It was doing its job. It feels badly about doing what it must do. But it was weird. I was looking it right in the eyes, and when I turned to Friz, I was the same size I am now. I don't understand what happened."

"How did you speak the high language?" Ex pushed.

"I am telling you the truth, Ex. I don't know anything about speaking another language. The last thing it told me was to prepare for pain. Well, *that* certainly was fucking painful," Cassian said.

Ex was silent for a long time. Cass said, "Ex? Are you still here."

"I am here, Cassian," Ex said.

"What do you think this means?" Cassian asked.

"Do not fear, Cassian. You have faced much in this life, and you are strong. But the power I have is not being pulled by either Franklin or Samuel. They may be dead," Ex said. "And I am no longer certain that *I* am the one providing *you* with power."

Cassian crawled over to Samuel. He was unconscious. Cass rolled him over and began shaking him and lightly slapping his cheeks, saying, "Wake up!"

Samuel was still breathing and he had a pulse. Finally, Cass slapped his face harder to wake him up.

Instinctively, Cass jumped back as Azazel filled Samuel and said, "You survived again! But don't expect to survive the next time, you fucking weasel. We know who you are, demon-killer, and I will personally torture you for eternity when you die!"

"No. You won't," Cassian said. "You will never touch me, Azazel. If I walked into your world, it will be *you* who feels fear. Fear and agony," Cass flexed some new feeling he had and Azazel screamed in pain.

"I don't know what deal you have struck with that Builder, you fool. But I will be there when you die!" Azazel said.

"You may be there when I die, Azazel. That is true. But that will be a day you and your kind will *not* be celebrating," Cassian said.

Azazel fled back to his place in the dark recesses of Samuel's mind as Samuel began to awaken. His voice sounded more like a scared boy as he asked, "Dad, are you still here?"

Cass put his arms around the giant man and said, "Samuel, I'm here. Are you okay?"

Something within Samuel snapped, and he began to cry in the arms of his father. Cassian pulled him close and said, "It's okay, son. I'm here now."

"That hurt so bad. What happened? I feel different. Am I okay? I mean, am I injured?"

Cass looked him over and said, "No, Samuel. You are fine. It was painful for me too. I feel strange as well. Can you stand?"

"Yes, I think I can get up. Where is everyone else?"

"I don't know yet. Let's see what we can figure out. But I think it's time to let Azazel go. You don't want this in your life."

Power flared in Samuel as he fought against the hold Cassian had on him. He should have been able to easily overpower Cassian. He was a Nephilim. But Cassian held Samuel fast.

"What is going on?" Samuel said. "How are you able to hold me?"

"I don't know. But let Azazel go. You don't need it," Cass said.

"But the power, Dad. You don't understand. It's immense," Samuel said.

It was Friz who spoke up and said, "It is not Azazel who gives you the power. It is merely a conduit."

"Friz? Are you okay? Where are Franklin and Malcom?" Cassian asked.

"I'm here," Malcom said as he pushed himself up on his knees. He was facing away from the hospital with a look of shock on his face as he gazed past Cassian. He said, "What the fuck…"

Cass turned and saw what Malcom saw. The area was laid to waste. It looked as if a bomb destroyed the whole city…a hundred years ago. Only ruins remained through the thick forest that now sat over it.

Franklin crawled out from under a pile of dirt and debris and stood. The five of them looked around in shock at the destruction. It looked like many years had passed as bits of homes and buildings were visible through the lush, green landscape, now covering everything north, east and west. Behind the hospital, to the south, it looked like a desert. The highway and hills were leveled for miles.

"How? How is this possible?" Cassian asked.

"I do not know," Friz said. "I do not believe anyone has ever survived a Builder. You spoke to it and spared our lives. You truly are the Chosen of this world."

"What do you mean?" Malcom asked.

"He is the one chosen to lead your world to the next level. Or the end of your existence," Friz said in awe.

"What happened here? Are we in the future or something? Why does it look like some place Indiana Jones would be exploring?" Malcom said.

Franklin turned and ran to the hospital. Samuel was right behind him. Cass and the others followed more slowly.

The front windows were broken, but the second set of sliding doors were intact. Samuel threw the doors open and they ran to the steps, making their way to the sixth floor where they left the others.

"Marissa? Lynn?" Samuel called as he opened the stairwell door.

"Victoria? Are you here?" Franklin asked.

A single door along the hallway opened. Corrina appeared and said, "Son? Is that you?"

"Oh, Mom!" Franklin said, running over to her and hugging her. "Where is everyone else?"

"Samuel?" They heard Lynn's voice from behind Corrina.

Other people began to walk out of the room, which appeared to be one of the exam rooms where a bunch of people took shelter together.

Phil pushed past everyone and started to yell at Cassian, "What the fuck did you get us into, you fucking crippled asshole!"

Samuel reached back like he was about to punch Phil. Cass began to protest as Samuel moved impossibly fast. To his surprise, Samuel gently, but firmly, put his right hand over Phil's mouth as his left hand held his head. Phil grabbed his arm and struggled to break free for a moment. Samuel's arms and hands were not just firm; they were as utterly immovable as stone. Fear spread over Phil's face, and he immediately stopped struggling.

Samuel spoke in a soft tone. "Phil, if you ever disrespect my mother or my father again, I am going to rip the spine out of your fucking body." He was looking Phil in the eyes when he said it, then nodded as he said, "You understand, don't you?"

Phil looked terrified as Samuel made his head nod in agreement. Samuel tossed him aside and said, "Marissa? Are you in here?"

"I'm here, Samuel, with your mother," Marissa said.

Franklin found Victoria in another room down an orthogonal hallway. He stood hugging Corrina and Victoria close to him.

Lynn came out and hugged Samuel as she said, "What happened out there? Why is it daylight? It was 10 p.m. when you left?"

Cassian asked Friz, "How did it go with Mike? Were you able to help him?"

"It did work. It will take much effort for him to recover. I rid him of the virus, but he is going to have to be the one to work to gain his strength back," Friz said.

"Mike?" Cass said above the din of people coming out from different rooms to see what was happening in the world.

Pamela, now in her late seventies, said, "Over here, Cass," from another hallway.

Cass ran around the corner to see his mother pushing Mike in a wheelchair. People were running around trying to assess who was still alive and who may have died.

Pamela hugged Cassian and said, "Your friends, Cass, are going to be the death of me."

He laughed and said, "Mike? How are you?"

Mike looked skinny and frail but managed a smile and a weak thumbs-up gesture. Cass gently hugged him and was happy that Mike was able to return the hug.

Friz was there and said, "He will be able to regenerate his adaptive immune system now. But it will be an uphill battle. You will need to replenish your normal bacterial symbiotic species."

"Are you sure you got all of the virus out of him?" Cassian asked.

"I'm not certain I understand. Get all the virus out? Are you asking if he is cured of this disease? If so, then yes. It was either this or he would have perished. There was no other option. I thought that I made that very clear," Friz said this all in a rush.

Malcom interjected and said, "It's okay, Friz. We're just not used to things always working in our world. So, Mike's okay, then?"

"Yes. He can make a full recovery…if he is willing to work to get better. Can you do that, Mike?" Friz asked.

Mike smiled and nodded. Then he whispered, "I'll fight!" in a determined voice that sounded like it hurt to speak.

Samuel, Marissa, and Lynn walked over to Cass, Friz, Malcom, Pamela, and Mike. Phil decided to sit in one of the waiting room seats and stay out of the conversation.

Pamela's eyes narrowed as Lynn approached and she said, "I thought she was dead?"

"Mom," Cassian said, "Stop. Lynn came here to help save Mike's life. And you should know that this man," he gestured to the large man next to him, "is *your* grandson, Samuel."

Pamela looked confused or perplexed and said, "My…grandson? I…I thought he died when he was young." She said tenuously.

"I'm sorry, Mom. I never told you that Lynn and Samuel were alive. I think that Bill tried to say something about it right before Grandma Betty blew him away, but I didn't find out until Beth told me in 1994 after she…never mind that now," Cass said, sparing a quick glance to Lynn.

Lynn nodded slightly as if seeming to understand at that point what probably happened with Beth. She knew Beth hated Cass. But she loved her sister and never thought Beth would go that far.

"Oh, my goodness," Pamela said with a smile as she walked toward Samuel, "He's a monster!"

Samuel looked angry when Marissa jumped in and said, "Easy! She just means you're a big guy…which you are!"

"Oh…um…sorry. I just hear people say that about me a lot," Samuel said to Pamela. "You're my grandmother? You're not some religious nut, are you?" he asked, smiling.

"What? No. Why would you ask me that?" Pamela asked, sounding offended.

"Mom! Can you please stop going on either full offense or full defense and just rejoice in this moment. This is your flesh and blood! Samuel is *my* son! *Your* grandson!"

Pamela looked annoyed by the rebuke and said, "I'm not being defensive. I just don't understand how my religion should mean anything. I'm sorry."

"You don't know the—" Cass began.

"It's okay…Dad," Samuel said, sounding genuine, "I let it go. That thing you told me to let go. I feel a lot better. It's nice to meet you… Grandma."

Pamela's face broke into a smile that spread from ear to ear, "It's nice to meet you…Grandson."

Samuel surprised her as he bent down and gently hugged Pamela close to him.

She hugged him back as she said, "Maybe we can have a family again after all."

"I think I'd like that," Samuel said. "I'm just not too familiar with that."

Samuel stood and said, "Agent Turner, this is my grandmother, Pamela Nazarovich. Grandma, this is Agent Marissa Turner. She's my…" He suddenly swept Marissa off the ground and kissed her.

She kissed him back, then said, "It's nice to meet you. I think he meant to say that…I'm his girlfriend?"

Samuel nodded.

CHAPTER 47

DEVASTATION

"WHAT HAPPENED TO THE CITY?" Cassian asked Friz as they looked out the window facing north where the ruined city was now overtaken with nature.

"It has been destroyed," Friz said, shaking his head.

"How far does this devastation go?" Franklin asked.

"I don't know yet," Friz said. "Anything from that world that touched a part of this world will perish. That includes the air…or particles carried in the air. However far that spread in the brief time the portal was open will likely be reformed. My lividan is still trying to connect to a signal. All that I can say for certain is that there is still a signal to be connected to. That means that your world may still be intact."

"Ex," Cass said, "why didn't you ever tell me about these Builders?"

"You should never have seen one, never heard of them, never known of their existence, and never survived seeing one. When they appear, it is Damnum Fatale. They are not of this world. And any who sees a Builder does not survive to tell the experience. They destroyed the city of Fe Ultrenbard. This is what you believe to be Atlantis."

"Atlantis was real?" Cassian asked.

"Did you not hear of Fe Ultrenbard in the first book of the stewards?" Ex asked.

"No. Nothing of that name. I think I would remember anything about the lost civilization of Atlantis!" Cass said.

"They also made an appearance after Fe Ultrenbard in Tell el-Hammam in the Jordan Valley. The hedonistic people under the influence of demons were instructed on the inappropriate use of the metal. Following an ultimatum presented by two angels, a Builder arrived and destroyed the cities known as Sodom and Gomorrah, as well as much of the surrounding area.

"The demons that provided the people with the metal, and the instruction on its use, presented themselves as ambassadors of peace. They were, in fact, ambassadors of death, Cassian. These are ones we are fighting," Ex said.

"Well, what about Fe Underwear or whatever? Atlantis? This is kind of a big deal," Cass said.

"It was a magnificent place…much more than a single city…that existed at the end of the Matriarchy in a place currently known as the Richat Structure in what is now Northern Africa. The country of Mauritania in the Maghreb is mostly desert today. But it was once a lush and prosperous land of great importance. It was surrounded by water leading many to believe that it sat amidst the ocean.

"The current inhabitants still believe that it will return to its former glory as the center of the world…a hub of tremendous technology. That will never happen. The people of Fe Ultrenbard became so powerful that they began to feel untouchable. Some believed that this society would be the ones to find Dese and progress your civilization to the next level.

"They did find the metal. But they did not do what was right. They succumbed to the Spurs and began to play with knowledge they did not understand. At the height of their technology, they used forbidden frequencies of the Builders to breach a passageway into another realm. There is now a sound disbelief by those who would call themselves experts that Atlantis ever existed. The people and their knowledge were thoroughly destroyed by a single Builder."

"Holy shit," Cass said, astounded. "Well, what about here and now? What do you know about this destruction? I mean, how much of the world did it destroy?"

"It is as Friz described. It depends on the depth of the transgression. How long the portal was kept open will determine what is destroyed. In the time of Atlantis, the entire northwestern part of Africa was laid waste. We must wait and see what has been done," Ex said.

"My lividan has received signal," Friz said. He moved his finger over the device and a map of the eastern seaboard of the US appeared for all to see.

Friz began, "According to your conflicting national news sources, this is officially being attributed to an attack with a nuclear weapon. Several countries are being targeted as scapegoats. At this time, however, authorities do not know what happened. The Builder caused massive electrical disruptions throughout the east, similar to an EMP. The destruction of an area sixty miles south, sixty-seven miles east, eighty-seven miles north, and forty-five miles west of our location have instantly…transformed," Friz circled a large area that included the city of Pittsburgh.

"What does that mean?" one of the nurses asked.

"Pittsburgh is destroyed!" someone else exclaimed.

The waiting room, filled with forty or fifty survivors began to bicker and cry as they heard the news. Soon people were coming to Friz and demanding answers. Some were sad and others were angry. All were worried about family.

Samuel and Franklin shielded Friz, particularly from the people who were angry. One man became violent and started punching Franklin. This had no effect on him, so he allowed the man to vent his frustration without raising a finger. But the man was left out of breath and confused. Franklin still tried to compassionately comfort the man. *Much easier to do when they can't hurt you*, Cass thought.

Cassian closed his eyes and began to feel the people and the wild mixture of emotions coming from the crowd. The underlying theme was fear. Cassian concentrated and sent out soothing vibrations. The effect was immediate. They all began to calm. Some felt tired and needed to sit or lie down. He was able to maintain this resonance with the people as he spoke to Friz.

Cass whispered, "Let's go into a private room to talk."

———————

Cass led them into the first exam room where most of the people had hunkered down. It was a large room with several tables and a lot of chairs. Cass thought it must have been one of the many underused triage rooms set up for the pandemic.

The attendees were Cass, Malcom, Friz, Marissa, Samuel, Franklin, Corrina, Victoria, and Pamela. Mike was already sleeping comfortably in another room after Friz gave him a food supplement, similar to what he gave to Malcom earlier. Lynn sat in the waiting room with Phil, trying to keep him calm.

Cass thought it better to leave Lynn out after she was eyeing Victoria with daggers. Victoria wanted to apologize, but Cass suggested that this may not be the best time while Phil was around.

Once the door closed, Cass began, "Friz, you need to tell these people that Pittsburgh may have been evacuated in time and that their families might be safe."

"But that is untrue, Cassian. The Builder has destroyed them," Friz said. "There are plots forming to blame this on a type of neutron bomb that they claim can destroy life without the detonation of a destructive bomb. That is also not true. Your government is currently taking actions to *prevent* any life from escaping this zone. This is bad news for us."

"Friz, can you please do as I say. I cannot maintain this frequency forever. They will panic and become dangerous to us and themselves if we do not control this situation and give them some hope. Do you understand?" Cass said.

"He's right," Samuel agreed. "People in a situation like this are dangerous. If you want to protect *their* safety, you need to tell them what they want to hear."

Franklin objected, "Cassian! How is this any different than what you were telling me the demons and Spurs are doing with our government? You are lying to these people! They deserve to know the truth!"

"I agree with you, Franklin," Cass said. "They do. But right now, they are confused, afraid, and suffering. Most, if not all of them, lost family. A human mind can only handle so much at one time. One person…we can help. Five people, we could absorb their pain as a group. Fifty or sixty people? Think about it. We need to buy some time to get them mentally prepared for what happened."

"This may seem cold to many of you, but perhaps we should consider eliminating them," Samuel said. "If what Friz said is true, getting this many people out of this area will be difficult. Afterward, if and when they do speak up about what they witnessed here today, they will be... silenced by our government anyway."

"We can't just kill these people," Franklin objected. "These are doctors and nurses and people who have dedicated their lives to helping others. What's wrong with you?"

"Franklin, what I am suggesting would be humane compared to leaving them here to fend for themselves. Or worse, allowing our government to find them alive," Samuel said.

"Stop arguing, please!" Marissa said. "We are not killing anyone," she gave a withering glance to Samuel. He simply shrugged.

Corrina was watching Cassian as she said, "What are you thinking, Cass?"

"Both Samuel and Franklin make good points. I am not in favor of killing these people. But getting them out of here may be difficult. Friz, what else can you tell us?" Cassian asked.

"I do not understand why we are still here," Friz said. "We should all be dead. I do not understand what is happening. Why were we spared?"

Ex said, "You gestured to the people behind you when you spoke to the Builder. Perhaps it believed you gestured to the whole hospital and spared everyone in it."

"That makes sense," Cass said.

"What makes sense," Friz asked.

"Ex said that when I asked the Builder to spare us, I gestured to those of you standing behind me. The Builder must have thought I meant the whole hospital. That would mean that if I hadn't made that gesture, maybe only five of us would have survived," Cass said.

The room fell silent for a long moment.

It was Victoria who spoke up. Her voice was soft and sweet, but the effect was powerful. "I spent forever trapped in the dark by something evil. Something I think we are fighting against held me down against my will. I have only recently rejoined this world...thanks to my husband, Franklin," she smiled and looked at him with pride as she said it, "but I love every bit of it! Every touch. Every smile. Every taste. Every emotion! You don't know what it's like to have life taken from you. To be trapped in the dark without any hope. I have hope now! And I intend to fight *anyone*," she shouted, "who tries to take that away from me again. I will not be part of any group that wants to take the life from these people."

Franklin put his arm around her and said, "I stand by my wife!"

Cassian smiled and said, "It occurs to me that we have the two most powerful men on the planet with us. It's time to make a stand. Franklin, how many Spurs do you have trapped?"

"I think three right now," Franklin said.

"How about you, Samuel?" Cassian asked.

"Sixteen Spurs and one minor demon," Samuel said.

"We can get out of here," Cass said, "…*with* all the people here."

"What do you plan to do to keep them safe after we escape, Cass?" Samuel asked. "They will find them and eliminate them. I know how they operate."

"I will take responsibility for their protection," Cassian said. "I see my pathway now…and that of our enemy."

"Cassian, I don't know how you think we can go against the US military if they come against us in force. I felt nearly invincible with Azazel, but even with him, I'm not so sure I could take on *that* much firepower."

Cassian stood in the center of the room and threw his arms wide. The power of Ex filled him along with his own power. The air thrummed with energy. They all shrank before him as he said, "This is the beginning of their end. We will no longer permit the masters of nothing to rule this world. The power from Earth will prevail over evil.

"Take my hands, my Nephilim allies…children of the Seraphim. Feel the power bestowed upon us. We must now right the wrongs of this world. Those with hate in their heart will perish in the dark past. Those who hold on to hope will rejoice in a bright future. Any who would deny what they witnessed this day will deny the sovereignty of God!"

Samuel and Franklin looked at Cassian's outstretched hands. Trepidation filled them as they slowly reached out to take his offered hands. Samuel on the right and Franklin on the left. When the three joined hands, a tremendous bolt of energy flared through them.

At that moment, people rose in awe as the whole planet shuddered. A glimmer of light filled every living being as, for a brief moment, the Spurs and demons lost control. Hope began to blossom where the roots of despair had dug deep into the ground.

Azazel, Semjaza, and the other eleven demons in the coven stood atop a cliff in the southern Mountains of Hell. Azazel burned with rage at its recent defeat. No memory of where or who the shrouded was could be found in its mind. A wave of fear and panic, unlike anything any of them had ever felt before, passed through the demons. Could it be that the Sword of God had been drawn? Doubt, and thoughts of betrayal, began to fill their minds.

The massive dragon turned her head to the sky. A smile formed on her mouth as Tiamat said, "God be with you, young soul."

EPILOGUE

"A WORD IN YOUR EAR, YOUNG man," said an elderly woman in a hospital gown.

Cass turned to see who spoke to him. He recalled seeing her as they took inventory of the surviving patients in the hospital. This woman was one of the catatonic patients from the third floor.

"You seem to be feeling better. What is your name, dear?" Cassian asked.

"You can call me Plato…like the clay children amuse themselves with," she said with a half-smile.

"Stu!" Cass said, excited.

She sighed and said, "You are in your fifties, for God's sake. Have you yet to learn discretion? Let's go."

She led him to an empty treatment room and closed the door.

"What are you doing here? How are you here now? I was expecting you around 2021, but you never came," Cass began.

"You are never going to quit with that question barrage of yours," she said. "First of all, the cycles are not circular but elliptical. You said our last meeting was fifteen years after our first meeting. The next one will be longer. Maybe thirty years. I don't know exactly. Our window could open next week, for all I know. I told you before that I am bad with time.

"Now, as I am a resonant steward, I am permitted to move any other steward out of the body they protect and use that body as I wish. It is frowned upon to do this, but it is occasionally done.

"There was an amusing movie called *K-PAX* that was based on one of us doing this very thing. They certainly took some creative liberties with the story, but the gist was there.

"The reason I have risked doing this is due to the urgency of recent events," Stu said.

"How did you know I would be here?" Cassian asked.

"Oh, I don't know. I just looked for where a Builder showed up and destroyed a few thousand square miles of your planet. As the people in this hospital are the only life remaining in this entire region, I figured, 'Hey, I wonder if Cass might be at the epicenter.' I took a chance that I could find you here.

"Clearly, the Grad stewards are allowing me to bend the rules due to the recent betrayal. How in the nights of hell you managed to pull off surviving this is something that is going to baffle the stewards for many spans. But you need to get your ass out of here soon. We are not the only ones who know you are alive.

"Since Semjaza was killed in your confrontation, the demons no longer know your identity. Very fortunate that it felt the need to gloat," Stu said.

"You mean Semjaza is gone?" Cassian asked.

"No, not like you have been able to kill demons and angels. Semjaza was physically killed here by the Builder. That means it was banished. But it is considered a loss in a battle against you. Thus, they lost the knowledge of *who* you are. Crazy rules.

"But," she held up a finger, "they will not have any problem finding a group of people in the middle of this destruction. They know the shrouded they want to kill is here…even if they don't know *your* identity. They will kill all the people…in this entire state if they must. Do not be surprised if a demon in the US government pushes to have a nuclear detonation in this region to kill you. It would be a perfect cover story for them to begin a war," Stu said.

"Could we survive that? I mean, with two Nephilim and an angel, could we withstand that?" Cassian asked.

"No. Even if you were able to shield your bodies from the heat, your physical body would suffer too much radiation damage to survive for long. None of the other people would stand a chance," Stu said.

There was a soft knock on the door. Cass opened it a crack and saw Malcom and Friz.

"What is it?" Cassian asked.

"I wanted to make sure you were alright. Wasn't that lady comatose?" Malcom asked.

"Send in the Gorwanian, Cass," Stu said.

"Gorwanian?" Cassian repeated.

Friz nodded and said, "With whom are you speaking, Cassian? I am from Gorwan."

"Stu wants to speak with you," Cass said. Over his shoulder he asked, "What about Malcom?"

"No. The fewer the better," Stu said.

"Sorry, Malcom. Can you watch the door?" Cassian asked as he allowed Friz in.

"Yeah. Sure. I'm only risking my life for all this shit. I would love to stand out here—totally excluded—so I can guard the door," Malcom said sarcastically.

"It's not me, Malcom. I asked. They get weird about who they talk to. I'll tell you everything after," Cass said.

"If he comes in, where does it stop?" Stu asked. "We don't have much time."

"Wait here. We won't be long," Cass said to Malcom and closed the door.

The elderly woman looked Friz up and down and said, "Nice outfit. Were you in a circus?"

Friz said, "That explains how you know from where I come. You must be one of the stewards. Presumably the one who resonates with Cass. What number are you?"

"Yes. Well, you are clever. I am Tinilfasela. What are you doing here?" Stu said, with an edge to the question.

"You are rather new. Not even Karma level," Friz said.

"Yes. I asked you a question, Gorwanian. Answer me!" Stu demanded.

"I am part of the Elder Quatran. Therefore, you know what I am doing and what I do to conceal my task. My choices were to risk diving through the portal or being tortured by demons. What would you have done?" Friz said.

Stu nodded and said, "I suppose I can understand. But you could cause a major disruption to this realm. Set your lividan and accessories to destruct if you die here. This is not something they should have at this stage of development."

"I have already done that," Friz said.

"Do you wish to go home?" Stu asked.

"Of course. I left my world behind. My family. But there is no way back. Not with the technology here," Friz said.

"I will see what I can do about getting your network to send you a return portal. But you would be taking the same risk as when you came here. It could kill you," Stu said.

"I know the risks," Friz said.

"You are to tell them nothing about how to use Desemilnoct. Take out your lividan and set in the code 42463117 and then hand it to me," Stu said.

Friz pulled out the golden lividan, pressed it twice and handed it to the old woman. She pressed it on the top and spoke a strange language into it. When she was done, she pressed the top and handed it back to Friz with a disapproving look.

"You may go now. I will try to help you return home," Stu said.

"I have something interesting to tell you. My theory now has a strong piece of evidence. Listen to the last recorded spoken record before you spoke," Friz said, holding the lividan out to Stu.

She took the device, pressed it twice and said, "I'm listening."

Friz did an odd blink and the lividan began to replay a recording of Friz in a rapid language. It did not last long.

When it was done, Stu looked surprised and said, "Very interesting observation. I know your identity. If this turns out to be true, I assure that you will be credited with this discovery. Thank you for trusting me. I am sorry if I have been terse with you."

Ex spoke in Cassian's mind, "Interesting concept. It seems Jimmy was able to study Limbo when he was locked in the dark during his possession."

Friz took the lividan back and said, "I understand your anger. And I appreciate your help and kindness. Thank you, Tinilfasela."

"One more thing," Stu said to Friz. "There is a Peitho with Cassian's son. Do not allow her to question you."

"That is…" Friz looked briefly at Cass, "unfortunate. I will avoid her."

Friz gave a slight bow to Stu and left the room.

"What was all that about?" Cassian asked.

"You can ask him later. You will have time to speak. We do not.

"It seems there is now a Nephilim-Peitho pairing in your group. Your son and the young woman with whom he arrived. This is concerning to us," Stu said.

"Yeah, I don't know anything about a Peitho. Ex told me about it. What are they?" Cassian asked.

"As you may have noticed, the Peitho have a strong and natural ability to resonate with others. They do not know they do this, and they have no control over it. People who talk to them will find themselves spilling their deepest, darkest secrets to a Peitho. They also have a powerful ability to influence others. They are exceptionally rare. More rare than a Nephilim. So, the pairing of the two is of no statistical concern," Stu said.

"What's the problem then? They seem to get along well. She was able calm Samuel enough to keep him from killing me. At this point, I *more* than approve of her as a good match for my son," Cass said.

"It was this coupling that led to the dark era of the Matriarchy. The death of billions of people. While Nephilim are susceptible to the influences of women, the Peitho binding is stronger than iron. A Nephilim will find peace in their presence. They exude a comforting resonance that takes away the constant, unheard voices of those trapped within. And their physical contact with a Nephilim will bring them back to the person they are, without the influence of any trapped entity," Stu said.

"This was never in the book! Why didn't I hear about the Peitho when I learned of the Matriarchy?" Cassian asked.

"They were left out. Specifically, because they are so rare. It should never have been an issue," Stu said.

"Left out. You mean like the Spurs leave things out of our history?" Cass said angrily.

Stu looked down and said, "Yes. Exactly as the Spurs do. But this was not done to influence you. It was considered to be of no true value to your situation."

"Even if this is so, I still don't see what the problem is," Cass said.

"What would happen if the Peitho were taken by a Spur? Or worse, a demon? What if she is a willing host to a demon or has some other contact with them?" Stu asked.

Cassian sighed and said, "I see your point."

"She may not be as big a prize for the demons as you, but she would make a great second place for them. You need to check her as soon as you can. Then you need to make sure she does not fall into their hands. Tell your son, but be careful. His bond to her will supersede all others," Stu said.

"Practically speaking, Stu, what does that mean?" Cassian asked.

"It means that he would kill every person on this planet before allowing someone to do so much as raise a hand to her," Stu said.

"Okay. I will have to keep them close to me," Cass said.

"Yes. Now, get these people out of here as fast as possible. If you cannot get them mobilized soon, take the Nephilim and those close to you and run. The Gorwanian can help you but warn him not to use the Dese unless absolutely necessary. If we have another traitor, they will be pinged of your location. Good luck, Cassian."

"Good to see you again, Stu. Tell Khalima I said hello," Cass said.

The old woman smiled and left the room. She sat in a wheelchair in the hallway, and a vacant look replaced the smile.

TO BE CONTINUED…

I hope you enjoyed this sequel to *Envious: A Fictionalized Tale*, book one of the Resonance of Souls trilogy. Please visit your favorite online bookseller and leave a review. I would greatly appreciate your feedback.

ABOUT THE AUTHOR

I grew up in western Pennsylvania, in an area where the steel industry dominated the economy through the '70s and '80s. I was like many kids whose father worked in the unimaginable (by today's standards) conditions of the steel mills to support his family. It was a time when getting by on one income was starting to become a thing of the past. By the time I hit fourth grade, my mother also began to work to make ends meet. Many parents at that time made sacrifices to assure that their children would not have to suffer through the hardships they had experienced. My parents have recently passed away, and I hope they both know I am eternally grateful for what they did.

My mother had a special way of fascinating me with extraordinary subjects. It was she who pushed me into the creative process of learning rather than simply memorizing information as we were taught in school. Consequently, I did well in my standard education but found I had very little interest in the standard educational curriculum. In other words, I sponged up information on subjects I liked and treated the rest as a toddler in an insurance seminar. This often presented as an apparent disregard for authority, but that would be an inaccurate conclusion. It was much later in life when I realized that it wasn't a disregard for authority I felt, but a disdain for a biased or unjust authority. Perhaps I unknowingly formed a mental shield around my mind to the indoctrinations of the status quo.

Our family attended Presbyterian church with many in our community. I even occasionally attended Catholic services with my father.

Perhaps it was this same indifference to indoctrination that led me to feel as though I had no particularly strong religious or spiritual foundation. I had no interest in religion because, frankly, it bored the hell out of me. The hypocrisy from the parishioners, along with the depressing pipe organ music, soon made me dread Sunday mornings. I couldn't wait until the service was over. Apparently, I wasn't alone in that feeling since the people trying to get out of the parking lot were damning to Hell the very brethren with whom they had just shared warm greetings of "peace be with you."

Growing up, I wrestled, took judo, and played basketball, football and the saxophone. It wasn't long before I had to face a harsh personal reality—I had no talent for athletic endeavors…or music for that matter. Have you ever heard the practice pieces of third-string saxophone players? There exists no semblance of any song you may know. It sounds like traffic noises with the rhythmic honking of car horns. In addition, running for a school bus while lugging around a saxophone case became a daily tribulation. Despite the investment in the instrument, neither of my parents struggled very hard to reverse my decision to quit playing.

I began playing Dungeons & Dragons with some older kids when I was in the seventh grade. One of my friends encouraged me to read a book he was reading by Stephen R. Donaldson, titled *Lord Foul's Bane*. While it was rather adult for a young mind, I immersed myself into the fantastic world created by the author. When I finished the trilogy, I felt sad and lost, as if the characters had left my life forever. After that, I was hooked on reading books of fantasy, horror, science-fiction…anything that would cater to the creative side of my mind.

Despite my general lack of athletic ability, I started playing golf at a young age (long before 3D movies became ho-hum for me) at the urgings of my great aunt, who was actually quite great. By the age of twelve, I began using her old wooden clubs to discover a type of rage I never knew existed. On occasion, my friends and I would walk several miles to the pitch-n-putt course where I could hone my profanity skills. Whenever I could gather enough money and a ride to a real golf course, I would spend a long afternoon on well-landscaped grounds, cursing at a small white ball along the periphery of the neatly trimmed fairways.

I won't bore you will all the minutia of my life, but I do have a point. So on to some of the more defining moments. At the age of eighteen, I survived a gruesome car crash, suffering severe debilitating injuries, including the loss of an eye. The reason *Envious* is considered *fictionalized* is due to many of the very real nightmares and incidents experienced during my recovery. Some of these nightmares continued to recur for many years.

After being released from the hospital, fear of possible brain damage led me to change my college major to the topic I dreaded the most—Chemistry. Perhaps it was this very hard-headedness that spared my life. I figured if I could still grasp the complexities of such a scientifically strenuous subject, maybe I could still manage to complete college and fulfill my lifelong dream of having a job and retiring with a pension. (It is this type of humor that keeps me both optimistic and happy.) I earned my bachelor's degree in 1993. Through great luck (or by the grace of God…or possibly Satan), I was offered a genuinely wonderful dream job performing biomedical research. This came with the acceptance of performing tasks that would later haunt me…maybe forever.

While studying the effects of chemicals on the body and the effects of the body on chemicals, I eventually earned both my master's and doctorate degrees in chemistry. Unfortunately, by the time I finished my doctorate, pension plans were a thing of the past. (Yet another shattered dream…insert laugh track.)

Years later I began to golf with a friend (a very sincere thank you to him) who taught me the true nature of the sport. Swinging at the ball with rage transferred that rage to the ball, which urged it to run away from you and into the woods. Peace was required to keep the ball happy in the sunny fairway. We also never kept score. I began to realize the profound joy of golfing. Those delightful days are recalled as wonderful moments in nature, in a world less and less inured by the modern world.

In many ways, golf is a reflection of life. It is not a competition against yourself or others. It should be something we do to find happiness as we play. The more you find peace and forgive yourself from past mistakes, the better you will do!

To date, I have written or participated in the writing of over 60 peer-reviewed published items of scientific research. My focus now is

primarily on reducing or ending the need for any form of animal testing in the future. I have worked at several companies in major scientific
hubs throughout the northeastern coast. My ongoing multidisciplinary
research into multiple disease states has become a career I very much
enjoy.

But the science I perform is very niche. I have many wild ideas I
would like to share with the world. Ideas that border closer to the science
side of science-fiction. There are many brilliant people out there who
may be better equipped to realize these ideas, but what I really hope to
achieve is to show people the gray areas in life and possibly open their
minds to non-canonical prospects.

For humans, life on Earth is very short in the grand scheme of existence. Far too short to dwell on hate and anger. I believe that creation is
the purpose of life. I also believe that conflict drives that creation. The
only way to peaceful creation is by the allowance of communication
through disagreements. Perhaps ambivalence is something to embrace
as much as love and happiness.

I invite you to become part of the ever-growing community of readers and dreamers who may find solace or excitement in the pages of my work.

Follow the author on social media:

https://www.facebook.com/profile.php?id=61560463770969

Learn more about the author and other books, subscribe to his website for exclusive updates, and join the conversation about stories yet to be told at his website:

https://azenzik.com/